D1239491

**Books by
A. Claire Everward**

The First

Oracle's Hunt
Oracle's Diplomacy

Blackwell: A Tangled Web

A. CLAIRE EVERWARD

ORACLE'S DIPLOMACY

BOOK TWO
IN THE ORACLE SERIES

Author & Sister

First published in 2018 by Author & Sister
www.authorandsister.net

Print ISBN 978-965-92584-2-0
eBook ISBN 978-965-92584-3-7

With this one completed,
a future can be charted.

The Disputed Region

List of Acronyms

ARPA	Advanced Research Projects Agency, previously DARPA
IDSD	International Diplomacy, Security and Defense
IDSDATR	IDSD Advanced Technologies Research
SIRT	Serious Incident Response Team
USFID	United States Federal Investigative Division

Chapter One

"Thank you," Ambassador George Sendor said in a distracted tone as the steward placed a cup of Earl Grey tea with a touch of orange flavor before him. He didn't look at the young man, instead keeping his gaze on the endless sky outside the window.

The steward was not offended. The ambassador was not a rude man, nor one to disregard those who worked for him. He was kind and caring, and took to heart any offense he might have caused. And the steward, the entire crew of the official executive jet, in fact, had been with the ambassador for the past two and a half years in his extensive travels. They knew he appreciated them. No, the distinguished man was not rude or uncaring. He was simply preoccupied, and for a good reason.

The assistant sitting across from Sendor acknowledged the steward with a smile as he accepted a cup of coffee. "How're we doing today, Cyril?"

"Very well, sir. Clear sky, no turbulence. Looks like a quiet flight all the way." The steward's tone was calm, practiced.

They were flying home to Belgium—Brussels, to

be exact—after four days at the negotiating table, long days that were the final milestone in an endless line of negotiations. The main terms and covenants had now been finalized, and all that remained was for the two sides to confirm their respective governments' acceptance of them. If all went well, within days, weeks at the most, they would be on their way back on this same jet, not for further negotiations but for a festive treaty-signing ceremony.

The assistant waited until the steward left, then resumed watching the man he had served for many years now, long before Sendor became an ambassador, before the assistant himself knew the kind of difference the older man could make in the lives of so many, that he would succeed where no one else had.

"Your tea, Ambassador," he prodded.

"Yes. Yes, of course." Sendor turned to him with a sigh.

"What are you thinking about, sir?"

"Hoping, more than thinking, I suppose, Lucas."

"It seems to have gone well." In fact, no one had ever gotten this far in mellowing the tense relations between the sworn enemies.

"Indeed." Sendor sipped the exquisite blend, let its warmth, its aroma, wash over him, tried hard to surrender to its calming effect. "Indeed," he repeated. Nothing he had done in his long decades in diplomatic service had been as important to him, had touched him as much as this, the negotiations that had been going on for more than two years and had now finally matured into what looked like a viable peace treaty. Bitter years of hatred and fighting, unspeakable suffering, were finally about to end. Still, Sendor couldn't help considering it all—the situation, the negotiations, the peace treaty itself, the prospects for the future—again and again, worried he might have missed something, concerned that what had been so painstakingly achieved would not stand up to the test. Fearful there would be more deaths.

"Are you considering their request?"

Sendor's brow furrowed. The previous evening, he had been asked to remain in the region after the peace treaty was signed, as the ambassador to both countries. Rather unusual, true, but in this unique case it was most likely the best way to keep what would undoubtedly be a fragile peace alive. Except that at sixty-eight, he had been looking forward to retiring, finally spending much needed time with his family. His sons had both settled with their families in the Ardennes, their birthplace, and he would have liked to settle there himself, move back to the house he had brought them up in, spend more time with his grandchildren.

But that might have to wait. How could he live the rest of his life enjoying precious time with his grandchildren, watching them grow up safe and protected, when so many other children were dying because he wasn't there to ensure their safety? Both sides in the negotiations trusted him, his motives, his ability to stand behind his words. This would not be an easy peace, and someone had to be there to take it through its first steps, make sure it did not fall apart. After so many years of conflict, there were so much anger and bitterness, terrible pain to deal with. The two nations, the people behind this peace treaty, needed to heal, rebuild, make it to a day when they could meet on a peaceful street without instantly feeling animosity, without the risk of resorting to raging violence.

So much work to do, and only he could do it, he was all too aware. No one knew them as he did after all he had been through with them.

He took in a deep breath. "Yes, I do believe it will be for the best if I—"

A distinct shudder passed through the aircraft. The ambassador and his assistant both sat up, startled. In the galley, the steward steadied himself against the countertop and darted a bewildered glance at the closed cockpit door.

In the cockpit, Captain Laura Yates frowned at the autopilot. Beside her, her copilot turned to look at her, perplexed.

"What the hell was that?" he asked.

"I have no idea." Yates's eyes were on the flight instruments before her. "Whatever it was, it didn't show on our instruments."

"The autopilot is working properly."

"It wasn't an internal—"

The aircraft shuddered again, more violently this time.

"What on...?" Yates's hand hovered over the instruments panel, and both she and her copilot stared in astonishment as the autopilot disengaged, relinquishing control to some hidden hand. The jet kept going, level. Yates touched the panel once, then again. Nothing.

Moments later, the altitude indicator showed the altitude changing, even as the pilots themselves felt the aircraft turn, then begin to descend.

"Who the hell is flying this jet?" The copilot looked out the window, then realized the absurdity of the act at forty-one thousand feet.

Yates flipped switches, operated touchscreens, went through every procedure she could think of that could do something, anything, to give her back control of the jet. Beside her, the copilot followed suit. But the aircraft didn't respond. This is no malfunction, Yates thought as the altitude indicated on the screen before her kept decreasing, the aircraft steady in its descent. Someone is controlling this jet, and it's not me.

Her precious cargo in mind, she wasn't about to take any chances. "Mayday, Mayday, Mayday," she repeated, her tone urgent, then relayed the aircraft's identification and position and prayed someone was listening, would come to their help.

But she already knew no one would, and could

only watch helplessly as the radio shut off. Her next thought was the ACARS message system, but a quick check found that it had been turned off, as had the ADS-B aircraft tracking system. Thinking that with the ADS-B disabled she might be able to activate the GPS uplink independently, she checked it, only to find that while it was still working, the uplink had been rerouted and she had no access to it, either. She no longer had any way to communicate with anyone on the ground, nor were there any remaining means on board the aircraft that would have allowed it to be tracked.

Still, she recounted what was happening in detail, hoping that the cockpit voice recorder would, together with the flight data recorder, at least give those she hoped might eventually find them what they would need to make sense of this.

The last thing she did as pressure throughout the aircraft dropped was pray that she would see her daughter again.

At the headquarters of International Diplomacy, Security and Defense in Brussels, the Internationals' High Council was meeting with the heads of IDSD's branches worldwide to review strategies past and future and their implications for the present. Everyone sitting in the upper-floor conference room of the building designated for the High Council's governing functions within the impressive complex was pleased. It had been a good year. A new, South Asian member had joined the alliance of peaceful nations, and another country had requested to join it just days earlier, in thanks for the alliance's help in a recent incident, assistance it gave without asking for anything in return. African Independent Territory was in one of the more precarious spots in the world, and its acceptance into the alliance would be the first successful diplomatic footprint it made in the continent. Granted, there was still a lot of work to be done there, but as the executive body of the founding member of the alliance, IDSD was more than ready to do what it took. It always was.

And then there was the promising news from the one place in Europe that had until not too long ago been rapidly going from bad to worse, in the region where the political divide between Eastern and Western Europe had once been. Two small countries that could have been a symbol of unity, cultural safe havens that would have set an example for so many, had instead been entangled in an endless feud that some years earlier had spiraled out of control, sending the two neighbors into a destructive conflict and sparking mutual atrocities that had not been seen in that part of the world for more than half a century. No one had been able to make the two nations talk, try to stop what was happening. No one until the Internationals' own Ambassador George Sendor had stepped in and, refusing to give up, had stuck with them through flare after flare of renewed distrust and violence, until he managed to get them to listen to him and had helped them see a better future for themselves, real hope for future generations. And now, after all the time and effort, the High Council could finally welcome news of an imminent peace treaty.

Ambassador Sendor was on his way to the meeting now and would be joining it sometime during its second half. The High Council was hoping he would accept their request that he remain in the region and watch over the implementation of the new treaty as the ambassador to both countries. The remarkable man was worthy of their trust, their respect, their support.

Council Head Ines Stevenssen was about to proceed with the next item on the agenda when the conference room door was flung open and a pale aide rushed in, followed by IDSD HQ's head of security, Julian Bern.

"Ma'am." The aide deferred to the council head.

Stevenssen motioned him and Bern in. Through the open door behind them, she saw people gathering, their agitation evident.

Bern approached the conference table. "I've just received a call from Mons Area Control Center," he said. "It has lost contact with Ambassador Sendor's jet. The last contact it had was a distress call from the pilot on the emergency frequency, which was cut off almost immediately but was without doubt relayed while the jet was still in the air. It has informed IDSD Global Flights Monitoring Station, and they've both initiated a search protocol." He paused. "So far, neither has had any success making contact with the jet. It has vanished."

The trailer was silent.

From the outside, it and the tractor unit it was connected to could be mistaken for an old semitrailer not worth the trouble of a second look, parked carelessly off the road, its driver apparently having sought a quiet place to catch some rest. And there was in fact someone in the driver's seat, a man who was seemingly asleep, a black cap pulled down over his eyes. Even with the windows up and the heater running, he had a short coat on, and his hands were crossed on his chest. To hide the gun.

The other armed guards—and there were quite a few of them—were deployed at varying distances around the trailer, all hidden from view. Not that they had to be hidden, or would even be needed at all. There was no one for miles around, and no one knew anyone was there. And even if someone happened to stray into the area, perhaps stumble upon any of the hidden men, no one had even a remote chance of guessing what their mission was, what they were protecting.

Still, it didn't hurt to be cautious, considering the stakes involved.

Inside, the trailer was far from simple, nothing

innocent about it. It had been converted to house, power and protect a system unlike any other in the world. Few knew this system existed, and fewer yet knew it was already operational. In fact, it was fully active now, working to the limit of its capacity in this, its maiden task.

The two men overseeing the system's activity were silent. They worked with precise efficiency, noting every single datum on the screens before them, knowing they must miss nothing. There was no time for words.

They were too busy controlling the jet flying high above them.

The initial shock had worn off, and the mood in the conference room was somber. Council Head Stevenssen had adjourned the meeting for an extended break immediately after hearing the news, to give everyone time to settle and to at least begin to adjust to what was thought to be a tragedy that had befallen one of the Internationals' most revered diplomats, a friend to many of them. The break was also intended to give Bern a chance to collect more information and, perhaps most important at that point, to give Stevenssen herself the time she needed to make sure the news would not get out. Until more was known about what had happened, she had to do her best to ensure that the two nations whose future was on the line would not find out prematurely that their best, perhaps only, chance for a lasting peace was gone. If they would blame each other—and they would, their history had shown—there would be no stopping the tragic consequences ever again.

Having reconvened the meeting, and with a pang of regret as she realized Sendor would by now have been there with them, Stevenssen took a long look at her peers sitting around the table, their eyes expectant on her.

"I have been given additional information," she said. "However, I suggest Head of Security Bern impart it himself, since he has been in direct contact with the parties involved."

Bern stepped forward. "They don't think the jet crashed."

He had everyone's attention.

"Signals from all systems on board designed to communicate the jet's location disappeared more or less simultaneously. So together with the pilot's emergency call the first thought was catastrophic failure. However, the emergency locator transmitters on board whose activation would have been triggered by a crash were not activated. Also, the jet was over land when it disappeared, and our satellites would have found a crash site by now around its last recorded position or we would have had reports from local authorities or witnesses. There's nothing.

"The monitoring station has attempted to access the flight data recorder remotely—I don't know if you're aware of it, but this capability was developed to avoid a possibly critical delay in having to search for the recorder in the event of an air accident or an attack, and the risk of being unable to find it if its locator beacon ceases to operate. However, the recorder cannot be accessed." He paused. "It seems we are being actively locked out."

"Could a signal jammer have been used?" The man asking was Admiral James Helios, head of IDSD United States. It was the recent Oracle incident involving his IDSD branch that had brought to their attention the existence, in the hands of the wrong people, of a sophisticated type of jammers one of the applications of which was to conceal the flight path of an aircraft.

"No, sir, we don't believe so. We don't know much yet about that jammer I'm assuming you're referring to, how it works, but I believe a jammer would have caused a different type of interference, not what we're seeing here."

Helios nodded, although he clearly wasn't entirely convinced.

"Couldn't the emergency locator . . . what was it, transmitters? Couldn't they have malfunctioned?" the High Council's deputy head asked.

"There are two of them installed on the jet, sir, as a safety measure, given its designation, and it is unlikely both would have malfunctioned at the same time," Bern answered.

"Could something have happened on board it,

incapacitating everyone? In which case, wouldn't the aircraft still have continued to fly on autopilot?" The speaker, Council Member Sloan, had been a combat fighter pilot in her past. She would know her stuff, Bern knew.

"Theoretically, yes, ma'am," he said, "and the jet certainly had enough fuel. However, if that were the case, we would have been able to access the auto-pilot and take control of the jet. We can't. We have ascertained that the autopilot has been turned off. And no, the one thing we already know is that the jet did not continue on its predesignated route." He cleared his throat. "Also, once the monitoring station realized it is unable to contact the jet, it calculated possible routes for it beginning with its last known position. So far, satellites have found nothing along any of these routes." He hesitated. "I think at this point we can safely assume that the jet is no longer in the air."

Silence fell as the implications of what he was saying sank in.

"Are you telling us that it was somehow taken?" the head of IDSD Southern Territories asked.

"That seems to be the most likely possibility. The question is by whom and how. The jet went through the mandatory pre-flight scan. Other than the ambassador and his personal assistant only the regular aircrew and the protective detail were on board, and I can tell you we can vouch for every one of them."

"Where the hell is it then?" Council Member Richmond, an old friend of Ambassador Sendor, was understandably upset.

Before Bern could answer, his phone rang. He glanced at it, then excused himself and took the call. Everyone in the room remained silent, waiting expectantly.

Bern muted the call and looked at them. "The monitoring station has located the jet. It seems to have landed on the artificial extension of Cres, the Croatian island. From above it looks intact. Our air-sea base at Split has dispatched helicopters to the area."

The room was hushed as they waited. No one dared think of the possibilities. Everyone hoped.

Bern, too, waited, listening on his headset. He was patched through, heard it all. After endless minutes, he finally ended the call, stared at his phone. "I'm sorry. The jet's aircrew, the protective detail, the ambassador's assistant, they're dead. They're all dead."

He raised his eyes to the stricken leaders before him. "Ambassador Sendor is gone."

Chapter Two

While Ambassador George Sendor was still sipping his orange-flavored Earl Grey tea forty-one thousand feet above Europe, contemplating the fate of nations and mercifully oblivious to his own, Lara Holsworth was just waking up in Washington, DC. She had left the blinds open so that the sun would shine into the bedroom, and it did, another clear autumn day. Winter would be here soon enough, but she was glad it hadn't arrived just yet. She got up and put on a light, lace-trim robe she had laid at the edge of the bed, then went to the window and looked out at the house's back yard, planted to emphasize the best of each season. Delaying, she realized. It was simple, really. She was delaying starting the day.

Donovan wasn't here.

This is crazy, she thought. How can I miss him? How can I miss him already? Shaking her head, surprised at herself but not entirely displeased with this new feeling, she descended the stairs to the quiet of the first floor, the late morning sun greeting her here, too, in a renewed attempt to distract her. The main security console was silently active, and for the first time in days she had no reason to give it even a cursory glance. The coffeemaker purred in the kitchen, and she contemplated it, then reconsidered and turned to go back upstairs to shower and dress when her phone beeped upstairs, then automatically sent the arriving message to the media screen closest to her. The text message made her smile.

"Have breakfast, the kind I would make you."

So he wasn't asleep. And he wasn't at his place, otherwise he would already be here, with her. He had brought her back home earlier that morning just as the sun peeked over the horizon, after first insisting on another visit to the IDSD medical center. The agents guarding her and her home were, to her relief, gone by then, all except the two who had stayed behind to formally pass the house security back to Donovan. After making sure she would go straight to bed, he had gone back to his own house next door, to get some sleep. Apparently that hadn't worked out so well. But then, being a United States Federal Investigative Division senior investigator was no less demanding than her own job.

The smile wouldn't go away. "Where are you?" she dictated back.

"On a case," was his answer. "I'll come by as soon as I get back. How're you doing?"

She sent him a smile.

This is crazy, she thought again as she made herself breakfast. But the smile was still on her face.

She was on her way to open the patio doors, intending to sit down on her favorite couch, log on to her secure laptop and get some work done, perhaps dig into the operations and unrests updates her aide, Aiden, would have sent her already, when the house security system let her know she had a visitor. A look at the closest security console showed her that Donna Howard was at the door. Lara let her best friend in, and a moment later the colorfully dressed woman rushed into the living room, visibly agitated.

"Hey, I couldn't come in! Why couldn't I come in?" Donna was used to simply walking into Lara's home, whether here, in this house Lara had moved into only weeks earlier, the house Donna herself had renovated for her, or in her previous apartment, right next to the one Donna still lived in with her common-law partner, Patty, and their young child, Greg.

"It's okay, Don, the security system has been upgraded. Come on, I'll enter you in the new one, it will recognize you next time."

"Upgraded? Why? It was installed just before you moved in!" As Donna approached Lara she gasped, her hand going to her mouth. "Oh my God, what happened to you?" she said, rushing to her.

Lara was at a loss for a moment, then remembered. Her face still showed signs of the recent attack on her. The sleep she got, exhausted, together with the painkiller Donovan had asked that she take, made her feel better, and the aches were now only background static, a reminder that no longer needed to be helped away. She was glad her friend couldn't see the already fading cuts and bruises on the rest of her body. The accelerated-recovery treatment she had received twice, both on the night of the attack and on the following night, at Donovan's prodding, ensured that she was healing quickly, and soon there would be no signs of what she had been through. Unfortunately, not soon enough to hide them from her worried friend.

She contemplated how to explain this. Delaying, she turned and walked to the kitchen, and busied herself with making some tea, a fruity blend she herself didn't like but that Donna craved, hot or cold. She put the cup on the dark cherry red countertop and finally faced her friend, who continued to stand where she was, unrelenting, her hands planted firmly on her hips. Waiting. And Donna would never back down, not if she thought anything might be wrong with Lara. The fact itself that she was there—

"Wait a minute. Donna, what are you doing here? How did you know I'd be at home?" The thing about Lara's job was, there wasn't a nine-to-five routine about it, not even close. Yes, there were those quiet, even ordinary days, ordinary for her, that is, in which she ran post-mission analysis or received updates about alliance operations in progress, global hot spots or deployments she needed to know about. But more often than not her work involved her working missions that could last days, preparations

that would last weeks. Unpredictable days that started or ended at odd hours, times when Oracle took
over and that not even she could know how long
they would be. Donna knew this and wouldn't just
drop by and expect her to be at home. Yet there she
was.

"Donovan called me," Donna stated.

"Donovan...?"

"Yes. He said you're at home and that I should
come over because you might need me."

"He did what?" Lara fumed. "I can't believe he
did that! He can't babysit me himself so he sends
you? The nerve of this guy!"

Donna's jaw dropped. "Look at you. Lara, you
never lose your temper. Certainly not because of
a man! And Donovan? What's going on here? First
he calls out of the blue, he doesn't tell me anything
but he has me promise I'll come over, and then I
find you looking like, well, like you've been in a
brawl! What on earth is going on? Come on, spit it
out!"

Lara was too busy fuming to answer. "That man
is impossible! It's not like I'm in any danger anymore, and I certainly don't need to be taken care of,
I've done very well alone, without him!"

"Lara!"

"Okay, okay." One thing she definitely couldn't
do was avoid Donna's need to know. "This thing
our agencies, IDSD and USFID, were cooperating
on? Well, Donovan and I ended up working on it

together, and it got complicated. Long story. Anyway, it's just that . . . he sort of ended up saving my life."

As Lara spoke, Donna's hands dropped to her sides, and she simply stood there, gaping. Finally, she approached the counter with a measured step. "Donovan . . . what?"

Lara shrugged. "He saved my life."

"Saved . . . ? How? What's there to save, you work at IDSD, you're in an office, how would he . . . you said danger? Why would you be in any danger? Wait, you two get along now? The last time I saw you together you were at each other's throats. In fact, I clearly remember that Donovan actually threatened to shoot you!"

"Things kind of changed after that." Which was, admittedly, an understatement.

"Really?" Donna sat down at the counter. "I don't know where to begin. With the fact that for whatever reason you needed saving, or with this very interesting turnaround in your attitude toward Donovan. Donovan, of all people. Or maybe I should say, you, of all people."

Normally Lara would have gladly used the opportunity to steer the conversation away from her work and the circumstances that led to the attack on her, but turning the conversation away from Donovan and her—she still had to wrap her own mind around that one—seemed to be the more attractive option right then. And so she gave her friend a generalized, and quite skimpy, account of what happened. Not enough to increase Donna's worry or divulge too many details of what was a highly confidential incident, but enough to let her know that it happened, was over, and was unlikely to ever happen again. While Donna knew about Oracle, in fact she had been there when it first came into existence, she had no idea what it had become since, how far it had come. And while she knew it had Lara working hard, too hard, she often said, she had never thought, and must never again think, that it could actually put her best friend at risk.

"Wow." Donna's tea sat forgotten before her, shock evident on her face. And that was only the abridged version she got of the story, Lara thought with some amusement as she got up to replace the tea.

Still, apparently it still wasn't enough to distract Donna from what interested her most. "So, wait. About Donovan. You two are okay now?"

Lara walked back slowly, handed her the hot cup, then sat down in a way that Donna knew there was something else there.

"Lara?"

No sense delaying. Donna would find out eventually, and who would Lara tell if not her best friend? She braced herself. "He kissed me."

Donna almost dropped the cup.

"Last night, he kissed me," Lara repeated, wonder in her voice, her eyes distant. "I think he . . ." She found it difficult to complete the thought. Say the words.

But Donna understood. "Do you?" Her voice was gentle. She knew more than anyone that this was delicate ground she was treading on.

Lara turned her eyes back to the one friend she could talk to about anything, the one friend who knew everything. She opened her mouth to speak but then stopped, ended up retreating into herself as the struggle inside her took over. "Donna, what am I going to do?"

"I think you're already doing it."

Lara shook her head. "I'm not doing, I'm just..."

"Feeling. Finally. But the past is still there, you're still pulling back."

Lara looked away, focused on the view outside the backsplash window that lined this part of the house, and her eyes fell on the red, yellow and orange leaves of the shrubs that separated her back yard from that of the man who had elicited this conversation she never thought she would have.

Donna leaned forward and put a hand on hers. "It will be okay, nothing is going to go wrong. Let it happen, sweetie. Just let it happen."

"I am," Lara admitted to Donna, to herself.

"So where is Donovan anyway?"

"A case, he texted me."

"Texted you?" Donna asked and marveled at the smile that appeared on her friend's face.

"Yes, he does that." The emotion was evident in

Lara's smile, and Donna felt her eyes tear up. After all this time, all the pain, it was finally happening. Lara had finally fallen in love.

At IDSD's headquarters in Brussels, Council Head Stevenssen took a deep breath to collect herself. Someone had to, it was that simple. The devastating news about Ambassador Sendor had sent a ripple of shock through everyone present, and the meeting she had reconvened had broken up again as mayhem took over. The questions were numerous, and none could be answered. All they had were the jet and the bodies of everyone who had been on it. Everyone but the ambassador. Which lent itself, Stevenssen thought, to some hope. Surely if he was not killed with everyone else who had been on the jet, he might still be alive somewhere. The questions remained, however, where, and to what end.

She stood up, placed her palms flat on the conference table, and waited, a tall, slender woman with somber eyes that had seen a world of worry, her long years in leadership etched on her face. One by one her peers noticed, quieted down, prodded those closest to them to do the same. Soon they had all sat back down, and the room fell silent.

Stevenssen remained quiet for a moment longer, looking around the table, including all of them in her gaze. When she spoke, her tone was resolute. "This incident must not be made public." She raised her hand at the protests. "At least until we know more. I am aware that it will come out eventually. However, if we make it known now, with the scant information we have and without any explanation as to what might have happened and why, this could lead to the peace talks that are so important to our friend crumbling, and we all know what the implications for the region are certain to be. Of course, if we do not make it public and whoever is behind it releases the information before we do, we will be seen as having failed to disclose news we had no right to hide." She let out a heavy sigh. "This is a fine line we have no choice but to walk."

All heads in the room nodded in agreement. The risk had to be taken, for the sake of everyone involved.

Lara finally convinced Donna to go home and spend what was left of the day with Patty and Greg, then settled down on her comfortable, soft cream-colored couch not far from the now open patio doors and dove into work. When she looked up from her laptop again, Donovan was leaning casually against the doorway, illuminated against the falling darkness outside. Handsome in a dark gray suit and a white shirt, its top button open. Looking at her. He seemed to do that a lot, watch her. It amazed her, how his gaze had changed since they first met. From anger and rage, to scrutiny, to this look he now had in his eyes that made her heart flutter, easily penetrating through the defenses she thought she had put up so well around her.

In the past she would push any man interested in her away, not let anyone in. But not anymore, not him. He had awakened in her something that she had thought long gone, and maybe, she had begun to think in the still dim morning hours, a moment before she fell asleep, maybe there was no need to push him away. Maybe she could risk letting him in.

His lips curved up a little, the smile deep in the blue of his eyes. He's reading me again, she thought, standing up and walking over to meet him, and might have done something about it except her heart was too busy picking up speed as he straightened, came toward her and, just as he had that first time, the first time he had kissed her, put his hand on her waist, his other hand on her cheek, caressing, then leaned in and touched his lips to hers, his kiss as soft now as it was then.

She didn't move away, but wondered. "Another kiss."

"Just fulfilling a promise I made to you. And I will never break my promises to you." He pulled her closer to him, touched his lips to hers again. Found himself surprised at how good it felt, kissing her, being this close to her, as his body, his entire being, reacted, not letting him let her go. He had meant to do this slowly, still not knowing what it was in her that had resisted him until so recently, what it was she was hiding that had been an impenetrable wall between them. But now that he was here all he could think, feel, was her. He kissed her again, a long, deep kiss, holding her close to him, unable to stop.

Her arms came up around him. "You already fulfilled that promise, you know. You kissed me," she said softly. Their first kiss, the one he had promised her amid the chaos they had found themselves in until mere hours before.

"This is a new one," he murmured against her lips. "A new promise I made when I couldn't stop thinking about you today. That I will never stop kissing you."

No fear, she wondered as she answered his kiss. Where did the fear of loving him go? Did the attack on her take it away? Or was it all him, her confidence in him, in what she felt from him, in what could be?

Did it matter? she mused before she lost her train of thought, drowning in him as the kiss deepened and he wrapped his arms around her. His hand slid down her back, his fingers tightening as need flashed, as he realized it was more than a kiss he'd been waiting for the entire day. Finally, he thought as he felt her body respond to his.

His phone signaled an incoming message. He was grumbling in protest when hers indicated one, too. They pulled away from each other with some difficulty.

"Mine's a new lead on someone I've been looking for. This morning's case, a guy who escaped SIRT's net a year ago and has resurfaced now," he said absently, glancing at the phone. He shook his head. "A bad guy who loves being a bad guy. Unfortunately, it means I have to go in again now. Yours?"

"Oracle." It was enough, she knew. He knew all about Oracle now.

"You're supposed to be off today. You need the rest."

"They wouldn't call me in unless there was no choice, you know that." A frown crossed her face. The code in the message said it all. She looked at him. "And never mind me, I slept, had the entire day to rest. Did you sleep at all?"

"Don't worry about it."

"Goes both ways." Her eyes narrowed slightly. "Donna says hi, by the way."

He laughed. "Fair enough. Once this one's over I'll catch up on some sleep." Although, he thought, even then sleep just might have to wait. He now had something else on his mind.

Unfortunately, for both of them work could not wait.

"Any idea what it is?" He indicated her phone.

She ran missions in her mind. "None of the pending missions have matured yet, so it's most likely an emergency. The code is immediate." She turned to go upstairs, change, get her IDSD ID. But then she turned back.

"Did you see the car?" she asked. Donna had alerted her to the unfamiliar car in her driveway. Going out, she had discovered that, sometime when she had slept, IDSD had placed a car out of its executive car pool in her driveway. It was thoughtful of them to do that, make sure she had a comfortable—and yes, secure, she knew—replacement to her own car, giving her the independence she wanted instead of just assigning to her an interim ride with a driver, which she would feel limited with. But she still hated the car.

Donovan nodded. "It's temporary. We'll figure it out."

"Yeah." She shook her head, miserable. "There's no way Frank is going to let me choose my own car again."

She turned back to go upstairs, and Donovan smiled. He'd already thought about that.

Chapter Three

Council Head Stevenssen raised her head. Her eyes were tired and felt so very gritty, but she was still here, in her office, in the same building where the meeting took place that had seen cheer turn into grave concern. She could not bring herself to leave and felt compelled to wait for news. It was surreal, all of it.

George Sendor, her good friend and a valued colleague, had disappeared.

News from Cres was scant, and not in the least helpful. But of course the search would take time, as would the investigation into what happened. She had to be patient, and it would not do to let show her horror at the events taking place, the potential outcome, the devastating consequences. The people around her looked up to her leadership, and she had to give a show of robustness and provide them with the stability they needed. It would be a necessity if events unfolded the way she was praying they wouldn't. Nor would it do to disturb the work of the investigators. Or of the search teams, for that matter. They were the best, and she should let them do their job, as she would do hers.

So far nothing had been found. The search teams were canvassing the area around Cres at a growing radius, land and sea alike, but whoever had perpetrated the abduction had obviously planned and executed it in a way that no evidence leading to them had been left behind. The jet had landed on the hard surface of Cres's artificial platform, and no vehicles had driven up to it, or so it had so far been ascertained. Sendor, the investigators on site now believed, must have been taken away through the sea, just a short distance away from where the jet had been stranded.

After an initial examination, the bodies had been taken away, Stevenssen had been told, and arrangements had already been made to move the jet. Night had fallen, hampering further efficient forensic work at the remote, barren site. That, and the fact that the incident had to remain hidden for now, had prompted the decision to move the crime scene— the jet itself—as quickly as possible. Where questions were raised about its presence there in the first place, a mechanical malfunction in a privately owned transport was cited, an explanation that also helped justify the presence of the search and rescue forces around it. All signs on the jet itself indicating who it was really registered to were covered, to prevent questions that no one could, as yet, answer. As for the search, it would continue under the guise of previously scheduled military search and rescue exercises. Other than that, there was nothing more to do on site. They had nothing.

It has only been hours, Stevenssen said to herself. Patience.

Easier said than done.

At IDSD US's secure complex on the Virginia bank of the Potomac river south of Washington, DC, the opaque reinforced glass doors to the war room spanning the greater part of the top floor of the missions building silently slid open before Lara, the priority-clearance security system having already identified and tagged her as she entered the building, and followed her every move. She stood at the entrance and looked around her. As always when she came here something within her awoke, taking its place at the forefront of her mind. A focus, an alertness that she loved to feel. This was her turf. Here everything that she was came together seamlessly, here she could be herself and was valued for precisely that. And even now, even after who she was had almost cost her her life, this was still where she felt most at home, where she belonged.

A step into the vast space was all she managed to take before the harried-looking Major Korrel strode toward her, trying hard to look as if he wasn't running. She skimmed in her mind over what she knew about him. Mike Korrel, forty-four, head of the team that dealt with peacekeeping missions in the

Middle East. Not someone she had had the occasion to work with directly, since usually if anything went wrong she worked the military oversight and intervention side. But he was a familiar face.

"Ma'am." His voice was urgent. "Our peacekeeping force on the former Syria-Jordan border was attacked. Our people managed to strike back, it looks like they're managing to fend the attackers off and we've dispatched backup, but five of our peacekeepers were taken and we can't track them."

As Lara walked to Mission Command, listening to Korrel's account of the events, Aiden Jenor, her trusted aide, approached her from his station outside her office. Without a word, he took her briefcase and handed her the headset that would allow her to communicate with anyone she required access to, in IDSD or outside it, in or outside the field.

"I need a run-through," she told him, and he nodded once and hurried away. A run-through, a concentrated run of all data available done while she was already working a mission, was something she had to do only when she was called on to intervene in a mission in progress that she had no prior involvement in, an urgent intervention that did not allow any preparation beforehand. Not only did it demand more of her, since it involved the intake of a substantial amount of data within an impossibly short amount of time, it also left significant gaps in the information she had for her use and required her to take a considerable leap to fill them. She didn't like that, didn't like the added risk to the lives of those who depended on her to bring them home. But sometimes, like now, there was simply no other choice.

The armed security agent standing before Mission Command moved aside and its heavy door slid open before her, and she didn't slow down as she walked up to the multipurpose holoscreen that covered the entire length of its main wall. Stepping on the operations platform stretching the length of the screen, she issued a series of commands into the slender microphone of her headset, and the left half of the screen blanked for a split second before it erupted with a flood of information—data and images—the run-through information flow Aiden had already activated in her office. She never took heed of anyone else in Mission Command, never took her eyes off the screen. There was simply no time.

Around her, Mission Command fell silent as those present realized what was going on. That she was there. That Oracle was there, already working. They all fell back, retreating to the rows of seats that lined the back wall, all except for the two system operators in their designated stations on each side of the screen and the officers who had been overseeing the situation in the field, including Korrel. Normally they too would move back, but this was different. She might need them to provide information, having had no time to prepare.

Not far from her, she noticed Vice Admiral Frank

Scholes, the second-in-command of IDSD in the United States and the head of IDSD Missions as well as the global missions commander, and the only person authorized to oversee Oracle's work. He was the one who had called her in despite the hectic events of the past days and her place in them, which meant, she knew all too well, that there had been, simply, no other choice.

"They came through a tunnel," Korrel was saying behind her, an edge of panic to his voice. "We had no idea it was there, that they had dug it, it runs so deep underground, and this isn't the type of thing . . . tunnels have never been used in this area before, much farther southwest, yes, and some northwest from there, but never in this area, nowhere near it. And the peacekeeping mission has been in place for twelve years now, and successfully so. Why would anyone do this?"

Lara didn't care why. Not now. She wasn't here to understand the why and how, these could be left for the post-mission debriefing and analysis that would lead to the required reaction, redeployment, and re-securing, through both military and diplomatic channels.

She was here to bring the captive peacekeepers back before they were taken too deep into unfriendly territory. A hostage situation could escalate into years in which their captors would use them as leverage against those who cared about their fate. And if her assumption as to who did this was correct, that was exactly what would happen. Those who didn't care about human life facing those who valued it over all—that never ended well. But even more of a consideration was the suffering the captives were facing, if they were even still alive. They, and all those who loved them and would want them safely back home.

Were they alive, all of them? She knew that the abduction of five peacekeepers at once was a rare occurrence for that region, and close to impossible in the type of incident Korrel had described, a fast escape through a tunnel by what would necessarily be a small group holding the captives. That if their abductors found them too much to handle they might kill them, some or all. Bodies were easier to handle, did not resist, and could still be used as leverage, all the more so if the abductors managed to hide the fact that the hostages were no longer alive.

No. They were alive. They had to be alive. All of them. And they had to be found now. And the abductors, they would be stopped before they managed to hurt the innocents they had taken. That was the only outcome she would allow in her mind.

She tuned out Korrel, who was still speaking behind her. What he was saying was no longer relevant. Tunnel. That was all she needed to know. She faced the screen, didn't see Scholes put a hand on Korrel's arm to silence him, didn't heed the tense anticipation behind her.

Her mind filled with the data and images on the screen before her, absorbing it all at a staggering speed. The shortage of time was a major hindrance, but the immediacy of the situation, the lives of the people she was here for, served, as always, to focus her, and she gave it all she had. Information flowed on the screen, and she added to it what she already knew from past experience, combining it all—the region, the peacekeeping mission, the day's events, past and ongoing conflicts, resident and transient groups, angers dominating, interests ruling, methods used. Anything, everything.

Tunnel.

Abruptly, she turned but not to the current view of the focus area, which she had placed to her right on the screen. Instead, she turned to Scholes, who was still standing close by, waiting, watching her. He nodded slightly. So that's why he called her in to do this. He was one of only two people who had recently seen something that would have led him to think Oracle just might be the one who could cut short the peacekeepers' abduction, something she herself had no idea she could do until then, until just the day before. She knew exactly what he was asking her to do. He wanted her to seek an unknown at an unknown location. Which was, for all intents and purposes, impossible.

She turned back to the screen, now showing, at her command, a stationary drone view of the incident area and the arriving back-up defense forces deploying, the remaining peacekeepers mixing with them. The minutes ticked by on the rows of clocks hanging on the back wall of Mission Command, but not in her mind. Thinking about the advance of time, the urgency, wasn't a priority. It got in the way. Time, in this instance, had only served her for the split second it took her to realize this had to be done, to decisively end, now.

Although she might have use for it again later.

She took a last look at what she had, then uttered a quiet command and the entire screen blanked. Everything useful to her right now was in her mind. This wasn't like other missions, there were no satellite feeds and drone footage of hostile forces moving around trapped allies. There had been nothing except the shocked peacekeepers and raging defense forces in the live images she had removed from the screen before her. There was no one to guide here, no one for them to stand up against, not until she could tell them where the missing peacekeepers were.

She kept her eyes on the blank screen and locked on to the mission-relevant information in her mind. Gradually, everything around and within her faded away—sounds, sights, data and thoughts—until nothing remained but that which mattered here, now, what she needed to work with. She was completely, entirely focused.

But it wasn't enough. There wasn't enough. No sufficient information, no likelihoods to be used or deduced, no certainties to grasp on to.

Just five people trapped in their own private hell, which no one could bring them back from. Not in time. Perhaps not ever.

I can, she thought. I have to. I have to bring them home.

Turning into the depths of her mind, she took a leap.

For anything from a split second to eternity she was in nothing. There was, quite simply, nothing. Not even familiarity with her own abilities—this was new, she had done this only once before, once just the other day, and then the constraints were, in a way, so much . . . less.

Unafraid, she stayed where she was. Where others needed answers to hold on to, guidance to follow, certainty to live in, she didn't. She accepted what was not there. Lived with it. Existed within it. Turned without hesitation into it when she needed, took confident steps deep into the unknown where others would be too fearful to venture.

And did within it as she wanted. She restructured some probabilities, closed some gaps, left some for later, turned away from others. Deduced, decided. And when she was ready, went beyond. It happened, was happening now, somewhere, someplace real, she couldn't see it but it was there, still happening in that someplace and sometime she would be able to return to in the future, look to, analyze, but by then it would be too late, she needed it now. She needed to be there, to be then, to see it, now.

And then she did. Just enough.

Just enough to know.

Mission Command was dead silent. No one dared to move or speak. Even those who had seen Oracle at work before, and many of those present had, had never seen her this way. Standing like this for so long, silent, eyes closed now, head slightly bowed. Of course, she had nothing to work with. It was impossible. Not even Oracle could—

Oracle raised her head, opened eyes intense with focus that had Scholes take an involuntary step back when she turned them to him. Yes, he thought. That's it. You have them, don't you?

He never had any doubt she would. In the five years since he had brought her here, as he built the war room and Mission Command around her, he had seen her take step after impossible step forward, advance, develop. Walls only stood in her path until she found a way to break through them. And she always did.

Her eyes turned back to the screen, her commands already bringing up multiple localized views and alerting the field commander assigned to her, who would relay her orders to the forces on the ground that were ready to go on the hunt.

Oracle was ready to bring the captives home.

Chapter Four

When she finally came out of Mission Command, a gray autumn morning greeted her through the window wall that stretched along the entire length of the war room to her left. She stood for a moment looking at the overcast sky, focusing. This was the difficult part of finishing a mission. Winding down that part of her that was Oracle, and focusing back on here, now. Normally this last incident might have been easier than other missions, some of which left her exhausted, fighting to return to herself. This one was short, one night, that's all. But it was a time-sensitive mission with a high uncertainty level and she had worked under tremendous pressure, and that was a recently found skill—very recently—she had used in there. And then there was the toll recent events had taken on her, mind and body, and the fact that they themselves had come on the heels of long weeks of a hectic workload, a line of successive missions. But then, that was what Oracle's days looked like more often than not.

Letting out a breath, she turned right, passed the entrance to the main conference room, skirted the hub of activity comprising the enclosed workspaces that took up a large part of the war room's midst, and approached the critical mission experts' offices, the nearest of which was hers. Aiden followed her into her office, a cup of coffee—her favorite strong blend—in his hand. She sat behind her desk with a sigh and gratefully accepted the coffee. Around her the wall screens were blank, as was her multitouch desk. Normally, as soon as she entered the war room and its internal security recognized her, the mainframe would activate the secure closed system in her office, and all screens would be waiting for her with the IDSD Missions symbol rotating on them. But Aiden had been in here and had blanked all screens, thinking, and rightly so, that she would prefer her office calm and quiet after the long hours behind her.

She squinted at him. "Didn't I tell you to take some time off?" Aiden had stuck with her throughout the events of the past days, the mission that she herself had been the center of, and before leaving the war room the night before she had asked him to get some well-deserved rest. And yet there he was.

"I did, I was off part of the day yesterday," he said, scrutinizing her. "Long night. May I suggest you go home, ma'am? You're still officially off duty, and there really is nothing urgent."

"No." She put the cup down and rubbed the knots out of her neck. "No, it's okay. Since I'm already here, I'll run mission analysis and go through the updates. Of the pending missions first."

When Aiden had left, she swiveled in her chair toward the window spanning the wall behind her and settled back. But it wasn't the view outside that she saw, nor the increasingly gray autumn sky, clouds overpowering the new day's sun. Instead, her mind went back to days past and to new attractions and revelations that promised different tomorrows, and she marveled at how right things had turned out despite everything that had happened and that had come so close, too close, to ending so wrong. After a while she turned back to her desk, swiped her hand over it, activating the multitouch platform, and went to work.

Aiden walked to his workstation, his eyes pensive. No, he wasn't tired. He was used to working this way, in the same hours Ms. Holsworth did. She never allowed weariness to stop her—like now, he had seen the deep weariness in her eyes—and so neither did he. He was used to taking time to rest when she did, although even then he was in charge of the updates she received and kept an eye on each and every pending mission she was scheduled to guide.

And, as always, he was alerted about the emergency mission when she was. He had set that up a long time ago, ensuring that he would be there when she was. He'd been with Ms. Holsworth since her very first day at IDSD, and would have it no other way. Specifically chosen and carefully trained to be an aide, he had initially been assigned to her temporarily, but the fit was immediate, and he hadn't left her since. Now, five years later, he could easily anticipate her needs, and ran everything both Lara and Oracle around her with unequaled efficiency and loyalty. Even when he was off duty, he never really was, just like she wasn't.

Ms. Holsworth's phone indicated an incoming call, and Aiden answered it. He'd taken it from her, as always, before she entered Mission Command, and had planned to keep it for a while longer so that no one would bother her after the mission she'd just completed. He was now glad he did.

The name by which the man on the other end of the line introduced himself and the first words spoken had him halting in place, then turning and walking briskly not back into Ms. Holsworth office, but to Vice Admiral Scholes's office on the other side of the war room. As he burst in, not heeding the indignant protests of Scholes's aide, Celia, the look on his face had the vice admiral stand up in apprehension. Aiden was not one to be easily shaken.

The movement at the door made Lara raise her head. The ready smile that appeared on her face at the sight of the vice admiral faltered, then dimmed, then was replaced by a frown.

"Frank?"

"Lara." He stood in the doorway, hesitating.

She would have asked him what was wrong, but something clicked in her mind. Out of nowhere, a memory surfaced, a distant one she had not thought about for a long time. It was the look on his face that had triggered it. A look she had only seen once since she'd first met him. Only once, on that day five years before.

Only on that day.

She froze.

"No, it's not like that, not like then." Scholes realized he'd made a mistake. He should have waited a beat, collected himself, planned this ahead. But he had been there, back then when it happened. He'd barely known her then, not at all, really, and even then it had been difficult, what he had had to do. And now he knew her well, and he cared. Now she was like family to him. And this was painful.

"Listen." He spoke fast, wanting to explain, to give her all the details, to show her it wasn't the same, not necessarily. Not yet. He hoped to God it wasn't. "Director White called you, Aiden took the call. White just wanted. . ." He faltered. He couldn't believe he had to do this again. He'd seen Lara and Donovan grow close, saw the way Donovan looked at her, how he had put himself in harm's way to protect her. Saw Lara react, push back, then finally respond. Finally, after all this time.

No, he couldn't believe he was doing this. Again.

He gave it to her straight, knowing who he was

talking to. He didn't want her to fill in the gaps herself. "Donovan flew to New Mexico last night, as part of an investigation. Apparently he was chasing someone he'd been after for a while, together with the local marshals. Donovan and his agent followed the guy into the desert hills, and White says the agent called for backup, but the call was cut off."

Her eyes remained on his.

Scholes braced himself. There was no sense in hiding this, not from her. "Last thing they heard were shots and the agent shouting Donovan's name."

She closed her eyes.

"Lara, it's not the same." It can't be, oh God, it can't, not again.

She said nothing.

"White sent in agents from their local office, and the marshals had already gone in, but there's nothing. Nothing yet," he corrected. "Before he left, Donovan asked White to call you if he's delayed, he didn't want you to worry. White waited before he called, he only did so when after the sun came up they still found nothing, and he thought—" He stopped, realizing he was rambling.

Lara couldn't breathe. The past came rushing in, mercilessly drowning too recently awakened emotions, too new an attempt, a hesitant decision to let a present, a different future in.

Scholes skirted the desk and eased his huge bulk to the floor before her, his knees protesting. He took her hands in his. "Lara, it doesn't mean anything.

He could be safe, this could be . . . there could be a dozen reasons why he hasn't made contact yet. You know that." But even as he spoke he knew it didn't matter. This wasn't a mission, something for her to assimilate and resolve, this wasn't Oracle he was talking to. This was Lara, Lara of the past, before Oracle ever existed. These were old emotions, pain so deep it never healed, had only began to heal with the man whose death he feared she might now have to deal with.

"Listen," he said, "White has an open line to me, as soon as he knows anything he'll call."

She said nothing. There was nothing. Threatened by overwhelming emotions she knew she had no way of dealing with, she had already shut that part of herself down.

Donovan, the thought unwittingly came to her mind, and with it his face, his eyes on hers, his smile for her. His kiss. She clamped down on it with everything she had.

And hoped it would hold.

Leaving Lara's office, Scholes stumbled into Aiden, who was standing immediately outside. Scholes nodded but said nothing. Aiden would watch over her. It wasn't by chance that the aide had taken the call to him rather than directly to Lara. All those years ago, Aiden had learned the truth about how Lara came to be recruited to IDSD from Scholes himself, who had seen the young man's immediate rapport to her. He had been there at the very beginning, and in the first weeks and months as she had fought to take step after step forward and rebuild her life. Even now only a rare few knew the whole truth. Aiden was one of them. He was loyal, and had never said a word.

As Scholes walked away, Aiden stationed himself at the doorway to Ms. Holsworth's inner office, where he could see her. He didn't worry about her seeing him. She had turned back to the window and was staring out. Locked somewhere inside herself. Damn. He liked Agent Pierce and trusted him with Ms. Holsworth. He liked what the agent brought out in her. It was the first time he had seen in the remarkable woman something that was different from what she had been like until then. It was the first time he had seen that pensiveness that accompanies deep-rooted pain ease.

He resumed watching over her, praying silently that this was all a mistake.

The doors of hangar A506IDSD-T slid shut and locked with an audible click.

"Alfa-five-zero-six secure," came the affirmation, even as manned security moved to surround the imposing structure. Normally technological means would be deemed sufficient, however in this case IDSD Security opted for the additional measure, noting the necessity that no information about what was going on here would leak out.

Inside, the military hangar, specifically designed for the inspection of malfunctioned aircraft, housed only a single executive jet at this time, and yet the number of people working on it was staggering. Aviation accident investigators, crime scene investigators and intelligence agents, they were all there. Behind the transparent divide separating the main floor from the primary inspection lab overseeing it, Dr. Rebecca Tanner watched the rare sight with awe. They were like ants, swarming the aircraft inside and outside, yet not getting in one another's way. Everyone worked with somber efficiency.

The aircraft was empty when it was brought here, to IDSD-Alliance Defense Forces Europe Air Base at Mons, southwest of Brussels. The bodies had already been taken away when it was still on Cres, and the medical examiner's team was still working on them, no findings there yet. All the investigators had to work with in their efforts to piece together the story of what had happened was the sleek aircraft and its systems, now dormant.

The oddest thing was that there was nothing wrong with this aircraft. When the first search and rescue teams dispatched from the air-sea base at Split got to it, it was simply standing there, silent. All its systems were shut down, but otherwise it was intact.

There had been no apparent attempt to damage it, nor to hide it. Whoever had perpetrated the hijacking had taken what they wanted and left the aircraft as is, with the gruesome testimony to what had happened inside, the bodies. And so, ironically, the aircraft was fully usable. Theoretically, all its finders had to do was turn it on and fly it to their airport of choice.

Of course, that wasn't what they did. The aircraft had not been activated and had instead been brought to this hangar as the inanimate object it was now, hoisted by a military heavy-lift transport helicopter in the deep of night and flown above dormant Joint Europe countries in the hours when it was least likely to be seen, arriving here just before the sun first appeared over the horizon.

Dr. Tanner took in a breath. "Right. Let's hook it up," she said, and her own technicians and engineers joined the agitated swarm of those so desperate to solve this mystery.

Hoping the missing ambassador was still alive.

The call came directly to the vice admiral's phone. He snatched it up. He had given this number to USFID's director Leland White, Donovan's boss, to ensure there would be no delay in giving him any updates. As he took the call his hand shook. As he listened, his eyes closed.

He wanted to rush into her office, giddy with the news. But this was far too complicated, and so instead he walked in with a measured step. He found her sitting with her back to the door, her eyes on the world outside the window.

"Lara," he said, his voice gentle.

She didn't move.

"Lara, he's safe. Donovan is fine. He checked in."

She turned to look at him and his heart broke. He began to walk to her, but she stood up. He halted. "Apparently, during the shootout the person they were after escaped into a cave and Donovan and his agent followed," he said, "and this was a blind spot for all comms. They didn't return until they got the guy. White says they will be back in DC in a few hours, they're scheduled to return on a designated USFID flight."

She was hearing every word, he knew. Yet she simply stood there, looking at him. And there was too much in her eyes.

His news was enough, but too late.

"I'm going home." Her voice was quiet, controlled. Empty.

"Yes, of course. How about I drive you?" He was worried. Terrified, more like it. He hadn't seen her this way since . . . No. No, this was different. And he could understand why. After all this time, she had finally taken the risk and had allowed Donovan in. And he ended up almost getting killed. For a while, a short while perhaps but too long for her, she had thought he might be dead. The old loss had been too much. This new one would have been unbearable. Scholes had no idea what to do, how to fix this. How to help her.

"It's okay, Frank. I'm fine. It's just been a long night, a long couple of days," she said with a forced smile, meant, he knew, to keep him at a distance. This only made him more concerned.

She was shutting life out again.

Council Head Stevenssen did her best to preserve her focus. She was tired, worried, and felt as if she had the world on her shoulders—and considering the situation here in Europe, this was more than an abstract observation—but there was much to be done, much that had to be accomplished to ensure the sense of certainty of those who needed her leadership and strength.

She had finally gone home the night before, realizing there would likely be no news for a while. But she could not rest and had returned to her office in the early hours of the new day.

And was still waiting.

"Ma'am." Her personal assistant stood at the door. "The Chairman of the Joint Europe Civilian Command is on the line."

Stevenssen nodded. She had already spoken with André Lerner as soon as she had adjourned the High Council's meeting the day before. Faced with the possibility that Ambassador Sendor would not be found within the time frame after which the consequences facing the region would become inevitable, she had realized Lerner had to be told. And now that night had come and gone, and they were no closer to understanding what happened, let alone finding the missing ambassador, the steps she had discussed with him had to be implemented. Delaying was no longer an option.

Considering the volatility of the situation, the representatives of the Joint Europe countries who made up the Joint Europe Civilian Command—the civilian administration of the Joint Europe treaty—would now be told, in a secure videoconference that was already being set up. The Joint Europe Military Command, located, like its civilian peer, in Brussels, would follow—its chairwoman had already been updated by Stevenssen together with the head of IDSD Defense Europe Command, although so far only the IDSD command had gone on alert, in an effort to avoid the disputed region understanding too soon that something was wrong. And next would come talks with the leaders of alliance nations outside Joint Europe, who would be called on to assist if it came to that.

But first, she and Lerner would update the leaders of the two countries most affected by the unfortunate turn of events. Stevenssen had already broken the news to both of them, together, as soon as the ambassador's jet was found without him. Their trust at least, if not that of their people, had to be maintained at this crucial time.

War, Council Head Stevenssen thought with a flare of anger, war they had all worked so hard to eradicate, was threatening the alliance once again.

Lara didn't remember leaving the war room, taking the elevator down to the building's lobby—Frank, she remembered him there with her, couldn't recall what he said, if he had said anything at all, just the concern in his eyes—going to the car, getting in, letting the autodrive take over and drive her home, passing that spot off the road where Donovan . . .

She pushed away the memory, the emotions it awoke, held herself in check, focused on the distance left to her house. Finally there, she walked in, dazed. She stood still in the middle of the living room, seeing nothing but the past in her mind, feeling nothing but the pain in her heart she couldn't breathe through. She couldn't seem to get a handle on this, on what was happening to her. Couldn't think.

Couldn't allow herself to feel.

She sat down on the closest couch.

Her phone rang. Then her home system. Then her phone again.

She didn't answer.

Chapter Five

Donovan was eager to get to Lara. The guy he'd been after, an elusive killer who had made it a point to kill diplomatic personnel worldwide—specifically American ones—and quite unpleasantly at that, was safely in custody. Finally, after a chase of over a year. He'd sent Supervisory Agent Ben Lawson, the investigator who headed the team that had worked the case with him and whom he'd taken with him to New Mexico, to USFID with the prisoner and an escort of USFID agents as soon as they landed after the short flight, not accompanying them himself. White had informed him, while Donovan was still on the flight back, that he'd spoken to Scholes while the chase was still ongoing, and that Scholes had said he would update Lara. He also knew that White had later updated Lara again through Scholes, this time with the news that he was safe, but he still wanted to go to her, see her himself. He remembered what it had been like for him when he had thought he had lost her, and the idea that she might think the same about him was unacceptable to him.

He tried calling her, but there was no answer. He frowned. This wasn't like her. It didn't make sense that she wouldn't answer the call, especially if she knew he'd been in trouble, and if she knew he was on his way back to her. Which she did, he was told that, too. And he knew she wasn't on a mission, Aiden would have taken the call if that were the case. He thought again about the situation, reversed, just days before, about how it had felt for him.

So why wasn't she answering his call? The way things were between them, he would have expected her to be eagerly anticipating it, him.

He got into his car, considered for a moment, then activated the security tracker he had on his phone for hers. She was at home, her phone active. Already driving, he called her again, routing the call through her home system this time, but she didn't answer that one either. He called her phone again. Nothing. He drove faster, the frown on his face deepening.

Arriving at his house, he pulled into the driveway, got out of the car and skirted his garage to his back yard, then crossed to hers, as had become his habit, half-running to the patio doors that opened before him as her home security system recognized him. She was coming slowly down the stairs from the second floor just as he entered the living room. Her hair was damp and she was dressed in casual jeans and a sweater, and he thought she looked so—

She turned toward him, and he stopped in place, then resumed walking to her, his gait hurried. She was pale, too pale, and her eyes were dark, devoid of any emotion.

"Lara?" He reached her, but when he tried to put his arms around her, she raised her hand and lay her palm on his chest, to keep him back.

"It's okay, everything is okay now," he said, his voice soft.

She took a step back. He let his arms drop, not understanding. She had changed completely. He had expected relief that he was unharmed, lingering worry perhaps, but certainly not this, this was the last welcome he had expected from the woman he had thought had the same feelings for him that he had for her.

"What's going on?" he said. "Lara, I know you were told what happened. Leland knows about you, about us. So he wanted to make sure you—"

"Go."

"What?" He stepped back, moving away from her. He couldn't possibly have heard right.

"I want you to go."

"Lara, what are you doing? We—"

"There is no we, it was a mistake. I made a mistake." She shook her head, and he thought he caught a whiff of anguish, of pain, before her eyes hardened again and she turned and walked away from him. It was, he realized, very much like the pushback he had felt from her when they had first met.

Walls, he thought. Walls again. Walls he had thought broken.

He was tired, too many long, sleepless nights behind him, and he'd had enough. This wasn't how he had expected it to be, expected her to be, now. The anger came out of nowhere. "The hell there isn't!" he said. "Damn it, Lara, after all we've been through, I thought we were past this."

She turned back to him, ice in her eyes. "What do you want from me?"

"I want you. All of you," he shot at her, striding up to her again, forcing her to step back.

"All of me."

"All of you, yes. Whatever is behind that facade you put up."

"It's too complicated."

"No, it isn't. God knows we've done the complicated part of it already. The rest is just love. And life. Ours." He was trapping her against the wall now, his palms flat on it on both her sides, his body close, so close, but not quite touching hers. His eyes were dark, and he was angry with her, with himself, with this damn resistance. With wanting her the way he did.

And then he saw it in her eyes. The fear. Not of him, but—

"You're afraid." His eyes narrowed to blue-gray slits. "You know what, I don't get it. As Oracle you wield great power, do you even realize that? You go into your Mission Command and you control soldiers and satellites and drones and fighters and ships, you control people's fate. And just the other day you knowingly walked into a trap to face those who you knew wanted you dead. Yet here you are, afraid of this. Of us. Because that's it, isn't it, you're afraid of what's between us, aren't you?" He held her eyes for a long moment, then pushed away from the wall, from her, in a sudden move that made her breath catch.

"Or maybe I'm wrong. Maybe I've been wrong from the start and you're just not interested, maybe this, us, isn't to you what it is to me. Were you even worried about me today? Did you want me to come back?"

The look in his eyes pierced into her, awakening new pain, a sharp sense of loss. Too late, she realized. She already cared about him too much for her to once again put up any defenses, to protect herself against what he was saying, leaving her defenseless to deal with what it meant for her, for them, in the worst possible moment for her. And still she could do nothing, couldn't take that step, couldn't—

"I still don't know who you are, do I, Lara?" Donovan's eyes were full of anger. "Even now, you're still hiding from me."

He was right, she knew. But after all this time, she could no longer release herself from the prison she had been in for so long.

"I can't," she said. She closed her eyes, needed him to go, wanted him to stay, and when she finally opened her eyes and he wasn't there anymore, she let herself slide down against the wall, and finally, now finally couldn't stop the tears. But even when they came, the pain, too deep inside her, didn't ebb. It only grew stronger, reaching places she didn't even know still existed, as fear and love fought a battle that finally had to be won. But as they did, her emotions reached proportions she couldn't begin to deal with, the loss of the past mixing with this now final loss of Donovan. He was gone, she was sure. He would never come near her again.

She ran.

Donovan strode angrily into his house and threw his jacket on the sofa. That's it, he fumed. He went upstairs and took a long shower, washing off the desert sand, the past day, her. He began pulling on something thoughtlessly but then reconsidered and chose a more formal shirt to go with his pants, a fresh jacket. He would go to his office at USFID, he didn't want to be here right now. He descended the stairs two at a time. Christ, he was crazy to have permitted this, to have let her in this far, to have allowed himself to care this much. She had too much effect on him. And of all women it had to be her he'd fallen for. Well, he was done. He would leave it all behind him, go back to the way it was before her, back to when it was simple. He'd move, yes, do everything he could to stay away from her.

Never see her again.

"Damn!" In an uncharacteristic rage, he flung the badge he was holding at the wall. It hit an encased holographic image standing on a recessed shelf, one of a boat in a stormy sea, and sent it to the floor in a deafening crash of breaking glass. That made him stop, breathe in deeply. He walked over, crouched between the shards, gingerly picked up his badge and slid a hand on the image, carefully pushing glass away. He looked at it for a long time. Finally, he stood up, walked over to the downstairs safe and opened it. After a moment's contemplation, he placed his badge inside beside his gun, slammed the safe shut and walked out.

Damn you, Lara, he thought. Damn you, he raged, even as he crossed over to her house again. You're not going to push me away that easily. He knew there was no way he could let her go. The idea of being without her just wasn't something he seemed to be able to accept.

And the thing was, the one thing he trusted most were his instincts. And his instincts about her. He knew he'd made no mistake. He wasn't wrong about her, about them. He would get to the bottom of this once and for all.

He strode into her house again, through the still-open patio doors. The place was ominously silent. Frowning, he looked around him. And halted. Her phone was on the coffee table, exactly where he'd noticed it before. He stared at it.

"Lara!" he called out, but no answer came, and he found himself running across the living room and up the stairs. He flung her bedroom door open. It was empty. He went to the wall safe and opened it, the home system recognizing his security override authorization. Her IDSD ID and work laptop lay inside. He slammed the safe shut and ran downstairs, and crushed through the garage door. The IDSD-issued car was there. He took a step back. Her coat, a light autumn coat she'd taken out of her closet just two days earlier, hung near the garage door.

He turned around and looked at her phone again. She never went anywhere without it. This was how Oracle was called in. And it was one of the ways Oracle was tracked to keep her safe, especially after the danger she'd been in.

And without the phone, the laptop, the car, he had no way of knowing where she was.

He was taking out his phone and dialing before he realized it, his heart beating fast, fear taking over. She wasn't in danger again, he knew, not from the outside. There was no one after her, not anymore. But this . . . He thought about the way she had been with him the day before, the open emotion for him in her eyes, her acceptance of him, of them, a given. His mind returned to the way she had been with him earlier. Stupid, he thought, knowing now he should have stayed with her, knowing something was very wrong.

He considered calling Scholes but realized that

in light of recent events, this would lead to the kind of panicked search his instincts told him was wrong for her now. So he called the one person who knew Lara more than anyone, the one person who would know.

"Really? Twice now? I'm beginning to think—"

"Donna."

His tone was enough to stop her flow of words. She listened, then interrupted him. "No!" she said, her own tone enough to send Donovan's concern up a significant notch. "Donovan, you're wrong, she does care, that's the whole point, you got in. Oh God, I knew it, I should have told you, I should have told you! The one time I listened to her and shut up about it, and look what happened!"

"Donna, what the hell are you talking about?"

"Something happened. What happened? Not now, not what you told me now. Before that. Did something happen to you? It had to have been that. Just tell me!" Donna was almost shouting now. Donovan had never known her to react this way.

"What? I . . ." Impatience was the first to rise, but then he realized she was right, something did happen. "Yes, last night I had to go away on a case. I got into some trouble and for a while the people I was with thought—"

Donna got it. "Did she know?"

"USFID made sure she did. But she was also informed once they knew everything was fine, and I came back to her as soon as I could."

"It doesn't matter. The damage is done, she had time to think you might be . . . God, I have to go, I have to find her. Where's my bag? Come on. No, I must have left it in the car again. Okay. I should go. Wait, I have to call Patty, I'm supposed to meet her after she picks up Greg from daycare—"

"Donna, wait, just stop. What do you mean it doesn't matter?" He needed to know. Now. "Damn it, Donna, what aren't you telling me? What the hell happened to her?"

On the other end of the line, Donna forced herself to calm down. "I guess it's okay to tell you now, you need to know." She let out a deep sigh. "Five years ago, there was an attack on an alliance military base in Kuwait."

"Yes, Camp Vrede." It was one of the deadliest incidents in the alliance's fight for peace. The large base was located near the Kuwait, Iraq and Saudi Arabia tri-border, its presence there sanctioned by the three countries, which welcomed its assistance in maintaining the area's stability. The attack, by insurgents who opposed the alliance's presence in the region, came in the middle of a heavy desert storm, and the number of dead and injured was high. Donovan remembered the incident clearly, USFID had been one of the agencies put on alert following it. "The United States lost people there, too," he said. "Fifty-nine were killed there that day."

"The man Lara loved was one of them," Donna said quietly.

Donovan sat down, stunned. Everything fell into place in his mind. The hints from both Donna and Scholes, the way Lara had refused to let him in. The walls she had put up between them, meant to keep him out.

"She and Brian, they were together since college." Donna's voice was full of pain. "They were it, you know. They were happy. When he was killed, she just . . . it changed everything."

Donovan turned to look at the photos on the fireplace mantel, photos he'd looked at the first time he came into this house but didn't get a chance to have a closer look at since. He stood up and walked over to them. Lara laughing with Donna by her side. A younger, different, carefree Lara. A man with a little girl on his shoulders, both waving at the camera. The same man, in uniform, a civilian beside him, smiling.

"The two men in the photo. On her fireplace mantel. The soldier."

"No, Brian's the civilian. The soldier is Jason. Her older brother Jason. He was killed there that night, too."

Donovan stared at the photo. "How did I not know about this?"

"Because you haven't known her long enough to find out. And even then, she doesn't allow anyone to talk about it." Donna sighed. "You need to understand, she was gone, Donovan. They didn't just kill Brian and Jason that night. There was nothing left of her, she shut down. It changed her. She hasn't let anyone near her since."

He understood now. "Until me."

"Until you. And you're wrong, I understand why you reacted the way you did but you're so wrong. I've never seen Lara fight herself this way. It's like she's inside this invisible cage, fighting to get out. To you. You did that."

"And then I walked away." He cursed under his breath. "I need to get to her. Where would she go?"

"Their old house maybe, although no, I don't think she's ever gone back there. No, the cemetery. She'll be at the cemetery. They're both buried at Arlington National Cemetery's extension, the newest one to its north. Brian was one of us, an American, and Tom, that's Lara's remaining brother, he got permission to bury them side by side even though Jason was an International. I'll go to the cemetery first."

"No, I will."

"But—"

"Donna." Donovan's voice was quiet but left no room for argument. "I'm going to her. This is for me to do. Now, it's for me to do."

She was silent for a long time. Finally, she let out a breath. "Okay. Okay. Call, text, anything, if you find her. I'm not calling Tom yet, he'll want to come right over. It'll break his heart to know she's hurting like this."

She told him where in the cemetery Lara would

be. Donovan was already grabbing Lara's phone, ordering the home system to lock down the house and running to his car. She had to have walked, and he had no doubt she would know how to get to the cemetery from her house. And if she left immediately after he'd left her, she would have made it to the cemetery just about then or would be there by the time he arrived.

He turned on the grille lights of his USFID car and pushed through everyone and everything in his way, making it to the cemetery in record time. He didn't need any help to find his way around, easily getting to where Donna had told him Lara would be. Leaving his car at the side of the road, he got out, looked around him, and was relieved to see her a distance away. She was sitting under the heavy sky of this day when winter finally decided to make its appearance, on the meticulously cut grass between the orderly rows of nearly identical headstones. Fighting the urge to run to her, he approached her slowly, quietly. She never moved as he came to stand just a few feet from her in the gentle drizzle of the gray day, oblivious to him, immersed in a cloud of pain so thick he could almost see it around her.

She was sitting, he could see now, before two headstones, positioned squarely between them. Jason Holsworth was the name on the one immediately to her right. The name on the one to its left was Brian Scott Jensen. The dates on the two headstones were the same.

His gaze returned to her. She was pale, dried tears under eyes that had none of the light he was used to seeing in them, no gold flecks. Staring vacantly at the graves before her, at a past she had been trapped in until he came along, a past she now probably thought was once again all she had.

She was wrong.

The drizzle was heavier now, turning into the first light rain of the cold season. Lara wasn't dressed nearly warm enough, still in the clothes she wore earlier, and they were wet. Donovan took off his jacket and wrapped it around her, kneeling down on the grass beside her. She started slightly, raised her head and looked at him, and it took a moment for her eyes to focus.

"Donovan?" she said, looking dazed, as if only now realizing he was there. "You came back."

The way she said it, the bewilderment in her voice, tore into him. Did she mean that he came back after he had left her earlier, or that he had come back alive? Perhaps both. But then, it didn't really matter. All that mattered was that he intended to never leave again.

"Always," was all he said.

He stood up, pulling her gently up with him, and took her in his arms.

She resisted, struggling against him. "No, let me go." Her words turned into a sob, and she stopped struggling and rested her head against his shoulder.

She crumbled to her knees, and he kneeled with her, never letting go, his arms wrapped around her.

"No, I can't—"

"Lara."

"No, let me go, I can't, I can't lose again. I can't lose you." She tried to push him away, crying. "I can't love you."

"It seems it's too late for that," he said softly, tightening his arms around her. He stood up again, holding her gently to him. "Come on, let's go home."

As he began leading her away, she stopped and turned back to the two graves and the terrible loss they signified for her. She then surprised him by turning and looking at him, her brow furrowed. As if trying to understand, to find some answer. For the past, for what was happening now, and, not least of all, he thought, for the future.

She didn't resist anymore as he walked with her slowly back to his car, never letting go of her. He helped her in gently, then got in himself and drove to her place. That was all he wanted, to bring her home, take care of her. To show her that he was there, that he would always be there.

He parked at the curb before her house, and she didn't move as he got out, walked around to the passenger side and opened the door. He crouched down beside her and touched his hand to her arm gently. When she looked at him, he stood up and offered his hand. After the slightest hesitation, she took it. He helped her out, then walked with her to the front door, much like he had done on the night he had almost lost her. The similarity made him pause. Never again, he vowed.

Inside the house, he watched her as she went up to her bedroom to change. He then called Scholes, who had left concerned messages on both his and Lara's phones, and then Donna, as he'd promised.

"Put this call on-screen."

Donovan frowned, but complied.

"Good," Lara's best friend said. "I wanted to see your face."

"Donna, what—"

"I wanted to see that you love her. I heard that you do. When we spoke. The way you . . . But I wanted to see."

Donovan said nothing. He just let Donna look at him, see the obvious truth about him. He knew why she needed this. She didn't only know everything about Lara and her past, she also knew a bit about his. Her grandparents had been his neighbors for some years, they had already owned this very house, the house Lara now lived in, when he moved into his. He was a single man, living alone, and being with women was easy, with his looks. And it suited him, the transience of it.

Until Lara came along.

He remained silent and looked at Donna. She was protecting her friend, would naturally feel the need to do so. She had trusted him with Lara so far, and he wanted her to see it on him, see what he was now, what Lara was to him.

He needed this for Lara.

Donna finally nodded. This, Lara and Donovan, was the one thing she never thought of, had never even considered. And yet that's exactly what was happening, and she accepted that it was real. Gladly so. Donovan was a good man. "Look, it was more than that," she began, then stopped, hesitating.

Donovan looked at her questioningly.

"Ask her how Oracle began."

"You know about it?"

"Sure. I was there when it started. We don't talk about it, we have this rule about talking about work, and I told you it's better that way, it's how I get her to not always think about her job. But I know."

His brow furrowed. "What do you mean how it began?"

"Lara should be the one to tell you. Look, after it happened, she went there, okay? And she never really came back. In a way, I think only Oracle returned. Too much of Lara is still back there. And it was fine with her. All this time, she's never tried to change that. But then you came along. And now she's finally trying to come back. But she's doing it alone, because she doesn't know how to do it differently, not anymore, by now she is used to being alone." She shook her head, the memories, what her friend had been through, bringing tears to her eyes. "She is never going to be the same person she was before Brian and Jason died. That's just the way it is. And that's okay, she's done so much since then, been so much since. But that part of her you need is there, five years ago, where living stopped for her, and you can bring her back."

"Donna, I don't understand. What—"

"Just ask her," Donna said. "Ask her what happened five years ago. Get her to tell you everything. *Everything*." Donna couldn't believe she was saying this. "If you want a life with her, you've got to break into her first."

Ending the call, the furrow in his brow deeper now, Donovan turned to see the woman he loved descend the stairs.

Chapter Six

Once she was sitting comfortably huddled on the sofa, wrapped in a soft robe and with a mug of hot soup in her hands, he came to sit on its opposite end, sipping from his own mug. She was here now, safe, with him. That's all I need, he thought, that and for her to be happy, and even as the thought crossed his mind, he knew Donna was right. Lara had to go through it all, had to go back to those painful days in her past and to take him there with her. Otherwise, she would never be able to live now, in her present. With him.

He watched her silently, let her sit quietly with her thoughts, her gaze lowered to the mug she was holding. Eventually she raised her eyes to meet his, and he held them. She nodded slightly, then lowered her gaze again.

"Jason and Brian were high school friends, unlikely ones at that, I guess," she began after a pause. "Jason had an unruly streak in him. He was a good kid, but a tough one. Never thought twice about intervening in situations others would walk away from. He would protect the weak and could do so easily—no one messed with him." Her lips curved up a little, the sadness in that slight reminiscing movement sending a pang through Donovan's heart.

"He really was a good kid, you know. I was always protected, everyone knew he would beat up anyone who came anywhere near his little sister. Tom, that's his twin, the brother I still have, he preferred to reason. Anyone talking to Tom would understand very clearly that any action taken that Tom did not approve of would be certain to lead to dire and long-term consequences that would impact their lives in a way that would make them regret they ever met him. Even at that age he had the words, the posture. That effect on people, kids and adults alike. Tom reasoned, Jason battled. And Brian" —she smiled—"Brian was the one who stepped in, who pulled Jason away, who healed instead of fighting. An improbable friendship, Tom always said about the two of them. But it held fast.

"When they went to college, all of them, Tom was so obviously going to be a lawyer, Brian was set on being a doctor, like pretty much everyone else in his family, and Jason, about a year into college he knew it wasn't for him. He enlisted to IDSD Defense and was instantly at home. He had found his calling. My brother, the protector of the innocent. Our parents would have preferred he stay close to home, join the police or something if he had to, but Jason was military at heart, a combat soldier. And that's where he went.

"I'm six years younger than all of them, six and a half, and when I went to college, Jason was already deployed overseas, and Tom had graduated from law school and was interning with IDSD Legal in Brussels." At Donovan's surprise she laughed. "Yes, the original Holsworth at IDSD was Tom. He's now a senior partner at a law firm affiliated with IDSD Legal, here in DC."

He sat up, remembering. "Wait a minute."

"Right," she said. "You must have come across the connection when you were investigating me."

He did, and now finally understood. Trying to find out who Lara Holsworth was, he had found that the house they were now sitting in was registered to IDSD, as was her car, and that all mail was sent not to her home but to IDSD Legal.

"I tend to be preoccupied, obviously. So Tom, who's also my attorney, takes care of all the official bits and ends of my life, behind IDSD Legal's cover. And IDSD prefers it that way too because it's a way for them to balance their need to hide me with the fact that I refuse to live in their secure residential complex."

"He knows about...?"

"Oracle? Yes. Nothing specific about missions, of course, but yes. He knows quite a bit. He's my cover outside IDSD, because he's connected to both, well, Lara and Oracle. And he's very protective."

"You're his little sister."

"And the only sibling he has left. Losing Jason

was tough. It would have been entirely unbearable for him, for both of us, for our parents, if not for Sarah."

"Sarah?" He was finally learning more about her, and he wanted to know it all.

"Jason met a woman on one of his tours overseas, a foreign area officer, an International. Jenny. She died a year before Jason was killed. Sarah is their daughter."

Donovan winced inwardly. That was a lot of loss in one family.

"She lives with Tom and his family, his wife and two kids. They're like siblings anyway, the kids, Sarah stayed with them when Jason returned to duty after Jenny died. And it has made it easier for her, Tom being her father's twin and all. And Tom's wife, Milly, she's absolutely amazing. Sarah is eleven now, and she's doing great." Lara indicated the photos on her fireplace mantel, and Donovan remembered seeing children's photos there. Happy children. Must be one hell of a family, he thought, and somehow this only accentuated more the loneliness the woman with him was trapped in.

She was looking at the mug, her eyes distant, remembering. Abruptly, she put it on the coffee table and folded her hands in her lap, the thoughts too painful.

"Is that where you and Brian became closer? College?" Donovan prodded, recalling what Donna had told him.

Lara nodded slightly, still not looking at him. "Jason and Tom asked him to look out for me. Brian was in med school by then, and I was enrolled in college not far from there." She smiled a little. "And he was always around. We were . . . together since my last year in college." She paused, and Donovan gave her the time she needed, knowing how overwhelming her memories must be. "Jason always tried to talk Brian into joining the military, but Brian just wasn't the fighting type. He was a healer at heart. Still, he was affected by Jason's stories and by the fact that his best friend was in situations that could harm him. So he went into trauma care, and when he finished his residency, he took a fellowship at the US-alliance military hospital here in DC. That's where they bring those who were injured in the field, you know. The bad ones. He joined as a civilian, but trauma doctors are always needed, and he convinced them to take him by doing a stint in the trauma unit at the IDSD-alliance military hospital in Brussels and agreeing to join forward surgical teams in the field when they had a shortage of doctors. He eventually became a permanent member of one." She raised haunted eyes to Donovan. "He loved what he did, you know. Helping people."

She was silent for a long time. "He wasn't even supposed to be there, that day. Neither of them was. Camp Vrede, that's where they were. Did I tell you that? Camp Vrede, in Kuwait. That's where Jason was stationed at the time, and he was supposed to be out of there a month before, it was his last tour. He asked to be transferred back here, he wanted to come back to Sarah for good, raise her himself. But he extended his tour by a month because the guy who was supposed to replace him had a new baby and wanted to be there for his family for the first few weeks. That month was over the day the camp was attacked, Jason was scheduled to fly out the next day. And Brian, he stopped there on his way back to me after three months at a field trauma unit in the region, thinking he'd fly out with Jason."

She shifted, just a bit. It hurt, talking about it. Thinking about it. "I was at work, that day. I was a junior civilian analyst at IDSD Intelligence, of all places. Tom's idea. I wasn't like my brothers and Brian, I didn't seem to belong to any specific profession and none of them attracted me, but I had a good memory and this ability to cross information, make out-of-the-box connections, so Tom suggested I work there until I figured out what I wanted to do. They put me on one of their task teams. The Asian Territories. And I was there for a while." She paused again, then spoke quickly, as if trying to get through it, through the pain. "I remember looking up because everything was so quiet all of a sudden. And these man and woman in full dress uniform walked into the analyst teams' open space, and they passed by my desk and went to my supervisor's office—not the head of the Asian Territories team I was in, but the head of all task teams, Solly—and I breathed again. If anything happened they would come to me, I knew, because I was Brian's contact for the military. But they didn't come to me, they went to Solly, and they talked to him. And then he called me to his office."

She still wasn't looking at Donovan. "Frank was there, you know. That day. I'd seen him before, we never talked, though, he probably never even noticed me. He and Solly, they were friends, still are, and Frank had just been appointed second-in-command of IDSD Missions, so they would meet there sometimes and go out to lunch together—the intelligence building is not far from the missions building in the IDSD complex, I don't know if you've seen it. Anyway, he was there that day. Solly, he had no idea what to do, but Frank, he's been in the field and in command most of his life. He knew what to do. And then, I remember, this giant of a man came and sat beside me, and I had no idea what they were all saying except Brian was dead." The tears flowed freely now, and Donovan had to hold himself not to take her in his arms, take the pain away.

"The notification officers, that's who the man and woman were, they finally left. And Frank and Solly stayed there. I remember everyone outside Solly's office was so hushed." She looked at him then. "I never went back, you know. That was my last day there. I never set foot there again. Solly was so nice about it, he and Frank had everything done so I wouldn't have to, later. Even now, I never go to that building, they come to me.

"They wanted to call Tom, but then he called. My phone. It rang. Frank took the call. And he went so pale, and I thought maybe someone had already told Tom except that Tom was at our parents' house. I took the phone and Tom said that they're still there, the notification officers. Telling them that Jason was gone. I didn't tell him Brian was dead too. He was heartbroken because of Jason. He said I should come immediately. Jason was his twin, did I tell you? Yes, I did, didn't I?" Her eyes were lowered again, her entire being in a world of hurt.

"They were gone by the time I got there, the officers, Tom had sent them away. My parents, they were devastated. And Sarah. She was so little, just six. Tom was trying to hold everything together. And then he took me aside and asked if I managed to get through to Brian. He was the only one who knew Brian was there, too, at the base. We didn't want to worry anyone. But he knew. And he asked. So I told him."

Her voice was hollow as she fought to keep anguish at bay, and Donovan's heart broke.

"Tom and I and Brian's sister, we took care of everything. The funeral, everything. The casualty assistance officers did everything they could, we had them from both sides you know, the US and the Internationals, and IDSD was amazing with Tom and me. And Donna was there, she and Tom's wife were trying hard to take care of all of us, of the family." She was finding it difficult now not to fall apart, and Donovan, fighting the urge to take her in his arms, moved his leg slightly. Contact, just the slightest. She stared at it, at the point of contact, moved slightly closer. Hanging on. Hanging on to now, to him, to this man she was finally letting in.

"The day of the funeral, after people left . . . we were all at my parents' house, I was staying there, I couldn't go back. Couldn't return to the house I'd lived in with Brian. I was outside, sitting on the front porch, I remember. My parents were inside, with family that came to help, friends. And Tom came to me with Sarah, said he was taking her home, taking them home, his family. Trying to maintain some normality. For the kids, for Sarah. He asked me to come with them, to go with Donna, anything. Anything but just sit there that way. But I really didn't care at that point. No one could get through to me. And then as they were turning to go Sarah ran back to me and she hugged me and then that little girl said something. She asked me if it was true that the bad people got away with killing her daddy and Uncle Brian." For the first time, she raised her eyes to Donovan's. "And she had all that pain in her eyes, she has Jason's eyes, you know." She shook her head. "I saw her entire life in her eyes, the question that would never go away, of how someone could take them away from us forever and get away with it. She'd just lost her mom the year before and now her dad. So I said no. And I remember Tom standing there, and he was about to say something, he almost did, but then he nodded, and he picked her up, hugged her, and they left. I don't think he ever thought I would do what I did, didn't know I could. No one did, not even I. He just wanted something done, by anyone."

She breathed in deeply. When she spoke again, some of who she was now, some of who Oracle was, was in her voice. "I knew quite a bit, analyzed enough situations, followed enough missions from afar. I never acted on it before, never needed to, was never asked to. But apparently I could. I knew enough to know what to do. Who to go to. I knew that those who were still alive from Jason's unit came back, they were at the funeral, the too few who survived and came home."

Donovan sat up. What was she saying?

"Three days later, I was in the base Brian and Jason were killed in."

"Impossible," he blurted out, but then remembered who he was talking to. Wasn't Oracle herself an impossibility?

"And yet," she simply said, "that's the way it was. I talked Donna into bringing me my personal laptop from . . . the house. She wanted me to come stay with her and Patty, they were already living together then, and I told her that I wanted to stay with my parents for a while. She knew me enough to know something was up, but at that point she'd let me get away with anything. Anyway, I used my laptop and my work authorizations to break into the right places, stole some higher authorizations to get to others, and got all the information I could about the incident and its investigation, which at that point had pretty much stalled. They knew who did it, who attacked the base, just not where they were and how to get to them." She shrugged. "And then I talked Jason's unit into taking me to where my brother and the man I loved died. Which was easy. They had an open door—they could go back whenever they wanted to, they weren't ones to quit and Camp Vrede did, as you probably know, continue its operations. It was just a matter of getting me there. And for the record, I fixed everything so that all blame would fall on me."

Donovan gaped at her. "Exactly how many laws did you break?"

"Internationals, US federal, alliance joint command, you name them, I broke them." She gave him a small smile. "You fell in love with a criminal mastermind, my United States Federal Investigative Division agent."

His heart missed a beat. This was the first time she acknowledged his feelings for her directly. And it sure sounded as if she was accepting him, and them.

"I knew I would be caught. And no, I really didn't do anything to hide what I was doing, just enough so it wouldn't be discovered until I got to Camp Vrede. I just had to get there. I had no idea what I would do, if I could do anything. I just wanted to go to where they died, and I had nothing to lose." She moved a little, the contact between them more pronounced now.

"I actually used the mess of the aftermath of the attack on the base to get to it pretty much unnoticed. We took a direct ride, military transport—please don't ask me how I got those orders through—and on the way, they, Jason's guys, told me everything they knew. I was, for them, family. They told me about the base, the region, the time they spent there. And everything they knew about what happened that night." She was quiet for a beat. "Everything they thought I would need for closure, I think. Except with me, it worked differently. I just didn't know it yet.

"When we arrived, they showed me around the base. Showed me where Brian and Jason were killed. And on the way, they just happened to show me everything else that had to do with the attack. No one questioned my being there, none of the troops still there. I was an IDSD Intelligence analyst in an alliance military base under IDSD control, and I just happened to be the family of two of their peers, and Jason, he was their friend. Everybody knew I wasn't really supposed to be there. But..." She shrugged. Donovan got it. "And the place was under lockdown, kept safe by then. But then the order came, so they had to detain me."

"Order?"

"Yes. Everything I did unraveled, which was fine, I just wanted to get to the base. What would happen after I got there, that I didn't care about. So shortly after I got there IDSD figured out what I'd done and already had agents on the way. In the meantime, I was to be detained by the military police on site." She said that as a matter of fact, and Donovan realized that back then she really had thought she had nothing more to lose. "The base commander, he was a good guy. And you need to understand what it was like then. It was just days after the attack. They were still picking the place apart, the death and destruction were still too real around them, and they were constantly sending out units to try to get to those who did this, who injured and killed their friends. There was a lot of anger and frustration there. And now the base commander was being asked to arrest a family member of two men lost in the attack. So he didn't. Officially. He just brought me to their secure command and control center, so that I wouldn't just wander around and he could keep an eye on me himself.

"And there we were, with all those screens, all those live views. Most views were of the base and the surrounding area, all the places that were now alive in my mind along with everything I knew about that night. But a series of screens right there before me were locked on the view from low-flying drones following the progress of soldiers looking for the attackers. And there was constant chatter around me, and someone was trying to explain to me what I was seeing, and I was focused on the screens and then I couldn't hear him anymore and I could see it myself. As if I was there, myself." She shrugged. "And then I knew where they needed to go."

Anyone else might have needed to know more to understand, but Donovan didn't. He'd seen her at work.

"At first no one listened when I talked, and then the mission coordinator who was communicating with the soldiers outside realized that I was saying things that no one could know. I couldn't go forward then yet, see what was ahead of them, either in spatial or in temporal terms, but I could see them in the immediate context of their surroundings. And I could see some of the people who participated in the attack on the base. Their images, taken by security cameras on the night of the attack, were on the walls of the command and control center. And it clicked, I could see them in my mind." She looked at him, her eyes focused. "See, they were there. The attackers."

"There where?"

"Not far. Flanking locations. They had waited, hidden, and had returned, hoping to take advantage of an old trick. The base was still devastated. In shock. They'd watched, knew who was there. Were on a suicide mission this time. Double back and destroy, and kill anyone looking for them on the way, that was their aim."

"Except there was a new element in the base."
He frowned. "So that's how Oracle came to be."

She nodded. "Although I wasn't anywhere near
today's Oracle, it was just something that awakened
there and then, so that suddenly everything I needed was there to show me how to help them. Help
Sarah and everyone else who'd lost someone at that
base. Them, and the soldiers themselves, those who
would die if the attackers succeeded again." Her
brow furrowed. "I wasn't able to do what I do now,
and I didn't have anywhere near the knowledge
I've acquired since. But I was surrounded by people
who knew everything there was to know, and they
were guiding the search expertly. All I did was tell
them the attackers were there, guide the soldiers to
them, and make sure no one was hurt."

"Easy," Donovan said with a smile.

She laughed a little. "No, really. We all did it together. I told you, I wasn't today's Oracle yet." She
contemplated how to put it. "Oracle wasn't something I could always do and didn't. I couldn't do
any of it before . . . before then. I have no idea why.
All I can say is that it is as if what happened to
me, losing Brian and Jason that way, together with
this situation where I knew that the soldiers on the
screens were close to their attackers, in danger, and
I knew . . . I could feel what their families, everyone
who loved them would go through if anything happened to them, it's as if all this led to dormant
thought processes and capabilities awakening in my

mind, becoming dominant. And I was open to it, there was nothing else there by then, nothing of who I had been was left." She shrugged again.

"I remember the silence. The soldiers got the attackers, killed most of them, captured several. There were more troops out there by then, more firepower. Elation at the capture. And then the quiet in the command and control center. Everyone was looking at me. That's when I realized what I'd done. But I didn't care. I did it. I could go back and tell Sarah that it was over. I could never tell her what I did, I didn't even understand it myself, but I could tell her it was over." She looked beyond him, her eyes distant again. "And it was over for me, too. There was nothing for me anymore."

She said nothing for a while, immersed in her thoughts. Finally, she looked at him, her eyes focusing again. "And then the quiet changed, and everyone was looking behind me."

"The agents."

"Yes. From IDSD Intelligence. And apparently they had seen enough. And they also knew who I was, that I was family to two of the fallen, I guess this factored into their treatment of me. The agent in charge, he approached me. Told me that his agents would take me to the transport they came on, where I was to wait until it was prepared for its return trip. I did as he said, without arguing." She shook her head with wonder. "He didn't even hand-cuff me or anything like that, just clarified that I was being arrested. He was very kind about it. His agents, too. One of the women on his team even volunteered to look after me, make sure I had everything I needed.

"The agent in charge, he stayed in the command and control center to talk to the base commander. Then he joined us for the flight back. He interrogated me at the beginning of the flight, and I didn't hide anything. Except for the role anyone else might have had in what I did. But he knew. Eventually—it was funny, I only thought about it later—he told me not to worry, that I'd covered everyone else's tracks well, that it was possible to ensure no one would be held accountable but me, that considering who else was involved, everyone understood. And then he asked me how I did it. Just like that, how I did it, what he saw in the command and control center. I told him the truth, that I didn't know. And that was that. He went to call someone, and for the rest of the flight I was left alone. I was exhausted, but it didn't matter, nothing mattered." She was quiet for a moment.

"When it was time, when we landed, he came to me. Told me he had to put handcuffs on now. I was officially under arrest, after all. We landed here, at the IDSD airfield, and disembarked inside a hangar, because what I'd done and the circumstances of my arrest could not come out. I was a security risk. A civilian who was a security risk." This made her smile a little. She shrugged impishly. "Can't blame them, if you think about it. Anyway, they put me in a room at the hangar for an hour or so, and then the agent in charge came alone and took me to Donna's."

"Sorry, what?"

"Exactly. Well, it was all very formal, really. He told her he was releasing me to her custody. She was ready, he'd called her, told her the bare minimum. It was the middle of the night, I remember, but once the agent left, I called Tom. Asked him to wake up Sarah. He didn't ask me where I'd been or what I'd done. He just put her on and stayed on the line with her and I told her. I said, 'Sarah, they didn't get away with it.' And she was quiet, and then she just said, 'Thank you, Aunt Lara.' Just that. And I heard Tom crying."

She was silent for a long time. "She was better after that, you know. She began recuperating. Smiling again. Tom, too, and Milly and the kids. They're a good family, a real family, now."

"And you?" Donovan asked softly. He remembered what Donna had said, about Lara not having really come back from the place where living had stopped for her, which he now knew was Camp Vrede. He understood better now. Understood both her and Oracle.

"I don't remember much of the two months after that. Donna and Patty were there. They were amazing. They didn't let me out of their sight, one of them was always with me in their apartment. I never went out. They said Tom came by, and Sarah. Milly. My parents. But I don't remember. I was done. Gone. For a while I expected, waited even, for someone to come and make the official arrest, take me in. Get it over and done with. But no one ever did. No one even came to talk to me about what I'd done.

"Then one morning there was someone at the door, and Donna and Patty argued with them, but eventually let them in. It was Frank, and another man I didn't know then. IDSD US Intelligence, he was then, now he's in Brussels. They came to talk to me. They wanted Donna to leave, but she planted herself at the living room doorway and refused to budge. I remember all of this mostly because of Frank. When he came in, it connected in my mind, even in my haze I recognized him, remembered him from the day I was told Brian and Jason died. And they talked to me, but I didn't listen, didn't care. Frank told me later it was like walking in there and looking at a ghost of who I'd been when he first saw me. But he had to try. He said he knew that if he walked out of there without me, not only would the others die, but I would too."

Donovan frowned. "The others?"

Lara nodded. "He came to sit before me, made me look at him, see him, and said that he needed my help. He had fourteen soldiers trapped in Mali, and no one could get them out. 'I need you to do whatever it was you did in Kuwait,' he said, and I heard him." She smiled. "Donna wouldn't let them take me without her. She didn't trust them, didn't trust anyone with me, the way I was. So they took her along. That's how she knows today about what Oracle is. Or was, back then.

"That's the first day I actually remember, you know. They took me to IDSD, to the same place I work in today except it looked very different back then. We've since changed the war room and Mission Command, as Oracle became, well, Oracle, and as we became the main IDSD Missions for all our missions worldwide. I wasn't anywhere near what I am now, and I wasn't entirely there physically, and I had no idea what I could do, but Frank said he'd take a chance. I walked into what later became the Mission Command you know, and there were people there and they were trying to figure things out, and I saw what was happening on-screen, just helmet cams, that's all they had, and I could see they had nowhere to go and I thought about Brian's family, about Sarah and Tom and our parents and me. I knew how those like us, like me, would feel. I could feel what would happen to all those people, all those who loved them." She was looking at Donovan intensely.

"And then I could . . . I connected to them, somehow. To the soldiers on-screen. And I knew what to do. So I did. All I had was a short briefing in the car on the way, but I had enough experts around me. Now when you see me work you see five years of knowledge and experience, but none of it existed back then, I needed those who had the necessary knowledge to interpret for me what I was seeing and to relay my instructions accurately to those in the field. I couldn't just step in and take over like I do now."

She took in a deep breath. "When it was over, I remember everybody was staring. Again. Mission Command was smaller then, and it was packed. I had no idea when they all came in. And then Frank took me out, didn't let anyone talk to me. And when I came out of Mission Command that day, I was in focus again."

"You were Oracle."

She nodded. "Although that designation, the code name, came months later, and, seriously, it took a long time to get to what I am now. They crammed so much information into me, plus with every mission I pushed the boundaries, tested, improved. Still do."

Now Donovan knew how Oracle began. And he finally knew that it was true, amazingly so—Oracle was all her. Just Lara and that unique, brilliant mind of hers. But for him, Oracle wasn't what mattered. "Yes, but you. What happened to you?"

She knew what this man who loved her was asking. For him, Oracle came after the woman she was. "An officer took Donna and me back to her place, and I slept. First time I'd slept peacefully since Brian and Jason died. I was dead tired, but finally for the right reasons. The next day I sat in Donna and Patty's living room again, but near the window this time. Looking out. First time in two months. I wasn't sure what would happen now. The life I'd had was gone, along with everything I ever thought I wanted, and whatever it was I now did twice, seeing things this way, I wasn't sure what to do with it. I only knew I could do it again. This time, at IDSD, I sort of made it happen intentionally, and it was still there, I simply knew that I had this ability, whatever it was.

"And that's when it also occurred to me that I was never brought to justice for what I'd done. Now I know that they had no idea what to do with me. And that there had been discussions about what I did at Camp Vrede, finding the attackers that way and making sure the soldiers were safe. Which was how Frank knew to come to me." She shrugged. "Anyway, that day Frank came back. Asked me to come work for him at IDSD Missions, said we would figure it out as we went along. Donna said yes. The rest is history."

"Donna said yes?"

"Don't tell me you're surprised." She smiled.

He chuckled. "No, I really shouldn't be, should I?"

"The two of them brought me back. Donna kept me alive those first two months after I returned from Camp Vrede, and then Frank brought me into IDSD, and he watched out for me. He had IDSD's medical center and physical trainers on my back until I was completely healed, at least physically—the rest came with time, and with what I did as Oracle. Patty negotiated the apartment next door, and she and Donna prepared it for me, and I moved in. Lived there for five years almost, until they had little Greg and I decided they should have it, expand their own apartment. The rest you know."

"You've been alone since?" he asked bluntly.

She watched him. "I dated. Sort of. After a long time. Donna would set me up, she said I needed to stay alive." She laughed a little. "She drove me crazy. I'd go to meet her and Patty, and she'd have a blind date there. And I got asked out. And yeah, sometimes, okay, rarely, I said yes. But just a date, I always cut it short, and I never..."

He nodded. He understood what she wanted to say. "She isn't planning to set you up anymore, is she? Donna, I mean."

Lara laughed, as he hoped she would. Then the laugh subsided, and she watched him for a while. Struggling, he saw. He waited. She needed to go that last stretch. From then, to now. To him.

"I thought you were gone," she said, her voice barely more than a whisper. "When I heard what happened... I thought I lost you."

"I tried to call as soon as I sent away the guy we captured. You didn't answer my calls. And then when I came back, you pushed me away."

She just looked at him.

"Was it easier that way? Keeping me away?"

Her gaze was tired. "No. Too late."

He grinned. "See? You love me."

Her eyes narrowed. "Go away."

"Like hell." But then the grin disappeared, and his voice softened. "My Lara."

They were both half lying on the sofa now, comfortable against each other. She looked exhausted. And he was, too, he realized. He'd barely had any sleep, and this, finally knowing what had kept her from him, took away tension he hadn't even realized had accumulated in him.

She had leaned her head on the back of the sofa, and her eyes were heavy. He got up, and at his movement she opened her eyes, but didn't resist when he picked her up.

"You keep doing that," she murmured, her head against his shoulder. It felt so good, being in his arms this way. He was here. He was safe and here, holding her.

"I'm taking you to bed. You need to sleep."

"So do you, you haven't slept yet, have you? Go, get some sleep, I'm fine." Her voice was already blurry with sleep.

"I will." Reaching her bedroom, he put her down, lingering just enough to hold her to him, touch his lips to her forehead. Then he walked over to the bed, turned the covers down and waited while she slipped her robe off and lay down, then pulled the soft blanket on top of her.

She turned on her side, to face him, tried hard

to stay awake. "I'll sleep if you will."

"I will," he repeated. He touched the bedroom console to activate the fireplace set in the wall opposite the bed to a continuous low, to add to the comfort, the cozy warmth of the room, and ordered the lights off, then undressed to his underwear and got into bed with her. She didn't stir when he slid over and wrapped himself around her, let him draw her close.

"Donovan?" Her voice was drowsy.

"Yes?"

"I thought I lost you."

"You never will. To you, I will always come back." His arms tightened around her. "Sleep, my Lara, I'm here," he murmured in her ear, felt her body relax against his as she slipped into exhausted slumber.

He watched her in the fading evening light. She slept on her side, facing away from him, and his hand rested on her hip. He looked down at her, at this remarkable woman sleeping by his side. He was actually sleeping with a woman not in the spoken sense of the words, without having made love to her. It occurred to him that he was thinking about it as making love, not just the casual sex he had always been careful to allow, and was no longer surprised that the thought didn't bother him, not anymore.

He realized what it would mean for them both to be together. Understood the complications of that life, their life, considering whom they were, the work they did—the past days had accentuated that all too sharply. But he didn't care. He knew now that he would do all it took to be with her, to have her as his.

He stroke her cheek, caressing soft skin. Her long dark hair framed her face, the light from the fireplace, gradually becoming more dominant in the room over the darkening sky outside, playing with its soft auburn hues. His gaze traced the delicate curve of her neck down to the rise of her breasts under the thin undershirt she was wearing, then down to where the blanket covered her under his hand. He raised his eyes back up to her face, his wonder at the emotions this woman had awakened in him never fading away. He touched his lips to her brow, lay down, and tightened his arms protectively around her, to let her know that he was here, that she was not alone, that he would never leave.

He was still marveling at how it felt, holding her this way, when he fell asleep.

Darkness reigned outside, deep and silent, when Lara woke up, the only light in the room from the fireplace, burning low. Donovan, it was Donovan in bed with her, she realized even before she opened her eyes, had a dim recollection of him carrying her to bed. And getting in with her, this time. His arm was around her and she lay quietly, feeling it, feeling him, his body warm and firm against her back. He

was here, in her bedroom. In her bed. She hadn't allowed that since Brian died, always kept men away.
But Donovan was different. With him, everything
was different.

Her heart beat hard, and she could do nothing
to calm it, nothing to order it to obey her. She
turned slowly in Donovan's arms, her legs brushing against his, and met his eyes, dark blue in the
flickering light, hiding nothing. Fully awake now,
and close, so close. The blanket was up to his waist,
and his chest was bare. He had taken most of
his clothes off, she remembered, blushed with this
knowledge under his gaze and hoped he would not
see this in the dim light of the fire. But then he
could read her so well, just as she could read him,
knew that he wanted, but knowing what he now
did, why she had resisted him, would wait, let her
decide if she was ready.

She wondered at this man who loved her no
matter what he saw, what he knew about her, and
who had somehow managed to get in. Before the
thought even crossed her mind, she extended her
hand, soft fingers tracing the lines of his face, down
to his chest, found that his heart was beating as
hard as hers. She raised her eyes back to his. Let
him see her, no longer hiding from him.

He shifted slowly, rolling her onto her back. He
touched his lips to hers, deepening the kiss as his
hand pulled the blanket away and moved up her
side, subtly brushing the gentle curve of a breast,

felt a soft intake of breath that reverberated through him at his caress. He leaned back, his gaze tracing the slow movement of his hand along her body, the gentle touch of his fingertips awakening in her sensations long forgotten, thought dead and buried together with that part of her she hadn't imagined anyone would ever again get through to. As his hand moved back up he rounded to the inside of her thigh, up to her panties, stopping short of touching them, touching her. He raised his eyes to hers, saw her watching him, didn't take his eyes off hers as he moved his hand up on bare skin, under her undershirt, pulling it up as he did. Slow, giving her time, feeling her respond to him as he touched her, wanted her, seeing the glimmer of need in her eyes as he aroused her.

She touched her hand to his, and his heartbeat quickened when she helped him take her undershirt off. Even as his hands were back on her he kissed her, his mouth seeking, craving more. His lips traced the gentle curve of her throat, down to her breast, his tongue teasing soft skin as she bowed back under him, erupting awake, already drowning in the sensations, already lost in him, in them. His hands and mouth explored her body, and this time he did not stop, did not hesitate when he reached her, found her wanting him, his moan mirroring hers, and he rose just enough to slip her panties off, trying hard not to let his wanting her so much control him in this, their first time. Failing.

There is nothing separating us anymore, the fleeting thought crossed her mind as he pulled off his underwear and shifted on top of her, bringing his mouth down on hers as her arms came up around him, pulling him down to her.

"Lara," he mumbled against her lips, "my Lara," and, unable to wait any longer, he pushed himself inside her, heard her gasp as he filled her, felt her close tightly around him, moved inside her, his eyes never leaving hers, wanting to see her, let her see herself in them, the intensity in his eyes mirroring the intensity of his movement, their movements as their pace quickened, matching that of urgent need finally unleashed, allowing what was right to be, any remnants of the walls that had been between them dissipating as they finally gave themselves to each other.

They lay, quiet, wrapped around each other, for a long time after. His breathing was calm, his body relaxed against hers, and she marveled at this, at herself this way, with this man in her bed. She wondered quietly to herself, there in the gently flickering light of the fire, savoring the feel of his strong body. She shifted a little, and his arms tightened around her, holding her close to him. But then she'd known he was awake, his wasn't the relaxation of sleep. She raised her head from his shoulder and looked at him, at this man who had her . . . who had her, that was just it, the 'it' that still perplexed her so.

His eyes were closed. Hers moved on him, followed the tips of her fingers as she caressed softly, exploring him. She skimmed over his shoulders, his chest, lingering, taking her time with him, with his body that lay so naturally against hers, frowned over an old scar just under his ribs and kissed it tenderly. His stomach muscles quivered under her touch, no longer relaxed, nothing about him calm, his eyes open, on her, and he was already hard when her fingers skimmed along him. He caught her hand and reversed their positions in a quick move, easily pinning her under him.

"Hey!" she protested, wriggling under him, which really wasn't helping his self-control. "I was doing something there!"

"Yeah, I noticed." He chuckled softly, amazed at how easily this woman could take him to the verge of control, and embarked on some arousing of his own.

Chapter Seven

"This can't be right." Dr. Tanner stood up and contemplated the jet beyond the thick divide. It looked forlorn now, standing alone on the inspection floor, with no people inside or around it. Just the aircraft itself, an overwhelming variety of hardware hooked up to its systems, all access doors and panels open. It looks so helpless, she couldn't help but think. Hard to believe it could be at the center of an ominous plot.

And yet all evidence was pointing to just that.

The crime scene investigators had found nothing useful, or so she heard them say among themselves. That part of the investigation was not hers to deal with. All that mattered to her was this aircraft and its embedded systems. This was what she and her staff did, figured out what made aircraft behave other than they were designed to. Which was why the aviation accident investigators had left, too, sometime during the night, as did the intelligence agents, knowing the best way to getting some answers was to let her and her people do what they did better than most.

And yet they had been unable to reach any helpful conclusions of their own. They had run all the mandatory checks of the aircraft's components, all of which were still connected directly to the unrivaled range of machinery in the lab. They had then run a check to look for any systems that shouldn't be there, something that might have been installed in the aircraft, although they hadn't expected to find anything. This same check was mandatory in every IDSD and allied airport before any manned aircraft, civilian and military alike, took off, especially now, with the recently discovered signal jammer they knew rogue groups might already have. The fact was that this aircraft had been thoroughly checked each and every time it was used, and nothing unknown had been installed in it.

No matter what they had tried, Dr. Tanner and her people had found nothing to explain what happened to this aircraft. Nothing until she herself had gone through the information provided by the cockpit voice recorder and the flight data recorder, which allowed her to hear what had gone on in the cockpit and view control and sensor data logs on the lab's screens. She had gone through the information twice, in fact, and had then had her techs repeat some of their earlier testing of the aircraft's systems, hoping she was wrong. But all these tests ultimately did was confirm what the initial checks had shown, that none of the systems in this aircraft had been infected with malicious software, hacked or otherwise interfered with in any way. They all worked perfectly. In fact, the aircraft standing on the other side of the divide could be refueled and sent up again right now.

And yet, as the last words of the pilots attested, this aircraft had been controlled from the outside. No way around concluding that that's what happened. Something had taken control of it, and, once it had been landed on Cres, whatever had done that had disengaged again. All without making any apparent changes to the aircraft's avionics.

Anyone else might have been confounded, reaching the conclusion that there was no way this could have been done. But eight months earlier, Tanner had assisted in the testing of a technology just entering the implementation phase, right here, in this hangar, on an IDSD-MIL Technology Demonstrator UAV. And those tests had just about mimicked what seemed to have been done with this aircraft her lab had just finished inspecting. The problem was that she wasn't part of the development process of that technology and had no ready access to it, and so she couldn't directly ascertain her assumption. But she did have something that could give her a clue.

Tanner accessed a secure partition in the lab's mainframe, one only she was cleared for, and went straight to the data she knew was still there, the UAV tests conducted under the project manager's strict supervision. While she wasn't privy to the exact structure and operation of the technology in question, she was privy to the test parameters and results and had in fact assisted in their analysis. Which was how she knew what to look for—the detection parameters for a specific signal, residual signal to be exact, generated whenever the technology was used to control an aircraft, and that would never be picked up unless those searching knew specifically what to look for. This signal, an intentional feature built into the technology, was no less confidential than the technology itself, for all the obvious reasons.

She was alone in the lab. Her staff had been working the entire day and most of the night before, and she had sent them to get some rest, knowing the importance of a fresh mind and seeing the signs of frustration in them—they weren't used to failing. But she had stayed, unable to let the mystery of this aircraft go, had caught a few hours of fitful sleep on the sofa in her office and had then returned here to try to understand what was bothering her, what her mind was telling her she was missing. Which was how she came to be where she was now, about to test the only possibility left.

She made sure the lab door was locked, just in case, then returned to the workstation and consulted the information in her secure files again, and calibrated a signal receiver accordingly. She then selected specific systems and controls in the aircraft and activated them one by one. She watched not the aircraft, but the signal receiver's screen. Nothing. She let out a relieved breath and turned away, then stopped, thinking. She wasn't taking these measurements like she should be. The technology she was thinking of would have been used on the aircraft while it was in flight, operating in its entirety, and after all its systems had been fully active and interacting with one another for a time. Once the technology was activated, the residual signal would appear, its strength depending on the length of time the technology was at work. When the technology relinquished control again, the residual signal would remain for a time, eventually fading.

This aircraft had been under the suspect technology's presumed control well over a day before—almost two now—but had been shut down since it had landed, and since it had been brought to the hangar had only operated in a controlled environment and in a compartmentalized manner, its systems never active all at once. This meant that a shadow of the residual signal she was looking for might still be there, but it would be detectable only if all systems were simultaneously active. And it would be far less evident by now, requiring more sensitive measurement parameters.

She recalibrated the signal receiver and activated all the aircraft's systems remotely, from the lab, switching them on in an exact flight simulation sequence. And then she waited, her gaze on the screen, counting the seconds silently in her head. Long minutes passed, and she finally began to relax, to think that she was wrong, when the receiver screen came to life, pulsing with a steady, albeit faint, shadow signal. Tanner closed her eyes. She now knew it was not only possible, it was in fact likely. This aircraft must have been controlled from the outside using technology no one was supposed to even know about, let alone have.

She listened once again to the cockpit voice recorder audio file, to the last words uttered by the dead pilots. Her eyes returned to the silvery aircraft on the other side on the divide, the innocent pawn in the now all too likely ominous plot. Then, deciding, she called the inspection lab's administrative aide.

"Get me..." She struggled with herself, agitated. She would have liked to get to the bottom of this herself, contact the same people she'd assisted eight months before, but her orders were clear. This investigation was not only of the highest priority, the security around it was at a maximum to prevent information leaking out. She was not allowed to talk to anyone other than the person specifically designated to receive any findings that came out of her lab.

She tried to remember the name of the man she had no choice but to call, then waved the attempt away in frustration. "Get me the agent in charge of the ambassador investigation," she finally said.

The morning after sound, tension-free sleep followed by lovemaking that felt so right, was carefree and relaxed. As Donovan cleared the kitchen counter after breakfast, Lara stood leaning back on it, watching him. A faint blush rose on her cheeks when he turned and saw her eyes on him, when his gaze met hers, unveiled, then flickered down her body. He walked over to her and pulled her into a kiss, not holding back, and she leaned into him, responding.

"How can a day that began so bad end so good?" she asked in wonder, and lost herself in his answer, another kiss to remind her, remind them both, that the events that nearly resulted in both their deaths were over, that they were finally together.

He untied the short robe she was wearing and slipped his hands inside, touched soft skin. He was nuzzling the hollow of her neck when his phone, laying on the counter beside hers, sounded his unit's priority call-in tone.

"You've got to be kidding me," he grumbled. "I specifically told them to call me only if the world ends." But he reached for the phone and frowned at what the caller told him.

"A dead US Air Force major," he told Lara when he ended the call.

"So why you?"

"It's at ARPA," he said. He was the agent in charge of the USFID unit that handled interdepartmental, interagency and intercountry investigations with a potential for sensitive entanglement, the Serious Incident Response Team, USFID-SIRT. And since whatever this was involved the highly secretive Advanced Research Projects Agency—previously

DARPA, renamed and reorganized more than two decades before to reflect a new era of projects and international cooperation—if he was called in, there had to be a good reason.

"I have to change." He looked down and corrected himself. "I need to put some clothes on." He touched his lips to Lara's, then kissed her again, wanting more. "You staying here?" he asked as he considered going upstairs for his clothes, then figured he'd simply cross to his place next door through the back yard. He'd need a fresh change of clothes anyway.

"I'll go in. I left rather abruptly yesterday, Frank must be worried. Aiden too."

"I updated Frank yesterday, after you and I came back here. He knows you're with me. I spoke with Donna, too. I'll see you as soon as humanly possible, my Lara." He kissed her again and left her smiling.

In hangar A506IDSD-T at the IDSD-alliance air base at Mons, Belgium, the same aircraft was still standing alone on the otherwise empty inspection floor. But this time its systems were all active, operated from the main inspection lab.

"See?" Dr. Tanner was sitting in one of her lab techs' chairs. Her own, before the main console, was taken by Brendan Ailee, the aviation engineer who had appeared there a short while before accompanied by the same stern agent who had first appeared in her office early the previous day, closing the door behind him and letting her know of her new priority assignment, giving her just enough time to clear the hangar and prepare her lab and her people.

"That's impossible. We're not even using it yet," the engineer said, staring aghast at the signal receiver's screen. At the faint, yet clearly visible, proof of how this aircraft had been taken.

"And yet, there it is."

"Yes. But it's impossible. I mean, technically it's possible, the technology is functionally ready, or almost ready. But it's not fully operational, we're just in the testing stages. I don't get it. How could anyone get their hands on it?"

"Is it or is it not?" Special Agent in Charge Marcus Emero of IDSD's Office of Special Investigations approached behind them.

The engineer nodded reluctantly. "The residual recognition signal is the same as the one detectable when we use our technology. Whatever did this, it's ours. This is ours."

Emero's eyes hardened. He turned to one of his agents, standing silently in the otherwise empty lab. "Get me a list of everyone involved in this project. And track them down, find them all." He took his phone out and put in a call to the man he answered to directly in this investigation, the head of IDSD HQ Intelligence.

Chapter Eight

Lara put the car on autodrive. She loved to drive, but not this car, it wasn't her choice. She moved uncomfortably in the driver's seat and huffed in frustration. There had to be a way to convince Frank to let her choose another one herself, something she would actually like. The problem was that her new security status meant IDSD had now limited her choice to models approved for the high-clearance ranks. The result was cars too big, too heavy and too cumbersome for her taste—one of which she was in now—and she hated pretty much all of them. She had loved her convertible, that classy, elegant car, and had bought it herself, it was hers, even if she did have to let IDSD install some security measures in it. She would have liked to replace it, but it was no longer a viable choice, considering what had happened to her last one.

As the car made its way to the IDSD complex, she busied herself with calling Donna, placing the call through the car's communications system but routing it through her home to keep it private. The interior decorator came on-screen immediately. She was in her studio, Lara could tell by the level of noise around her, and her image wobbled as she walked to her office.

"Are you okay?" Donna asked before Lara managed to say anything.

"Morning."

"Morning? Your morning is, like, hours ago!" Donna looked at her quizzically. "You look good, by the way."

Lara raised her eyebrows, saying nothing.

"I know, I'm sorry, I had to tell him."

"I understand, I do. You did the right thing, Don."

Donna scrutinized her. "You really do look good, sweetie. I mean good good. Rested. Different."

"I slept. Anyway, Donovan said he called you, but I wanted to call you myself, too, to let you know everything is okay."

"Did you sleep with him?"

"Donna!"

"Sorry." Donna had the grace to look ashamed for about half a second. "Did you?"

"Yes. We slept very well, thank you. We were both exhausted."

Donna's eyes narrowed.

Lara smiled, relented. "Yes."

"Once?"

"What kind of a question is that?"

"Come on!"

"We spent the night together, okay? And that's

that."

Donna sighed. Finally.

"He came for me, Don. He just came and took me home, and he stayed with me. I told him every-thing, and he still stayed." Lara shook her head. "No matter what he finds out about me, he stays."

"He's in love with you."

"I know. He has never hidden it. I just didn't expect . . ."

"To love him back."

"Well, I was going to say that I didn't expect him to accept all of it, all of me. But yes, that too, I guess." That too, she was still thinking as the car passed through the massive main gate of IDSD US, the security system identifying her and not stopping the car for a further check.

Vice Admiral Frank Scholes was waiting for her in the lobby of IDSD Missions. As she walked toward him he scrutinized her face, and she saw the relief on his.

"I'm fine," she said before he had a chance to say anything. "I really am. Frank, I'm sorry I left that way yesterday."

He shook his head. "I'm the last person you need to explain that to, Lara. I'm sorry you had to go through it." He contemplated this for a moment. "I'm just glad Donovan is okay. That you two are okay. I mean, I assume . . ."

"We are." She gave his arm an affectionate pat

as they entered the elevator. "Don't worry," she said, but knew that he would, this man who had taken her under his wing on that fateful day her world came crushing down and had been a close friend to her since. "Were you waiting for me?"

"I had security inform me when you arrive. I just came from Jim's office, he's back from Brussels." The office of the head of IDSD US, Admiral James Helios, was at the IDSD Diplomacy building.

"What's up?"

"It seems we have a rather problematic situation on our hands." He gave her a brief rundown of what was known about Ambassador George Sendor's disappearance. Which wasn't much, but he had long ago learned it paid to keep Lara updated. She was that rare combination, a trusted friend with a security clearance equal to his and a unique mind, a great recipe for brainstorming.

And then there was his gut feeling. He didn't personally know Sendor, but he was more than aware of the situation the ambassador had been trying to untangle, and of the likely implications of his disappearance. Especially in light of the news Helios and he had just been given by the head of IDSD HQ Intelligence. Updating her was a good idea.

Still, Oracle wasn't directly involved in this, nor would she be.

Unless all hell broke loose.

The man had been dead no more than several hours, USFID's medical examiner would determine exactly how long. He would, Donovan thought, have been discovered sooner, but the room he was found in had prevented that. As for the cause of death, that was immediately determinable. The guy had been shot in the back of his head. A single, clean shot.

Donovan took a look around him. A large sub-basement room with equipment of all sizes lining the walls, all covered with opaque protective sheets. All except one machine, evidently an old one. This one stood on top of another in an inner corner, un-covered. A closer look showed that it had no traces of dust on it. In fact, it looked like it had been in use. Donovan crouched down near the body. No signs of struggle, no obvious marks other than the bullet wound. No matter. If there were any hidden clues that might help find out what happened to this man, the medical examiner would find them.

He stood up as behind him his people swarmed into the room. They were the only ones he would allow in here, trusted not to destroy any evidence. A few brief orders and the crime scene was being canvassed and imaged, the machine in the corner pounced on by his techs. One of his lead investiga-tors and the one who would be heading the team that would work this case with him, Supervisory Agent Emma Quinn, quickly took charge, and he walked out, knowing the evidence part of the inves-tigation would be properly handled.

Outside, the head of ARPA's Internal Security and Intelligence Directorate stood quietly, looking into the room with a grim expression.

"What can you tell me about him?" Donovan positioned himself between the man and the crime scene.

"Major Joseph Berman, liaison for ARPA level five projects," the man said quietly. Which meant, Donovan knew, that Berman had been in charge of interagency and intermilitary relations in joint projects at the highest confidentiality level. And that would explain why he himself had been tagged to investigate his murder.

"I'll need to know what he was working on, and who with. I also want his complete service file and his attendance and travel data going back one year. To begin with. And my people will require access to the major's office and his computer."

"His computer? I'm not sure I can provide you with this type of access without the permission..."

"I believe I can make sure you receive the more classified information about Major Berman. Provided, of course, that your security clearance allows it." The deep voice, with a trace of accent that Donovan placed in Boston, belonged to an authoritative man in his mid-fifties who was approaching them.

"Special Agent in Charge Pierce, I presume?" He offered his hand and introduced himself as Richard Bourne, ARPA's director. "This agency and I will provide you with all the assistance we can. However," he added, "I'm afraid you and I will have to continue this conversation in a more private setting." His expression was somber even before his eyes flickered to the dead man laying not far from them.

"I apologize for the theatrics," he said when they were in his office on the main administrative floor of the building, "but we try to compartmentalize project-related information to the extent possible. Strict procedures have proven to be highly effective, and quite necessary, you understand, as many of our projects often involve sensitive collaborations."

"What projects was Major Berman involved in?" Donovan came straight to the point. Experience had taught him that the people holding the most access to information in this type of investigations, his type of investigations, were usually guarded, careful with what they said. Which had, of course, everything to do with the type of organizations they were part of and the information they tended to be privy to. The director, the extent to which he was forthcoming, offering his help, presented a rather unique opportunity for Donovan to obtain valuable information at an early stage of the investigation, and it was an opportunity the seasoned agent wasn't prepared to miss. Still, the question lingered in the back of his mind—just why was ARPA's director so ready to jump in and offer his help? Normally, he might not have been involved in the investigation at all.

"Allow me to check." Bourne called up the information on a screen he kept carefully averted from

Donovan. "Ah. Yes. He is . . . I'm sorry, was affiliated with aviation projects. Most recently, and for more than a year, two years almost, I see, he has been assigned as the liaison to one specific project named Sirion, under our Tactical Technology Office. Unfortunately, other than to tell you what entities were involved in it, there is not much else I can disclose. I believe your USFID clearance is not high enough to provide you with the specifics of the project itself. If you would like, I can approach your director and the head of the project, and once we clear you I'm sure I can provide you with—"

"Entities, meaning it's an interagency project?" Donovan interjected. Interesting, he thought, how the man's readiness to provide information seemed to have cooled down, now that he had placed himself as Donovan's direct source for it. Was he stalling? Surely he knew that if Berman's work was so important, Donovan would eventually be cleared for more information, not only because it could hold the motive for his murder, but also to ensure the project was not at risk.

"And international too. Let me see"—Bourne consulted the screen—"yes, ARPA and IDSD United States' Advanced Technologies Research, IDSDATR, and both air forces, ours and the Internationals', are involved."

Donovan's face remained impassive, not showing his interest at what he'd heard. This was also an IDSD project.

As he was about to ask Bourne for the identity of the project managers, the director's phone emitted a quiet, classical tune.

"I apologize," Bourne said, glancing at the phone. "I must take this call. I assure you it would not have been transferred to me if it were not a priority."

Donovan was still wondering what took precedence over the life of a man, when he saw Bourne's face pale.

On the other end of the line, Paul Evans, the recently appointed director of the US Global Intelligence Agency, explained that at the request of IDSD's main intelligence division at its Brussels headquarters, made directly to him, ARPA's employees involved in the Sirion aviation project needed to be tracked down. As attempts to reach the project liaison, Major Joseph Berman, any other way had failed, Evans was contacting Bourne himself directly. This was, he reiterated, a matter of the utmost urgency.

"I'm afraid I can't," Bourne said, and in response to Evans's agitated protest he added, "Yes, I understand. But, you see, Major Berman is dead."

"What?" This, Evans did not expect.

"He was found here, in ARPA's main building, earlier this morning. USFID-SIRT is down here right now—"

"USFID's SIRT?" In his office, Evans sat up. "Who's the investigator?"

"An Agent Pierce. He's here with me now, I—"

"Give him any information he needs. I'll call him now, speak to him myself."

Bourne hesitated. "But surely his clearance—"

"He's got clearance."

"How could he have clearance? Our projects—"

"Give him what he needs." And with that, Evans ended the call. He wasn't about to be argued with, nor was he about to explain. Ironically, it was Bourne who wasn't cleared for that information.

Bourne was still staring at his phone when Donovan's signaled an incoming call.

"That's..." Clearly unsure of himself, Bourne looked up at Donovan, who didn't take his eyes off ARPA's director as he took the call. Was that a glimmer of panic he saw in the man's eyes?

"Pierce here."

"Donovan, it's Paul Evans, I was the one who just spoke with Bourne. This guy, Berman, you're positive it's him? How did he die?"

Normally Donovan would refrain from answering this last question before receiving the medical examiner's findings, but this one he took straight. Obviously, something else was happening here, and he knew Evans was a no-nonsense man. The fact that he would bypass Bourne for Donovan said a lot. It meant he needed to speak to someone he could trust, and Donovan knew Evans well enough to go with that.

"Visibly, looks like a shot to the back of the

head," he said.

Evans, who'd been updated by his counterpart at IDSD HQ Intelligence in Brussels about the details of Ambassador Sendor's disappearance and was all too aware of why Berman was being sought, was silent for a long moment. "Donovan, your victim is part of a larger, international investigation," he finally said. "I'd like you to stay on top of it at our end." He sighed. The complications here were stacking up. "I guess you're right where you're supposed to be, eh? Good thing. I'll call Leland, I'm taking you to us on this, you and whoever else you need. IDSD HQ Intelligence did the same with their agent in charge of this thing at their Office of Special Investigations, so that's a full team. You'll work directly with me, I can use an investigator I can bloody well trust in this mess, and you're the only one who can freely work all related agencies. Okay with you? We're meeting at IDSD later today. In Missions, it's a secure three-way conference, three countries."

Donovan consented without hesitation. For Evans to bring him into whatever was going on when he had his own agents, he must have a good reason. And anything IDSD was automatically connected in Donovan's mind to Lara. If there was a chance she would be involved in whatever was going on, he wanted to be there. Even though he'd been readily added to Oracle's security protocol by Scholes himself, his and Lara's recent history together and his proximity to her considering, Donovan still wasn't anywhere near trusting IDSD, or anyone else, for that matter, with her security. Not after their screw-up the last time.

Evans didn't provide him with any other information before he ended the call, other than the time of the meeting and another warning to keep a lid on all the details of his investigation. Bourne was bursting with curiosity, but Donovan wasn't about to satisfy it, and not only because Evans obviously chose not to bring ARPA's director into this. Whatever this was all about, Donovan still had a victim and an investigation to see to. And around here, everyone was a suspect.

Going back to his investigative team, he worked the crime scene with them and joined in on the initial on-site interviews. This also gave him a chance to already have a look at the dead man's service file, provided to him personally by a helpful Bourne, who hovered around for the duration.

Donovan didn't leave the scene until the last of his investigators and techs did, taking everything they had so far to work on at USFID. And once he did leave ARPA, his destination was IDSD.

Ambassador George Sendor opened his eyes, then closed them again against the bright light. His head was pounding.

"I do apologize, Ambassador."

Sendor started and sat up in apprehension. The

man the voice belonged to stood up and walked to the wall, and used a small, manual switch to dim the light in the room. Sendor could now look around him more comfortably, albeit with increasing confusion. They were in a smallish bedroom. He himself was sitting on a single bed, a bedside table beside it with a glass of water on it and a tall water pitcher. A desk with a chair beside it stood in the corner, shelves filled with print books hanging on the wall above them. The room had two doors. One stood open, and led, he could see, to a small bathroom. The other, heavier looking, was shut, and must, he thought, lead outside. The room had no windows, and the subtle hum of air came from shafts in the plain low ceiling overhead.

The man came back to sit on the only couch in the room, which stood with its back to the far wall, not far from the closed door. He leaned back, crossing his legs, and resumed watching the older man with an expression of quiet, and subtly arrogant, interest. He was short, sturdily built. Clad in black, all black, and his clothes were, while seemingly simple, rather expensive, Sendor could tell.

"What happened? Where am I?" He felt dizzy, disoriented. The last he remembered he had begun feeling lightheaded moments after those shudders went through the jet. Nothing since.

"Take it easy, Ambassador. You are feeling the effects of falling unconscious after pressure in the jet you were on dropped, and of the sedative you were administered subsequently." The words, spoken in English with an accent Sendor could not place, were uttered pleasantly, belying their menacing meaning.

Sendor reached for the glass of water beside the bed, then hesitated.

"I assure you there is nothing in the water. We no longer have reason to sedate you, nor do we wish you any harm. You will find that while you are our guest, you will be well cared for and treated with the utmost respect."

"Who are you? What do you want?" Sendor realized there was an underlying panic to his voice and fought to calm himself.

The man simply smiled. "Someone will be here shortly with a change of clothes and a meal for you. If there is anything else you require, do let him know." He stood up and walked to the door.

"Please, wait, what day is it?"

The man opened the door.

"No, wait. My assistant, everyone on my jet, where are they? What did you do to them?"

The man left without answering, shutting the door behind him.

Sendor breathed in deeply, steadying himself. He stood up carefully, testing his balance. Once his head cleared he made his way to the bathroom. Like the bedroom, this room was simple, yet it looked new and was spit clean. He washed his face with cool water, used a clean towel to wipe it. Stared at his face in the small mirror. Pale, haggard, gray stubble.

Ah, he thought. Stubble. So it must have been, what, a day? Two? He shook his head. He had no idea. He had no idea about anything. Except for one thing. One thing that had his heart go cold with apprehension.

His captor had not bothered to hide his face.

Chapter Nine

The IDSD gates loomed before Donovan. Security was back to normal here after the days of heightened alert mandated by the threat of an attack on this complex and the people in it. He drove up to the main gate and wasn't surprised when the newly installed barrier opened before him, the armed agents eying him with no suspicion. The automated security system had identified his USFID-issued car well before he even approached the complex's gate, then tagged him inside it. His security clearance here did the rest, even though the formal vetting process had not yet been completed by IDSD's Brussels headquarters. He was, after all, part of Oracle's security protocol now.

IDSD Missions was a distance away from the gate, deep inside the secure complex, and Donovan made the way in his car. Reaching the building, he pulled into a visitor spot in the attached parking lot and walked in. The place was familiar to him by now, and he headed straight for the elevator bank, then took an elevator to the top floor. Once there, he crossed the open-space work area with its humming activity to the opaque reinforced glass wall separating the war room from the rest of the floor, then walked through the doors that slid open silently as he approached them. This was where critical operations, missions worldwide that determined lives and fates, were overseen from.

No one stopped him when he came in here, not even those who did not yet know who he was. Besides the stringent security system that had allowed him in, he had his temporary IDSD ID on beside his USFID badge, identifying him by his image, his name and a code that allowed him in here, and near her. Those who did know him acknowledged him with a wave, a word at times, as he turned left and skirted the workspaces that dominated the floor, heading toward the offices of the critical mission experts.

The woman he loved was in her office, leaning back on her desk, her eyes on a wall screen running data. Oracle was evident in her stance, in the slight narrowing of her eyes. She was thinking, he could tell. Focused on whatever was on that screen that she needed to place in some context he had no idea about. He couldn't even make out what was on there, it was running, switching, too fast. Not too fast for her, though. He stood in the doorway for a long moment, watching her, then entered and came to stand beside her, leaning back on the desk as she was.

She smiled, never taking her eyes off the screen. "What are you doing here?"

"I came to talk to Frank. Then I'm due at a meeting here, a videoconference."

"So you're not here to see me?"

He laughed at the tease, at the new freedom of it, the new freedom of them. His hand went up to her waist, and he pulled her to him, nuzzled her neck softly.

She didn't resist him, not anymore. With him, with this man who from the start had been part of both Lara and Oracle, and had simply accepted her as a whole, loved her for everything that she was, this closeness felt so right even here, in her office, where Oracle took precedence.

"Now I know the story behind Oracle," Donovan said, throwing another glance at the data screen.

Lara laughed. "Like I said, it wasn't always like this. At the beginning I was on a lower floor of this building. Frank was in charge of me even then, because he hadn't worked out where I belonged and wanted to keep an eye on me, but I was down there, in a tiny makeshift office. Aidan was assigned to me from day one, but he was up here, to keep in contact with the war room as it was then. And there wasn't space for him anywhere near me anyway. But already on my first day at IDSD, I was called up here on a mission. And by a couple of months later, I was running up here for briefings and missions, or to work with the screens in Mission Command or in the conference room. And people were already coming to me, officers and agents would come to my tiny office to talk pending or running missions. And up here, they began more and more to look for me. Require my presence, so to speak, that's how Aiden called it. It became pretty crazy." She smiled, going back five years in her mind. "Then one day I came up here for a mission, and they were tearing apart the walls of some rooms that used to be right here, on this side of the floor. And a couple of weeks later, when I came to work my office was empty, and I was asked to come up here. When I did, Aiden was already organizing this space around the tech guys who were scrambling to understand what I needed to do my job. I had a new title, the fittingly obscure critical mission expert, and a code name."

"And so Oracle officially came to be."

She chuckled softly. "Yes. It all happened very quickly, I barely had time to settle into it."

"Frank said you changed with time. Evolved."

She nodded. "After I was moved up here, they began teaching me faster, completing what I hadn't learned in my short time as an analyst, or in my even shorter time here. I spent a lot of time in the field, so that I'd see everything first hand. From aircraft and ships and vehicles and all kinds of military technology to training and methods and ways of thinking and strategies and everything they could think of, for friendly and unfriendly militaries, and for others, too. I still do that, when there's something new I go to see it. At the beginning, with every mission there was something else I needed, something I hadn't encountered yet. Something new. The sheer amount of information, it was crazy. I barely ever got home.

"But eventually, when I reached a critical mass of knowledge and experience, and what I was doing wasn't that new to me anymore, I guess my mind was free to explore, see where it could develop, and I began pushing against what I could do, tried to break through every barrier I encountered. There really was no other choice, it was either that or leave someone behind in a mission because what I could do wasn't enough. Anyway, at some point, when Frank realized this, he had everyone take a step back and let me dictate the pace and what I needed. And it's been that way since."

Donovan let out an appreciative whistle. "That must have been one hell of a process to watch from the outside. And it must have taken some effort on your part."

It was like him to think about this, about her. She still wasn't used to it. "It suited me," she said. "I needed to get through that period, to find a way to cope, to . . ."

He wanted to complete her thought, say live, but that wasn't what she had done. Not then, not until now. "Stay alive. Rebuild," he said instead.

She leaned into him. This once it was nice that he read her so easily. She found that she liked that he understood. And that she liked the feel of him.

His arm tightened around her.

"Hey, what happened to the dead body?" She suddenly remembered.

"It's connected to why I'm here. At least, that's what Evans told me."

She straightened up and looked at him. "Wait a minute, you said you're in the videoconference. That means you're on the ambassador case."

"Ambassador?"

She nodded. "I don't know much about it, just the preliminaries. I've got this as a priority." She turned back to the screen, a slight frown on her face.

"What's that?"

"One of my pending missions is likely to go forward sometime in the next twenty-four hours. These are the latest updates and regional deployments. And another pending just went an alert notch up, and I've got a new one, if that will come in it'll be as an unscheduled emergency intervention, it's something outside the alliance that we might have to react to."

He frowned inwardly. She spoke as if this was the most natural thing in the world for her, dealing with these missions. And she was Oracle, after all. But he still worried about the pressure on her. "Will you also be in on this ambassador one?"

She shrugged. "Depends."

Which meant, he knew, depends on how wrong it goes. "Well, anything that doesn't target you is fine with me."

She smiled. "No, I think we're done with that."

"Good," he said, and kissed her, lingering. Wanted to linger some more but this wasn't the place, or the time. Stealing another moment of the kiss anyway, he turned to go, leaving her with a smile and more than a bit of flutter.

Scholes looked up as Donovan greeted Celia and walked into his office. "Well, good to see you here," he said and settled back in his chair, which creaked dangerously. He squinted at the younger man. "You gave us quite a scare, you know."

Donovan's eyes flickered toward Lara's office before he sat down.

Scholes saw the glance. "So now you know. Lara said she told you everything."

Donovan said nothing.

"I couldn't say anything. Very few know the entire story, and no one can access that part of her IDSD file. She made me promise her that back then. The offenses, by the way, whether Internationals, US, or alliance, don't exist anymore. That one was a collective decision by everyone involved, considering what she can do. Anyway, I couldn't tell you."

Donovan frowned. He understood Scholes better now, this hardened military veteran who was so protective of Lara. Not just Oracle, as Donovan had thought when the vice admiral had first asked him to keep an eye on her. But Lara, too, the young woman who'd lost her brother and the man she loved and had then gone straight into the war zone they were killed in, avenged their deaths, and then returned to do all she could to prevent what had happened to them from happening to others, and to prevent other loved ones from going through what she had. And he appreciated the fact that while the vice admiral had said nothing, he did try to hint, and that everything he had said and done was for her.

But he was still angry. "I understand," he said quietly. "But if you had, if anyone had told me any of it, I would have handled the incident I was involved in in New Mexico differently, in terms of the information she got from USFID. Certainly its timing. She didn't have to go through this."

"Maybe she did. Maybe you both did."

Donovan contemplated him. "I would think you wouldn't approve of us, her and me. My job has already put me in danger."

"True. But I've seen you with her. And I've seen her since she's met you. I never thought I'd see that." Scholes sighed. "I'll have to trust that you'll always do your best to come back to her, safe."

"No," Donovan said mildly, prompting a perplexed look from Scholes. "I won't try. I *will* come back to her. Always."

Even though what the younger man was saying was impossible to promise, Scholes found himself believing him.

"Of course," Donovan continued, "as far as you're concerned, you do realize I'll be a pain."

"How so?"

"I will do anything to protect her. She is your Oracle, but she is my Lara."

With everything that had happened, Scholes understood what Donovan was aiming at. He sighed. "Considering the fact that I was the one who asked you to protect her in the first place, I think that's only fair."

Donovan nodded, then turned to the other thing he'd been planning to deal with as soon as he could. He glanced at Lara's office. "While we're at it, let's talk cars a second," he said.

"What?" Scholes was caught off guard.

"She hates the car you gave her."

"I know. But you and I both know I can't just let her replace the car she had lost with an identical one. It's not secure enough anymore, Donovan, and IDSD will no longer be lenient about her safety."

Donovan looked at him thoughtfully.

"At least we have a new one on order, Lara has already been called in today for all the necessary additions, so that our car fleet techs can retrofit it when it arrives. But she refused."

"Is it like the temporary one she has?"

"Yes, just next year's model. It's our most secure car, Donovan."

"A secure car she won't like is as dangerous as the car she used to have. And may I remind you that she blew up the last one, and that one she liked."

"Yes, but my priority is to make sure she's safe—"

Scholes stopped, remembering who he was talking to. Donovan wouldn't allow anything that would put Lara in danger. They both wanted her safe.

And they both wanted her happy.

"Okay, I'll tell you what. Show me something she would like, and that security approves, and I'll authorize it." He stood up as Celia motioned to him from the doorway. "Come on, that's us."

The conference room of IDSD Missions' war room was nearly empty, but not for the lack of participants. The videoconference taking place here was being held across three countries in two continents. The room held Admiral James Helios, head of IDSD US and interim head of its diplomacy arm, Vice Admiral Frank Scholes, Helios's second-in-command and head of IDSD Missions, who made the introductions all around, and the only non-IDSD participants in the meeting, the director of US Global Intelligence Paul Evans and USFID-SIRT Special Agent in Charge Donovan Pierce. Other than them, wall screens featured two participants from IDSD's headquarters in Brussels and one from its temporary peacekeeping base at the Brčko demilitarized district on the border between Republika Srpska and Bosnia, tension and weariness evident on all their faces, and not only because of the lateness of the hour in Europe.

Hugh Jeffries, head of IDSD HQ Intelligence, came to the point without wasting any time. "Two days ago, an IDSD diplomatic jet disappeared over Europe. On it were our Ambassador George Sendor, his personal assistant, and the regular aircrew and a protective detail. They were on their way from Brčko District to Brussels via IDSD-Alliance Jadran Air-Sea Base at Split, in Croatia. The ambassador was due to join the semi-annual meeting of our High Council and the heads of IDSD's branches worldwide. A short time after its disappearance, the jet was found standing, apparently intact—something the inspection lab at our main Europe air base at Mons has already confirmed—on Cres, the Croatian island. The crew, the protective detail and the ambassador's assistant were found still in their seats, each killed with a bullet to the back of the head. The ambassador was gone."

Donovan sat up. A bullet to the back of the head, just like Berman.

Jeffries, sitting at his impeccably organized desk, paused, his intelligent eyes taking in everyone on the split-view screen before him. More than half a decade in this office, he knew all of them except for the USFID agent, who had been brought in by Evans. However, he certainly knew who the man was, and had concurred with Evans about involving him in this situation.

He considered, then decided to proceed with a brief account of the ambassador's current engagement in its immediate context, to ensure both the IDSD and non-IDSD participants would have the background required. Inconsistencies in the knowledge the people dealing with the situation at hand had could not be allowed, and its importance had to be understood by all.

"Two and a half years ago," he said, never appearing anything other than calm and composed, "Ambassador Sendor ended his commission in Italy. He had already been assigned elsewhere, but had first returned to Brussels for a month, intending to wait there until the ambassador he was scheduled to replace would end his respective commission.

"During that time, Council Head Stevenssen had asked him to assist in resolving the dispute in the Republika Srpska and Bosnia region. I remind you that despite the harsh lessons of the Bosnia-Herzegovina war at the end of the last century, and the decision of the former European Union two and a half decades later to allow the country to become a member in order to assist it in achieving political and economic stability and to keep its Republika Srpska enclaves from falling under control of the Russian Federation, something the latter had been close to attaining, another war eventually broke out between the Serbs and the Bosniaks. A brutal war that saw Republika Srpska with its Serb majority fight the Federation of Bosnia and Herzegovina with its Bosniak majority and each ethnicity turning on the other's minority within the two autonomies, once again committing acts that cannot be seen as anything but ethnic cleansing. In fact, on the way they had managed to chase out the third minority, the Croats, who were taken in by Croatia to protect them.

"That war finally ended with a forced ceasefire, but the ceasefire was precarious and as soon as the countries that had brokered it had turned their attention elsewhere, busy with their own problems— the European Union had broken apart by then—relations between the two main ethnicities, Bosniaks and Serbs, deteriorated, eventually reaching a point where they threatened to rekindle the war again. This time, we and what was then already Joint Europe were there to broker a rather unique agreement, backed by a referendum, under which, instead of resorting to war again, Bosnia and Herzegovina was officially split into two, with the Serbs keeping the name of their original enclaves, Republika Srpska, and the Bosniaks choosing to remain with the name Bosnia, in order, in their words, to make clear to their enemies who they are—Bosniaks.

"The split was deliberately done in such a way so as to ensure complete separation. Which was why the original divides, which would have meant the two parts of Srpska would have continued to be entirely separated by Bosnia in between them, were not kept, but rather the country was newly split in two, with a single border stretching from Brčko District, the country's self-governing administrative unit, to Croatia on the opposite side. Bosnia, which was closer to the West, took the north, and Srpska took the south. The split was done in a way that each of the two warring nations received the same area size it had prior to it, and the new border was created along existing roads, to facilitate monitoring and control.

"As for Brčko District, it was badly hit in the war, neither side respecting its self-governing status, both of them stripping it of much of its area. The different ethnicities in it ended up having to retreat, each to their own safety of numbers in Srpska and Bosnia. Most people, at least. Some stayed, insisting Brčko District should have its status back. And that's in essence what happened, as part of the split. A new border was negotiated for Brčko and it became a self-governing demilitarized district protected by both new countries. It was a natural choice, too, because of its location.

"IDSD Diplomacy assisted in the necessary relocation and rebuilding of whole cities and rural villages, where residents chose to move. For most people their homes, their livelihoods had been destroyed anyway, with too many dead, too many memories for them to remain where they were. It was a difficult decision to reach, but the two nations—unfortunately that's how they perceived themselves, as two separate nations—agreed that the mutual independence would be better than another war. And so many had been displaced by the wars, that it was a decision the people were willing to make to attain a safer, permanent home. By then, none of them had any hope things could ever go back to the way it was before the wars.

"Still, it was a difficult feat to undertake, one carefully done, with ample resources and complete transparency. And for some years it seemed that the two nations might take a new, separate course. However, tensions remained high, and eventually, a little more than three years ago, the cold conflict once again threatened to escalate into war. And this time, threats issued made us believe that it might also cross the border to the northwest, to Croatia, which is a member of Joint Europe and therefore a member of the alliance, and the one to the south, to Montenegro. Montenegro isn't a member of Joint Europe, but it has joined the alliance independently after we protected it back when the Russian Federation reached it in its renewed attempt to take over Southeastern Europe. Montenegro is already more than a little concerned about the prospect of another war on its borders."

Scholes nodded, adding, "The way that last conflict escalated had the clear markings of outside intervention, the deliberate meddling of an external hand. A village in the heart of Bosnia was attacked, and the attack mirrored a little too closely the attacks that began the first war. The only living witnesses were the village elders. Everyone else—men, women and children—was murdered. There were, the witnesses said, no insignia, no identifying marks, on the clothes worn by the attackers. But they had, apparently, accidentally identified themselves as Serbs by speaking that language."

"The attack sparked a reaction of shock and disbelief from the Bosniaks and the entire world," Hughes continued. "It was followed by more, equally sporadic attacks, all in Bosnia, spread over a period of several weeks. The Bosniaks went from shock to anger to hate. Old feelings erupted, and Srpska's claims that it wasn't behind the attacks fell on deaf ears. The hostility between the two countries spun out of control. We had our suspicion as to who was behind the renewed tensions, but there was no reasoning with the two sides, and there was no hope of avoiding a war. In fact, at the time, we were already working with Joint Europe to bolster our defense forces at the Split base and were mobilizing forces to protect the Croatian and Montenegrin borders. And I remind you that to the east, Srpska, the southern of the two countries, now shares its border with the Russian Federation." Jeffries paused, allowing the meaning of what he was saying to sink in.

"A regional war was a certainty. Or at least, that was what everyone thought. Even though Bosnia and Srpska are not a part of the alliance, Ambassador Sendor was asked to travel to the region, and he did, to see if he might, perhaps, get the two countries to talk, and, in the meantime, to undertake not to involve their neighbors in their dispute. And he succeeded. That war never broke out. Somehow, the ambassador prevented it, and he has been working to resolve the conflict between the two countries ever since. He ended up foregoing his scheduled commission and had taken it upon himself to save the two nations.

"That's what he's been doing since, for two and a half years now. And in the past year, he got dialogue within and between them to change. They initiated trade relations and established joint committees to promote their economic recovery, and he eventually got them to agree to a peace treaty. In fact, the last of the formal peace talks ended early the day of his abduction. And while we've been searching for him, both sides expressed their full support of the final terms he had agreed with them. The peace treaty only needs to be signed. At least, that was the case until he was taken."

The expression on Jeffries's face was no longer calm as a frown crossed his brow. He passed a hand through his meticulously combed blond hair. "The implications of this are unthinkable. The last war, before Bosnia-Herzegovina was finally split in two, had been horrific, with both sides committing atrocities we couldn't believe, equal only to the acts of the first war, a war that left more than a hundred thousand dead, two million displaced, innocents who were left unable to live a normal life again. These were dark times, and the two nations were scarred beyond repair." He shook his head. "All those terrible decades. We finally gave them hope. If war breaks out again now . . ."

Donovan listened raptly. He hadn't known any of this, hadn't known much at all about these two countries, or their history. But he did remember the news about the imminent threat of war, endless broadcasts with urgency in the words of journalists forecasting the inevitable, forbidding images of the previous two wars playing in the background. And then things seemed to slowly cool down. While between the people hate still raged, the governments of both countries began to speak differently, soothingly. The militaries followed. And slowly, so very slowly, the moderate tone began to reach the people.

But it was only a few months before that, just like everyone else in the world, Donovan heard the name George Sendor, the Internationals ambassador who was succeeding where no one else had, who was making two nations full of hate and distrust not only slow down, but actually stop and think. He was making them listen. And he wasn't trying to attain another uneasy ceasefire—he had brokered true peace, a new beginning to a path he had carefully planned well into the future to ascertain its success, to ensure that for future generations the hate and wars would only be a history lesson taught in classrooms.

And now he was gone.

"Any leads, sir?" Donovan asked.

"None." It was IDSD HQ Intelligence's Office of Special Investigations Special Agent in Charge Marcus Emero, sitting beside Jeffries, who responded. "There was nothing inside the jet or outside it. No useful trace evidence, and all bullets recovered from the bodies were untraceable. The jet landed close to the edge of the artificial platform constructed for Cres after the main island was hit by that earthquake that destroyed it eleven years ago. A stable, rigid surface that could easily take a landing from an aircraft of that size. No clues anywhere around, other than indications that the ambassador might have been taken off Cres via the sea." His black eyes rested on Donovan, assessing him. "I understand, Agent Pierce, that you have a death that is similar to those on the jet?"

"US Air Force Major Joseph Berman, the ARPA-IDSDATR liaison in a level five project, was found dead this morning in an ARPA storage subbasement. One shot to the back of the head, no weapon found. Security cameras and motion sensors were deactivated and then reactivated again at a cascading sequence, no one noticed it because of the low-priority of that part of the building. The only reason Berman was found was that the last-sector security camera didn't resume working, and security eventually went down to check it and made the rounds just to make sure nothing was wrong."

Emero nodded. He didn't like the fact that an outsider, USFID, was brought in, but this investigator, he seemed to be thorough.

"Which brings me to a no less troubling matter." Emero glanced at Jeffries, who nodded his consent to the disclosure. "We now know that control of the aircraft was taken while it was still in the air, and not by anyone on board but by an external system. The jet was then downed using this same system." He paused. "Our system. Our technology, to be exact."

"Ours how?" On the screen next to the one with the Brussels participants, the head of the military component at IDSD's peacekeeping base in Brčko District, Major General Zachary Slaviek, frowned.

Emero looked at Donovan as he answered. "It's a joint ARPA-IDSDATR project, nearing operational stage."

Donovan nodded his understanding of the reference to his investigation. Sirion.

"So, you're certain." Helios had been told by Jeffries earlier that day, in a call attended also by his second-in-command, about the technology suspected as having been used in the ambassador's abduction. But he had also been told that Emero had yet to speak to the head of the project on IDSD's end, to confirm his suspicion. Which he had obviously done. His brow furrowed. He was in this meeting in his capacity as the representative of the head of the High Council, but he was also George Sendor's friend, and all too aware of the uncertainty as to his fate, his and that of the innocent lives he had worked so hard to save.

"Wait." He suddenly caught on. "Nearing operational stage? But it was used. And apparently all too successfully so."

"Whoever used it has obviously taken it through its final development stages, making it operational. The ARPA-IDSDATR project team has already tested it, yes, but their current version can't be used in the field yet."

"I don't suppose it matters either way," Helios said. "If this comes out, consensus might well be that it was us, that we did it on purpose. That the Internationals and the United States are sabotaging the treaty, and the alliance that had placed itself behind it. Considering the volatility of the situation, this would have serious repercussions." He clenched his fist, the motion betraying the true emotion behind the quiet tone of his voice. "We cannot allow this to happen. And yet, does anyone have any idea how we stop this? Ambassador Sendor is gone, we have no idea where he is or even if he's still alive, and someone—and we have no idea who—is apparently framing us for this." He fell silent. There was nothing else to be said.

"Excuse me," Slaviek said, breaking the silence. He was looking not at them but to the side, "you'll want to see this. A government-owned Russian television station has apparently aired . . . Right. That's not good." He seemed to be listening to someone else in his office. "I'm told this is already being tagged by the major media outlets here, both in Srpska and in Bosnia. Ah, no, everybody is already picking it up. I'll let you see for yourself." He nodded to whoever was there off-screen and was instantly replaced by a somber-looking news anchor, speaking Russian. The broadcast was automatically translated.

". . . We understand that the ambassador was on his way from Brčko District, where the peace talks have been taking place, to Brussels. The United States and the Internationals' executive body, IDSD, have refused to explain how it is that the diplomatic aircraft was downed using their proprietary technology, or to defend their involvement in the ambassador's death. Nor would they explain why they have chosen to withhold the information about what happened for so long. Again, Ambassador George Sendor, the Internationals' envoy to the peace talks between Republika Srpska and Bosnia, has been found dead two days ago after the aircraft he was traveling in was downed over Croatia."

In Brussels, Jeffries nodded grimly. "That's it then. It's out."

Beside him, Emero cursed under his breath and stood up. "With your permission, sir," he said, deferring to Jeffries, and when Jeffries nodded his consent he continued. "Let's see if we can find who the hell tipped them off. General Slaviek,"—he addressed the IDSD representative at Brčko—"if I may, sir, I will transfer this call to my office, we'll continue the conversation there. I'll update you as soon as I have anything," he said to those present at the IDSD US conference room, nodding at Donovan and deferring to the two heads of IDSD US and to the director of US Global Intelligence.

"Yes. Yes, of course." Slaviek, who was not only the person trying to hold everything together on the volatile Srpska-Bosnia border, but was also born in what used to be Bosnia-Herzegovina and had experienced first-hand some of the harsh episodes in its history, was still looking at the news broadcast in his office, his brow deeply furrowed.

"I ask you to excuse us both at this time," Jeffries said, his voice controlled. "I need to update Head of the High Council Stevenssen. It appears we now have no choice but to resort to further action, diplomatic and perhaps also otherwise."

As the two screens blanked, Brussels and Brčko gone to face front-line events, those remaining in the conference room at IDSD Missions in Washington, DC, somberly contemplated what the head of IDSD HQ Intelligence meant.

"Who knew about the ambassador's disappearance? Before this news broadcast, I mean." Donovan asked. The secret had had to be kept, but IDSD was not one to let two days go by without preparing for contingencies.

It was Helios who answered, his tone preoccupied. "Since earlier today, Brussels time, the Joint Europe civilian and military commands, and alliance members who might in any way be affected by the situation. Everyone who needed to know."

"Including . . . ?"

"Including the prime ministers of Srpska and Bosnia, yes. They, however, have been kept informed throughout the duration," Helios said and stood up with a deep sigh. "Frank?"

Scholes nodded and added, as Helios left the conference room, "The heads of IDSD worldwide have also been kept appraised of the situation, since they are responsible for the Internationals living in their respective jurisdictions. Good thing, too. This news leak about the origin of the technology used to down the ambassador's jet and the claim that we have hidden his death both mean that the repercussions of this incident might well be felt outside the disputed region. There are Internationals in many places, and they need to be protected."

He passed a hand on his face, his expression weary. "General Slaviek has had the peacekeeping force in Brčko District at high alert since the ambassador's jet disappeared, but we couldn't provide them with immediate backup, this would have let on that something was going on. We will do so now, see that the necessary forces are at Split to assist them if it comes to that. They need to be prepared, now that the news has been made known this way to the two nations they are monitoring. Worse, since the prime ministers also knew and have hidden the information from their people—they've only informed their governments and the heads of the militaries—that might have repercussions for them, too.

"We will also be deploying on the Croatian and Montenegrin borders of the disputed region.

Obviously, this too could not be done until now, but we've already made preparations at our Mons air base and will now be deploying part of the alliance defense forces there to the Split base, it's ready to receive them. We've all scaled back all other non-urgent initiatives. The alliance drill in the Baltic Sea has been canceled, all navy ships are returning to European ports and fighter jets are being redeployed either to Mons or to secondary bases in the countries closest to the disputed region. We're ready, we've had this planned back when the risk of war still existed, before the ambassador came to the region. As you can imagine, our Europe front has been busy." That was how the alliance did things, something that the Internationals had started. Politics would take a backseat to the military and diplomatic professionals, who would discuss the situation among themselves and set out the optimal layout and possible reaction scenarios aimed at a peaceful outcome backed by unwavering strength.

Donovan turned to look at the war room outside. It looked too busy not to be actively involved in this, nowhere near the hushed hum he remembered from the last time he was here.

Scholes saw him look. "While Brussels will be the heart of the diplomatic efforts to contain the situation and the heads of alliance militaries in affected countries will run defense and security with the rest of the alliance prepared to assist, we, as the main IDSD Missions, will receive concentrated updates

from everyone and run oversight and mission guidance. We'll be the ones looking at the situation from
above as it evolves. Which is what we've in fact been
doing since this morning. There was a reason this
specific meeting of these specific hands-on persons
took place here."

"With the origin of the technology that downed
the jet out, Americans worldwide might also be at
risk," Evans said thoughtfully. "And since we stand
beside the Internationals on this, and our military
forces are right there alongside yours and everyone
else who will be deployed to the disputed region,
I imagine this is about to go from bad to worse for
us too."

Scholes nodded. "IDSD's branches worldwide, and
especially in Europe, are looking out not only for
Internationals but for all alliance innocents, with em-
phasis on US citizens, considering your shared role
in this."

Evans gestured his dismissal of the comment as
obvious. What the vice admiral said was, quite simply, IDSD's way, and another reason why the unique
body, and the Internationals in general, were unequivocally trusted.

And that, ironically, made the current situation
so much more dangerous for them. Inevitably, there
would be those who would be convinced by blunt,
uncompromising rhetoric that the Internationals really did have something to do with what happened
to the ambassador, and disillusionment tended to be

a powerful path to hate.

"Of course, somehow, God knows how, we'll have to convince even our closest allies that we are not behind the ambassador's disappearance and the unraveling of the peace treaty, and worse, the renewed risk of war," Scholes said. "Considering that the technology is being created right here in this complex, and its testing, now that it is known, can be traced to both our air forces, that's not likely to be simple."

"I'm just hoping it isn't us," Evans said, receiving stares from both Scholes and Donovan. "What I mean is," he continued hurriedly, "it's always possible that someone here, either ours or yours, or both, is or are responsible for what's happening." He shook his head and stood up. "Which means we'd better get to the bottom of this sooner than later." His phone signaled an incoming message, and he glanced at it. "Well, looks like it's time to deal with reality head on. Your High Council must have already updated my administration." Another message arrived, and he looked at it. "And that's Jeffries." He turned to leave.

"Why would they say he's dead?" Donovan's question had Evans turning back to him. He looked from Evans to Scholes and back. "You called it abduction. But the Russian broadcast claimed he was dead."

"Why wouldn't they? Can we prove he isn't?" Scholes spat out bitterly.

"No. But I don't think they can prove he is, either," Donovan said.

Scholes and Evans looked at him thoughtfully. But then Scholes shook his head. "They don't need to," he said somberly. "The damage is done. We are unable to show the world that Ambassador Sendor is alive and well, and so anything to the contrary holds. We need to be prepared for the fact that unless something happens to turn this in our favor, we may very well be unable to stop what's about to happen."

Chapter Ten

Donovan stopped outside the conference room, his brow furrowing as Aiden came out of Lara's office and began to close the outer door. The aide stopped when he saw Scholes approach it, and waited where he was while Scholes walked inside. A few minutes later Scholes came out again, and waited until Aiden closed the door, which automatically led to the outer office's transparent walls darkening, effectively isolating Lara inside. He then walked with Aiden back to the aide's workstation, a thoughtful expression on his face, and the two spoke briefly as Aiden indicated his handheld screen. Finally, Scholes nodded, tapped the young man on the shoulder, obviously pleased, then walked over to Donovan.

"What's going on?" Donovan asked the vice admiral, who came to stand beside him.

"That Russian news broadcast has changed Lara's role in this, she knows she needs to prepare."

"So she's being updated about what was said in the videoconference?"

"No, she was listening in from her office. I wanted her to keep updated just in case, it seemed the smart thing to do after we learned this morning that it may have been our technology that brought down the Ambassador's jet. But she can't sit in on a meeting if anyone present doesn't know about Oracle."

"Who in there didn't?"

"Major General Slaviek has so far had no reason to know. And even if the situation in the area he is in escalates, Lara is likely to speak not to him, but to the commander of the combatant forces we are deploying in Split to assist him. He's worked with her before."

Donovan indicated the closed office. "So what's that for?"

"There are a number of people she wants to speak with. That's what Aiden is doing, he's setting up the calls." Scholes's tone was somber.

Donovan looked at him questioningly.

"IDSD officers," Scholes said. "One is the head of our team at IDSD HQ Defense that knows all alliance military deployments at any given moment. He can give her data on what's deployed at an increasing distance from the disputed region—what's deployed now and what's expected to roll out in the next hours—including what the alliance members in Europe don't have available because of unchangeable deployments away from Europe. Then there's his counterpart for the non-friendly deployments. Another is at our air base at Mons, two are in Split and are overseeing the defensive deployment to the Croatian and Montenegrin borders, and there's the contact we've set up for her in the Joint Europe Military Command. All of them have worked with Oracle on several occasions, so it would be a seamless interaction."

"So for her it's the same as preparing for a pending mission."

"Yes. These officers have been privy to everything that has happened since this started, while she was only brought into it this morning, and even then, only partially, and she's been busy with her other pending missions. And she hasn't had a hand in Srpska and Bosnia yet, so now she needs to understand them, too, and quickly." Scholes's eyes were on Lara's office. "With this war room overseeing the region, she might be called in unexpectedly. She has to be prepared so that she would only need real-time on-site data.

"When she's done with them she's scheduled to speak with a diplomatic negotiator from IDSD HQ Diplomacy. He has worked with Ambassador Sendor since the start of the negotiations. He heads the team that helped the ambassador understand the situation in the disputed region—past and present—and its implications, and later helped him plan the logistics of the peace treaty and its future. He'll be taking over the negotiations for now, if that's even possible. Anyway, Lara can't speak to him as Oracle, so she'll do that under her cover, the critical mission expert designation."

He sighed heavily. "The irony. If things had been

different, this might have been a euphoric day, filled with preparations for the signing of the peace treaty. Instead, that entire region is on the verge of becoming pure chaos." He turned to Donovan. "Anyway, she knows what to do. She's getting this information so that from this moment on she'll be able to react quickly enough to any emergency on the ground. Later she'll call for whatever dry and background information she decides on, the surrounding context. And in the meantime, she'll be kept updated throughout the incident. Just in case."

Donovan nodded.

"Just in case," Scholes repeated thoughtfully, all too aware that the eventuality of the situation had just become so much more of a certainty.

Donovan was about to say he understood, after what he had heard in the videoconference, when Celia came over to tell him that Evans was calling from his car, and that she had put the call on-screen in the conference room. While Scholes turned to go to his office, Donovan returned to the empty room, to see that not only was Evans already on-screen, clearly in the back of his agency car with the aide who had waited outside during the videoconference, but that he had also added Emero to the call, on an adjacent screen.

"So. Director Evans says there are good reasons why you're being involved in this," Emero began, somewhat more accepting of Donovan than he had been earlier, although he obviously hadn't warmed yet to the idea of working with the US agent. "And you are heading the Sirion liaison's murder investigation, so I suppose we'll be cooperating on this."

So he wasn't one to mince his words. But then, neither was Donovan. "Makes most sense," he responded. "Both our nations are equally in hot water here. Best if we each work our familiar sector and bring this to an end faster." His phone signaled an incoming message, and as he looked at it his brow furrowed. He addressed Evans. "Paul, does Bourne —ARPA's director," he added for Emero's benefit, "know just how much access I have to information?"

"All he knows is that you have an indeterminate high clearance and that he should give you what you ask for," Evans answered, preoccupied with something on the mobile screen he was holding.

"Good. I'd like to keep him and everyone else at ARPA who has anything to do with Berman and the projects he worked on thinking I only have what I or my investigators asked them for directly when we worked the crime scene." Donovan made a mental note to make sure all information would in fact be obtained also otherwise, through his own resources. Including a few more pieces of information he now thought he might require.

"What are you thinking?" Emero recognized an investigator's look.

"I'll let you know," Donovan said thoughtfully.

"I can wait," Emero surprised Donovan by saying. A good investigator didn't speak half-thoughts, half-theories. Certainly not with the stakes involved here.

Donovan acknowledged the gesture with a nod. With the pressure on his IDSD counterpart, it couldn't have been easy for him to place this confidence in a non-IDSD agent, and one he was being forced to work with, at that.

"I understand you have full access to ARPA and its projects," Emero said. "I can let you have similar investigative access to the IDSDATR personnel for the Sirion project, and I will trust you to share all your findings with me. However, we cannot allow them to be questioned outside the IDSD complex, nor can we allow your investigators access to them unless you can produce a good reason for me to request that such access be given—the status of all our IDSDATRs mandate that, you understand. Anything beyond what you yourself can get from them will have to be done by IDSD agents, if need be I'll send one of my teams over to assist you."

"Access for me will be fine for now," Donovan said, again acknowledging the gesture.

"Good. Let me know if there's any background information about them you need, I'll see that you have it. Also, please note that any interaction with the project personnel will not—" Emero stopped and considered his words. "I guess you already know this, I understand that SIRT unit of yours has dealt with this type of sensitive investigations, and you'll have the same issue with the ARPA side of the project, won't you?" He sighed. "So. Any interaction with the Sirion personnel, both IDSDATR and ARPA, will not be easy. Neither side in the project will appreciate being looked upon with suspicion for the murder or for the theft of the technology. You'll be dealing with brilliant people who take great pride in their work and what it is done for, both Sirion and previous projects they were part of, the good it does in the name of peace. And as far as our people in the project go, I suppose I don't need to tell you that we would like to not lose any of them."

"No diplomatic incident. Got it."

Emero chuckled.

"Since you don't have the access I do to ARPA, I'll let you know what we find on that end," Donovan said. "Let me know if there's anything else you need."

"Everyone involved in the project is now under increased protection," Evans said, his eyes still on whatever it was that had his attention on the screen. "The Internationals can only leave the IDSD complex with a protective detail, although they're being asked not to do so at all, and the Americans are in a similar situation. Their project meetings are currently conducted remotely by secure channel or at IDSDATR, where the heart of the project is. However, if one of them is involved in this, if an insider killed Berman, then any measure we take is futile. Ultimately, we can't limit their access to each other." A note of exasperation seeped into his voice as he finally handed the screen to his aide and looked up.

"I doubt it matters. The technology is out there, and Berman is dead, so he can't talk. At this point, and with the protective restrictions on everyone working on Sirion, another murder of one of them would only lead to the investigation being centered on them. So if it is an insider, he or she would do well to sit quietly and hope we'll focus on an outside perpetrator. Even running is not an option." Even as he spoke, Donovan thought about the message he'd received on his phone. He wanted to call SIRT.

"I agree," Emero said. "Also, while the research and development were done at IDSDATR and ARPA, field testing involved a range of air force teams working with aircraft of varying sizes and complexity. The Office of Special Investigations I'm in works under IDSD Intelligence, so we have a global reach. I already have teams looking into the testing sites, any people of interest there. If there's anything you want with them, we'll take care of it."

"Either way this has to be resolved quickly. We need to find who killed Major Berman, and we need to find whom Sirion was leaked to. Security implications aside, our priority is proving we had nothing to do with this. Especially if we can't find what happened to Ambassador Sendor," Evans concluded.

"Well, you're in now," he said to Donovan once Emero signed off. "From here on, you and Agent Emero coordinate this directly between the two of you. Emero has better access to the global arena, and since he reports on this one directly to Jeffries, he's got the authority to mobilize a lot of good people anywhere he needs to. You're in charge of the investigation on our end, so you deal with the Berman murder and see what else you can find in our jurisdiction. Now that we know that the United States has been used here, we're as responsible for finding out what happened and tracking down Ambassador Sendor as IDSD is."

His aide spoke in the background. Evans glanced outside the window, and Donovan caught a glimpse of the White House drawing near. "Looks like we're here," Evans said. "Keep me posted, Donovan."

And with this, he ended the call. Donovan didn't envy him. The director of US Global Intelligence could expect to have his hands full until this incident came to an end, however that would be.

Alone in the conference room, Donovan called SIRT. The message he had received was sent by Reilly Thomas, one of his two best techs. She had been looking at the dead man's computer. ARPA didn't want to let her take it, but Donovan's mandate, with Evans's order to Bourne supporting it, gave his team the authority to take everything related to the investigation and to the Sirion liaison, and that's exactly what they did.

Reilly's initial check showed nothing out of the

ordinary, but she had dug deeper. And her message had briefly told him what she had found.

"Sir. Boss. Agent Pierce. Donovan," she greeted him cheerfully. He couldn't help but smile. She was pink again today, a pink outfit, pink hair, pink fingernails. Pink was good, it indicated a cheery, optimistic mood.

"Hey, Reilly. So?"

"So, like I said, the guy had been downloading data from the joint ARPA-IDSDATR secure Sirion database.

"And?"

"And he did that in the past seven months. Every month, twice a month. Like clockwork."

"What kind of data?"

"Component designs. Protocols of development meetings. Test results. Lots of test results."

"Anything practical that could be used to replicate the technology."

"Exactly."

"I see." Donovan thought for a moment. "Reilly, how difficult was it for you to find out what he did?"

She looked pained. He corrected himself quickly. "I know it wasn't difficult for you. I meant, how difficult would it be for anyone else? How careful was the effort to hide what he was doing?"

"You mean, was it really meant to be hidden?"

He nodded. She pursed her lips, thinking.

The fact that she even needed to think gave him the answer he needed. "Go back to his computer. I want you to play out a scenario for me."

With a theory now forming in his mind, he explained what he wanted and then asked her to patch him through to her sister, in the same lab. It took him a moment to realize she had—Sidney was equally as pink as her twin. A cheerful and optimistic day for both, apparently.

"Sidney, anything on the machine?" He had her working on the piece of equipment found uncovered, and apparently in regular use, not far from Berman's body.

"It's old. Like, ancient," she said wistfully. But since ancient for her might well have been technology six months old, the way she was gobbling up new gadgets, he asked her to be more specific.

"Did you see the size of that thing?" She shuddered. "It's a late twentieth century tactical radio."

"Tactical radio? Really?"

"Totally. Military."

"Used?"

"Looks like it. But I haven't finished checking it yet. It's a bit difficult, this technology hasn't been in use for a while. I had to call up some equipment from our off-site storage."

"So how could it have been used?"

"Whoever he might have been communicating with had to have had the same radio. If you think about it, it's brilliant. The technology used nowadays is far more advanced, no one would expect this type of communications, so no one would look for its signals. Plus, it's pretty easy to hide the origin, destination and content of any data message sent or received on this thing or any voice transmission made. It's rigged so it doesn't save anything, you can't go back later and trace what the user did. This guy was really paranoid with his messages. Anyway, I'll need more time with it. I've never seen anything like this before."

"Could files of the sort Reilly has found our victim had downloaded from the Sirion database be sent using this communicator?"

"No. I mean, I haven't seen the file format, but I would imagine not even close. They would be incompatible on so many levels, not the least of all size and complexity. This thing is far too ancient."

Ending the call, Donovan sat quietly, thinking. Finally, he stood up and left the conference room. He had considered going to his office, but since he trusted his people to do their job and since there wasn't enough, not yet, for the kind of in-depth analysis he wanted to do, he figured the next best thing was to understand what the technology was that someone had made such an effort to procure, kill for, and then use in such a way that—deliberately, it seemed—threatened to destabilize a significant portion of the world, or at least lead to a war between two nations.

Chapter Eleven

Donovan decided to make his way to IDSD Advanced Technologies Research's new building on foot. Walking through the comfortably lit roads, he ran in his mind what he knew so far about the investigation. Around him the vast complex was calm, empty except for the occasional car passing by and for a mixed group of uniformed peacekeeping officers and civilian diplomacy personnel who stood on the sidewalk, raptly discussing the situation in some place whose name he didn't catch, and who nodded to him as he walked by.

Impressive, he thought as he walked up to the ring-shaped structure's main entrance, but then IDSD tended to treat science and technology with respect. The Internationals' military, aimed at preventing war, not making it, and at reducing the probability of casualties where a war had already broken out, was, and had been from the start, a smart, advanced force, intent on quality more than quantity.

As he entered the lobby of the building, a security agent met him. The security system would have identified him as he approached, but this was one of the places in this secure complex where this would not be enough. The security agent led him across the floor, where some finishing works were clearly still being done, to the internal ring, and to a glass elevator mounted on its inner rim, overlooking the center of the building. As the elevator ascended, Donovan saw that the entire inner courtyard was designed as a lush garden, with cobblestone paths winding through it and tables of varying sizes and shapes strewn around, none occupied just then. A comfortable place for a momentary reprieve, he imagined, perhaps a place for the creative minds in this building to work in under the domed skylight above.

The elevator opened to a corridor that stretched to his left and right, disappearing from view with the gentle curve of the building. Across the corridor he saw a set of double doors with the Sirion logo on them, and as he walked toward them—the security agent remaining just outside the elevator—they slid open to reveal a technology lab. Spacious, built to facilitate easy interaction between the people working in it. Polished clean, although here too there were obvious signs that the place was still being adapted to its occupants, who had moved here less than two weeks before. Advanced computing and visualization technologies lined multiple workspaces constructed to optimize team work, and a simulator the likes of which Donovan hadn't seen before stood in a far corner. Behind a transparent partition ahead, he could see people working around a disassembled aircraft, no wings, all its systems exposed and connected to a staggering amount of equipment.

Despite the relatively late hour, many of the project's personnel were there. The ambience was quiet. Pensive, Donovan thought. None of the people he saw were smiling, and quite a few were standing in small groups, speaking in hushed voices.

"They don't want to leave, and are trying to occupy themselves, keep their minds on what they do best. This day has been difficult for everyone."

Donovan turned around. The voice belonged to a smallish, silver-haired man with old-fashioned spectacles sitting low on his nose, his eyes peering over them, not at Donovan but at the lab's obviously perturbed occupants.

"You must understand, this comes as a shock to us all," the man continued. "We have been working on Sirion for a long time, and all the amazing people involved in its creation have put their hearts and souls into it. To discover that while they have been working so hard, someone has been stealing it and has used it for the purpose it was used for, to hurt people, is a terrible shock for them. And not in the least, Joseph's death . . ." He shook his head and turned to Donovan. "I'm Dr. Dori Beinhart. Co-head of Project Sirion for IDSDATR. And you are Special Agent in Charge Donovan Pierce, USFID-SIRT." He offered his hand, and Donovan wasn't surprised at the firm, resolute shake. He turned back to where the disassembled aircraft stood and strained to see.

"It's not here. It's at our Mons air base, on its way back from a field test. That's why . . . that's how a Sirion team was there to confirm that what happened was . . . that it was our creation that did this." Beinhart's voice was quiet, pained.

Donovan frowned. "Major Berman wasn't with them?"

"He was until yesterday. We were using our main testing site this time, and they are prepared for us there, so he chose to return here early to set up our next testing site, a new one."

"What was Major Berman like?" Donovan let the older man lead him to a small office at the right end of the room, under the somber gazes of everyone in the lab.

"Joseph was an excellent man. Excellent. He was reliable, endlessly patient, and had a way with people. He was uniquely efficient in managing all contacts between ARPA and us, the people and the organizations alike, and between this project and all military and civilian elements whose assistance we required to test Sirion in its various stages. Thanks to him, all aspects of the Sirion project ran smoothly, smoother than in any other project I have ever been part of, in fact. You know, at the beginning he worked on other tactical technology projects alongside ours, and as we progressed into the more elaborate testing stage we—my ARPA counterpart and I—did not hesitate to ask that he be assigned exclusively to us.

No, he was not involved in this, in hurting us, and I'd stake my life on it. We all would." Beinhart nodded to himself with a finality that did not invite an argument.

Donovan said nothing. This would not be the first time people close to perpetrators were sure of their innocence. He never let that affect him.

"Who has access to Sirion?" he asked.

"The people working on it, whether IDSDATR or ARPA, we all have complete access, that's the way it works best. Project sub-teams participate in meetings according to the subject being discussed, but we place no limitations on these meetings being attended in real time or viewed later by anyone in the project, and we certainly encourage inter-team discussions. It is conducive both to the formation of new ideas and to critical thinking."

"What about administrative staff?"

"No, they had no access to Sirion, not at all. Joseph took care of that side of things, too."

"Is the actual work on Sirion done only here?" Donovan indicated the aircraft in the next room.

"Yes, this is the main working floor, used by all of us—some of the people you see here are ARPA, they were already here when . . . when we heard. We do travel for on-aircraft testing, though."

"I suppose I don't need to ask you what Sirion can do, all considering."

Beinhart sat down behind his desk, and leaned forward in his chair, agitated. "No, please, you must understand, Sirion isn't a bad thing. It's a great idea. It's a life saver, don't you see? It came about thanks to Jamey, Dr. Jamey Black, he heads the conceptual side of the project. When he was a young child, his parents were traveling, his father was piloting their small plane, there was a seal problem and they lost consciousness. When they didn't respond to the air traffic controllers' calls and crossed into restricted airspace, military fighters were sent to intercept them. The pilots saw them through the windows, apparently unconscious, but could do nothing but follow the plane until it crashed into the sea. The aircraft had an autopilot, but it wasn't engaged, Jamey says his father loved to pilot the plane himself."

He sighed. "Jamey himself grew up to become a pilot, he flew jets for IDSD for a while. Much like the one that was taken, the jet with the ambassador on it. His experience, together with his investigation of what happened to his parents all those years ago, have led him to come up with the idea of Sirion." He spread his hands beseechingly, desperate to make Donovan understand. "You see, Sirion was designed to take control of any aircraft, manned or unmanned. Eventually, when it is completed, it will be able to do so at any stage of the flight, no matter where the aircraft is, how high up, over land or over water, and regardless of its speed, maneuverability, stealth or cloaking capability. Anything you can think of, Sirion will be able to deal with. It will lock on the aircraft's systems, all of them simultaneously, take them over without anyone being able to break its control, or even being able to trace it, and bring the aircraft wherever we want it to go, safely.

"If Sirion had been in existence back when the plane with Jamey's parents in it ran into trouble, it could have been controlled from afar and brought to land remotely, and they might have been saved. And that's only one application. Think of the possibilities—aircraft that malfunction in the air, flights in which pilots lose capacity, aircraft that are being hijacked..." His voice tapered off as he remembered that Sirion had in fact been used to the contrary, not to save a hijacked aircraft but to cause the hijacking, to cause death and grief. "Jamey is broken over what happened to that ambassador, to the people on that jet."

"Can you explain to me how it works?" Donovan brought Beinhart's thoughts back on track. He needed to understand more about this thing, what made it so special, so unique that it was kept a secret, and that someone would go to the length they did to steal it and murder for it.

"I've already explained it to that other investigator from Brussels, I forget his name, he called me to..." Beinhart sighed. "Yes, of course, I understand you need to know. Of course. Well, as I said, say we have a situation where we need to take control of a malfunctioning aircraft, or perhaps a hijacked airliner where someone on board manages to block our access to the autopilot so that the airliner can't be controlled from the ground, to bring it to safety. Or we need to take control of an enemy aircraft on its way to an attack, in which case we want to take complete control to ensure that, say, a bomb can't be dropped or information can't be passed to whoever has sent it about what's happening to it. In any such case, in fact whenever an aircraft needs to be taken over, Sirion is designed to near simultaneously take over the entire aircraft, all its systems. Everything on board becomes our puppet, and the pilots —if the aircraft is manned—can't do anything. And this is done through the satellite data link which all aircraft now have."

"I thought it wasn't possible anymore, to do this. That data links are secure, that they can't simply be hacked."

"You're right. Lessons were learned. There is a layered authentication protocol for all aircraft—different for civilian and military, and between certain classes of aircraft, too, to accommodate not only security but also the various needs of, say, ground stations for drones and air traffic control for airliners. And in some cases, there are also entity-specific layers, like IDSD has for its military and diplomatic aircraft, as an example—the internal layers are IDSD only, allowing the aircraft to still communicate its location to authorized ATCs while adding the internal authentication layers to block unwarranted access to the aircraft, such as if, say, someone wanted to upload false flight path corrections to the autopilot, malicious acts such as that. Anything that might pose risk to the aircraft. Basically, they have to pass multiple escalating access authorizations within the layered protocol, and even then, they still can't take control of the aircraft, these options were neutralized over the years through reengineering or the isolation of in-flight systems from avionics or . . ." he fell silent, perturbed. "What Sirion does is use the layered protocol against itself. It runs a cascading takeover from the outside-most layer to the internal-most one, and then it rides on the internal layers while the ones immediately outside them are reconfigured to act as isolating layers that prevent interference with its function. I won't go into the technical details, you understand."

"So it takes over the autopilot?"

"Sirion takes over everything on board," Beinhart stressed. "Consider the ambassador's jet. As I understand, it's a three-year-old fly-by-wireless with fiber optics fallback systems. Full separation of its in-flight systems from its avionics, that's a given, but it wouldn't matter in this case, our technology uses a number of contact points to take over all the aircraft's systems. And once it does, once Sirion has a lock on the aircraft, no one can take control of it back."

"So you take and maintain total control."

"Sirion does, yes. To maintain constant control of the aircraft, reliably so, of course, we use overlapping satellite coverage. In the testing stages we're using only our own satellites, and we will continue to use them as the core control platform. But once Sirion goes into use, we'll use allies' satellites as backups, a secondary security layer to increase our assurance of continuous control. We have already developed this feature and will be adding it in the next revision. And, just in case, we have a team that is designing into the specs a tertiary security layer to ensure continuity of control, one that will employ the communications capabilities of friendly aircraft in the air at the time. This is an ad hoc backup network, as it were, to help bounce communications to and from the target aircraft. Since our own protocol is secure, we'll be able to do this without significant added risk. No latency, of course. That's the idea." Beinhart spoke with pride. "For the fully operational Sirion, when it's completed, we will effectively be creating a closed, isolated avionic network, and this would increase communication—and therefore control—stability, predictability and reliability, and reduce both latency and susceptibility to security attacks."

"Whoever hijacked the ambassador's jet wouldn't have that, backups they can use. So they took a risk," Donovan said thoughtfully.

"Not necessarily. They kept the jet in the air for a very limited time and a very limited distance—as I understand, it originally took off from Split and was landed on Cres. There wasn't much of a risk there."

"Could they have used IDSD satellites? If you're already capable of using them, can they?"

"Of course not, that requires external authorizations and satellite tasking. They must have changed that part of the protocol." He frowned. "No, we would have been alerted. We can't know whose satellite they used, not even if it's private or not. All we were able to ascertain is that it doesn't belong to anyone in the alliance. Look, we originally designed the protocol to mask certain information, for confidentiality purposes. I remind you that the existence of this technology wasn't supposed to be known. Not even the instances in which it might have been used, especially if non-friendly aircraft were involved."

"Okay. So they're holding a technology that can already now take over an aircraft's data link, access all the aircraft's systems, and take them over, and they can potentially continue to develop it as you would have developed Sirion, to eventually be able to take over any civilian and military aircraft."

"Eventually," Beinhart said with a somber expression. "That was our original aim, and the basics are therefore already built into the architecture. So theoretically they could do that, with time. I mean, they got as far as they did, so they obviously have what it takes."

Donovan contemplated what all this meant. That the ambassador and the people traveling with him never had a chance. That the capability to irreversibly take over an aircraft and get away with it was now in the hands of an unknown element that had already demonstrated its intentions. He shook his head. "What about a countermeasure? Somehow blocking Sirion, which now means also blocking their version of it?"

"Well," Beinhart began, then paused, suddenly hesitant, it seemed to Donovan. "One of the issues we faced was in fact the need to prevent attempted hacking into our protocol by someone who might realize that Sirion has taken control of an aircraft or is in the process of doing so and would want to take that control back. One of Sirion's strengths is in its ability to block such attempts to take back the aircraft or even just release it from its control. You see, we recognized that since people created Sirion's takeover protocol, we need to assume that at some point there will be people who can break it. So in addition to the designated encryption we created to prevent a network breach, Sirion can detect any attempt to interfere with it, and can block it."

"Okay." Donovan frowned.

"But it doesn't matter anyway. Even at the very moment Sirion begins its takeover, the way we designed it no anomaly will be detected by the aircraft's systems and so no defenses on board or in any watching ground station will be activated, certainly not until it's too late, and that also means that no fallback systems on board will be reverted to, something that could interfere with our hold on the aircraft's systems if it were to happen." He stopped, shifted in his seat. "Look, Sirion can override all protocols, all alliance and non-alliance technologies, current and . . ." He stopped again. "It just can't be interfered with, Agent Pierce. It's as simple as that. Just . . . yes, we'll have to develop a countermeasure, try to at least, but—" He shook his head in something close to despair. "It was supposed to be used by us, used for the right reasons, not—"

"Dr. Beinhart." Donovan met the eyes of the co-head of the Sirion project with unrelenting focus in his. "What aren't you telling me?"

Beinhart let out a heavy breath. "Yes, well, no real reason not to tell you, is there? Sirion is not a secret anymore, it's already been stolen. And you're here to find whoever has it, to prevent further use of it, I hope. Yes." He braced himself. "Right then. You see, Sirion can learn. Or will be able to learn once we reach that stage in its development. Learn new data link security protocols it encounters, detect attempts to hack it and learn from them, learn the system trying to interfere with it and how best to block it." He paused. "It's a smart technology. It analyzes, learns, then overrides."

The furrow in Donovan's brow deepened. "You're telling me these people stole a technology that can't be stopped?"

"Well, this feature hasn't been completed yet. But the intention is clear in the architecture. Someone with enough resources would eventually figure out what we were aiming at and complete this part of it." Beinhart passed a hand over his face. "It wasn't supposed to be stolen. God."

Donovan considered him for a long moment, then turned in his seat and took a look at the disassembled aircraft. "What does it look like, how big is it?"

"It's basically a flight deck," Beinhart said, clearly relieved to leave all thoughts of the implications of the theft behind. "It's complex, because of the need, ultimately, to take over and control all systems on board aircraft of varying complexity, from, say, an armed UAV to a jet fighter or an airliner. And, of course, the need to prevent detection of the controlled aircraft for as long as possible, by keeping it away from air traffic but also by scrambling signals, if needed. All means will be employed, that's the idea. The flight deck houses the computer systems that do the work but also the people needed to monitor these, intervene if needed. There are considerations they would be needed for, at least in the learning stages, such as if new information comes in that requires a course change or, say, if the need arises to incapacitate everyone on board by decompressing the aircraft..." He halted, then stammered, "As was the case with the ambassador's jet, I mean."

"So, stationary?"

"No. I mean, it's big, yes, it's an integration of systems and people and it requires quite a bit of power, and it's enclosed in a designated structure. But it is mobile, and it can be operated not only on the ground but also on board a ship."

"From the air?"

"You'd need to retrofit a suitable aircraft for that, and that would take more time than these people had. And remember, they stole an uncompleted technology. Operating it from an aircraft requires more development, more work that we ourselves haven't done yet. We haven't even decided which aircraft will be used, that will require some testing. No, we're talking just months since they began stealing the specs, so all they would have had time to do is complete it and use it in a way that requires the least adaptability, in terms of place. Which means using it the way we use it in our testing and therefore configured it in the specs they will have stolen—in a specially fitted container that can be moved on the back of a truck or hoisted by a helicopter or disassembled for a specially-fitted cargo flight. But anyway, it doesn't matter."

Donovan looked at him questioningly.

"You're thinking about finding it, right? No, it's long gone. We have no idea where it was when it took the jet down and because we can't be sure how far they completed it we can't know if there were any limitations to its use, such as in terms of operating distance. You should assume it has no such limitations, because Sirion doesn't. And anyway, it's been powered down since. So even we, who would know what to look for, can't find it."

"Wait, then how did they . . . how was it originally understood that Sirion was used?"

"You mean Dr. Tanner, at Mons? She heads the aircraft inspection lab there. We asked for her help in testing Sirion a while back and she solved some issues for us, so when the jet was brought to her she was able to recognize its use, or rather the use of the stolen version. See, we originally created a residual signal that appears when the technology is in use. You need to know it's there and how to detect it. We did this for us, to identify Sirion's operational efficacy in its testing stages, it'll probably be removed once Sirion is operational because once it becomes known it will be a telltale sign. Anyway, a shadow of this signal can be detected after Sirion disengages, as long as all of the aircraft's systems are operating all at once. Luckily whoever stole the specs didn't realize what the residual signal was for and built it into their copy, and Dr. Tanner knew to look for its shadow signal. Still, it's gone now, and it wouldn't have been strong enough to track their copy anyway, certainly not after the jet was moved and when the copy can be anywhere."

"Okay." Donovan contemplated what he heard. "Okay, so if Sirion isn't operational yet—"

"True. We have already tested components on UAVs, military aircraft—cargo planes and fighters. We've even been given an executive aircraft by IDSD and have purchased an airliner for extensive testing. But there are still functions that are incomplete and glitches that need to be eliminated. We haven't applied the technology as a whole yet. I cannot believe someone is already using—"

"What would it have taken to make it operational to the extent that these people have?" Donovan needed Beinhart to stay focused. He needed to understand if there was a way here to find out who did this. Somewhere out there, there was a technology that could be used to take control of aircraft. Any aircraft. And if whoever did this could replicate it as they had, they could also duplicate it. Sirion in the hands of rogue groups, of people who didn't care about lives, was unthinkable. These people needed to be stopped.

Beinhart thought about it. "I haven't seen yet what was stolen, but with enough of our technical data, all it would have taken to replicate what we did and then continue our work is the right people. And they could work faster if they were taking shortcuts."

"Shortcuts?"

"For us, it's safety first. If Sirion is ever used, it would land an aircraft with none to several hundred passengers on board without causing harm to anyone on the aircraft or on the ground. No exceptions allowed. But if that isn't your aim, if you have other uses for the technology that do not make safety or even a one hundred percent successful performance rate a priority, making it operational sooner would be easier and require less testing. It wouldn't be perfect, and I wouldn't be surprised if the copy is far from it, but unfortunately it seems to have been built well enough to do the job."

Donovan took a long look at the lab. "What will you do now?"

"Continue. The original purpose of Sirion still applies, its importance is not in question. But if our internal protocols have been exposed we will need to revise them, and either way we will be setting up another team whose job it will be to try to find a way to protect aircraft from this Sirion copy, to counter its functionality or to, say, allow a friendly to take over an aircraft from a hostile attempting to control it."

"To prevent a recurrence of what happened this time."

"Yes. I can only hope that these people didn't pick up on the self-learning intention within the Sirion architecture, so that we can still create a countering system, or that at least they will be stopped and the technology retrieved before they get to build on what we already did. And obviously if their copy is found intact, we will have more to work with." He hesitated. "Agent Pierce, I wonder, can you tell me what . . . how this happened, how our Sirion was stolen?"

"I'm afraid I can't—"

"No, of course not. Of course. I do apologize. It's just that everyone here is wondering. They all thought they were safe, you know. IDSDATR and ARPA are two of the most secure entities in the world. And now, not knowing who killed Joseph and

how our work was stolen, some worry they might
be in danger." He raised a hand. "I know you can't
say anything, and I imagine you might even think
one of us was involved, although that is not a
possibility, no one here would..." He stopped and
took a breath. "I understand. I do."

"I realize how difficult the situation is for you,
Dr. Beinhart."

Beinhart nodded absently, his eyes on his people,
in what was the still active, albeit subdued, Sirion
project.

Donovan left it at that. There was no reason to
disrupt work at the lab any further by talking to
anyone else. Not yet. These people were being treated with respect. Not as suspects but as a treasure
to be protected, and, in a way, as the victims of
a crime, and he could understand why. They were
scientists and engineers and technicians who dedicated their lives to developing technologies in the
name of peace. That was what they had done with
Sirion, and what they would continue to do once it
was completed. And so, while each and every one
of them, including Beinhart, was being investigated
without their knowledge, none of them would be
approached directly with questions that might sound
accusatory unless they became suspects, not even
with the time constraints here.

Chapter Twelve

"Donovan." The deep, resonating voice interrupted the USFID investigator's thoughts as he walked back into the missions building out of the night enveloping the IDSD complex. Scholes was coming out of the elevator. He had a coat on and his briefcase in his hand. "I was about to give you a call."

"Going home?"

"Nothing too immediate to do here. Brussels, Washington and the Joint Europe Civilian Command are on now, we here are just watching from above for now." The vice admiral sighed. "One thing you learn around here is to take a breather before the sky falls. Which is something Lara should do, too. Get her out of here, will you? Otherwise she's going to lose herself in her work, stay here the entire night. Run herself down. I need her sharp. One of her pending missions, for the Joint Europe Military Command, was postponed because of the ambassador's disappearance, but there's another that's still expected to be set in motion sometime soon. A few hours away from here would do her some good."

Donovan concurred. "Good thinking."

Scholes laughed heartily. "Never had this option before, you know. Someone who might actually be able to get her to take a bit of rest." And with that he turned and left, still laughing.

Lara was alone in her office. She was standing beside her multitouch desk, looking down at a map displayed on it in muted colors. An old map, of Europe as it was half a century before. As Donovan walked in, she stretched and rubbed her neck.

"Looks like you could use a break. How about calling it a day?" he said.

The day had been over for some hours now, Lara realized. The mission she would be assisting in hadn't been set in motion yet, the weather and forces deployment local to the target area would decide when it would be. She did have the Srpska and Bosnia entanglement in her mind, but the information she requested from the officers she had spoken to earlier would take some time to compile, considering the angles she needed. And it was, for now, the work of diplomats to try to reduce the tensions, heads of military forces to deliberate their and their opponents' end goals, and intelligence to try to understand what was going on. There was no trouble yet, not her kind.

Although something did tingle in the back of her mind, something that didn't let up. But she had learned long ago not to push it, to let it be. Let herself be. If it was relevant, whatever it was that was bothering her, it would come to her when it was time. Chasing it would only tangle her mind up in itself, while what it needed most was freeing. Still, the idea of leaving the war room when so much was on the verge of happening bothered her. She could look at what the IDSD databases had about the disputed region's past. It wasn't entirely what she needed, but still, context could add more certainty when the time came and Oracle was called in.

"Lara?" Donovan could see the wheels turning.

Her eyes remained on the map, the furrow in her brow—and in her mind—not letting up. "I think I'll have another look at the Bosnia and Herzegovina wars and the Russia takeovers in the region. Why don't you go home, I'll follow in a bit." It had been a long day for him, too.

"In that case, I'll also stay. I've pretty much commandeered this place's conference room anyway. I could see if my lab has finished analyzing the evidence from this morning," he said conversationally.

"Really? Is that some kind of attempt to convince me to go home and—" She turned to find him close beside her. He leaned in and kissed her, stopping her thoughts, both their thoughts, and they remained locked in the kiss for a long time.

"Let's go home," he whispered in her ear, an unmistakable huskiness to his voice.

Any thought of arguing escaped her mind.

He didn't bother going up his driveway, just left the car at the curb and crossed her front lawn as the car she drove entered her garage. He walked inside just as she was getting out of the car, hearing the door slide closed behind him, and his gait didn't break until he met her with a ravenous kiss. He pushed her against the car, pressing his body against hers urgently, felt her respond, felt her push her body against his. He was already slipping her jacket off, tugging at her shirt, when she managed to speak through a kiss.

"Sensors," she managed to say. "The car."

He realized immediately what she meant. At her IDSD protection level, one of the security measures installed in the car was sensors, which would alert IDSD Security if anyone was tampering with it or if the occupant might be in any danger. And what they were doing . . . he pulled her away from the car into his arms and backed her toward the inner door to the house and through to the living room, and they tumbled onto the sofa and from it to the thick rug, leaving a trail of clothes behind them.

"Is something beeping?" she asked later. She was still catching her breath, the thick carpet soft at her back, Donovan's body prone against hers.

Donovan raised his head. "You're right. Something is beeping."

"I didn't hear it until now."

He smiled and stood up. "It's your new message

system, it was replaced along with the rest of this place's home system and security layout. It still has its default sound settings," he explained as he walked to the main security console. "We'll get rid of that beeping, replace it with something friendlier if you want. Yes, there's a message here."

She got up and walked over to him, putting on the closest piece of clothing within her reach, his shirt, as he read out loud, "Left dinner in the refrigerator, didn't want you two to bother with it."

Lara smiled. "Rosie. She called me earlier. She understood I had a man here last night and actually wanted to make sure it was you. She said she likes you."

"Huh. So I *am* a man after all." And at Lara's quizzical look Donovan swooped her into his arms. "Just a conversation she and I had a few days ago," he said.

"Sounds . . . interesting?"

"It was," he said, amused, as he busied himself with dinner. Lara contented herself with watching him. Seeing him being handy in the kitchen was always enjoyable. Seeing him doing so nude was much more so. She smiled, still surprised at herself, at the way she was with him.

"And so, you're a man," she concluded with a laugh when he finished telling her the story of his first encounter with her devoted housekeeper.

He glanced at her. "And I intend to prove that again later."

She caught her lower lip between her teeth. She intended to let him.

"So what bothered you?" she asked him as they sat down to eat.

"Bothered?"

"In the videoconference. Something about the Russian news broadcast."

"You really were there."

"Yes. Had you all on-screen."

"So not just watching me?"

"Watching everyone. Listening to everyone. Not my fault you were the cutest guy there. So what was it?"

He laughed. "What do you think it was?"

"You think the Russians are certain that Sendor really is dead."

He looked at her, surprised. She shrugged.

"Could mean they're not behind it," he said, testing a theory. "Maybe they found out about all this happening from someone else, were tipped off. Obviously they know about the technology used to down the jet, so whoever tipped them off is either behind it and is intentionally giving them only certain information, withholding the whole truth, or is not behind it but knows at least part of what happened, for whatever reason. Either way, it is a stakeholder in all this. After all, why tell Russia in the first place unless you want to instigate a political dispute?"

"No, it's them. Russia did this. But indirectly.

They had someone else do it, and that someone was supposed to kill the ambassador but didn't and is now feeding them misleading information. And that's what you think, too. That the Russians don't know he wasn't among the dead, that they think we found his body along with the others'." Her tone was factual, and he marveled at how her mind worked. And at how well she could deduce his.

"You wouldn't by any chance have any idea who they used?"

"No. You're the investigator. I'm just the . . ." She tried to find a word.

"The one who forges ahead confidently long after everyone else is already lost."

"Very poetic," she mused. "So, my investigator, any ideas?"

"*Your* investigator?"

She threw a cherry tomato at him, and he caught it neatly, grinning, thrilled at her natural reference to him as hers.

"Unfortunately, no. No ideas yet," he said. "It's just . . ." He was pensive now. "It's all too neat."

"Your dead guy." She leaped again. Leading him. "There's something there, you think."

"All I have is a gut feeling." Donovan played with his food, moved things around on the plate. "And it contrasts with the evidence." He told her what Reilly and Sidney had found.

"What about whoever killed him?"

"I have nothing. You heard it. A clean shot to the

back of the head, no weapon. The bullet retrieved in the autopsy in the meantime was untraceable, like the ones used to kill everyone on the jet."

"But you don't think it was someone he may have been conspiring with, giving the technology to."

"I believe it's whoever was following his work and stealing the technology through him. Framing him for something he wasn't involved in." It came out of nowhere. He raised his eyes and met hers, focused on him. Realized she was two steps ahead of him in what *he* was thinking and had just brought him on the shortest path to what he was really going for. He might be able to read Lara the woman, but Oracle was obviously able to go right through her investigator's mind.

"So basically, no," he continued after a pause, "I don't think Berman downloaded that data about Sirion. My gut says this guy was a straight arrow. I'm thinking someone else did that, either directly from Berman's computer or by hacking remotely and using Berman's authorizations, then took care to remove any signs of what he'd done so that Berman wouldn't know someone was getting into the project through him. And then, when the time came to kill Berman, the real perpetrator restored the original download logs, making it look as if Berman had been stealing data all along and trying to hide what he was doing. Nor do I think Berman used that radio we found beside him. I think he was lured to that subbasement room and killed at that precise spot to point us to it, make sure he would look guilty."

"It would have to be someone with access. Do you know whether the actual downloads were done at ARPA or not?"

"Not yet, my tech is checking."

"So it's either someone who can move through ARPA unhindered or someone outside it who was able go into the ARPA building and kill Berman."

"Ever considered being an investigator? I could use someone like you in my unit." He traced a finger on the back of her hand.

"Sure. And we'll get a lot of work done," she said, laughing.

Good point, he thought. Damn, she looked so inviting in his shirt. "You're right on, of course." He tried to focus again. "With what I learned today at ARPA and at your Advanced Technologies Research, and knowing ARPA's security and certainly yours—IDSD's—so that even an insider couldn't easily do this, I'm thinking this murder was deliberately set up to look like something it's not, by an insider with considerable access. But then there's the main question. Why. Why steal Sirion, go to the trouble of completing it, then use it to take this particular person, this ambassador. I mean, beyond the obvious political motive—to stop the peace treaty. Why do it this way?"

She shrugged. "To use it as a means to an end. Their end."

He frowned in question.

"You're thinking about whoever is behind this. I'm talking about whoever actually did this. And whatever *their* agenda is, it's important enough for them to risk taking the ambassador instead of killing him. That's some risk, because if Russia finds out they did, it can still continue with its original plans, as if the ambassador is dead, because it knows we can't just claim outright that he's not dead because we can't prove it, but at the same time, it will go after whoever was supposed to kill him, and do so with vengeance."

"You've put some thought into this," he said.

"Sixty-eight years old, held by people who have no problem shooting innocents in the back of the head and double-crossing the Russian Federation," she said simply.

Yes, he thought. That would prompt her to get into this. An innocent in the hands of some very bad people, who needed to be brought home.

He wondered if she had considered the possibility that Ambassador Sendor really was dead.

Chapter Thirteen

Donovan was in his office, the animated buzz of activity on the SIRT unit's busy floor coming through the open door. He was surrounded with information about the Berman murder, and was going through it at a focused pace. He went through points highlighted by Emma, some questions the investigative team working under her had tagged, the answers they had found. He then called up all the interviews done at ARPA the previous day—the day of Berman's death—and some complementary ones his investigators had done earlier that morning. He went through everything, even though he suspected he would find nothing. Considering where his mind was going with this theory of his, before he went in deeper he wanted to make sure he'd been thorough and had missed nothing—and no one—in the investigation, and in the process to back up his gut feeling with the facts he did have.

He'd asked his investigators to run current in-depth background checks on several of the ARPA employees they had interviewed, and he called these up now and went over them. Where he saw reason to, he used his own clearance to dig even deeper. As the umbrella organization for what used to be the separate investigative departments of the different military arms, USFID had access to all their resources, and as the agent in charge of SIRT, Donovan could easily get what he needed. He then had a look at several of Sirion's personnel. For them he had the background checks periodically done for everyone involved in ARPA or IDSDATR high-level projects—to those working at IDSD he was given uncensored access thanks to Emero. He found nothing, just as he had expected.

He then focused on the two people he was most interested in. The first was Berman himself. Donovan had the full version of his file not many were cleared to look at, including the level five projects he had worked on, Sirion being the latest. There was nothing there. The man's finances were clean. His military salary had been enough for him. He had no life outside his job and had apparently spent all his waking hours in whatever project he was working on. He seemed to be nothing more than a reliable, efficient man, good with people, good at bridging over differences. ARPA's projects competed to have him as their liaison, and Sirion was not his first ARPA-IDSDATR joint project.

Donovan checked the man's travels and compared them with the Sirion project's off-site logs. Ever since he was assigned to the project full time, Berman had traveled quite extensively, all the more so since the technology became viable and required frequent field testing. All his travels, without fail, were for the project, were on IDSD or ARPA jets or cargo planes, and coincided with the Sirion project logs. Nor did he ever travel alone, he was always accompanied by others in the project as well as by the protective agents assigned to the project personnel in their travels.

And that was it. He was single, had parents and a sister, all living in Virginia. No apparent contact with anyone outside his work other than a few friends, all from previous projects he'd been involved in, people he'd met along the way. He could have rendezvoused with an accomplice in his travels—it was easy to slip away for a few minutes, bump into someone, or simply leave storage media somewhere with the project files on them. But then, he could have done this in the vicinity of where he worked and lived, no need to travel for that. All phone calls came back legit, too, although he could have owned another, an unregistered phone. But considering the apparent use of the tactical radio his body was found near, Donovan doubted that. Either way, his investigators had found nothing of the sort, and they were thorough.

Donovan leaned back thoughtfully. By all appearances, Berman was a boring, reliable man who had made his job his life and who had spent years building a reputation as the man to trust.

The perfect spy.

"Or the perfect man to tag as a spy," he said to himself. That was his problem here—too much added up too seamlessly. Berman looked the part too well. He had both access and unlimited freedom because of the trust in him. Motive? Could have been money, hidden somewhere it couldn't be readily found. Could have been ideology. Ideologies could be safely hidden away in one's mind.

Okay, that would be true if he was guilty. But what if I'm right, what if this is too perfect? Donovan played devil's advocate. What if this guy really is innocent? If not him, who?

Bourne, his gut answered without any hesitation. He'd tagged the guy since he had first met ARPA's director. Bourne had been exceedingly forthcoming when Berman was found. Quick to offer his help, quick to offer information. Donovan would have expected him to be reserved, agitated, to worry about the invasion of the swarm of nosy outsiders, the USFID agents roaming ARPA, considering the sensitivity of its projects. No one welcomed an investigation. Yet Bourne certainly seemed to go out of his way to help. He had voiced no objections, and had seemingly placed no boundaries, even as others present at ARPA at the time did. And yet the moment he had the chance, he had subtly tried to stonewall Donovan, de facto threatening to delay the investigation. And then there was the look on his face when Evans, US Global Intelligence's director, chose to confide in Donovan instead of him. For a split second there, before Bourne had regained his composure, Donovan thought he saw apprehension in his eyes.

And then, that morning, he had called USFID's director, in an attempt to show his cooperation with the investigation, Donovan thought, perhaps try to gain White's trust as his peer. Was he worried that the investigation was now backed by US Global Intelligence's director, that the lead investigator had access, too much access? The man was hiding something, Donovan was sure.

Donovan had Bourne's file, procured in a way that Bourne would not know it had been requested. Procured such that no one would know, in fact, using one of the ways Donovan had available to him for his most sensitive cases. It was the only file he had procured this way in this investigation. The ARPA director's service file—his intelligence file, to be more accurate—was highly detailed, as Donovan had expected it to be. Going over it, he frowned. The man was clean. Despite his position, he had no technical background. A degree in political science, rose up through the ranks, steady career over the years, asked and received the assistant director position at ARPA, was a natural choice for director in due course. Ran ARPA efficiently, no real enemies. The perfect background, the perfect career, his way to ARPA paved by his ambition, nothing out of the ordinary there. Sensible finances here, too. Family money, though not so much that it would stand out. His only income came from his job, a generous salary at ARPA. He wasn't military like Berman, but a civilian employee from the start. Still, that didn't stand out, either, since the backgrounds of ARPA's personnel varied. Married for many years, one adult daughter who lived in Brisbane, Australia and was a tenured political science lecturer. No outstanding political affiliation, no outwardly voiced opinions, not him nor anyone in his family. Nothing extreme. Nothing not extreme, either. The man was steady, dedicated, clean.

Donovan shook his head.

"Guess what I found." Emma stood at the door.

"Bourne?" he asked absentmindedly.

"No. Berman. A bank account in Detroit, under his brother's name."

"He doesn't have a brother." Berman's brother drowned in the family pool when he was eight.

"Didn't stop Berman from opening an account in his name. All legit-looking, opened remotely with all the right credentials. I sent the info to your screen."

Donovan had a look. The account was opened seven months earlier. Fifty thousand dollars had been deposited in it every month since, in two installments, almost immediately after the dates on which the Sirion files were downloaded. Until one month earlier, when a final sum of two hundred thousand dollars had been deposited, as a single amount.

"Must have opened it when he succeeded in selling the tech, then was paid off after each delivery until they had what they wanted," Emma said. "Nice pension cushion."

"Mmm." A neat closing touch on Berman's guilt. So perfect. Too perfect.

"You're not convinced." Emma looked at him quizzically. Donovan's investigators had long learned to trust his gut feeling.

"No, I'm not." Simply too neat, he thought again once Emma had left. How could everything point to Berman, if he was in fact innocent? How could nothing point to Bourne, if he was indeed the one who betrayed his country by selling Sirion? And did he sell, or did he simply give it away—was he also in on Sendor's abduction and the motives behind it? And did he kill Berman, who was killed in the exact same way as everyone on the ambassador's jet? But then, why kill Berman at ARPA, necessarily turning everyone there at the time, including him, into suspects?

Donovan leaned back again in his chair and ran his fingers through his hair in frustration. No answers there, while the case against Berman and his accomplice turned killer, whom they could not trace —there was simply no evidence there—was adding up too well. Cases that added up too well always made him uneasy. Every thread here was in place. Each and every thread. And they all led in the same direction.

He sat up. That, precisely, was the problem. It all led in the same direction. But there were two things missing. One was a motive. And he wasn't convinced money was it. Over the years, Berman had had access to many other technologies that were more straightforward in their use, some weapons that could do much damage, portable systems that could be sold to rogue militaries for huge profit. And yet Sirion was where he chose to betray his country? An unfinished technology whose success, when he had begun to sell it, was not yet entirely assured? Sold for the meager sum of, what, half a million?

And then there was the question of the buyers, for whom there were no leads. Which was interesting, since while they had obviously taken great care to conceal themselves, they had made no effort to hide the technology they had procured. It was completed and then used immediately, and this, even without Berman's framing and killing, revealed its theft, which could otherwise have been hidden for much longer. With the ambassador disappearing and the announcement of his death made to the world by Russia, this was looking more like the deliberate acquisition of a technology that someone—apparently Russia, pending the oddity of their inferring that the ambassador was dead—planned to use to discredit the Internationals and the United States and their efforts to bring about a peace treaty in a region that Russia bordered with and had had an eye on in the past. A region Russia might have controlled by now, in fact, had the Internationals not stood in its way.

Donovan's brow furrowed. Helping this type of people stood against everything Berman seemed to have believed in, this man who had wanted everything he was helping make to be used to do good. Did anything happen to change him? Did he do it after all for the politics of it, to destabilize the treaty? But if it was all about ideology for him, he wouldn't have been paid as he was. This looked more like a thief being paid regularly until he provided all the information he was hired to steal. And that didn't fit this guy's profile.

Was he blackmailed? There were no indications of that, either. Emma had already spoken with his parents. They were in shock and had no idea who would want to hurt him, and neither did his sister. Nothing, they said, had bothered him recently. He was, as always, happily engrossed in his work. He had been to dinner at his parents' only the evening before his death—the medical examiner had determined he had been killed early the morning he was found—and had brought his mother memorabilia from the country he had just returned from, the last in a line of locations he had visited in this latest project he was helping, he had told them.

No matter how Donovan looked at it, Berman simply did not fit in the context of this, of all of it—theft, hijacking, abduction. Berman was an honest man, a dedicated professional.

The problem was that the same could be said about Bourne. Donovan looked again at everything he had on ARPA's director. He simply couldn't shake the feeling that there was something off with this guy.

He was contemplating what he knew so far and considering having a talk with Emero when a call from Brussels came through to his office. He took it on his wall screen.

Emero eyed him. "So, now that it's just the two of us," he began, "you were in on that recent situation we had at our IDSD Missions over there, that's why they pulled you in on this one, isn't it?"

Donovan said nothing. The reason why Lara had not been in the conference room during the call the day before made it all too clear to him that he could never know what the person he was talking to knew, even if that person was from IDSD. Emero knowing about the incident that had involved Lara didn't mean he knew about Oracle, even if he was a senior agent and the agent in charge of the ambassador investigation at IDSD. And while Scholes had noted that Slaviek didn't know about Oracle, he never specifically said that Emero did. It wasn't about rank or position at the international organization. It was simply about need to know.

Emero laughed, clearly amused. "I originally started out as a protective agent at IDSD HQ Security before I decided to get the training required and transferred to the Office of Special Investigations. So a couple of years ago, when there happened to have been a need for it, I was seen as having the necessary expertise and was asked to head the protective detail assigned to ensure someone was protected when that someone happened to come to IDSD HQ. And it worked out well, despite someone disliking protection, because I befriended someone, we got alone right from the start. So on the occasion that someone comes here, I make sure I oversee the protection of that someone if I can. And I'm rather pleased to know a guy like you does that in the United States, too, knowing how someone adamantly refuses to be properly secured at our complex there. That someone is rather a miracle worker, one we wouldn't want to lose, isn't that right?"

Donovan's nodded in appreciation. The guy was observant. And he knew about Oracle. "Nicely put."

"Yes, well, we in intelligence love being all mysterious," Emero said with a chuckle, and then his eyes became serious again. "Meanwhile, I've got zilch here. So far, we've found no one connected to the theft, or any trace of the technology. I'm sending you the medical examiner's report on everyone who died on that jet. Basically, they were all unconscious when it landed, pressure drop did that—Dr. Rebecca Tanner, our expert in charge of the inspection of the jet, confirms the proper controllers in it were remotely manipulated to cause that and whoever did it also made sure the emergency oxygen system didn't work. And hypoxia set in quickly, which explains why there was no struggle. All the perpetrators had to do was land the jet, walk in, shoot the crew, the protective detail and Ambassador Sendor's assistant, and take the unconscious ambassador with them when they left.

"Also, all Sirion personnel and everyone either directly or indirectly involved in the project are accounted for. We have some of them working on the jet right now. I've cleared them, and they're working with Dr. Tanner in her lab. A senior aviation engineer, Brendan Ailee, you'll see his name on the Sirion personnel list, and several of his people who were on their way from a field test back to the United States when this happened. All clean, all eager to help. They've run additional tests and have confirmed that a Sirion copy was how the jet was taken and landed, and they're trying to reverse engineer it now, see if they can figure out which Sirion features would have been completed by the perpetrators, maybe even changes made in them or new features added—we've already told them which specs Berman allegedly stole—and perhaps use this to identify trademark practices of whoever may have participated in recreating the stolen technology. There was also something about the unique markers of the signal through which the technology communicated, whatever, I swear I tried to understand.

"Anyway, they think this will take time, so I wouldn't count on any help there just yet, even if some engineer or whatever did leave a methodological fingerprint we can use to trace him. Or her. Or them. Hell." He rubbed his face in frustration.

"You got anything?"

"Could be." Donovan began by giving him a rundown of what he had so far on Berman, including the hidden bank account.

"Interesting," Emero said thoughtfully.

"Isn't it just?" The way Donovan said it made Emero look at him quizzically. "Did you ever meet the guy?" Donovan asked.

"No," Emero said. "I just read his file after the videoconference. Same one you have."

Donovan lifted an eyebrow.

"You don't think it's him."

"Seeing how it looks, it's just too neat."

"Right." Emero knew to trust an investigator's instincts. "What do you need?"

"I want to look at Richard Bourne."

"As in ARPA's director Richard Bourne?" Emero sat up.

Donovan nodded.

"He is completely outside our circle of suspects. He wasn't involved with the project, hasn't been anywhere near it since he signed off on it and it passed go. You'd be more likely to look at ARPA's division head for the aviation projects, she would have kept a close eye on Sirion."

"And yet."

Emero assessed him. "It could be tricky."

"More than an ambassador going missing?"

Emero let out a breath. "You have a point there. Well, he's one of yours, a high-up one of yours, so

I don't need to tell you how it is. Problem is, you go after Bourne and he starts screaming bloody murder, this is going to bring whole new problems on our heads. He's got friends, and ARPA is well protected. As things stand now everybody is letting you and me do our jobs quietly because of the importance of this to all of us, but if someone like Bourne stirs up trouble, as in political allies, and they—your end, my end or both—think they have no choice but to intervene, this could cause delays we can't afford right now."

"He won't know I'm looking into him," Donovan said quietly.

Emero scrutinized him. "Not sure I want to know how you're going to do that."

Which was fine with Donovan. He changed the subject. "How're things over there?"

"Just grand. Our diplomacy situation room is putting out fires all over the place. The head of our High Council, Stevenssen, she's a strong consensus leader and a smart one. She is doing all she can to keep things calm, but everybody in and around Joint Europe is moving forces around like in a game of chess gone mad. Basically, unless anything changes, everybody is simply holding their breath waiting for the bomb to fall." He breathed out. "Literally."

"Did you find anything about how the Russian station got the news?"

Emero shook his head. "Nothing solid. They cite an anonymous source. I put some of my best investigators and some damn good intelligence agents working with us on it, found nothing so far."

"Wouldn't the news broadcast had to have been sanctioned by their government?"

"Oh, it would have, all right. And just listen to the station's reasoning for putting it out there, it says it was its duty to share the troubling news with the public, that the people have the right to know, for the sake of transparency and trust." Emero didn't even bother snickering.

Donovan nodded, was silent for a beat. "So, you got any thoughts about who did it?" he finally asked, his tone conversational.

Emero's brow furrowed. That part of the investigation was out of Donovan's jurisdiction. At least formally.

"Someone obtained Sirion. Completed it. Used it. And then delivered what Russia needed to blame you and us for standing in the way of the treaty."

"You don't think it's Russia."

"I think Russia doesn't know Sendor is dead. I think someone over there got someone else to do this."

Emero considered him. What the hell, he could trust this guy. He understood that Donovan needed a link to establish a trail to the killer, and to the seller—obviously the seasoned investigator didn't think the latter was Berman. And IDSD needed him to find this link, it could prove material in finding what happened to the ambassador.

He put what he knew out in the open. "We think Russia's administration did it when they realized that we, the Internationals, were making too much of a headway toward peace in Bosnia and Srpska. These two countries were unstable and tired even before this happened, and right now they're also in shock, at a loss as to what they should do next, and it wouldn't be that difficult for Russia to step in and take them over. Such a move would take Russia to the edge of alliance territory, and it could try to escalate the war across the border, south to Montenegro or even into Croatia. They could very well try to tangle Joint Europe and us, and the entire alliance, in a regional conflict, a full-fledged war. And yes, we think they probably hired outsiders, someone who is out of their reach enough to risk taking the ambassador instead of killing him."

Donovan nodded. This fit in with Lara's assessment. And that, he trusted. "Any thought on who?"

"A couple. Depending on motive. If we assume it's someone who didn't mind causing this much of a mess in Europe, hurting us and betraying Russia— so obviously not someone loyal to it . . ."

"And someone who can gather substantial technological expertise," Donovan added, "not to mention funds, to complete the Sirion copy within a short time. Someone who can operate without easily being traced."

"An independent group," Emero said. That was IDSD HQ's working assumption, too.

"With an agenda. It's got nothing to do with, I don't know, taking over the disputed region, because it's obvious that Russia would go for it and not let anyone else stand in its way. So, someone who likes a bit of chaos? A weapons dealer maybe?" Even nowadays there were still many of these around, and they didn't like the Internationals advancing their plans for world peace. "No, these guys are too smart, too refined even. Highly resourceful and careful. And not as traceable and exposed as a weapons dealer might be. They're adept at hiding, act surgically, infiltrate subtly, here for the long term."

"Someone like Yahna maybe," Emero said with a nod.

"Yahna?"

"Oh, for crying out loud!" Emero looked to the side. "I'm being called away here. Listen, you've got access to IDSD Missions over there. Ask for the information about Yahna. Talk to me if you need to know anything else." He was about to sign off, but then considered and laughed heartily. "And say hello to someone for me if you happen to see someone, will you?"

Donovan smiled.

Chapter Fourteen

Lara was leaning back on the side wall of Mission Command, watching. The Brunei mission was well on its way, and so far, it was going as planned.

This was the only scheduled mission for which Mission Command would put aside its assigned task of watching the Srpska-Bosnia region via designated satellites, temporarily transferring this function to the war room outside. No other mission was scheduled for now, they had all been postponed in light of the tensions at the Srpska-Bosnia border.

When Lara came in that morning, she was told that the night before, just hours after the news broadcast claiming that Ambassador Sendor was dead, the Russian forces had begun moving. It looked like they intended to deploy along the Russian Federation's border with Srpska—and with Brčko District, where IDSD's peacekeeping force still was together with the peace negotiation team Sendor had been working with at IDSD HQ and that had now gone to the disputed region itself, desperate to keep some sort of a grasp on what he had achieved. In light of the situation, the alliance's military redeployment in the region was being accelerated.

Her briefing had barely ended when the go was given for Brunei, and she had switched gears for that, so she hadn't received any further updates other than to be told by Scholes that IDSD was putting Oracle on priority standby for Europe. But she wasn't thinking about that now, nor about the ambassador or the too likely implications of his disappearance. She would let nothing but what was happening on Mission Command's wall-wide screen into her mind until it was over. That was how it had to be. Whatever else was going on, this mission was the most important thing right now. It had priority, and anything else would have to wait.

She wasn't the mission coordinator. She was on the outside, looking on, her role very specific in this one, a mission with known certainty gaps that could not be closed and that would potentially need to be dealt with. Which was why she was needed, and why this mission required her undivided attention. She was the one who dealt with the unexpected, and it was, after all, the unexpected that tended to be that which threatened lives.

This mission was given a go despite the ambassador incident because there was no other choice, postponing it would mean loss of lives. It was a rather unusual situation. A group of locals believed to be a terrorist sleeper cell disappeared from Indonesia five months before. They had been on the Southern Territories' watchlist but had still managed to hide any communiques that must have passed between them before their disappearance. And then, three and a half weeks before, an undercover counter-terrorism agent in Indonesia, working there as part of an operation under IDSD Southern Territories Intelligence and the Australian Security Intelligence Organisation and posing as a black-market racke-teer, was approached by one of them. The guy was fishing for radioactive materials the procurement of which could be made without the risk of alerting authorities.

In the time the agent took to obtain for him low-radioactivity materials modified to appear more potent in their contamination capacity than they actually were, he managed to use audio surveillance to discover, through the guy's communications, that the cell was hiding in Brunei and was preparing an attack on five major Australian cities, one in each province. Its plan was to simultaneously detonate a dirty bomb in each of the cities, its main objective in the attack being the psychological effect on the public more than anything else. It would cause per-sonal and environmental harm, it would cause panic, and it was only the first in a line of planned terrorist attacks.

The man disappeared again, with his purchase this time, and with a nano tracker injected into his arm by what he had only thought was a mosquito. The agent's work and the quick reaction and ef-ficiency of the intelligence agencies he'd warned were commendable, but they were only part of the process. The cell needed to be eliminated. Experts judged that since the cell had already planned its attack and had apparently procured the necessary expertise, it would not be long before they could complete the bombs with the materials they now had. Worse, no one had any way of knowing if they had otherwise obtained other hazardous materials. And so a plan was immediately put together to stop them, and Australia's Counterterrorism Tactical Assault Group was sent to do the job. But heavy rains delayed the mission, and the soldiers had had to stay put. Until now, until the rain let off enough for the mission to go through before the cell could act.

The terrorists chose the perfect hiding place, Brunei's remaining cloud forests. Which meant satellite coverage would be inefficient in the dynamic time and resolution required. The only support the soldiers had were specially fitted helmet cams that would send their data through a network of nano drones that would be dispersed in the forest all the way from the clearing the soldiers would land in up to the terrorists' camp as the soldiers progressed toward it. That was all they had. That, and Oracle.

This incursion was unexpected and unwelcome by Brunei. It had not been forewarned about it, and the mission was not sanctioned by Brunei's sultan, nor would it be if he knew about it. And so it was also crucial that the soldiers get in and out unseen, certainly uncaught. Of course, the upside was that while the soldiers couldn't use direct line of sight satellites or drones to facilitate their mission or warn them about unwanted interference, going in virtually blind, the terror cell couldn't either. It was just as blind under the cover of thick foliage.

On-screen, the stealth transports carrying the soldiers reached their destination, let them out and ascended again, cloaking as they did and remaining high above. Below them, the soldiers deployed, their helmet cams sending erratic images through the transmitter nano drones that followed them, dispersing according to their preprogrammed sequence and sending data to the designated receiver drones at the edge of the clearing, which in turn sent it to the tasked satellites far above.

In Mission Command, all those present moved uneasily. This was a high-risk, serious-consequences mission with far less ground information being received than they would have liked to have before them, conditions in the cloud forest worsening as the Tactical Assault Group ventured deeper inside it. The mission coordinator was focused.

So was Lara. The helmet cams footage transmitted via the nano drones was enough for her. She was already constructing it all in her mind, constantly updating the spatial reality the soldiers were operating in, with them in it. Even as she watched, she increased the activity level of her mind, putting herself among them. This enabled her to go deeper into that part of her that allowed her to do pretty much whatever she wanted. And what she wanted right now was to see—and anticipate.

It took only a little nudge, and she saw enough, just enough, ahead, pushing the temporal envelope just that much. She didn't need anymore. She stayed that way, just a bit ahead, through the minute, minutes, time stacking up, as the soldiers inched forward. Seeing on the screen, and in her mind. Hearing the rare chatter, a brief command here and there. Silence mostly.

Silence on the comms. Silence, but...

Her command, uttered quietly into the mic of her headset, had the forces on the ground halt and the mission coordinator standing on the operations platform before the screen turn to her. Him, and every rank present in this place Oracle reigned in, all with earpieces they could listen with, listen but never interfere. Her next words had all of them turn back to the screen, the mission coordinator wiping a drop of sweat from his brow. The soldiers had weight-rigged motion sensors waiting for them up ahead, and beyond these, she knew, could see them clearly in the mind, were remote-detonation land mines.

She never moved, never approached the operations platform, there was nothing on the screen she could use. Her next commands had selected nano drones break from the communications network their peers were forming behind the soldiers all the way back to where their messages could be received by the satellites, and she had a single drone position itself before each of the advancing soldiers. She had already changed the chosen drones' designation, taking over command of them from right there where she stood, linking them to the Mission Command mainframe and working them directly, ensuring they would now detect and warn of the booby traps set by those the soldiers were there to eliminate.

From that moment, she never let her guard down, never left them. The nano drones saw the ground and the traps planted under it, the soldiers saw the drones' guidance, and she saw it all, her mind going where she needed it to, not feeling the strain, not coming up against any boundaries.

She had intended to let the mission coordinator run this mission, he would have relayed any guidance she might have had without question. She would have remained in the back throughout it all. Instead, the circumstances, the reduced visibility and unreliable communications, and the added risk from the cell that had, apparently, not trusted even its invisible hideout, had her taking over, allowing her to keep the mission within the margins needed to get the job done, while keeping those risking their lives to do it safe.

The terrorists may not have trusted Brunei's heavy forests, but they did trust their added measures, the sensors and land mines she had helped the approaching soldiers get through without harm, un-detected. The soldiers were in the camp before the terrorists noticed them. It was over in minutes. They found five ready dirty bombs, all ready for transport, for use, for unthinkable harm.

When the soldiers were safely back in the trans-ports, successful in their mission to ensure that those who had been in the camp they had left behind would never get a chance to hurt innocents, and the mission coordinator in Mission Command turned to acknowledge her, Oracle was already gone, already back in her office, already engrossed in the conun-drum that had until now stayed in the back of her mind, awaiting its turn.

Where was Ambassador Sendor?

His fist came down so hard that the touchscreen embedded in the large, rectangular table cracked, colors mashing together as the map on it warped a split second before the mainframe shut it down in defense. The Russian Minister of Defense Dmitry Aleksandrovich Rostovtsev would have preferred to hit the messenger, but the man was smart enough to retreat to the door.

Rostovtsev had been busy with the deployment of the forces along the Srpska and Brčko borders, assisted by his loyal advisers. The actual deployment, not the plan for it. The plan had been in place for many months now, waiting for the right moment, the perfect opportunity to present itself. Which it had. And it had all been so perfect, so effortless, Russia's success assured. It would cross the border into Brčko and from there move into Bosnia, at the same time crossing directly into Srpska—his eyes hardened when he thought of that treacherous country, which Russia had cultivated for years, yet when the time came and it had been perfectly positioned for a takeover, it took a step back, choosing to remain independent, saying it did not want the fate of its former neighbor, Serbia, which had succumbed to Russia's promises and ultimately ended up being absorbed into it when the dominating country had decided to assert a single rule across its lands.

But now Russia would have Srpska *and* Bosnia, and that damn alliance would be too busy trying to understand what happened, trying to deal with allegations against two of its prominent members and to contend with suspicions from without—and within, he was certain. Human nature was like that, and could so easily be played against itself. No, no way for them to get out of this one, he had thought until just a short moment earlier when the message had arrived, delivered by the Russian envoy to the United States who was back in Russia for a hastily scheduled leave. The message wasn't delivered directly to Rostovtsev, of course, but to the president. To him it was delivered by this man, one of his many spies in the country's foreign intelligence service.

The message had been simple. A single image

of the cabin of an executive jet, clearly showing a number of bodies. The image had been accompanied by a single question, delivered verbally by the envoy, in the words given to him by the US representative who had personally met him to relay the message.

Where is Ambassador George Sendor?

"What do they mean where is the ambassador?" one of Rostovtsev's few trusted advisers asked, perplexed. "He is dead."

"They claim that his body was not on that plane. That they don't have him," the intelligence officer stammered, then took another step back when the minister turned his eyes to him.

"They are lying!" The adviser nearly shouted in disbelief. "They must have removed him before that photo was taken. It is disinformation, to throw us off track."

"We can analyze the image," another adviser, a younger man selected precisely for his technological savvy, said. "See if they doctored it, if there was another body there, one that had been removed."

"Nonsense. We cannot believe them. They are trying to undermine our success, to find a way to save themselves—"

"Enough!" Rostovtsev's voice and an even louder crash of his fist on the table had everyone in the room cowering. He stood silent, his dark eyes on his own warped reflection, even now every black hair in place—he didn't mind the gray ones, he thought they added dignity—his expression hardened by years of stubborn resolve, and by the unwelcome turn of events. It could not be. It simply could not, must not be.

Finally, he spoke. "I want to see him." He raised his head. "I want proof that he is dead."

Chapter Fifteen

Donovan's call to Lara, as the sun disappeared over the horizon, was answered by Aiden, who promised to relay his message to Ms. Holsworth as soon as she came out of Mission Command. Ending the call, Donovan stared at the phone, frowning. Another mission. The one Scholes had talked about, he figured. Two missions that he knew of and now the trouble in Europe, too, since the harsh incident she herself had been the center of, tense days that had been packed with events that threatened her directly. She had been attacked, injured, and the need for her to be actively involved in her own defense had taken its toll, and yet the missions never stopped.

It was unavoidable, he could understand that. She was, after all, the one and only Oracle. But what she'd been through with him just two days before, thinking he'd been killed, that had taken a toll on her too. He worried that she would exhaust herself. There had hardly been time for her to recuperate, none at all, really.

At least she had him and what was finally happening between them. He could already see something new in her, as though this, them, was giving her new life, as it was giving him.

He found himself smiling at the thought of her and marveled at that. He had every intention of taking her away as soon as it was possible for them both. Just the two of them, for a break they both needed. That first date, the one he'd asked her on but hadn't had a chance to do anything about, that could be so much more than he had originally intended now that they were together, that she was his. He already had it all planned.

Turning his thoughts back to the investigation, he turned back to his desk screen and accessed available information regarding groups that opposed the United States, the Internationals or the alliance. He then narrowed down his search to those that were not affiliated with specific countries, skimming over them quickly before focusing his attention on Yahna, and on the information he'd already asked for and had received from the liaison assigned to him by IDSD Missions in his previous case working with them, Lieutenant Commander Nathan Walker, who was only too happy to help.

Donovan had fleetingly heard about Yahna, but he never had a reason to give it a closer look. Yahna —originally an acronym of the names of its five founders—was an independent group, quite a large one, comprising citizens of multiple countries, the United States included. They had substantial financial backing and a say in parliaments and business communities worldwide, some of its members being former politicians and powerful business people, others seasoned lobbyists.

Yahna had been a vocal opponent of the Internationals and, as a result, of the alliance they had created. But it never operated against the United States, other than to voice anger at its close cooperation with the Internationals and at its decision to join the alliance and play an active role in its activities. And the same was true for the group's members in other alliance countries, none of them had gone against their own governments.

The group had been founded immediately after the Internationals were first granted their unique global status by the international court. It had voiced its objections with increasing vehemence as the world got used to the existence—and benefits—of the new nation, and as the Internationals became increasingly active in the global arena and began pushing for the formation of the alliance.

Yahna's concerns were mainly the disappearance of political borders and with them the identities of countries—a world order they did not agree with—and the idea around which the alliance evolved, of eventually reaching a global state of equal opportunity life. The fact that the borders remained and that the Internationals had actually encouraged a sense of identity and had never gone against people's sense of nationality, of belonging to a homeland they could always return to, if that's what they wanted, and had instead brought about beside such identity a sense of humanity, of caring for the world beyond their own home, never even slowed Yahna's objection to their existence. The years that followed the Internationals' inception, which showed marked societal and economic improvement in alliance countries, didn't convince Yahna either. It seemed that Yahna was, quite simply, seeing everything Internationals as a betrayal of the ways of the past, despite the new hope the Internationals brought with them for the future.

As Donovan read on, his brow furrowed. He was looking for something else, something he wasn't finding here. Whoever was behind the ambassador's disappearance was acting behind the scenes and did not shy from violence. That didn't sound like something Yahna would do. Back in its day it made sure it was heard, and it had never resorted to violence. All it did was try to convince people in positions of power in the dominant countries of the free world of its opinions, hoping to strike down all the Internationals' initiatives. And in the past decade or so, it was barely even heard anymore, and its rhetoric seemed to have been substantially moderated. In fact, it seemed that Yahna had become nothing more than a feeble opponent of the Internationals, one that no longer drew much attention.

Nothing about Yahna fit here. So was Emero mistaken? Donovan doubted it. The seasoned IDSD agent would have for groups opposed to the Internationals the same feel Donovan had for those that could endanger the United States.

Deciding to stick with Yahna a little longer and figuring Emero might have known something the IDSD liaison didn't think to send him, Donovan considered contacting him, but then reconsidered and instead used his SIRT authorization to go deeper into intelligence files and search for any extremism Yahna might have manifested. He didn't have to dig for long before he hit pay dirt. Some years earlier, acts were committed by Yahna that were enough to turn more moderate members away from it and that increased the objection of alliance members and even nonalliance countries to it—a bomb placed under the car of an IDSD diplomat in Milan, which injured him and killed his wife, arson of an IDSD building under construction while the construction workers were in it, injuring many, instances of violence against Internationals worldwide that in four known cases resulted in death. As a result, everyone associated with Yahna was blacklisted so that business and political ties with them were prohibited, which damaged Yahna's finances and its clout, and some of its members were tried in very public trials designed to deter a repeat of their acts.

This apparently didn't fit in with Yahna's survival agenda, and it ousted a number of its leaders and members, going so far as to publicly denounce these rogue elements, as it called them, subsequently becoming the more carefully subdued organization it was nowadays. Donovan read through some of the trial transcripts and checked the names in them against the information in the intelligence files. Every one of those involved, everyone who wasn't still in prison, had gone off the radar since then. There was literally nothing about them, which was odd this day and age. It wasn't easy to disappear.

The problem was that the actions that Yahna's rogue members had chosen to take didn't fit in with the patient, sophisticated, and critically damaging act of stealing a technology no one was even supposed to know about from a highly secure organization, completing its development and making it operational, and then using it to abduct an ambassador right out of the sky over Europe. And then using that to discredit two powerhouses—the Internationals and the United States, destroy an alliance that spanned half the world, and cause war in the middle of a continent on the way, destabilizing a third powerhouse, Joint Europe.

He needed to know more. He tried to contact Emero, but his IDSD counterpart wasn't available. He leaned back, considering his best way to get what he needed. He could call US Global Intelligence's director, Evans, for what he wanted, but realized he would face questions he didn't want to face. Considering Emero's reaction to his interest in ARPA's director, he didn't want this to come up again yet. Nor did he want to be pressured into providing answers about Berman just yet, not when he wasn't at all sure the guy was guilty, while the general consensus seemed to be that he was. And anyway, for what he needed, the best way to go was with those who would know all there was to know about groups who were a threat to them.

He called Frank Scholes.

"Good, I was hoping you wouldn't be in Mission Command," he said when Scholes answered, sounding preoccupied.

"Going in and out throughout the day, we're running the mission in there and Europe from the war room in the meantime. It's wrapping up soon, by the way, the mission. Lara, how should I put it, took care of everything." Scholes chuckled softly. "You know, until not that long ago, no one would have dared approve a mission with those levels of limitations and risk, and yet with her, we did, and success was never a doubt."

"Is she okay?"

"Sure, she's just watching over their departure now," Scholes said. "She does that. She's doing the debriefing immediately after the mission's over, by the way, to clear her time for Europe. Since we're overseeing all operations in the disputed region, and with the Russians on the move, unless an unexpected incident comes up that's all she'll be dealing with from now on."

"Actually, it's you I wanted to talk to," Donovan said. "I need something. I've been looking at groups that are anti-Internationals, some anti-United States and anti-alliance. And I've been looking at Yahna."

"Right," was all the vice admiral said.

"Yes, I assumed you'd know all about it. Thing is, I need to know more than I have. Not about the original Yahna. I need to know the extremes."

"You want the dry info or someone who can do some in-depth explaining, answer questions that are, I suppose, immediate to your investigation?"

"Both. And I'm thinking it would take more than an analyst. I need someone with hands-on knowledge. Current knowledge."

Scholes didn't hesitate. "I know exactly who can get you the right person to give you what you need. But you'll have to talk to them on an IDSD secure line, and at maximum privacy mode. You could do that here, but since I can't be sure when they'll call, you might as well do it at Lara's place." IDSD's upgrade of Lara's home security following the change in her security status after she'd been targeted included also a more secure communication line.

Donovan agreed and ended the call, then glanced through the open door of his office. By now, the floor was nearly empty. Impatient and with nothing immediate to move on, he grabbed his jacket and headed to Lara's place.

The man was sitting in the same couch again, although he had turned it to face the chair beside the desk, where Sendor was sitting. The ambassador had been writing. In an old-fashioned paper note-pad, with a pen. They had given him no computer, not even a media screen. To prevent him from see-ing what was happening in the outside world, to keep him completely isolated in this cage he was in. But he had asked for, and received, simple paper to write on. Will anyone ever see it, what he was writing? he wondered and then immediately chided himself. That was no way to think. His being alive was obviously of value to these people, whoever they were. And as long as he was alive, there was a chance. He had a chance.

The man, the same man as before, had come in while Sendor was deep in reverie. He had knocked on the door, oddly enough, before coming in. To give him a false sense of security? To taunt him? Sendor didn't know, nor did it really matter. He was the man's prisoner.

"Do you have everything you need?" the man asked now, his voice calm, pleasant, as it was before.

"Everything except for my freedom," Sendor replied. And it was true. He had done his best to acclimate and had requested certain items he wished to have for his comfort. Such as a shaving kit, one such as he was accustomed to using. Or a kettle and some tea, so that he could choose when to prepare it himself. And they had given him all he had asked for. A silent man, elderly, had brought it all to this room, a man who did not meet his eyes and never said a word. They seemed to have been prepared.

Down to his favorite tea, they even had that. How long had they been planning this? How long had they been watching him, learning?

The man nodded slightly. "I'm afraid freedom is the one thing you cannot have."

"You will kill me," Sendor said quietly.

"Will we?" The man raised his brow slightly, and Sendor thought he saw a glimmer of amusement in his eyes.

"Otherwise you never would have let me see your face."

"I could disappear, go into hiding. This is not a small world."

"We have made it smaller. And we have allies everywhere. You will be found, and you will not be forgiven for this. Even if you change your face, they will find you."

"When this is over, the Internationals and their blasted alliance will be fighting for their very existence. They will be powerless to do anything but scramble in panic." Anger flashed in the man's eyes for a mere second before he collected himself and leaned back in the couch again, crossing his legs in a facade of calmness.

"Then that is what this is all about. You are using me somehow to hurt the Internationals, the alliance." Sendor contemplated his captor. The man sat quietly, clearly amused at the older man's attempts to understand why this was happening to him. "I don't understand how. How could my disappearance hurt them? It will not even stop the treaty. It is too far along, the two nations—"

"Are already blaming each other for trusting the Internationals, for not truly wanting the treaty, for standing in the way of peace by killing you, for collaborating with the Internationals, with the alliance, to conquer them. They are making up so many absurd allegations, and no one can do anything about it, simply because there is no proof to the contrary. They all think that you are dead, you know. The entire world does. Your two protégé nations, they will be at war soon enough. And Russia is already moving its forces to the borders. Oh, I have revealed too much," the man added with mock innocence, clearly enjoying the shock and anguish on the ambassador's face.

"No!" Sendor's voice trembled with despair. "Why? Even if you are against who we are, what we do, what have these two nations ever done to you? Have they not suffered enough?"

"We have no interest in them, they are but an excellent means to an end, as you are. This war will last, it will bring destruction and change Europe, and the world will not forget soon the Internationals' part in what happened. Even the alliance is already unsure what to think."

"Who are you?" Sendor thought hard. His years in diplomatic service had given him valuable knowledge and good instincts. Surely, he thought, I can figure this out. He tried to bait the man. "You are one of those groups, those who oppose our existence. What we do."

"Very good, George. You don't mind if I call you George, do you, seeing as we are likely to be spending some time together? And to your question, yes. We were once a part of Yahna." Sendor nodded his recognition of the name, and the man smiled. "In fact, we still are, in a way," he said. "We have members who are still working within Yahna, using its resources and contacts. Which also helps us to keep an eye on it. See what it does, what it knows. Which is, of course, nothing. It is an anachronism."

Sendor heard the arrogance in the man's voice. Good, that will push him to talk. Sendor wanted so desperately to understand, to know more.

"But surely Yahna knows of your existence. It will stop you," he said.

"It has no idea. It is too busy with its meek lobbying, too busy living the cushioned life of making endless backroom speeches to politicians who do not listen. It is outdated and has done nothing, nothing at all for far too long. We are what it should have been from the start, and we are smarter. We do not even have a name, intentionally so. Names have a way of coming out in documents, in communications. In conversations. We exist as a group of people with a common cause, a common purpose. Only we know who we are, who is with us and who is not. This way, we are hidden."

The ambassador clinched his jaw. He was being

held by a group no one knew about, in a location it seemed to be sure could never be found. The anger erupted out of nowhere. "Why keep me alive?"

"While you are alive we have the option to use you as leverage, if we find it necessary." The smile was slow, cruel. "We can keep you here for a long time, George. No one will ever find you."

"How do you know I will not kill myself? Then you will have no leverage."

"You, Ambassador George Sendor, are the symbol of hope. You know that your death will take away any hope of peace for those you have fought to attain the treaty for. And you have a family. A person like you always retains the hope of seeing his loved ones again. No, you will not end your life, life is too precious to you. Life and the hope it carries with it, the hope that the future will be better."

The man rose, walked to the door and opened it. He took a step outside, then stopped and turned back to Sendor. "But you are right about one thing. We will kill you. Eventually."

Scholes found Lara in her office, leaning back in her chair, the sky outside the window behind her brightening with the occasional star as the clouds separated, then darkening again. The screens on one wall were still on the Brunei mission, showing satellite feeds of the navy ship the soldiers of the

Australian Tactical Assault Group were now on, and no movement on the ground at the site they had left back in Brunei. Nothing there, nothing other than anticipated. But that's what she did, followed missions through, closing them on site and in her mind.

Her eyes weren't on the Brunei feeds now. They were on a screen on another wall. One with a smiling image of Ambassador George Sendor on it. She didn't react as Scholes came in and set his huge frame down carefully in the corner, on the recliner he'd long before requisitioned for her, for those long days she spent working on missions.

"You really should let me replace this with something more fitting," he said for the thousandth time as he tried in vain to find a comfortable sitting position.

"This one fits just fine," she said, as she always did, and finally turned to him. She contemplated him. He had that look again, the one he never could hide from her when he was worried.

"Smooth job on Brunei," he said. He wasn't comfortable with what he was about to do, had to do.

She continued to contemplate him.

"What would it take—" he began, then realized it wasn't a question that could be answered, nor would he understand the answer if it could. "How long would it take if we asked you to find him?"

He didn't have to say who.

"You're assuming I can." It was a quiet observation more than a question.

"I'm assuming you might have to. We are not making any progress finding him."

She said nothing. She'd been giving it thought, tentatively probing into her mind. So far, she had locked on to nothing. There was nothing to lock on to, she had nothing but too implicit information and the face, the life of the missing man.

"The peacekeepers, that's not anything like it, is it?" Scholes sighed. "This is bigger. It's bigger than what you did before that, too." And it would require much, perhaps too much, from her. He was torn between his role as the head of IDSD Missions, his responsibility to do all he could to prevent tensions in Europe from coming to a head, and his need to preserve the unique resource IDSD had in Oracle. Making it even more complicated, was his caring about her. But there really was no choice. He was well aware, had been from the moment he had heard the Russian news broadcast in the conference room the day before, that if all else failed, if nothing else was enough, Oracle might well be their only chance.

"Can you do this, Oracle?" he finally asked the question he had no choice but to ask.

"I don't know," was her answer.

Chapter Sixteen

The call was rerouted from IDSD Missions to Lara's home two hours later. Donovan started. He'd been watching the news reports. They were all the same, on all media outlets. Russian forces had been mobilizing throughout the day, beginning hours after the news broadcast alerting the world about the ambassador's death was first aired. Too few hours, which, Donovan knew, made Internationals and US officials wonder if the Russian Federation had been prepared, planning this move for a while. But the media wasn't wondering about this, nor were the various political analysts who were voicing their opinions to every media outlet that would listen. No one seemed to care about how organized the Russian forces were, how prepared to move, how fast to move. They were too busy targeting the alleged guilt of the Internationals' High Council and the US administration, trying to analyze the how and why of something they had no idea about, taking the Russian news broadcast at face value. Only some, too few, mainly seasoned broadcasters who remembered the lessons of the past or correspondents who had seen too much while covering bloody conflicts in too many places, only they questioned, raised doubts, tried to caution discretion, to maintain reason.

The incoming call tone sounded again, more insistent this time, and Donovan switched from the media system to the home communication system and heard the main security console behind him beep to indicate secure mode had been initiated. The man who came on-screen standing in a tiny, grimy room was at least partially of Filipino origin. He was scrawny, his hair unkempt, his beard wild, his shirt missing the odd button. His eyes were red, phlegmy. He and Donovan stared at each other for a long moment. And then the man straightened up.

"Oh, sorry. Hang on a sec, will ya." His speech was clear, coherent, and he spoke Australian English. He turned to the side, removed a pair of contact lenses and turned back. His eyes were now a clear dark brown, intelligent and alert.

"Better, I bet." He laughed cheerily. "Sorry, I live the role. Forget sometimes. Good morning! I'm Jon. Agent Jon Agawin, IDSD Southern Territories, Intelligence."

"Agent Donovan Pierce, USFID, SIRT unit. Good morning?"

"Morning here. Micronesia."

"Micronesia?"

Agawin laughed again. "Unreal, right? Tell you, though, once you get used to this place, you never wanna leave."

"Wait. Yahna isn't in Micronesia." There was no mention of the place in any of the records about Yahna. The group seemed to be partial to the more affluent and internationally significant countries.

"Yahna isn't. But my boss's boss says you want to know about the extremes. And they're here. At least, this is where they hide, meet, plot, however you want to look at it."

"In Micronesia."

"Pohnpei."

"Where?"

"Pohnpei. An island state in the Federated States of Micronesia. Specifically, on the main Island, you guessed it, Pohnpei." Agawin laughed at Donovan's surprise. "Makes sense, if you think about it. Nobody ever looks at Micronesia, other than to have an exotic vacation in, maybe. It's got damn near more islands than people, and it really is a rather easy place to hide your activities in. Especially if you're going against a global nation that's got its footprint pretty much everywhere. This entire area is independent nowadays and is not a part of the alliance. It's not a part of anything. It's a quiet place, keeps to itself, and, most important, it couldn't care less about alliances and global disputes. This group, if you can call it that, causes no problems for Micronesia, puts a lot of money into it—and I do mean a lot of money—and is therefore a very welcome resident. The local administrative authority doesn't allow law enforcement near any of its members. Hence, yours truly lives here, begs for pennies here, moves around freely here. Sees stuff, you guessed it, here."

"You say they're not a group."

"Not per se. They're smart. No name, no tangible identity. They know who they are, we think that all members memorize the members and locations they need to know about. They're small, but damn powerful. We have no idea what their exact hierarchy is. We haven't been able to infiltrate them yet, they are endlessly careful."

"But something made you look for them there."

"Tireless observation and painstaking analysis." Agawin chuckled. "And even now I can tell you we know the identities of too few of them."

"Problem is, I have to tell you, the little I read about them while they were still part of Yahna, they don't seem . . ." Donovan considered his words. He had to be careful not to link this conversation to his investigation. At his request, Scholes didn't tell Agawin's boss—or his boss's boss, apparently—what investigation this inquiry was linked to. It was, for them, a favor of sorts to a senior USFID agent, requested by the vice admiral. "They don't seem to be very sophisticated in their actions," he finally said.

"Ah. You read that. No, that's old stuff, back before this faction split off from Yahna. Or, to be more accurate, were shunned by Yahna, because they were too extreme, willing to go to more violent lengths. No, see, they were quiet for a long time after that, after the trials and their ouster. Intelligence thought that that was pretty much it, but then they turned up again, and when they did, they were different. As if they had thought things through, planned. Focused. When we began to notice them, they were already well organized. Careful, calculated. Damn smart. Money, clever use of resources. And they never slip. We think they're extra small and extra zealous because it helps keep them safe."

"Zealous against?"

"Us," the IDSD agent simply said. "As in us the Internationals, first and foremost. And then us the alliance, which means you, too, the United States. Although we think they work a dangerous mix of ideology, money and power. They don't care who they hurt as long as they get what they want. And what they want is for things to be their way."

"You said clever use of resources. How so?"

"Their actions cannot be traced back to them. Only to whoever they were using. A politician who hired them for a whole lot of money but for whom they were an anonymous group that did the job provided that he didn't ask questions, the makers of components that can be used for bombs who had their signatures all over their work but no idea what it was being made for or who hired them. You get the idea."

"Go back a minute. Bomb makers who didn't know they were making bombs?"

"Yeah, and techies who had no idea they made circuits for surveillance devices, that kind of stuff."

That, Donovan thought, was certainly interesting. But he left it at that, not wanting to hint at what his aim was in the conversation. "So what's in Pohnpei?"

"A leader. The only one we've so far been able to identify as a leader, at least. Makes sense, there has to be someone at the top who is calling the shots, coordinating, whatever. Anyway, these people, this faction if you want, they have a meeting place here. In a privately owned mansion on a ridge overlooking the city of Kolonia. It's a conservation building that was bought by this guy two decades ago after he promised to have it restored and keep it properly maintained, and to allow visits. Ironically, tourists go there for the sightseeing. If they knew what's right under their noses . . . Of course, I've never been anywhere near the place when they hold one of their meetings. They close it for miles around, damn near the entire island, plus the airspace above. No way of knowing even who comes and goes. Anyway, this guy who owns the place, he's the assumed leader. We have nothing on him, not even a clear image. We're not even sure if he's ex-Yahna or not. But several others we do know used to be in Yahna live around here too."

"Have you ever heard of a guy named Bourne?" Donovan asked.

"No. You think he's one of them?"

"Could be."

"You find something, let me know, maybe I can dig on this end. Either way, we'd love to have more leads on these guys, bring them down."

Donovan ended the call and sat back, his eyes narrowed. Something he'd seen in Bourne's file and hadn't assigned any importance to was now at the forefront of his mind. Bourne traveled regularly on ARPA business. He didn't oversee projects directly— program managers did that—but he was still required to travel to the higher-level meetings, where executive decisions were made. Always for a day or so, only a little longer for the longer travels, as would be expected for a business trip. Other than that, and the occasional visit to his daughter in Australia, he traveled only to one place, never elsewhere.

He had a vacation home on the main island of Pohnpei, in Micronesia.

Donovan stretched, removing the kinks in his neck, then got up to make some coffee. The problem was that this wasn't enough to link Bourne to Yahna or to its extremist faction, and it would certainly not stand as clear and convincing evidence. Nor would it likely be nearly enough to bring Bourne in and rattle him into a confession, and perhaps even into leading them to the ambassador, if Bourne even knew where he was. Donovan shook his head. An ARPA director with a clean record, who just happened to have a house on the same island as an extremist faction no one knew much about, which might or might not have had anything to do with taking the ambassador and instigating the events in

Europe. Two major links were missing here—the extremists' connection to the ongoing events and Bourne's connection to them.

Although the first link wasn't Donovan's job, not in this investigation—it was Emero's—the two were connected. Donovan sent Emero a message, updating him on what Agawin had said, and then returned to concentrate on the second link, the one more accessible to him. Bourne was a US citizen who, as far as Donovan was concerned, was suspected of murdering a US Air Force officer. Even if he didn't put the bullet in Berman's head himself, he had something to do with the murder. Donovan wanted him for that, but linking him to Sirion's theft and making him lead them to his accomplices, which just might bring IDSD closer to Sendor, was the more urgent priority.

The problem was that so far the only break he'd gotten trying to connect Bourne to anything was that vacation home he had. Still, it was a connection that could pan put. Unless of course he was wrong, and Bourne was innocent.

He didn't think so.

Before coming here, he had dropped by his house next door and had picked up his work screen. He now took it to the kitchen and sat at the counter with his coffee, and took a look at the Federated States of Micronesia. The place wasn't well known. As Agawin had said, it kept to itself, was independent, and had long nurtured a reputation as a tourist attraction. But emigration had taken a severe toll on it. There was a big world outside the small islands, and as the gap between the simple, modest life on them and the advancing world beyond grew, many had left to seek new opportunities. For a while Micronesia's future was uncertain, but it had found a new way to survive. It became a place the rich flocked to for some peace and quiet—and privacy in a world in which exposure was the most prevalent commodity—and Micronesia was only happy to accept them. But that meant that it became extremely expensive to live in. A man with Bourne's finances, as generous as they were, could not hope to buy and maintain a vacation home there.

He opened a secure channel and accessed his office, then brought up the records of Bourne's house on the island of Pohnpei. Right. Apparently Bourne had not bought the property, he had inherited it from his grandparents. Other than that, there was nothing there, nothing to speak of. There was a photo, a date of purchase, dry details. Not much more than that.

The problem was that Donovan couldn't look any deeper without attracting unwanted attention. He'd already had to use his own resources to get this much on Bourne and had managed to do so without alerting anyone to what he was doing. But going deeper, and further using US resources to investigate this specific high-ranking US citizen who necessarily had political connections, would likely raise an alarm somewhere. The eyes that routinely tracked ARPA's employees, for their safety as well as that of the United States' defense secrets, were far more alert following the ARPA liaison's murder at its building and the technology theft, both serious breaches of security, and Donovan couldn't risk being tagged as digging into the director's life. Nor could he risk Bourne finding out he was a suspect.

No, Donovan needed something else, another way to learn more. Something . . .

He had an idea.

His call to Lara was once again answered by Aiden, who explained that he hadn't had a chance yet to relay his message to Ms. Holsworth but would do so as soon as she came out of the mission debriefing. Donovan asked the loyal aide to let her know where he was, knowing that if Aiden told her that, she might decide to come home. Maybe, he hoped, he could even convince her to get a few hours' sleep.

Chapter Seventeen

When Lara came home, Donovan was sitting on the living room sofa, his work screen on the coffee table before him. He raised his head from the forensics of the Berman crime scene that were leading to nothing, not even when he compared them to what little evidence was collected in the jet, which Emero had sent him. He was touched that he'd been right, that his being there brought her home. He was thrilled that it seemed as if it was natural to her that he was there, hoped it had less to do with the fact that he'd been around since she had first found herself entangled in the plot to destroy Oracle and more to do with their new relationship. And he was astounded to find himself crossing right over to happy when she came over and slumped close beside him on the sofa. He put his arm around her, drawing her to him, and she leaned her head on his shoulder. She snuggled up against him, fitting so perfectly.

"Seriously, I hate that car." She contemplated the thought a bit. "What do you think Frank will do if I, oh, I don't know, blow it up?"

Donovan's brow furrowed. The memory was still

too raw.

She felt him tense and looked up at him. "Sorry," she said.

He kissed her. "It's okay. I guess it's good that you can joke about it."

"It's easier now," she said. With you, she thought.

His arm tightened around her, and she wondered how he could know, how he could read her so easily.

"You hungry? I made dinner," he said.

"Not a bit." She smiled. "You know, you can just have Rosie cook. She's been doing that for me forever now. And she loves cooking."

"You know I like to do that sometimes. Rosie will still do most of it, I mean I do tend to be rather busy, but once in a while I'll probably do some of our cooking myself."

Lara's heart quickened. He was talking as if this was, as if they were... "Well, you do make great breakfasts," she managed to say.

He smiled.

"She seems to let you get away with it, too. If it were me, well, she's made it clear to me long ago that I may not cook in my own kitchen."

"Really?"

"Really. But then, I'm useless there. And I keep being called in whenever I try to prepare anything anyway."

He laughed. "I spoke with Rosie myself. She's quite happy to share the kitchen with me."

"I have a feeling she'll let you do whatever you

want. More than she does me, that's for sure."

"That's because she loves you and loves taking care of you. And she told me that I love you and that I love taking care of you."

Lara pulled back and looked at him.

"I do love you, Lara," he said.

She began to speak, but before she could say anything he pulled her to him again and kissed her, not giving her a chance to answer, giving her time to accept. She contented herself with responding to his kiss in a way she could not yet do with words. Her head on his shoulder again, his arms tightly around her, she let her eyes close, let herself be with him.

"Lara," he said after a while, knowing this had to be done. "Your brother, Tom. He hid you well."

She raised her head and looked at him, not understanding.

"I need to look deeper into Bourne, and I can't touch him." He updated her about Yahna and about his talk with Agawin, and explained what he was looking for.

Lara let out a breath. "This is going to be fun."

It was Donovan's turn to furrow his brow.

"I didn't . . . you see, I never told him about what happened. Any of it."

"You haven't had a chance to talk to him," he realized.

"Well, yes. But also, I didn't want him to worry or to know that Oracle could potentially be at risk.

I mean, we checked on each other, like we always do, but by messages only, I haven't actually spoken to him." She took a deep breath. "He tried to call me earlier, but I didn't have time to get back to him. Can't call him now though. It's late. What time is it? We'll do it in the morning, we can catch him at home before—"

Her phone rang with a pleasant classic, and the call was automatically transferred to the home system. "Oh, that can't be good," was the only thing she said before she accepted the call on the main living room media screen.

The man who came on-screen was older than the one Donovan had seen in the photo on Lara's fireplace mantel, who he now knew was Jason, but there was no mistaking that they were twins. His eyes, the same soft hazel as his sister's but without the gold flecks, were somber. And angry.

"It's the middle of the night, why are you still awake? Are Milly and the kids okay?" Lara tried. Her brother was calling from his study.

Tom Holsworth was not about to be pacified. "How do I find out about this now?"

"Oh. You heard. I asked them not to tell you."

"You asked them . . . ! Well isn't it a good thing then that Legal sent me today the report on your car and the insurance settlement over it?"

"Damn, missed that one," she mumbled.

"Good thing you did. What the hell happened? And why am I only learning about it now? And just so you know, I had a talk with Frank. He called me after I called Legal to find out what happened, when I received the papers from them. At which time I was informed that my sister's car blew up! With her damn near in it!" He never once raised his voice, but the sentiment was unmistakable.

Lara let out a breath. "Donovan, this is my brother, Tom. Tom, this is Donovan Pierce."

Tom was not about to relent. "Pierce. Yes, the USFID agent. You're involved in this. Frank says you saved her life."

Donovan nodded once.

"Exactly how much did he tell you?" Lara asked, but Tom was too angry to answer her directly.

"It seems, then, that I owe you a debt of gratitude," he addressed Donovan. "Thank you for keeping my sister alive so that I can kill her myself!" He turned exasperated eyes back to Lara.

"I love you too, big brother."

He pointed an admonishing finger at her. "You are not going to get out of it that easily! Why haven't you told me yourself? And what if anything had happened? You want to explain this to mom and dad? To Milly and the kids? To Sarah? Jesus, Lara! You want to explain it to me? Exactly how many siblings do you think I have left? You joined Missions under the specific promise to us that you would not be in any danger! I will not lose you!"

Donovan heard the fear in his voice and had to agree. He nodded again.

"You got anything to say?" Tom turned on him.

"Oh, I'm right there with you. The danger part. You'll get no argument about that from me."

"Ah. See, I like you already." Tom stopped abruptly and contemplated Donovan, as if just now fully realizing the man was there. "What are you doing there anyway?" His eyes narrowed, and he turned back to his sister. "Lara? What's going on? Are you still in danger?"

"No. Really, absolutely not. No danger. All safe. That was a one-time thing, Tom."

Tom looked at Donovan, then back at her. So what was the agent doing there in the middle of the night?

"All right, moving on." Lara squirmed.

"No no, now I really want the whole story."

"Not now. Something's going on, and Donovan needs your help." She really wanted to divert his attention elsewhere. Like, now.

"Donovan, not Agent Pierce?" Tom put the agent in the context of the information he'd been given, the actions this man had taken to protect Lara, and considered that he was there now. Days after the incident in question was over. In the middle of the night. He wondered if maybe there was something there. Could his sister finally be moving on, living again? He hoped so. He made a mental note to run a background check on the agent.

Lara gave up, and motioned Donovan to please, please speak.

"I don't know what your home security and your clearance are," Donovan said.

"And you're speaking from Lara's home."

Donovan understood. "System security here has now been upgraded to top level. Status and safety."

"Of course it has." Tom glared at Lara again, but she was purposefully avoiding looking at him. "Communications security is quite high here, too. Comes with the IDSD Legal affiliation. As for clearance, I don't have Lara's. Or yours, I imagine. But I have enough. Lara will stop you if you go beyond what I'm allowed to know."

Donovan nodded. "Okay. You hid Lara. I tried to find her."

"Yes, I know. The system alerted me too, not only IDSD. But Lara told me it was nothing."

This time Lara didn't manage to avoid his glare. She sighed. Still, she was willing to face his anger now. It had been worth it, keeping the truth from him in real time. He would have worried, and as it was he was constantly afraid for her since Jason's death.

"I couldn't find her," Donovan continued. "There was nothing about her. I live next door and I still couldn't find—"

"You live next door?" Tom put several exclamation marks beside his mental note to run a check on this guy.

Lara glared at him.

"Fine. Later," Tom said with an exasperated sigh.

"IDSD does most of her hiding, but my firm and I are their peripheral, civilian venue. Considering my connection to both IDSD and her, this creates quite an impenetrable envelope."

"Yes, even I couldn't get through. And I can get through a lot." Donovan hesitated. "First, I have to make sure that nothing you do, if you do, is traced back to you."

"Lara wouldn't let you talk to me if she thought that could happen," Tom said easily.

Donovan turned to Lara. She nodded her agreement. "Okay," he said, and came to the point. "A man travels to a certain location once in a while, always for a short duration, always to the same place. Never alone. Takes his wife, sometimes also his daughter. He claims he owns a vacation home there, and he does have a house there, in his name. Purportedly he inherited it from his grandparents, who retired there. The location is home to a certain little known... call them resistance group. There's a mansion there that belongs to a man who is assumed to support and perhaps lead them. And others of this group might be living there, too. I need a connection." He considered for a moment. "I also want to know if he got the house the way he claims he had." He didn't believe in coincidences.

"Got it." Tom was listening raptly.

"This guy leads a clean life. He works, has a salary, savings he'd accumulated legitimately, some money he's inherited, low-risk investments, normal expenses. And that vacation home, considering where it is it has to be an expensive piece of land but the house itself isn't big, it's pretty old, too, it wouldn't have been that expensive at the time his grandparents purchased it. Doesn't look like something it would be expensive to keep, either, and some related expenses do appear in his finances. He has no hidden bank accounts, nor aliases that I can find. Everything about him is transparent and pretty much ordinary." Donovan paused. "Now let's assume the guy and that group are connected. There has to be something changing hands there, could be they're keeping money for him. Bank accounts, or even assets, maybe."

"That's the connection you need."

"Yes."

"What are your limitations in obtaining this information yourself?"

"That location the group and the house are in is supposedly neutral territory. It doesn't allow the official representatives of any country to enter it for any reason, law enforcement included. In practice, it's enjoying the group's resources—which are more than enough to buy its loyalty—and will therefore provide no information about any of its people. In fact, it might go so far as to alert them if questions are asked. Also, if I look deeper into the guy myself and get caught, this would have serious implications for my investigation."

"What makes you so sure this is your guy?"

"Two things. The first is information I can't use, otherwise I might expose the person who gave it to me. The second is my gut feeling."

Tom nodded. This agent saved his sister. And she had obviously put her trust in him. Tom would go to any lengths to help him. "Where?"

"The Federated States of Micronesia."

"No less." Tom chuckled.

"Gets worse."

"Can't wait to hear."

"I need this as soon as possible. A man's life is on the line, and that's just a small part of it."

Tom scrutinized him, then turned to Lara. "How do you figure into this?"

She didn't answer. He shook his head. "Lara, what happened to you was..."

She took a step toward the screen. "No, this isn't anything like that. Tom, I'm behind the scenes here. It's like it always was. I'm working from Missions, and no one outside it even knows I exist. I'm not part of this, not like that."

Tom shook his head again. It had been a shock to him, what he was told had happened to Lara. He worked hard to keep who his sister was hidden from the outside world, did his part to disguise the connection between Lara and Oracle. He never thought this could happen.

"I won't let anything happen to her."

The voice broke into Tom's thoughts. Not the words, not just the words were what focused him, but the way they were said. His eyes met those of the man who spoke them. He nodded his belief, and his agreement. But once Donovan had given him the necessary additional details, warning him once again to be careful and to communicate anything he found only to him directly, and to stop searching if at any point he believed he might be exposed, he resumed his worrying hat one more time.

"I'll see what I can dig up," he said. "And, Agent Pierce?" He was now back to being the big brother. "When this clears, you and I are going to meet. Have a chat."

"It's a deal." Donovan threw a glance at Lara. "I wouldn't mind a chat either."

Lara let out a breath. Great. Micronesia sounded good right about now.

The war room on the top floor of IDSD Missions' imposing building deep inside the secure complex south of Washington, DC, was always organized and efficient, but these days it was also packed and intense. Operations oversight had been transferred here, while IDSD HQ Diplomacy in Brussels was still working hard to try to resolve the crisis vis-à-vis the countries involved, in an attempt to prevent an escalation that would be catastrophic for Europe and that was already threatening to take the alliance and the Internationals decades back.

All workstations on the main floor were occupied,

the teams for the Joint Europe Military Command and for Bosnia and Srpska, the Russian Federation, and the immediate surrounding geographical regions all at work and taking precedence, along with the team in constant contact with those painstakingly searching for the Ambassador. Alongside them, alliance coordination and global oversight teams kept their eye on events that might affect Internationals and their allies worldwide.

Mission Command stood open, the officers who would be acting as mission coordinators if trouble arose working with their counterparts on site in Brčko District, on Croatia's border with Srpska and Bosnia, on Srpska's border with Montenegro, and watching all borders with the Russian Federation. On the wall-wide screen in Mission Command, satellite views of the region dominated, stern officers on the operations platform engaged in a hushed discussion before a view on the right showing the deployment of the Russian forces. The forces had stopped aggregating on the Brčko and Srpska borders, but the fact was that their numbers were still substantial. And so was the firepower they had brought with them. Fighter jets stood in nearby airports commandeered for the purpose, and armored vehicles stood in orderly batches along the borders, drones incessantly buzzing above.

But the Russian forces were not the only ones there. Opposite them, on the Croatian side of Bosnia and Srpska, equally powerful forces headed by IDSD land and air units were being positioned to protect the alliance's closest members to the west, north and south. Views on the left side of Mission Command's screen showed combat drones scouring the skies, surveillance aircraft hovering high above them. At the alliance's Split air-sea base fighter jets took off and landed, keeping a constant presence opposite Russian ones that teased the tense borders, and at Mons their peers stood in orderly rows, ground crews busy around them. They would be ready to assist any point in Europe, the disputed region a priority, if it came to that. And all the while the rhetoric from the eastern side was provoking, aggressive, blaming, while the western side was quiet, reassuring. Unwavering.

The main problem was the area in between the would-be conquerors and the steadfast protectors. Both the Bosniaks and the Serbs were angry, feeling betrayed, scared—of each other, of the Russian Federation's plans for them, of the future—a range of feelings, exacerbated by shattered hope, which needed only a spark to explode into a fire that would never again be controlled. News was scant, rumors spread, and people shut themselves in their homes in fear. Flags were pulled down, and decorations that had been bought when both sides thought a new future was near remained haphazardly thrown in garbage cans or rolling, forlorn, with the wind on the streets. That was not the future they had envisioned. And yet instead of uniting to protect the new life they had hoped for, the sense of betrayal, combined with distrust set so deep in both nations, overtook too many, and they were all but ready to turn on each other.

And in the district of Brčko, near the tri-border with the two unsettled countries, the Internationals' peacekeeping force still remained, refusing to leave. Originally stationed there with the agreement of the two nations and tasked with creating a safe zone in which the peace talks were conducted, now they themselves were besieged in the protected area they had created, under threat from the people they were there to help.

With their eyes constantly on the disputed region, the Internationals' High Council and the US administration cooperated and did their best to work with their peers in the alliance, some of whom were now eying them with unease, even suspicion. They were alone in the midst of a storm of confusion, blame and disbelief. So far, no matter what they did, the diplomatic efforts of both nations were unable to stop the escalation, not even slow it, and certainly not fix it.

Something had to budge, soon.

In Vice Admiral Scholes's office, the wall screens showed views of the same satellite and drone feeds as in Mission Command, far smaller but zooming in whenever the vice admiral gave the mainframe the command. The views that dominated, though, were those of the feeds showing the Russian deployment and Brčko District. Night vision might have been inconvenient for some, but Scholes and his counterpart, who was watching the same images in his own office at the Pentagon, barely noticed it. The expressions on both men's faces were somber as they watched the forces there to protect, and those there to destabilize.

"It worked," Scholes remarked. In the day since the news about Ambassador Sendor's fate first began washing over the world like an angry tsunami, the Russians had been steadily moving their ground forces. But then, all at once, they had stopped and had since only organized their troops along the borders, no longer adding to them.

In the Pentagon, Major General Scott Anderson nodded. "We've contacted the Russian president, as decided. Told him that Ambassador Sendor wasn't among the dead, wasn't even on the jet when it was found. As in, you know and we know that it wasn't us who downed that jet, that it was you, and that the goal was to get rid of the ambassador who was standing in the way of your plans and frame the Internationals and United States for it in the process. We assume that this means the ambassador was supposed to be found dead on the jet along with everybody else. Except that he wasn't. So either you are lying and you have him, or you didn't know he wasn't there."

"Think they'll buy it?"

"Your guess is as good as mine. Still, all this has to do is seed doubt, and considering that they've stopped moving forces, could be it's done the job, that they're now not sure where they stand. Which buys us time. I hope."

"And they just might turn on whoever they used, demand answers."

"Which could flush them out. Who knows, maybe they'll make a mistake." Anderson let out a long breath. "Hey, it could work, Frank."

"It could," Scholes said. But would it matter? Ultimately, Sendor was the most crucial part of the equation. If he was alive, they had to get him back. If he was dead, nothing else mattered. "In the meantime, we have restless, trigger-happy Russian soldiers on the borders. An hour ago a fighter jet— a manned fighter jet—crosses the Srpska-Russia border not far from Brčko District, shoots down a Srpskan surveillance drone, then crosses the Srpska-Croatia border into alliance airspace, buzzes IDSD drones sent to intercept it, and crosses southeast, back to Russian airspace."

"That's risky."

"Baiting us to make the first move, which would make us look guiltier than we already do." Scholes rubbed his face. This was not good.

After a lengthy pause, Anderson took his eyes off the mayhem in Europe and met those of the man who had what they needed. "Do you have it ready?" he asked quietly, careful not to specify his precise meaning.

Scholes knew what he was asking. "It's being prepared, so that it can be deployed on demand if and when."

Chapter Eighteen

Donovan was looking at cases his investigative teams were working on. Some were in the closing stages, and there was nothing in the rest his lead investigators couldn't handle without his involvement, other than perhaps the occasional guidance, a word of advice. Still, he was the agent in charge, and these were his teams, his responsibility. And while the investigation that held the fate of too many tugged at his attention, there was nothing he could do right now, not without risking consequences that weren't his but the multitudes' whose fate was uncertain.

"Sir, you have a visitor."

"Who is it?" Donovan asked, preoccupied, his focus on his desk screen, but raised his eyes to the junior agent at the door when he heard the answer.

"A Mr. Tom Holsworth, sir. He's been cleared and is on his way up."

Donovan reached the elevator just as it opened. He nodded at the escorting agent, and only Lara's brother got off the elevator. The two men faced each other. Nearly the same age, the same height. While Donovan had strength and years of training written all over him, Tom was slighter, sharing some of his sister's delicacy of posture. Dressed in a meticulous black suit and tie, unlike Donovan's equally meticulous but slightly less formal ware. Suits were fine, he was used to wearing them in his job. But ties, those he stayed as far away from as he could.

He scrutinized his visitor. The man bore a distinct resemblance to his sister, but there was something different in him, something Donovan couldn't quite put his finger on.

Tom laughed, the smile easily reaching his eyes, and Donovan remembered a photo of a younger Lara, at a time before death intervened, in which she had an equally easy laughter in her eyes. There was some of that back in them, more recently. He made another promise to her in his heart, to make sure it came back, that happiness, and stayed.

"Yes, she gives a different impression, my sister," Tom was saying. "There is an intensity about her, an awareness that you must have already seen, that I don't have. Unlike her, I'm just a regular person." He extended his hand. "Agent Pierce."

"Donovan, please." The firm handshake didn't surprise Donovan.

Tom nodded. "Yes, well, I guess there is no place for formality between us. Call me Tom."

"I suppose I shouldn't be surprised to see you here." Donovan led Tom to his office.

Tom nodded. "So, what's going on between you and my sister?"

Donovan settled in his chair, saying nothing.

"I managed to talk to her earlier, albeit rather briefly," Tom said, sitting down on the other side of the desk. "She's told me more about how you protected her. The inside details, so to speak. And I know she's told you what she hasn't told anyone, about our brother and Brian. You were in her house in the middle of the night—I'm not asking what you were doing there, she'd kill me. But she brought you to me, and she wouldn't do that, case or not. I'm her family." He stopped.

Donovan remained silent. Tom was understandably inquisitive. And normally, Donovan wouldn't go along with this. His and Lara's relationship was just that, theirs, and too precious for him to risk. But the man before him was there because he himself was protective of her, and they were obviously very close. And he'd only just recently had a scare, learning of what had happened to his sister, that he'd almost lost her.

"It's serious," Donovan finally said.

Tom contemplated him. "Yes, well, what you said last night, about not letting anything happen to her, that kind of gave it up." He nodded. "I haven't seen her this way with a man since . . ." his voice trailed off and a flicker of grief crossed his face.

"Brian was your friend," Donovan said quietly.

"Yes. Yes, for many, many years. He was Jason's best friend, but yes, he was my friend too." He paused, his eyes on Donovan, thoughtful. "You two are very different. You and him, I mean."

"You seem to be okay with this."

"I want Lara to be happy. And you seem to be a good man. I'm worried about what you do for a living, though. It obviously allows you to protect her, but it could come at a price that she's already had to pay once and had barely survived it."

"I promised her I would always come back to her," was all Donovan said.

Tom contemplated him. Donovan's eyes held his without wavering. Finally, Tom gave a slight nod. "It's that serious."

"Yes. And it's also new, and Lara has a lot to overcome. So."

"So you want me to butt out."

"No. You're her brother, and you're here, which says a lot. And I get that this wasn't just Lara's tragedy, what happened. It was yours, too. But I'm with Lara, first. I'm here for her, first. And what we have, she and I, it will require some building. And that's for her and me to do. Ourselves."

Tom felt torn. Lara was looking, sounding, different. Better. Something he'd begun to think would never return was back in her eyes. And this man was responsible for that. But Brian he'd known for a long time before he began dating Lara, while Donovan he didn't know at all. Despite what he knew, having checked about the agent using his contacts, and despite his instincts about this man, he was afraid for his sister.

"Don't break her heart," he finally said, his voice quiet.

"It's already broken. I'm going to mend it and keep it mended. I'm not going anywhere, Tom." Donovan leaned forward in his chair. "It's time for Lara to live again. And she's going to do that with me."

Something inside Tom loosened, as if he'd been holding his breath for five years. Ever since the day he had watched both his brother and his friend being lowered into the ground, his sister standing on the opposite side of the two graves, her eyes empty.

"Well then. But just so we're clear," Tom began, waited.

"Big brother. Got it." Donovan nodded and for the first time in the conversation allowed a smile to cross his face.

"So. Now that we've taken care of the important things, let's talk shop." Tom settled back and crossed his legs, all business now. "Your guy's grandparents owned the house. They originally lived in the United States, but the grandfather had some business dealings in Micronesia, and when he retired, he and his wife chose to live there. The Micronesian authorities allowed it because he'd visited the place a lot, had made friends, was known there. When the grandparents died, your guy inherited the house."

Donovan waited. He knew most of this already.

"All nice, dandy and backed up by enough records. Except that the grandparents were killed in a car accident on a trip to Singapore five days after the retirement. And they never even owned a house in Micronesia. Certainly not this house." He placed before Donovan a small screen with images of the property. Donovan skimmed through them. This was not the image he had seen in Bourne's file, of a simple one-story house with an acre or so around it. The house he was looking at and the grounds around it spoke of luxury. And it looked relatively new.

"It's situated in a restricted area, a gated community. There are several parts of the island that are private nowadays, all are luxury gated communities. The residents of this particular one guard their privacy jealously, and the Micronesian authorities assist. Among other things, they don't keep any updated records of ownership, purchase or sale, nothing. The properties are maintained by people who live either in Pohnpei or on the adjacent islands and who, may I say, are very generously provided for, them and their families. And everything, anything, is paid for from a single central account."

"So how do you know the house is Bourne's?"

"The property you saw in your files is in fact the property you see here. Same plot. Or rather, a small part of it. The image is of a house that stood there years ago, before these people purchased it from the Pohnpei administrative division. It's still the photo in Micronesia's formal—and very outdated—property records. And the original house is formally in his name. Every property in the gated community has a different owner, that much I've managed to ascertain. Interestingly though, I couldn't access the vast majority of these names, they are all hidden under the guise of a single umbrella ownership. Bourne included, although he has a certain visibility, probably because of the need due to his job. Even more interesting, the mansion you mentioned is also registered under the same umbrella ownership."

"So, whoever is behind these properties faked Bourne's background and inheritance, which if anyone looked into would stand to scrutiny, while in reality they paid for the house and maintain it."

"Chances are no one ever looked too deeply. Bourne has enough friends, enough clout, and, as you already know, a clean record. And these people are good. They only put close enough to the surface information that would be required for the background checks Bourne's job mandates. Anything else, I had to look for otherwise."

"And the checks wouldn't go any deeper because by the time this 'inheritance' came to be, he was already in a sensitive position at ARPA, although he wasn't its director yet. He'd been checked several times already over the years and was known to be trustworthy and reliable. And he has a daughter in Australia, so it wouldn't seem far-fetched for him to travel with his family to the not-so-far Micronesia, a place his grandparents were supposed to have lived in for years." Donovan shook his head. So much for foolproof security vetting.

"And no one looked into the grandparents, if they were even alive to retire there. They had been to Micronesia in the past, in fact they lived outside the United States for years at a time for business purposes, and they died outside the United States. And after the initial security vetting they were no longer persons of interest, Bourne could easily lie about them."

"And he did. One small lie. And he got away with it for years." Donovan chuckled in appreciation. "How did you get all this, and so quickly?"

"First," Tom said, "I have to admit that if you hadn't told me something was fishy there I never would have thought to look deeper either. Everything about the Bourne-Micronesia connection looks legitimate unless you actually know there's something to look for. As for how I got it, well, that's a trade secret." He laughed. "Let's just say IDSD Legal has certain cover entities for this very purpose."

"And you can use them."

"My firm is closely affiliated with Legal, it is in essence its arm in the private sector. We are all either its veterans or family members of IDSD personnel. In my case, I am both."

"And then some."

"True." Tom laughed again. "So what's got my sister working so hard this time? She was in her office when we spoke and was called away rather urgently. What, she's involved in that Europe debacle?" The laughter died as Donovan stayed quiet, serious. "God. She's involved in the Europe debacle. No wonder she is working this way."

Lara had received the call informing her of the incident status change for her early that morning, while Donovan was still at her house. She would now remain at IDSD Missions, with updates streaming live to her office, until this was over. There were many points of contact where the situation could go wrong, and a black swan would be needed. "Don't worry," he said to Tom. "When this is over, I'll take her away for a few days. Make sure she gets some rest."

Tom nodded thoughtfully. He could worry, but there really was nothing to say, nothing to argue. It was simple, really. His sister was Oracle.

As soon as the elevator doors closed behind Tom Holsworth, Donovan returned to his office and called Emero.

"You secure?" was the first thing he asked when the haggard-looking agent came on-screen. He was in his office.

"It's only us here," Emero replied, frowning.

Donovan told him what he now had, leaving the how and Tom out of it.

Emero knew better than to ask. "Right," he said. "Right. This does change quite a bit. How did we miss it?"

"It's simple, if you think about it. Bourne is a

US citizen and the director of a prominent US institute, who is monitored by a US agency that has had no reason to doubt him. This extremist faction he belongs to is unknown, is based outside the United States—and outside the alliance—and is being looked into only by IDSD Southern Territories Intelligence. The chances of the connection being made were near impossible."

Emero shook his head in disbelief. "What a mess."

"Listen, I can use this on Bourne."

"You think you can rattle him into giving up enough?"

"Yes."

Emero considered this. "If you're wrong, and if he clams up or, worse, if he manages to get word out to his co-conspirators, this could blow up in our faces. And then nothing will matter. But then, seems you've been right about Bourne all along, haven't you? And I suppose there's no more time, no choice really, is there?" He nodded. "Go for it."

Donovan ended the call, stood up and signaled his lead team in the investigation. Time to pick up Richard Bourne.

"Well?" Rostovtsev did not bother to turn around when the man came in, closing the door behind him as quietly as he could. He was intent on the strategy table with its newly replaced top. The others in the room—military ranks, trusted advisers—did turn.

The man stood fidgeting. He was, and would be until he delivered his news, in charge of the Foreign Intelligence Service. He knew the news would cost him his hard-earned job. He just hoped it would not cost him his life.

"We have nothing, Minister," was all he had to say.

Rostovtsev had to force himself not to react. The Foreign Intelligence Service—or those loyal to him in it, which were the majority of its people, he had ensured that over the years—had been tasked with attempting to contact the man who had been paid to kill the Internationals' ambassador. The death of that particular official had been the pillar of Rostovtsev's plan to loosen the Internationals' grip on the former Bosnia-Herzegovina, a strategic region that the Russian administration wanted for itself.

Not only had this enigmatic man, who had insisted on remaining as anonymous as the group he belonged to was, agreed to do this, he had come back to Rostovtsev with the claim that they could kill the ambassador in a way that the Internationals would be blamed. The Internationals *and* the United States. The man had cautioned patience and had then come back again, months later, just as the peace treaty was looming and Rostovtsev was impatiently considering another venue, and had laid before him an elaborate plan. A brilliant plan that would ensure a clean kill and the permanent unraveling of the peace talks in the region, paving the way for Russia to step in, save the day, and take over the warring countries and perhaps even venture beyond with the crumble of trust in the alliance.

Rostovtsev would have liked Croatia to be next, all the way to the Adriatic Sea. If he could make that happen, take this stronghold and advance beyond the line Russia had been forced to halt at all the way north and south all those years ago, and with the mayhem such wins would cause in the West, he was sure that Russia, his Russia, would be unstoppable. But with the alliance forces permanently stationed in Croatia, and with Croatia itself a strong member of Joint Europe, it would make more sense, he had to concede, to next take over the remaining countries in Southeastern Europe, which would then be cut off from the rest of Europe and from the alliance. This would strengthen his Russia's hold on the region.

Next would be the taking over of the countries in Eastern Europe that were not in his Russia's control yet. Its victories, the Internationals' betrayal of Srpska and Bosnia, and the weakening of the alliance would be enough, he was sure, to make these countries afraid. Regimes and citizens could be either swayed or intimidated, and alone without the alliance to turn to, with the Internationals no longer able to convince them with promises of empowerment and hope, surely they would easily fall.

His eyes were on the map, but he did not see it, in his mind he saw only the map of his dreams.

In it, his Russia would finally be the only remaining superpower. The alliance would crumble into the cluster of fearful countries they had been in the days when the United States and Europe—not yet Joint Europe then but its predecessor—were too weak, too hesitant to stop it and his Russia was able to do so much more, freely march forward into states that had dared claim independence from the once formidable union. And perhaps, when all went according to his plan, the presidency of the once again great country would be his. All proof was in place to position him as the hero who had returned Russia to greatness. The president was weak, so weak, seen as having bowed down to the Internationals back when they had stopped Russia's successful incursion into the territory the West had stolen from it all those decades before. He had followed a ruthless presidency and had thought he could keep the power his predecessor had, but the unexpectedly strong-minded Internationals and the alliance they had created had been his undoing. The image of strength counted in Russia, and he would be easy to impeach. And the people, without the lure of the Internationals' promise of new possibilities, and with their homeland once again a source of strength and pride, he was sure they would heed him, follow him, allow themselves to be controlled by him.

Yes, he had a plan in mind, a map to dream of. And it had required patience. As it was, it had been excruciating for him to convince the president to go with his plan—the part the weakling was allowed to know—and it had taken long, almost too long. But he had finally succeeded.

And it had all looked so elegant, so perfect. So final. Until the message had come from the United States, admitting that they had found the ambassador's plane and his dead crew, but not him. The first reaction had, of course, been disbelief, but the question could not be avoided—what if they were not lying? If that man and that elusive group of his had taken the ambassador, if he was not dead, if he were to turn up alive in the wrong moment . . . the implications were unthinkable.

True, so far the man had said nothing, asked for nothing. But he could. At a time of his choice, with the price of his choice. Money was not a problem, a hefty sum that would not embarrass a small country had already been paid. But there was no doubt in Rostovtsev's mind that money was not the issue here.

It had all been a mistake. He should have used an insider, a Russian, a loyalist. Instead, he was now in the hands of some unknown group with—apparently—its own plans. All because he had wanted to make sure this would never be traced back to him or to his beloved country.

The door crushed open and Rostovtsev started. President Sizov entered the room. A slight man, age having taken a toll on his body earlier than it should have, he nevertheless shoved the soon-to-be former head of the Foreign Intelligence Service aside and approached Rostovtsev with a determined step, never taking his eyes off the defense minister's. His gaze was angry, accusing. "This is unacceptable," he said. "Find them!"

"We can't." It was the man cowering in the doorway who answered. Panic had him raising his voice, but he didn't care, it didn't matter anymore. For him it was over. "The way we had contacted him before, it is not there anymore. He is gone, they are gone."

"Then find another way! We must have something!" Rostovtsev's voice was dangerously low.

"We can't." The intelligence officer's voice was feeble, defeated. "Minister, we can't. We have tried everything. They are gone. We allowed anonymity. We . . ." We have been used, he wanted to say, *you* have been used, but he did not dare speak out.

A crash had everyone in the room turning away from him. This time it was President Sizov who had broken the delicate touch top of the table. Disregarding everyone else in the room, he took a step closer to Rostovtsev and jabbed a finger in the bigger man's chest. "Fix this!"

He turned and left.

The room was silent. Rostovtsev stood motionless, thinking.

Finally, he turned to his advisers. "Move up the schedule."

Chapter Nineteen

ARPA Director Richard Bourne sat in his office, its only screen showing and having shown nothing but the news since he came in that morning. He couldn't focus on anything else, although if anyone happened to come into the room he feigned being busy at work, quickly getting rid of them. It was all over the news. None of the major networks had stopped talking about it. None of the minor ones, either, or the online media outlets. They were all showing endless footage of the disputed region, with field correspondents speaking dramatically about the dire situation in Bosnia and Republika Srpska, of what was sure to be another war between the two nations. And what if Russia's forces crossed the borders? Would it succeed in taking over the two countries? What did it want—was it really just looking to help stop the war if it broke out, help the people, or did it have the same ulterior motive it had had in the past? And could its anticipated actions lead to a region-encompassing war? How would the free world react, would it move to protect Bosnia and Republika Srpska? Could it? Was there anyone left to help, with the growing internal mayhem in the only alliance of nations that had any power to do so?

Their futile speculations amused Bourne. The alliance was falling apart. The United States had offered its help and was blatantly rejected, and already there were voices from within it calling for it to perhaps rethink its support of the Internationals and their agenda. The Internationals' peacekeepers near the Brčko District tri-border with Bosnia and Republika Srpska were suffering abuse. And even the Croatians, whose territory IDSD was apparently planning to launch the alliance's defense forces from, forces that included also Croatia's troops, were unsure if the Internationals were still friends or perhaps the new foes.

It was all going so well, better than he had expected. He was exhilarated. He wanted so much to contact his peers, his friends, wanted to be there with them in their meeting place in Pohnpei. But he must not. He wasn't allowed to contact anyone lest he was being watched. He wasn't worried about being caught, he had done so much over the years without ever being observed. Still, this was different. ARPA was at the center of a double investigation, the murder and the theft, and he could not risk drawing unwanted attention to himself.

Thinking about the murder clouded his mood. The theft of the technology had been easy, he had no compunction about it and had been in the perfect position to pull it off. But the murder, that was

terrible. Terrible. He had not had a quiet moment
since. He had never killed before, had never been
required to do so himself, there had always been
others far more suitable for it than him. But this, it
was worth it.

It was all worth it.

He was basking in the news reports that fore-
told doom and blamed it on the wrong people when
the door opened. He looked up with a carefully impassive expression, but it wasn't his administrative
assistant, nor any of the other people he had worked
with for so many years now at ARPA.

USFID Special Agent in Charge Donovan Pierce
walked in, other agents flocking into the office behind him. One of them approached Bourne, stood
him up unceremoniously, and handcuffed him. The
agent was saying something, but Bourne wasn't listening. His gaze was locked on the steely blue-gray
eyes that held his. His heart beat fast. No way. There
was no way they had him.

As the arresting agent led him out, others positioned themselves around him. He looked back to
see yet others with gloved hands walking into his
office, beginning to tear it apart, keeping everyone
else away. All the people who worked with him,
for him, stood shocked, watching, whispering among
themselves. He was urged forward and huffed indig-
nantly. How dare they do this to him, parade him
this way? A man in his position and with the kind
of friends he had! He was good at politics, and the

contacts he had in high places could attest to that. He would have their heads. Yes, he would destroy them, destroy that Pierce guy, destroy that arrogant USFID, as he and his friends had destroyed the Internationals.

He was placed in a small, claustrophobic interrogation room at USFID-SIRT. He had no idea how long he sat there, alone, deliberately visible cameras on him. He was being watched. Yes, of course he was. To make sure he would not hurt himself. Why should he? He had the upper hand. He would not let these puny people demean him into taking his own life. He had a future ahead of him, a brilliant future, with the elite group he was a part of. With what he had done, his crucial role in the events taking apart the Internationals and the alliance, he could expect prestige. Respect. Yes, respect.

Behind the wall that was, in fact, a holographically masked glass divide, Donovan watched him in silence. Every shift in position. Every gesture. Every small change in the man's expression. When behind him Agent Emma Quinn came into the room and informed him that connection with Emero was established and that the IDSD agent was standing by to watch the interrogation remotely, Donovan exited the room. Emma remained in it. The interrogation would not be disturbed.

Donovan entered the interrogation room and sat down opposite Bourne, who looked at him with a seemingly confused, indignant look on his face.

"I don't understand. Why are you doing this?"

Donovan remained silent, impassive.

"Have I not offered you my assistance in your investigation? This is about Joseph Berman, is it not? Why would you be acting this way?"

Donovan watched him.

"You cannot do this!" Fear flared, and Bourne switched tactics. "I am a high-ranking official! I have the most important projects in the United States, in the world, under me!"

Donovan's lips curved up a little. Just enough to remind the man before him that this was precisely why he was there.

The investigator's silence, those cool eyes, disconcerted Bourne. He remembered their first meeting, the efficiency with which the investigator had dealt with the murder, the way he and his people had gone through ARPA without hesitation in their efforts to investigate first the murder and then the Sirion theft, not the least bit intimidated by ARPA's status. The way the director of US Global Intelligence had gone around Bourne directly to Donovan, that first day.

Bourne fought to conceal sudden panic. Had he missed anything? Was there an omission somewhere, something that the investigator could have found? The killing had been clean. Berman had not questioned Bourne's request to meet him and the deputy director of the Facilities and Logistics Directorate in the subbasement, to discuss getting rid of the obsolete equipment stored there, to make place, perhaps, for more usable rooms. Space, after all, was always needed, and Berman had thought he was being asked to assist in suggesting which current projects might warrant the musty subbasement's conversion. He had been surprised that only Bourne was there, but it was easy to lie, tell him that the deputy director would be a few minutes late, delayed in traffic on his way to work. Nor did Berman think twice about turning his back to ARPA's director. It had been a single shot, with a gun that no longer existed. And then it had simply been a matter of returning to his office, trying to appear as calm as he could, which wasn't easy, granted, then waiting for the body to be found and for all evidence to be discovered that would lead to the major being implicated in the theft, which Bourne himself had so brilliantly laid.

No, they had nothing.

Bolstered by his own thoughts, his own logic, his arrogance returned. "I want a lawyer."

"You have committed an act of treason."

Bourne froze.

Donovan's smile was as cold as his eyes. "It's just you and me."

"Wait. No. You mean you suspect me of an act of treason. A ridiculous allegation." He was ARPA's director. Did this man think he was a fool?

"No, you did it. You stole sensitive technology through Major Joseph Berman and then you killed him. And you gave what you stole to people who didn't mind hurting your country," Donovan said conversationally. It was, for him a given, and he went with what his gut had told him since day one. It was simple, really. There was no time to go around it, interrogate, give the suspect time to consider, then interrogate some more. This would end now.

Bourne struggled to feign disbelief, indignation. "What? Why would I do that?"

"To eventually use that technology to abduct Internationals Ambassador George Sendor."

"Who?"

Donovan smiled again. Waited silently. The seconds ticked by, yet he did not move a muscle, never took his eyes off Bourne's.

Bourne shifted in his seat. "You mean the man in the news? You think I had something to do with that? You are out of your mind!" He laughed. "Yes, of course. It was all me. I stole the Sirion specs, then I killed Joseph Berman to cover my tracks and point the finger at him, and then I built a copy of Sirion myself and used it to down that jet the ambassador was on."

"Pretty much, yes."

"You are out of your mind." Bourne's eyes were wide.

"Except that you gave the Sirion specs to your co-conspirators. Your ex-Yahna buddies. *They're* the ones who completed it. *They* used it to down the jet."

Bourne choked. How on earth did the investigator know all this, make all the connections? He had to think. No, Pierce had to be fishing. There was no proof, he had made no mistakes.

"You didn't want to kill Joseph." Donovan's voice cut into Bourne's thoughts. His tone was almost regretful. This made Bourne's gaze waver.

"He was a good man. Reliable, committed. Everybody liked him," Donovan continued, going for the one weakness he knew Bourne couldn't overcome. This was, after all, why the director couldn't keep from involving himself in the investigation. The profile Donovan had prepared for him had been clear. Remorse about the life he had taken would be the one thing he wouldn't be able to deal with. His mistake was killing Berman himself, physically taking the gun and shooting the man at close range, seeing him die, seeing the life he himself had taken. The first time he had killed, Donovan had no doubt.

"Yes, he was a good man." Bourne's voice was barely audible.

"And you are not a killer, Richard."

Bourne's eyes lowered with regret he couldn't hide. "No, I'm not," he said, as the thin pretense of self-justification he had done his best to maintain to keep away the reality of what he had done finally fell apart and his mind betrayed him, replaying that horrible moment in the subbasement when he had shot the innocent man in the back of the head. In the back, of all things. His own involuntary intake of breath when had skirted the body and had seen the open eyes, staring lifelessly at nothing, surprise etched forever into the man's face.

That was the last thing he had seen before falling asleep, then waking up again with a cold sweat, in the nights since.

"You didn't want to kill him," Donovan said again, his voice soft this time, almost tender.

"No, I didn't, I never did," Bourne said before he realized what he was saying. His head rose sharply, his eyes wide. But the eyes that met his weren't victorious, none of the coldness was there. Just that same gentle tone the investigator had in his voice.

On-screen in the room behind the wall that only looked like a wall, Emero chuckled incredulously. "Damn, the guy knows his job."

"You don't know the half of it," Emma, in the same room, said. Most outsiders learned quickly that Donovan had a way of making connections others couldn't hope to make and following them without hesitation to his goal. Few got to see him breaking a suspect.

"You had to kill him. You had no choice, he found out," Donovan said in the interrogation room, his voice quiet, sympathizing. Reilly had run the scenario, the one he had asked her to run for him, after she determined that Berman's computer wasn't used by anyone but him. With ARPA's security and the Sirion project's restricted access, the only way to steal Sirion remotely in a way that the theft was hidden was to access it through Berman's ARPA account for the project when Berman was logged in. But then, ARPA kept track of all its personnel's computers, and as its director, Bourne would know when that was. In her simulation, Reilly had found that all the director had to do was use his own over-riding authorizations to get into the ARPA system, masking his entry, then enter the Sirion project piggybacking on Berman's account, take what he wanted, and then remove all logs as he backed out of the system again. He could also easily set it up so that if Berman logged out this would immediately disconnect him, too, to avoid discovery. Who better to steal from an ARPA project than the person who had unlimited access to it all?

But Berman must have found out. The co-head of the Sirion project, Dr. Beinhart, had said something that caught Donovan's attention—that Berman had returned early from the last testing site because he wanted to prepare the next one. But what if that wasn't the real reason? It would explain the place he was killed in. After all, it wouldn't make sense to kill him at ARPA, unless there was no choice.

Bourne's eyes were still on him, something almost beseeching in them. Seeking justification, Donovan thought, and used it to get what he wanted.

"You accessed the project when he wasn't in his account. Until then you only accessed it when he was logged in, you knew when that was because just as you could access his account, you could also access

ARPA's system that tracks its personnel's use of its resources." Between Bourne's override authorizations and the fact that he would have had the experts who replicated Sirion to provide him with the necessary technical guidance, this wasn't far-fetched to assume. And then again, Reilly had ascertained it in her simulation. "But something happened and you had no choice but to access it when he wasn't logged in, and he found out."

Berman said nothing, but his eyes moved away from Donovan's for a split second.

"Something was wrong with the Sirion copy. Your accomplices needed to use it, but, what, it didn't work? A test they ran to check it failed maybe? And they needed the fix quickly because they knew when the ambassador was scheduled to leave the peace talks and planned to get him then." This one, Emero was still looking at. Obviously, those who downed the ambassador's jet knew where and when it would be, possibly through someone who knew enough about the negotiations or about the ambassador planning to attend the meeting in Brussels, or someone at the Split base the jet took off from. The extremist faction had a man at the top of ARPA, so why not elsewhere? Unfortunately, Emero and his people were not even close to finding whoever it was yet. But that didn't matter now, not in this interrogation. "So you went in and took what they needed and Major Berman found out."

"He was in the field, where they were testing

Sirion, and later he saw that someone accessed the project through his account. He didn't know who." Berman spoke quietly, haltingly, the investigator's description of what happened unsettling him. How did he know so much? "He knew it had to be someone high enough, to do that, and he was afraid to trust anyone, so he called me."

"He trusted you, ARPA's director."

Bourne put his hands on the table before him. They shook, and he wrung them. "I told him I'll take care of it, I told him not to tell anyone so that whoever did it won't know we knew about the breach, and to stay there until they finished Sirion's testing, but he came back."

Donovan thought fast. "He was supposed to die there. Suicide?"

Bourne shook his head slowly. "Mugging," he said in a whisper.

"But he left before your accomplices could carry out their plan. He didn't tell anyone why, he gave Dr. Beinhart a reason and he returned. He went to his parents' straight from the airport, as he did every single time he traveled, and early the next morning he met you, the man he trusted to find out who was endangering the sensitive project he was working in."

"I didn't know. They called me, said he was back and that I had to take care of it."

"You had no choice. It was an order. It had to be done for the cause."

Bourne nodded and straightened up a bit, some weight off his shoulders with the deflection of guilt elsewhere, just as Donovan wanted. He needed to make sure the man would not fall apart.

"Getting him to the subbasement was easy."

"We need more space, and he is . . . he was so good at organizing his projects, I said I wanted his opinion on renovating the subbasement, that I was already scheduled to meet there the person in charge of these things at ARPA, that we would talk immediately afterward. That he shouldn't worry because I was already taking steps to find out if in fact the project had been breached and to secure it."

"The radio was to make us think he was working with an accomplice on the outside. An attempt to make sure we won't look inside ARPA. To point us away from you."

"There was no time, I needed something . . . I remembered the radios, my predecessor tinkered with them, he left several in his . . . my office when he retired, and I had them stored down there. He never asked for them." He stopped, hesitant.

"Well, I suppose it was clever." Donovan needed him to focus, and he got what he wanted.

The arrogance surfaced again. "I've been at ARPA for many years. People only assume I have no technological knowledge. You learn quite a bit there."

"Obviously. You did steal Sirion without being discovered." Donovan didn't tell him that it didn't take Sidney long to find out that the radio hadn't been used other than to try to make it work some-time during the night before Berman was killed, try to make it look as if it had been in use.

"You killed him the same way the people on the ambassador's jet were killed. You did that uninten-tionally." Donovan changed direction unexpectedly. He had grappled with that one. There was no real reason to kill Berman in that exact way. "You already knew how they died, and it stuck in your mind, didn't it?"

Bourne shook his head, and Donovan frowned. "I didn't want to see his face. I did it . . ."

"Before you could change your mind."

Bourne nodded, his gaze on his hands.

Donovan had now confirmed his assumptions about Berman's death and the Sirion theft, and he had a confession. But that wasn't all he needed. He let out a long sigh. "Too bad. A good man. A true patriot," he said sadly.

"I am a patriot!" Bourne was offended. He had served his country his entire life. Everything he had done was to ensure that things would go back to the way they once were.

"Sirion was ours. The whole world is blaming us," Donovan said. And got what he needed.

"Sirion was also the Internationals'! And they are behind the treaty, not us, and George Sendor was their ambassador, not ours! The world is laying more blame on them than on us, and if we, if the United States wasn't so intent on standing beside them, we could easily shift the blame and get out of it clean. We keep doing that, making the same mistake. That's why Yahna was forced to—" He stopped, his eyes widening in shock as he realized he had said too much. "You bastard," he blurted out, then collected himself, breathed in, calmed down. It didn't matter. The goal he had done everything for had already been attained.

"Yahna?" Donovan's eyes narrowed. He thought fast. "Yahna would never go along with this. Unless you're working from the inside."

The slightest flinch.

Donovan leaned forward. "You still have people inside Yahna. Does it know, are you some kind of an only seemingly unsanctioned spin off? Or, what, you're manipulating it from inside, using it to pressure the United States to distance itself from the Internationals and to break apart the alliance?"

Bourne didn't answer. Donovan didn't care, he had said that for Emero's sake. Perhaps Yahna, too, was not as harmless as everyone thought, whether it knew what was going on among its ranks or not.

"So was killing the ambassador also something you people were 'forced' to do?" He pressed on.

Bourne's brow furrowed for just a split second, with just the slightest tilt of his head, and Donovan's focus heightened, although he didn't show it. Was that an admission of death or a proof of life?

He leaned forward, his tone now low and dangerous in an intentional show of intimidation. "It'll never work, you know. What you're trying to do. And when this is over, what do you think is going to happen to you?"

The response was the one he'd hoped for. Despite having been rattled, Bourne still believed in his ideology, in the group he was serving, in the victory he was sure he had helped them attain with everything that he had done. He laughed. "It doesn't matter. You can do whatever you want. Imprison me, whatever. We've already won."

"Have you?" This time there was the slightest sneer in Donovan's smile, and he turned his eyes to the screen laying on the table before him, feigning interest in it rather than in Bourne. He wanted the man to talk, brag. With what he'd now learned, he wanted Bourne's obviously overinflated ego at work.

Bourne misread him, just as Donovan had hoped he would. He had the need to show just how successful the destruction of the Internationals and the alliance at whose helm it was would be, and how important his role was in this, and in the group he was a part of.

"You will never find him," he said. "He will remain hidden for as long as we need him to be and there is nothing, nothing at all you can do about it. And if we want, whenever we want, the order will be given for the Internationals' precious ambassador to die. His body will be handed over to the Russians, with a little present from us. A bullet from an IDSD-issued gun in the back of his head." He straightened up arrogantly. "We have had a few of those lying around for that very purpose."

"So Ambassador Sendor is still alive." Donovan finally raised his eyes to Bourne.

"Not for long! He—"

But Donovan was already standing up. "That's all I needed."

"What? Wait! What do you mean? You have nothing!" Fear lanced through Bourne again. It can't be, he can't know. What could he know?

Donovan took his screen and walked to the door.

"Hey, wait!" The realization was dawning on Bourne. The investigator was behaving as if he knew enough to what, find, who, the ambassador? His peers? *Could* he find them? Had he given up too much information?

"Wait, you can't just leave me here! What's going to happen to me?" he shouted.

Donovan turned back to him. "IDSD will take you. You'll be flown to Brussels."

"What? You can't do that! I'm a US citizen!" Here, at least, in the hands of the United States, he knew his contacts would have enough influence to make sure he would not face an embarrassing trial, perhaps he could even escape a trial altogether if interest in the murder died down and they would help him get away.

Donovan shrugged, indifferent. "The way I see it, the Internationals have every right to do whatever they want with you. You've done everything you could to get in their way and endanger their people in the process, along with many, many other inno-cents. And just look at the deaths you've already caused. Don't worry, they'll work with us to make sure you face justice for Major Berman's murder, they have an interest in seeing you punished for that, too." He turned away again and was almost out of the interrogation room when Bourne shouted be-hind him.

"They will kill me!"

His suddenly frantic tone had Donovan turn back to him. He was pale, trembling. Only a moment ear-lier confident, ARPA's director was now terrified.

"No. Unlike you, they do things the right way," Donovan said.

"Not them!"

Donovan's interest piqued. "Who then?"

"No, I can't, they will kill me! They will know I gave them up!"

"You mean your accomplices? They won't know of your arrest, we're making sure it doesn't come out just yet. By the time it does you'll be safe."

"No, I won't, you don't know them. They will find me. I know too much, they will kill me." There was despair in Bourne's voice now.

Donovan considered him. "Because once you're in the Internationals' hands you'll be out of their reach. They won't be able to influence what you do. Right. So much for their loyalty to you."

Bourne didn't answer.

"Nothing? Okay, good luck then," he said and turned to the door.

"No, fine, I will tell you what you want to know. But you have to make me disappear. You have to. You need me! You will never find them without me!"

"Where is the ambassador?" Donovan turned to him.

"I . . . I don't know," Bourne stammered.

Donovan turned to leave.

"I really don't! Only the ones who have him do! But I can give you names, locations, I can!"

Donovan believed him. Agawin had described a highly compartmentalized group that would certainly not risk one of theirs being caught by those they considered the enemy and giving up sensitive information. Bourne might well have no idea where the ambassador was. As for what he did know and was now willing to provide, it was valuable, but it could wait. He couldn't give them Sendor, and there wasn't enough time to go about picking up and interrogating his peers to see which one of them had the information they needed. They had to focus on finding the ambassador, who, if Bourne was right, might still be alive somewhere.

"I'm sure IDSD will make sure you're protected in return for that information," he said. "For now, you're safe here."

And he left.

"You heard him," Donovan said to Emero, on-screen in the next room.

"We need to stop these people. I'll pass this on to all the needs to know here and to Vice Admiral Scholes, and we'll prepare to move on Yahna and on Pohnpei. We'll use what Agawin and Southern Territories know. Bourne's knowledge can help with their prosecution later, and maybe with names we will have missed." Emero shook his head in frustration. "Problem is, we still don't know where Sendor is, and without him we can bring all the logical proof we want, we can even run this entire interrogation on all media outlets, but it still won't stop anything. No one will listen, sentiments are too heated over here."

Donovan concurred. Even with the headway they had made, the very heart of the investigation, the one critical unknown that could determine the fate of Europe, was still missing.

Ambassador Sendor.

"Where do we stand?" the leader asked.

"We are safe. There is no way they can find us."

They had initially been surprised when, contrary to the strict agreement between them and Russia, the latter's Foreign Intelligence Service had initiated a frantic search for them, despite the fact that, as far as Russia was concerned, they had fulfilled their end of the deal. Luckily, since they had long learned to trust no one, their designated team of hackers had been monitoring the Russians' communications since they had first been contacted, which was how the hunt had become known.

It had been Yahna the Russians had originally thought to approach, but they had felt their way to it carefully, unsure of what the dormant organization would agree to do and if it would betray their plans. It was pure luck that had them stumble instead upon an operative of what Yahna had years before termed its rogue elements, just before they had concluded that Yahna would not agree to do what they needed done and had withdrawn. By then the Russians themselves seemed to realize what they had been about to ask Yahna to do, that the stakes, for Russia more than anyone, were huge. That if what they wanted ever became known, the consequences for them would be disastrous. But the operative in question had coaxed, explained, lured, and the Russians had ended up hiring him and the group behind him and agreeing to the plan eventually brought to them, which included killing the ambassador.

But of course, the ambassador was not dead, a small detail that had intentionally been kept hidden from the Russians. Which was, of course, why they were so frantically searching for the group now. Interesting that the Russians knew the ambassador had not been among the dead. Interesting and troubling. It had been pure luck that the Russians had been so shocked that enough communications had gone around between them before someone had been clever enough to clamp down on all unnecessary talk. But not before the group had learned it was now being targeted by Russian intelligence, and why.

Which begged the question. Just why would the United States provide the information about the ambassador's disappearance to Russia so readily? There was no trust between the two administrations, and there should have been even less, a complete disconnect even, once Russia had openly blamed the United States and its cooperation with the Internationals and had moved substantial forces as it had to borders the alliance had laid claim to. And there was no doubt in the leader's mind that the United States would have surmised that Russia was somehow involved in the ambassador's disappearance. And yet it had chosen to approach Russia directly.

The group and select senior Russian officials were, or at least were supposed to be, the only ones who knew the truth about the group's part in the current game of power and control taking place in the European arena. And the leader was certain that, with the most to lose from its exposure, the Russians would never risk saying anything to either of their sworn enemies. And yet this move by the United States, letting the Russian president know it did not have the ambassador's body, showed that it, and therefore the Internationals, too, had somehow come to suspect there was someone else behind the downing of the jet, someone other than Russia, and that Russia hadn't been told the entire truth about the incident either.

How could that be?

The leader had known that the Internationals would search for the ambassador, and that the United States would help, if not immediately then as soon as it learned that it was a technology it too was responsible for that had downed his jet, and that this was publicly known. But he had never imagined that the United States itself would communicate the ambassador's absence to Russia, and had instead expected it to attempt to find him first and use this to take down its old opponent once and for all, resolving the problem in Republika Srpska and Bosnia in the process. Thus, of course, giving him and his group time to proceed with their own plans.

At least it had no hope of finding the ambassador. No one did. That was the only thing the leader was absolutely confident of. Still, now Russia too was searching for him. And that was bad.

If only they had killed the ambassador. If only his body had been left in the jet with the others. The United States would then have been helpless to do anything, would have had no alternative to turn to. Perhaps then it would have finally go against those damn Internationals, if only to save itself.

Had it been a mistake to keep the ambassador alive?

His man was still talking, detailing Russia's failed attempts to locate those it now knew had betrayed it and had kept the ambassador alive and hidden. But the leader was no longer listening. He was gazing thoughtfully at the closed door of the room that held their strategic captive.

It was time for a consult.

Chapter Twenty

Lara was in her office, in what seemed to Donovan to be a quiet moment in a day that, if the activity in the war room outside attested to anything, must have been quite hectic. She was leaning back in her chair, facing wall screens that showed real-time satellite images of the disputed region. From where he stood, Donovan could see there were multiple feeds, from inside the countries and all borders, the same ones he'd seen as he passed the teams working outside. A single screen on her left was running intelligence updates, flashing in and out as new data came in. Her eyes flickered to it, an eyebrow raised for a brief moment, and then her attention turned to a feed showing IDSD's peacekeeping force in the safe zone in Brčko District. Something there, and she didn't like it.

He entered the office and sat on the opposite side of her desk. She turned her chair to face him and smiled, but there was a shadow in her eyes, something haunted. He stood up and skirted the desk to her side of it. A look at what was running on its embedded screen had his eyes widen. He turned his back to it.

"Christ, Lara. Is that what you're studying? Those horrific wars?" To get a better grasp of what was happening in the region, he'd read a bit about both wars, the one half a century before and the no less horrific one that had followed it, and the violence in the images running on Lara's desk could only have come from them.

She shook her head slightly, her eyes on the desk, although she made no move toward it. The way she was sitting, the angle didn't let her see the images. And this suited her just fine. She'd been doing this, studying the region, the past, contemplating the present, possible futures, for long hours now. Some of it was excruciating to take in. Too much of it would be etched in her memory for a long time to come.

"These aren't the wars," she said quietly.

He glanced at the images again and then turned back to her. "You've got to be kidding."

"No. This is intelligence from less than three years ago. About the time Ambassador Sendor began working the region. That's what their reality was like then." Her eyes turned back to the satellite feeds, where the militaries of too many nations were waiting, ready for war. "And it's nothing compared to what will be if we don't find a way to stop what's happening now."

Donovan had known Oracle was given all necessary information whenever she worked a situation anywhere in the world. But this was the first time he realized what that information might include, the type of things she just might have to know about, to look at in order to understand the circumstances she would have to coordinate a mission in, the kind of people those she would be guiding might have to face, the horrors she might be called on to rescue innocents from. The consequences if she failed. Once again he marveled at how strong she had to be, how strong she was. Thought about all the years she'd had to do this by herself, return home, exhausted and depleted, to deal alone with the consequences to herself of the missions she had guided.

At least that part of it was behind her. She wasn't alone now, not anymore. Never would be.

He hid his concern and changed the subject. Took her elsewhere, far from where she was now. Just to remind her of that new side of her life that was there whenever she needed it. "You know, your brother helped figure out the lead on Bourne." He'd spoken to Scholes and her after ending the interrogation and signing off with Emero, telling him he'll update Scholes himself. "He gave me the deciding information. He came by my office today."

Lara turned to him. "He came by. . .?"

"It makes sense that he would want to check me out, Lara. I'm perfectly fine with that."

She looked up at him with unveiled wonder. "You're pretty great, you know."

"Yes, I am," he said easily. "Which is why you're coming away with me when this is over. Think of it as an extended first date. I still owe you a first date, remember?"

"Away? Where to?"

He just smiled.

"Come on! Nothing? Not even a hint? A tiny one?"

His smile widened.

Her eyes turned away from him to the doorway, where Aiden came to stand. "The Joint Europe Military Command team is asking for you, ma'am."

She stood up, passed by Donovan, taking his hand in hers for the fleetest of moments, and walked out. Donovan remained where he was, staring out of the window. Abruptly, he straightened up and strode out.

IDSD US's car service garage was empty, the day over for all but Pete Quentin, who reigned over the substantial car fleet. He didn't mind the hour. Cars were his great love, and this place gave him ample opportunity to immerse himself in them.

He was busy planning equipping schedules for the three executive cars due to arrive in just over a week. The three were identical but had different designations. Two were designated for Diplomacy— one for the guest pool and one for a newly hired high rank, and the third car was for Missions. He sighed. Pity that the car that one was replacing had met with such a sad fate. It had been a pretty thing, classy, and he had attended to it himself whenever it came in. It was the only car in his fleet in decades that he hadn't chosen himself. He had initially been indignant when it was bought without his consent, but he had to admit it was a beauty. And its owner had treated it just like he himself would. Yes, she did.

A car slid into the huge garage, and his eyes followed it with interest. It wasn't one of his. Strong, robust, quite an engine under that hood. A working car, not one of those toys built for vanity and meant to make some silly impression. He liked a serious car. Yes. Spit clean and not a scratch on it. He bet the car was well maintained inside, too, as it should be. Agency-issued. A US agency. He knew every model they used. Them, their militaries, their diplomats. Them and everyone else.

Cars were his life.

The man who came out of the car was about half his age, he guessed. Give or take. Taller than him, but then most people were. Strong, robust, like his car. A working man, too, he bet, like the car. Intelligent eyes that took in everything around him and then locked on Pete. Pete sighed. He didn't want any disturbances. That was why he had stayed here after his crew had left. Just him and the cars. So much easier to deal this way with those boring administrative tasks that were part of his job. But then the man seemed to respect his car, so he might be worth a moment of Pete's time.

"I'm Agent Donovan Pierce, USFID," the car's owner introduced himself. Despite the formality of the introduction his demeanor was relaxed, his countenance pleasant. "I'm hoping you can help me with something, Mr. Quentin. The red convertible."

Ah, yes. Vice Admiral Scholes, this was the young man he had called about. When was that? Yesterday, at exactly seven-thirty in the evening. Yes. Pete never forgot a detail. Good man, the vice admiral. Took good care of every car Pete had ever prepared for him.

"Sweet car," he said. "Dead now."

Donovan suppressed a smile. Scholes had said Quentin took his cars seriously. Good, that was the exact reason Donovan thought it worthwhile to talk to him in person. And precisely why he had identified the car, rather than the woman it belonged to.

"What do we do?" He dove right in, giving Quentin the helm to see what he would do with it. Donovan knew what he intended to achieve, but he had no problem letting Quentin get there his own way.

"No no. I will not agree to this again. Absolutely not." Quentin waved a hand in irritated dismissal and turned away.

"It was privately owned, the convertible, I understand."

"Yes, privately owned. Holsworth, she insisted,

although I absolutely did not approve." Quentin was busying himself with his screen again, shaking his head, not looking at Donovan. "But Vice Admiral Scholes and Head of Security Ericsson overruled my decision. And it was so different from my other cars. So different. She didn't even let me buy it. No, she bought it herself. Of course, it was registered to us for security. And I maintained it, from cleaning to fueling to periodic service, I insisted. But she was adamant on choosing and buying it herself. Highly irregular. Never seen such a thing in my entire time here. Never. And to be allowed that car."

Apparently Quentin had no idea that everything about Lara was highly irregular. "She loved that car," Donovan pitched in.

"Yes, she loved it. Treated it properly, too. I can tell you such stories about too many who don't. There is a colonel at—"

"She wants to replace it, you know, the convertible," Donovan interrupted gently, needing Quentin to remain focused and to go where Donovan wanted him to get to.

"That's out of the question, she can't do that now. She can't just choose anymore."

"Security," Donovan said.

"Yes. The alert came with the notice removing the convertible from my car pool after it . . . after the incident. Holsworth's status has been upgraded in my system, too, and she doesn't get that choice anymore. I'm supplying her cars from now on, and that's that, that's the way it should be. And they've got to be secure. No convertible. A pity, she loved that last one. It was a good choice for a car, a good choice indeed. Fit Holsworth so well, too." Quentin was mumbling to himself now.

Donovan nodded. The man cared. And he understood how much Lara liked her car. Good. "You're going to assign to her something like these, are you, Mr. Quentin?" Donovan looked at two new cars currently being retrofitted with security sensors. "Like the temporary one she's been given, just a newer model, isn't it?" He contemplated the cars quietly, knowing Quentin was watching him. "She'll hate it, you know. She hates the one she has now." He said it straight, the way he knew Quentin would understand. "I get why, I do. You know her. She likes sleeker lines. A car that would fit her, agile, strong, feminine in a way. Something she would enjoy driving. She really drives, I don't have to tell you. She doesn't like to use that autodrive like others do. I can understand that, I never took to it either." He let Quentin hear the feeling behind his words.

"What's it to you, anyway? You're not even IDSD, and here you are, you drive in here, you've got this type of access. Doesn't fit, agent or no agent." Quentin looked at him with sudden suspicion. "What's she to you?"

Donovan turned his gaze to the photo on the desk behind Quentin, one that had caught his eye the moment he got out of the car. Quentin and a woman his age. They looked happy. They looked like they'd been happy together for a long time.

He kept his eyes on the photo for a long moment, then turned his gaze back to the man before him. Saying nothing.

Pete fell silent and scrutinized the young man for a little bit longer. Then he nodded, his demeanor softening. That, he could relate to. In his mind, nothing was more important, even more than cars. Yes, the only thing that was more important, his wife of fifty-one years had taught him that. Still did, every single day.

"The way things are," the young man was saying, facing him, "she doesn't get to choose much, my Lara, and it's even worse now with her new security status. This is one thing at least we can get around, you and I. Something we can give her to make her happy."

Pete looked at him with a lot more interest now. He was nice. They both were, Holsworth too. He knew exactly what the young man was talking about, he saw things, heard things, the job did that. And she always took such good care of her car. Yes. He sighed audibly. "I don't have any leeway on this. Even if I wanted to get her something she'd like. But yes, she treats her cars right. It would be nice if there was something she would like. It would have to be something that could be retrofitted to the proper security standards, of course, not like the convertible. No, I don't see how that could be.

The one I chose for her is the one that will have to do. I don't see how—"

"Actually. . ." Donovan walked over to Quentin's screen and brought up what he had in mind. "How about this?"

Quentin squinted at the screen. "No. No way. I could never . . . it would have to be ordered with changes to the specs, this would have to be planned in advance. You think I just order cars? There are requirements, changes we work out with the manufacturer. And after it gets here, I would need my crew to complete . . . No. Absolutely not. Interesting, though." Donovan could see the direction of the man's thoughts change even as he spoke. Quentin skimmed through the specifications. "Yes. Interesting indeed. Yes, I can do that. Oh, yes I can." He gave Donovan a sly look. "You sure you can get this through the vice admiral?"

"You sure you can retrofit it to your security standards?" That was the first consideration.

"Yes. Yes, young man, I can." He tapped Donovan heartily on his shoulder and went to make some calls. Donovan remained in front of the screen, a small smile on his face. She'll like this.

In the dark of night, a hospital in the Bosnian city of Zenica erupted in flames, the explosion and the ensuing screams of the injured and dying tearing through the surrounding neighborhoods. As people in nightwear streamed out of homes, a middle-aged couple was bumped into by four figures clad in black, their faces masked. The figures pushed them roughly aside and rushed away, shouting to each other. The couple stared at each other in horror. Their assailants had spoken Serbian.

Just before dawn, several masked figures entered a small agricultural village in Republika Srpska, just miles away from the IDSD peacekeeping force's camp on the Brčko District side of the border. They broke down the doors of houses at the edge of the village and swarmed in, killing everyone inside. Only when the alarm was raised, and other residents appeared at the scene, did the figures begin calling to one another to hurry up and leave before disappearing into the fields beyond. They spoke Bosnian.

Hours later, people began assembling in front of the government buildings in each of the two countries, angrily demanding retaliation against the other. At the same time, riots erupted on the tri-border where Bosnia and Srpska each bordered with the Brčko demilitarized district, close to the IDSD peacekeeping camp. The rioters demanded that the Internationals be banished, calling for them to be brought to justice before the international court for their betrayal. The respective militaries, Bosnia's and Srpska's alike, flanked the camp, denying the rioters access to the peacekeepers and to the negotiators, even if halfheartedly so.

Unlike the people, both prime ministers had been

contacted by their counterpart in the Internationals' High Council and had been given the entire picture. They also had the unwavering insistence of both the Bosnian and Srpskan representatives to the negotiations that everything they had seen and heard in the course of the talks had shown them that the Internationals were honest in their intentions, that they had supported the ambassador, giving him all he had asked for. And they had, after all, placed in Brčko, virtually on the border between the two countries in crisis, a force that for a long time had kept the peace at its own peril, and had just recently began to prepare for its anticipated role in assisting in the implementation of the treaty. In fact, with the risk of violence gone, preparations had already been made for the Internationals to land there teams of experts, professionals who would be given anything needed to assist in rebuilding the broken countries. Funds had already been committed. The ambassador himself had been asked by the Internationals to remain there. Surely they would not have done all that if they had no intention of proceeding with the treaty.

And unlike the people, the prime ministers knew exactly what their Russian neighbor was doing, the truth about its intentions and its role in initiating the potentially catastrophic events, and exactly the kind of forces it had been amassing at the borders.

Unfortunately, anger and fear, distrust and disbelief, all borne of a too long, too violent past, dictated the actions of the people. Gruesome images on the news, of rescue forces desperately searching the rubble of the hospital and of the bodies of entire families being taken out of the raided homes, only fed fear and hate. And so the people would not listen. When their prime ministers tried to caution, explain, they found themselves facing their rage. Rumors ruled. That the Internationals planned to take over both countries. That they were collaborating with Russia, helping it conquer them. Bosniaks claimed that the Internationals had betrayed them and were preparing to help the Serbs in Srpska and those who, seeing the ambassador's success, had returned to live in Bosnia, take over, even as the Serbs thought the same about Bosniaks, and neighbor turned on neighbor. They blamed the Russians, the Internationals, each other. Those few with a voice of reason quickly retreated under angry threats. The prime ministers spoke, but the people raged, would not listen.

By the end of the day, military transports had landed on the Croatian border's intersection with the border between Srpska and Bosnia, ready to enter both countries to bring out any Internationals and US citizens living there, after many had had to take refuge in the only recently established consulates. A plan was already in place to open a venue to the peacekeeping force in Brčko District on the opposite side of the long border between Bosnia and Srpska, to get them out if it came to that.

At the same time, the Russian Federation's president appeared in a rare interview, explaining that he would ultimately have no choice but to send his country's troops across the borders to assist in keeping the peace in both Republika Srpska and Bosnia, and to keep any Russian citizens residing in the two countries, and mainly in its neighboring Republika Srpska, out of harm. Already, he added, these citizens had begged him to help keep them safe. He further offered, quite generously, to replace with his own the Internationals' peacekeepers in Brčko who were obviously bringing upon them the wrath of the people. Through no fault of their own, of course, it was not their fault that their nation's leaders had felt it necessary to join forces with the United States to destroy any hope of a true peace. And the replacement would only be a temporary one, he assured. After all, the Internationals would do well to distance themselves from the region, at least for a while. Perhaps, he suggested, the alliance should concentrate on clarifying what had happened, focus on resolving their internal issues. And in the meantime, Russia would gladly assist in keeping the peace in the disputed region, he offered, as he carefully avoided any question about the fate of the Internationals' ambassador.

Immediately after the interview, Srpskan forces began deploying on Srpska's border with the Russian Federation, ready to fight for their country's independence, and Bosnian forces deployed on Bosnia's border with Srpska, in case the Russians succeeded in reaching it. Opposite them, on the Srpska side of the joint border, additional Srpskan troops amassed, nervous at their presence. And with too much experience in their past, the disillusioned and more than a little subdued residents of both countries began stocking up on food, water and medications, in preparation for war the likes of which even they had never seen. Soon, desperate silence descended on dread-filled streets.

The leader stopped the car inside the warehouse, got out, and closed the driver's door behind him. The place was empty, abandoned, pitch dark except for the headlights of his car, but he had no doubt he was being watched. There were many ways, too many, to watch someone nowadays.

Many ways to kill someone, too, without ever being seen, but he wasn't worried. He was too valuable. And he had done his part in this elaborate scheme, and quite well at that.

He leaned back on his car and lit a cigarette. Wretched habit, so rarely encountered nowadays, long prohibited. But here, no one would know. Except for whoever was watching him.

And the man he was here to meet.

As if on cue, a limo entered the warehouse from some obscure entrance he could not discern. He walked toward it, tossing the cigarette away and subconsciously straightening his tie.

The bodyguard that came out of the front seat of the limo as it stopped before him made Mount Everest look like an anthill. He didn't even dignify the leader with a look as he opened the back door of the car, and the man the leader was meeting got out. Slowly, confidently, as if he owned the world.

Which, in a way, he did. The air of power and money sat on him naturally. As did the obvious expectation that he would be obeyed.

The leader did. Always. Which was why he could almost convince himself he wasn't worried.

He did not speak. He would not speak unless given permission to do so, that was how the man who was approaching him required it. It was a rare honor, the man taking the time to meet him this way. It was also cause for concern. He did not do that unless something happened that was important enough to warrant his own special attention, and failure in such an instance was utterly unacceptable.

Of course, the leader did not intend to fail.

The man scrutinized him, his eyes boring into the darkest corners of his soul. He indicated for him to speak. The leader did, succinctly. That was how the man required it. When he finished, the man spoke briefly. He then returned to his car and left.

So did the leader. He had his orders now.

It was time to bring this to an end.

As the black limo slid away into the dead of night, the man sitting inside it leaned back and turned to the side window, his eyes thoughtful.

"Sir?" The young man who sat facing him spoke with reverence.

"When this is over, kill him. Kill them all. I want them to be a dead end."

Chapter Twenty-One

Vice Admiral Frank Scholes shook his head. In the news broadcasts from Bosnia, tires burned near the government building, thousands of angry protesters standing beside them, chanting and throwing the occasional Molotov cocktail or rocks at the police who were trying to keep them back with little success. The equally unfortunate Srpskan prime minister's office had long since been ransacked by a raging crowd, smoke coming out of the windows, police officers helplessly scattered. As for the prime minister, who had enraged the people now trampling through his office by trying to reason with them, futilely trying to explain what was really going on, he had been whisked away to the safety of the Federal Police Administration building two blocks away.

"Doesn't anyone there stop to think about the coincidence of just two incidents, hours apart, one in each country, or the fact that the people who did this just happened to speak the languages they did, and so openly and carelessly?" Evans, sitting not far from Scholes in the conference room, said. "Don't they get that these perpetrators were masquerading as the enemy? And what about how the Russian forces just happened to be prepared to move so fast? Or—" He gave up. It didn't do any good to try to rationalize this mess.

Scholes rubbed his eyes tiredly. He hadn't had a chance to go home yet. No rest for his people, so no rest for him. His eyes returned to the mayhem on the screens. It was just the two of them here. Everyone else working the disputed region was either in the buzzing war room outside and in its Mission Command, or in the situation room in the Joint Europe Military Command or working the diplomacy side in the Joint Europe Civilian Command, where the IDSD Diplomacy professionals had also assembled. They were all working around the clock.

"At least they're keeping this inside their own borders," he said. "Let's hope it stays that way."

"So far the worst of it for us outside Europe were a couple of small demonstrations in front of US embassies against our alleged role in the Bosnia-Srpska mess, and mainly, as this one guy said to some reporter, against our insistence on standing beside the Internationals despite their betrayal and our intentionally hiding the development of technologies designed to drop airplanes with people in them out of the sky for whatever dreamed-up reasons these protesters choose to chant at a particular moment they see television cameras in front of their faces." Evans huffed bitterly. "Our people are handling it well, though."

Scholes heard the tone. "You miss it? Being out there in the field?"

Evans nodded. "Sometimes. Still trying to get used to being..."

"The boss."

"Yeah. You've headed IDSD Missions for, what, five years now? You're used to it."

"You'll get there. Eventually you realize you save a lot of lives doing what we do. Someone has to run the response to situations like this." He indicated the sporadic fires on the screens, in both countries. The sound was muted, but the images were all too clear.

"Yes, I suppose so," Evans said. The vice admiral was right. As much as he missed the hands-on part of the job, he had very capable people for that. He was needed for the orders no one else could give, for whatever came up that needed his authority to break through walls without delay. And here at IDSD was where he had to be now. The treaty had been the Internationals' work, it was their jet that had been downed, their people killed, their ambassador taken. And it was their peacekeeping force that was under threat in the disputed region, their people worldwide who were taking the most heat. The alliance of their making that was at risk.

And they had the lead role in the response to the situation. He also had to admit they had the best global intelligence. Before this happened, he had no idea about the extremist faction of Yahna, no one had. It was IDSD that had discovered their existence, had patiently tracked them, and had followed them without their knowing, all the while managing to keep it all under wraps. That was impressive, especially this day and age.

At least it was a USFID agent who had made the crucial connection between them and the ambassador's disappearance, he thought with satisfaction.

"Right," Scholes said, turning away from the troubling scenes. "We're preparing for Pohnpei, our agent on location and his support team at IDSD Southern Territories have provided all the information needed for the raid and are standing by to advise. We'll be ready to move as soon as the combined task team we've put on this are in position. As for Ambassador Sendor, we have our Special Mission Units currently in Europe and those available outside it preparing to move on command. And I spoke with Jeffries earlier, he got the Joint Europe Military Command to put more units alongside ours on standby in multiple other locations." Since no one had any idea where the ambassador's abductors had managed to move him to, the idea was to have as many special forces units as possible available in scattered locations, to reduce the distance to wherever he was found to be and get to him as quickly as possible. One man could easily be hidden, taken away and made to disappear, and in the time since his disappearance, the ambassador could be anywhere.

Evans nodded. "Southern Territories has given us

the names of everyone it has identified as being active members of the extremist faction who are not likely to be on the island during the raid. We're aware there may be others we have no knowledge of, but we ourselves have already identified current Yahna members who have been making aggressive attempts to pressure some of our high-ranking officials to turn against the Internationals, and who have more recently tried to force them to unequivocally blame you for what happened to the ambassador. We're working broadly here, we'll be taking in as many of Yahna's members and affiliates as we can, and we're preparing to move on them not only here but through our peer agencies worldwide." Knowing now, following the interrogation of ARPA's director, that at least some of Yahna's members were in fact part of the extremist faction, too, meant that, since the identities of the dual members were not all known, every possible Yahna member had to be apprehended and questioned, to ensure that as few as possible extremists got away. "Until then we're only watching them, we won't risk them knowing we're after them until we're ready to take them all in. And we can't make a mistake here, this also has to be done simultaneously with your raid on Pohnpei, to make sure they won't get any warning that would allow them to order Sendor moved or killed."

"Killed, I'll bet," Scholes said. "They can't risk him being found alive. That would not only allow us to refute Russia's claims that we were responsible for his death, but would also enable him to talk, tell the world what really happened to him."

"And perhaps also provide clues about the identities of those who took him, and thus proof of their guilt. No, you're right, if this extremist faction's ultimate goal is to permanently scar trust in your— the Internationals'—motives, there's no way it can allow Sendor to remain alive." And so, to try to prevent the ambassador's death and his captors' escape, the arrests of Yahna's members would begin as soon as the raid on the extremists in the Pohnpei mansion that served as their center and in their gated community on the island was underway.

"Still," Scholes said thoughtfully, "it's not perfect. Southern Territories worries that its intelligence operation is being cut short too early here and that it hasn't managed to get all of the identities of the extremist faction's members, not even all of their nationalities, which would have at least provided some clues that might have helped us find them."

"Worse, there could be others like Bourne, in more or less prominent positions elsewhere in the world," Evans added. "They infiltrated ARPA years ago, they could be anywhere. I guess we're all going to live with that. You, us, everyone else in the alliance, none of us will be able to let our guard down while these people are out there working against us."

"If they ever try to get back to action, revive their plans, we'll stop them," Scholes said, unhidden anger in his voice. "Eventually, they will all be found. And this raid on them, the fact that they were even discovered, should be enough to show them and others like them that no one can escape justice."

Evans frowned and looked at the muted scenes on the wall screens. "Of course, none of this solves the most critical problem remaining—Ambassador Sendor himself. Even if your raid and our arrests are successful, there's still the risk that one of these extremists, someone we'll miss, will find out about it and alert his captors. If this gets him killed—assuming he is, in fact, still alive—none of it would matter."

Scholes nodded his agreement, his own somber gaze on the scenes playing out half a world away. There was nothing else to do or say. The fact was that while everything was prepared, nothing could move forward.

Once again, the key to it all was finding Ambassador George Sendor, and in time.

Sendor hadn't realized he had gotten used to his daily conversations with his captor until the door opened and someone else came in. Not his recent companion, nor the silent old man who brought him his meals and cleaned up after him, but a much younger man he hadn't seen yet.

"Is there anything you need?" the man had asked. He was of an origin Sendor could not immediately place, and his accent was heavy. Sendor tried asking him where the first captor was, but the man only repeated the question, his face impassive. Something about his demeanor was different. Ah, yes, Sendor thought. Of course. The first man, his original captor, far outranked this one. He was sure of it, had seen enough hierarchies in his life.

He had declined, there was nothing else he needed, and the man had left without another word. Sendor had waited a beat, and had then made himself some tea.

He stirred his tea now, the movement controlled, his mind concentrating on the teaspoon, on the whirl of the aromatic water. Suddenly realizing what he was doing, he let the teaspoon go with distaste, stepped away, and sat at the edge of the bed. How long had he been standing there, stirring the blasted tea? He stared at it. Thought about his assistant. The young man had always carried a small pack of Sendor's favorite tea in his briefcase, always made sure the ambassador would be comfortable wherever he was. Sadness washed over Sendor. He was dead, wasn't he, his loyal assistant? Were they all dead? Those who had taken him only needed him, he knew now. They would not bother with the others. Although, perhaps, since his assistant, the crew, and the security agents had all been unconscious when the jet landed, was it possible they had left them alive? Hope, he reminded himself. You must hope.

But not knowing was difficult, preying on his

nerves. He wondered how his family was. He had no doubt that they were being well taken care of, but they must be so worried. And the treaty, the people, all those who had trusted him, to whom he had given his word that he would be there for them, that he would do all it took to help them. He had no idea if . . .

He sighed. That was the problem, wasn't it? He simply had no idea.

I must find a way to escape, the thought came to his mind. This cannot, will not, end this way.

The war room was as busy as it had been when Donovan had left it. He wouldn't have been surprised if anyone had told him he was the only one who had managed to go home since he was last here, and even he had only done so to shower and change, and to pick up a fresh set of clothes for Lara that she had asked Rosie to set out for her. He'd been eager to return not to USFID, where his investigation was no longer a priority, but here, where the events of the past days would culminate into a resolution, one way or another.

He headed to Scholes's office, to hear what was being done with the information he had gotten out of Bourne, but then slowed down near the conference room. The vice admiral was sitting inside, alone, staring at a screen. All the screens in the room showed the satellite feeds from the disputed region, except the one he was staring at. That one was dark.

Donovan stood in the doorway, watching him. "Frank?"

The huge man turned to him. Contemplated him for a long time. Finally, he let out a breath and motioned him in.

Donovan joined him at the conference table and waited. Scholes leaned back and just sat there, his eyes on him. Troubled, tense. It's as if now I'm that blank screen, Donovan thought. He wondered what it was like to have the world on his shoulders like the head of IDSD Missions did.

He also wondered why the vice admiral called him in here.

"You solved the car issue?" Scholes asked in an absentminded tone.

"Yes. Quentin will send the approval request directly to you as soon as he finalizes the specs."

"Good, good." Scholes nodded slightly, then continued to stare at Donovan. Struggling with himself, Donovan thought, alert now. An uneasy feeling was growing in the pit of his stomach, an instinct.

A newly acquired instinct. This could only have something to do with one person they both had an interest in, albeit for very different reasons.

"Can you stick around?" Scholes seemed to come to a decision. His gaze focused, although it was still full of thought.

"Yes."

"Good, good." Scholes nodded again, his eyes still resting thoughtfully on Donovan.

Donovan waited.

Scholes took in a deep breath and glanced at the door. No one was anywhere near. Still, he uttered a command, and the door closed.

"I've asked Lara to do something she can't do." His eyes returned to Donovan.

Donovan's eyes narrowed, but he remained silent.

"But she'll try to, she'll give it all she has. It's her way. And if she fails it'll crush her, given the consequences."

"But you don't think she'll fail."

"No, I don't. She won't allow it, there are too many lives at stake. I'm betting she'll do whatever the hell she does in that mind of hers and succeed. She'll push herself until she does."

Donovan had to keep from letting sudden anger erupt. He knew what the stakes here were. But he was the one who had held an exhausted Lara in his arms more than once these past weeks. "She nearly crashed, what, a week ago?" he said. "She was attacked, Frank. Injured. And still she came back here, and she pushed herself to get the job done, and she damn well nearly crashed. Right here, in your Mission Command. And she's barely had any down time since. It simply doesn't stop. You're pushing her too hard."

"I know." Scholes rubbed his face in frustration. "I know, but I have no choice. I need her, Donovan.

We haven't managed to find the ambassador, none of the intelligence agencies has made any progress and the search and rescue teams have no idea where to go next. And I'm under a lot of pressure to use Oracle. This is one of those cases where there simply is no one else who can do this, who can end this in time." He got up, glanced at the screens showing the reason for the difficult decision he had had to make, then turned away from them and walked to the windows lining the back of the conference room and stared out, his hands in his pockets.

Finally, he shook his head. "The night you were in New Mexico, Lara assisted in a situation where a group of peacekeepers on the former Syria-Jordan border were attacked, and several were taken. We needed to act quickly, and she found them, told us where they would be, and guided their rescue."

He chuckled mirthlessly. "What she did there, the fact that she could even do that is in itself incredible. Until now she has always locked on those she was guiding in whatever mission she was working, people she knew quite a bit about and could walk the mission through, with them as an anchor of sorts to the relevant time, place and situation. This, the peacekeepers, she's never done before. Never." He turned to Donovan. "What you said, what she did after she was attacked? That was the first time she's ever done anything close to this, and even that was directly connected to her, she had something personal to lock on to."

By now Donovan knew enough to understand what Scholes was talking about. "So you want her to combine these two things, and, what, take it even further?" He thought about the situation. A man she didn't know, who was being held, if he was even still alive, by people she had very little information about, somewhere, anywhere in the world. An impossible situation, with little if anything to go on. "And do it all as quickly as possible," he completed his thoughts aloud. "Before Sendor is killed, before war starts, before Russia invades, before the situation is no longer reversible."

He watched the vice admiral, a frown on his face. Scholes was clearly making an effort to explain his actions. Donovan stood up and joined him by the windows. The man looked haggard.

Scholes stared at the sprawling complex outside, peaceful in the early morning light, but was seeing none of it. When he spoke, his voice was quiet. Perturbed. "Aiden, you know, he's a godsend. He organizes everything around her, I've never seen anything like it. He looks after her while she's here. She relies on him. He works her schedule around so she can let out some of that tension she's accumulating in a swim, he even clears her favorite pool for her so she's there alone, God knows how he does that. He convinces her to get an hour's rest in her office on the long nights she's here, and he himself doesn't go home if she doesn't. Hell, he makes sure she eats even when the world is falling apart around her, and he thinks we don't see that he slips a bottle of water into her hand when she works Mission Command, or a cup of that coffee she likes, which he always makes for her himself. If he decides that no one comes near her, then no one does, not even me. But"—he nodded to himself—"he can only get that close to her. She is his superior, and she's far more tenacious than he is. He can't make her stop, or even slow down. And what she goes through, the effects of being Oracle on her, she keeps bottled up inside. And then she leaves here, goes home alone and deals with it, I have no idea how.

"And I agree with you. These past weeks, the sequence of missions you've seen—and even before you came into the picture, Donovan, we've had a busy year. That, combined with the pressure of her having been targeted like she was, attacked. And now this, her being positioned as the only remaining way to prevent a war and having to push even further than she already had, take Oracle to another level or whatever it is she'll do, has to do. So yes, I'm worried." He turned to look at Donovan. "Donovan, no one has ever gotten as close to her as you have. I'm thinking you can do what no one else can."

Donovan understood now the vice admiral's clear struggle with himself, a struggle between reluctance and realization. Reluctance to put anything or anyone between Oracle and the job she had to do, and the realization that she needed, in a sense, to be protected from IDSD itself and from those who needed Oracle and who had no choice but to push her beyond her own limits. In a sense, Scholes was doing exactly what he did the first time he had brought Donovan into IDSD. Asking him to protect Oracle.

"You want me to watch her. Catch her when she falls," he said quietly. "Well, you don't have to worry about that, I have no intention of leaving here until this is over."

Scholes nodded his thanks. "It's been a busy day for her. She's now watching the region from above, with the ground updates coming in in real time, and she has just finished reworking the deployment scenarios with the alliance commanders. We're IDSD's operations center on this one and she's right in the middle, working the entire war zone. Every border, every force, every scenario. So far she's been called twice to advise, and at some point she's going to be called on to take over, you've seen how it is. At times like this, we have no choice but to use Oracle. There simply is nothing else like her."

Donovan knew that all too well. He wondered once again about the pressure she was under, how strong she must be.

How much she still had left in her.

"As soon as this one's over, I'm taking her away from here." Distancing Lara would, he thought, be the only way to have her rest for longer than a few hours, recharge properly. And a change of scenery would do them both some good.

"Fine with me," Scholes said, nodding.

"I do mean away. For a few days, weeks, however long she needs."

"You got it. We need her, we'll call her in."

Donovan waited. No deal.

"You can't be serious. Donovan, you realize if I agree to go through you to find her when she's away with you and is needed, instead of contacting her directly, she'll have both our heads."

"I wouldn't expect less of her."

Scholes chuckled. This man had come into Lara's life right in the middle of a crisis that had accentuated everything that she was and what her life was like. From the very beginning he'd had to deal with her strength of will, even before he knew her extraordinary capabilities and what she had to deal with to do the kind of work she did. And he had done so without hesitation. Already then all he saw throughout it all was Lara the person, the woman. She was the one who mattered to him. And she had found her way to letting him in, after all. So perhaps the best thing would be to let these two just be together and work things out between them themselves.

"I know I was the one who asked you to protect her, but you do realize this means you'll find yourself standing up to her at times," he gave Donovan a fair warning. "I'm not doing all the pushing when it comes to Oracle. She does too good a job of that herself, too many times. And stopping Oracle in midstride is something I haven't seen anyone able to do."

"Let me worry about that."

Scholes acquiesced. Good. Donovan didn't put anything before Lara, Oracle or not. As the one who was increasingly finding himself having no choice but to pressure her, and running the risk of burning her out in the process, Scholes was relieved there was now someone who didn't think twice before putting himself between them.

"Very well. So"— Scholes changed the subject— "I'd like to hear sometime how you did that, get all the connections related to Bourne in place."

Donovan sat back down and shook his head in frustration. "It's still not enough, though. Bourne has no idea where the ambassador is being held."

"No, the people he's working with made sure he only knew what he needed to know. But then the fact that we stopped them once before would have made them careful. Anyway," Scholes added, "I understand you don't think Bourne has had any contact with his people since your investigation began. So I doubt he would know that the United States informed the Russians that Sendor is missing."

"We did what?"

Scholes laughed. "Yes. We agreed on it, thought it might rattle them enough to hopefully put a dent in their plans to rush in and conquer Bosnia and Srpska. And we were right, their military hasn't crossed any of the borders yet. But also, US Global Intelligence has since intercepted messages indicating that the Russian defense minister has directed its Foreign Intelligence Service to search for certain people, and specifically a certain man he had been in contact with, so we know they're looking for whoever took the ambassador. Which would, of course, also lead them to him. Which means we have to move faster than them, we can't have them get to him before we do."

Donovan frowned. "So if there was time, you could use this as an opportunity to flush out everyone involved. But under the circumstances, this could mean the ambassador's abductors will feel the pressure and kill him ahead of whatever their original plan was."

"A chance we all took, especially not knowing if he's alive or not. Russia was moving too many forces too quickly, and the fact is that once they cross the borders into Srpska and Brčko it's all moot."

Donovan could understand the reasoning. "It will still happen, at some point, won't it? Unless the ambassador turns up."

Scholes nodded with no little exasperation and glanced at the satellite feeds. "The special forces of a number of alliance members, including our Defense Force-Europe Special Mission Units and some others we've got available elsewhere, are standing by in multiple locations to go where Oracle tells them the ambassador is. Once she does, our designated Combined Special Ops Task Force-Micronesia is ready to raid the extremist faction in Pohnpei, and agents are standing by to apprehend extremists not there at the time as well as Yahna members inside and outside the United States, Evans has set that one in motion."

"This is unbelievable. We have the person who killed Major Berman and stole Sirion, and the connection to the extremists who took the ambassador, and yet none of it is enough to stop what's happening. A war, of all things. Without Sendor, nothing we have is worth much, is it?" Donovan shook his head in frustration. "How the hell does it come to this, everything coming down to one person making the difference between life and death?"

Scholes's eyebrows shot up, and Donovan motioned to him that he got it. Not one person, one special person who could change destinies.

Or one person who could see what no one else could. He marveled at that, at the rare existence, if the world was lucky enough, of people who could do what no other could and who ended up changing life for the better. Like Ambassador Sendor.

Or Lara.

On one of the screens, a satellite feed was replaced with a news broadcast showing images from a siege on a building, fires burning, people raging. Someone in the war room must have decided to go to live coverage, Donovan thought. The images

changed as whoever was doing this switched restless-
ly between news outlets. The reality on all of them
was the same grim one.

Scholes shook his head. "We're running out of
time. Spirits are heated over there, the people won't
listen to reason. I suppose you heard, it's all over the
news already, someone is making sure everything
that happens in Bosnia and Srpska is made public almost before it happens. Someone being the Russians,
of course." He gave Donovan a brief breakdown of
the latest developments, then chuckled bitterly. "It's
a hopeless 'I know, you know' situation. They know
we know they're behind it all and that we can't
prove any of it. Not that it would matter, the way
things are now, with the people raging this way.
Neither nation is noticing what's being done to
them. That they're being manipulated, that the violent incidents are conveniently placed to turn them
on each other and away from peace and to prevent
them from seeing that they're about to be taken
over by a third nation, and it's not the Internationals
or the United States. At this point, explanations are
no longer enough. It's wildfire anger. They're deaf
to anything anyone says, even their own prime ministers. Hell, the Serbs burned down their government
building. We are not sure about the fate of anyone
inside, the protective detail managed to get only the
prime minister out."

Donovan shook his head. "Lara said it was them,
you know, she said Russia did it. On the day of that

conference call we had here, she already knew. And Emero thought so too, when I spoke with him."

"Yes, I know," Scholes said. "I was with her when she explained it to him."

Donovan turned to him. Scholes shrugged.

"I really should have known by now." Donovan turned back to the screens, bemused.

Scholes's phone indicated an incoming call. He took it and listened briefly, then activated the internal comms and spoke, his eyes on Donovan. "Aiden, I need Oracle in Mission Command." He stood up. "Well then, here we go. Our peacekeeping force in Brčko District is being attacked."

Chapter Twenty-Two

IDSD's busiest and most advanced Mission Command was operating with practiced efficiency. Everyone's attention was on the main views showing drone imagery of the peacekeeping force and the negotiation team it was intent on protecting. The impromptu safe zone created for them by the military forces of the two countries flanking the Brčko demilitarized district was smaller now, the rage of protesters from both nations pushing the forces deeper into it. The safe zone's position, close to the Bosnia-Srpska, Bosnia-Brčko and Srpska-Brčko tri-border, had originally put them safely away from the border with Russia and right in the midst of the people they had come to help, but these same people had now turned on them, effectively leaving them trapped. And the forces guarding them had themselves also dwindled. The soldiers were finding it impossible to stand up against their own countrymen, all the more so since they knew their rage was fueled not by malice but by fear and disappointment, and by anger at what they were so sure was the Internationals' betrayal. They had been close, so close to a new future and had allowed their guard down and their hopes up, and their reaction was therefore that much more unchecked in its rage.

While the mission coordinators standing on the operations platform before Mission Command's wall-wide screen seemed intent on their work, speaking on their headsets, it didn't seem to Donovan as if anyone was actually moving anything. Nothing was changing on-screen, and he said so to Scholes.

"Patience," Scholes replied quietly. His eyes were glued to the views on the screen. Those were IDSD soldiers out there. He had trained many of IDSD's now-commanders in his day and knew quite a few of its servicemen and servicewomen. "When I called for Lara, she was talking to the designated extraction overseers working this. She's still with them in her office."

"Let's hope they stop advancing," someone remarked beside them, meaning the raging civilians. There was a bitter edge to his voice. "Our guys will never turn a weapon on them, no matter the cost to themselves. They were there to give them peace, not more of the same violence they've known all their lives. If only these people would remember that."

As the man spoke, the protective military force on the Bosnian side was suddenly forced back into the safe zone. Just as it fell back under the onslaught of angry protesters, the main views of the incident suddenly moved aside sharply along with all other views on the screen, out of the way, and a single view took their place at its center, a satellite feed of the peacekeeping force. Around the satellite feed, new high-flying drone views appeared, intermixed with additional fast-moving images. It was only when one of the drones was at the right angle and position that Donovan realized the dynamic images came from dual-purpose transports flying in formation among them.

Time seemed to crawl by until finally the transports descended, and everyone in Mission Command watched tensely as they landed, one by one, at the heart of the safe zone, each picking up IDSD personnel and rising smoothly into the air again. Finally, the safe zone was empty except for what looked, in the zooming satellite feed, like a small secure compound in its center. It was, the man who had spoken earlier told Donovan in response to his question, the original safe structure built for the peace talks back when there was still danger to the lives of the ambassador and the representatives of both sides who dared speak with him when he had first initiated the talks. It hadn't been used for the past year. There had no longer been any need for it, until now.

As Donovan contemplated what he was seeing, two uniformed IDSD officers with an insignia he didn't recognize came into Mission Command and approached the operations platform, taking in the views on-screen that now showed the transports heading west to the alliance's Croatian border, where they had originally been dispatched from.

"A small force stayed behind to protect the negotiators, who are refusing to leave, sir," one of them told the vice admiral. "It'll keep them safe in the secure compound."

"General Slaviek is staying with them," the other added. "He would have stayed anyway, earlier he was worried that if they all left, there would be no chance the talks could ever be resurrected. He refuses to accept that with Ambassador Sendor gone, it's all over. Certainly now, after this attack on the negotiators."

On the screen, the views from the transports slid to the left, now less of a priority as the transports approached safety. At the center of the screen, the previous satellite views returned, again showing all forces in the region, although a low-altitude drone remained immediately above the now much smaller safe zone. One by one the views zoomed in and out, as if someone was taking in the current situation.

Donovan turned to Scholes, who nodded, confirming. Lara was manipulating the images.

"These are our extraction overseers," Scholes said, indicating the two officers who had joined them. "She had them initiate the removal of the peacekeepers from the area, this was the best way and the latest possible timing to execute it." His eyes returned to the screen. "But as long as we still have people there, that's a problem."

"What if someone had tried to shoot at the transports?"

"You didn't see the air cover they had. I assure you those on the ground did," the extraction overseer closest to them answered Donovan somberly. "Oracle limited the views from above to the point rescue, so you didn't see them. It wanted to have close eyes on the extraction while it was going on, and it activated on its own screens additional views that you don't see here, for its eyes only. Ask to see the broad views later, you'll be surprised."

"Yes," the second overseer said beside him, "you should have seen it. The air cover disabled electromagnetically a launcher from above. Oracle saw it before they did, I've no idea how, and gave the order. Nasty thing, too, could have brought down a transporter."

"The force commander at Split also had more fighters deployed," the first overseer added. "They'll stay up there to protect our remaining people. Some of the low-altitude drones are armed, too. The problem is that none of them can do much, we can't run the risk of hurting civilians while protecting our peacekeepers and the negotiators. We are still the good guys in this." He fell silent and listened on his headset. "Oracle says to expect Russia to move just about now. And it says it has already spoken to all force commanders."

Donovan frowned.

"Damn," a mission coordinator said loudly, then

glanced around him and apologized. On the screen, the Russian ground forces began trickling across the Brčko-Russia border into Brčko District and toward the area the IDSD force had vacated.

"And here they go," the extraction overseer in direct contact with Oracle stated the obvious.

"How far can we expect them to move?" Scholes turned to him.

"Oracle says that for now they'll only come in through this section of the border, the Brčko-Russia one, and stop before they interact with our people or with the Bosniaks and Serbs. They won't risk either nation seeing them as the aggressors, they want to maintain the illusion that they are the saviors in this." He listened on his earpiece. "Their plan is to, at some point, incite a more aggressive riot among the protesters, maybe let some of ours get hurt, jump in to heroically save them, and just happen to move them all the way along the Bosnia-Srpska border to the Croatian border, leaving their own ground forces deployed along the way, de facto taking over both Brčko District and the entire Bosnia-Srpska border. Oracle says we've got some time, though, they will move gradually so that the two nations won't grasp what's happening to them until it's too late."

"And Oracle tends not to be wrong, so I'd say that's our premise," the other overseer pitched in.

Donovan noticed that they were speaking about Oracle as if she were "it", a thing, not a person. His first instinct was to react, but then he remembered what Scholes had explained to him back when he was first told what Oracle really was. That this was the instruction to all operational levels, to only re-fer to Oracle this way. That she was being hidden behind such a description, that her voice, when she spoke to those she guided from Mission Command, was disguised as that of a computer. An artificial intelligence. To protect her, limit the leakage of in-formation about her very existence.

Feeling uneasy at the reminder of the risks she faced just by being her, dangers he'd seen material-ize first hand, he turned to leave Mission Command, go to her.

And stopped in his tracks. Oracle stood just in-side Mission Command's open door, her headset on. Her eyes were fixed on the screen. He wondered how long she'd been there, choosing to look from afar, speak through others. She didn't seem to see him watching her. Her eyes were intensely focused, her brow furrowed.

Abruptly, she turned and left.

Ambassador Sendor was exercising. Slowly. Deliber-ately. Like a man in captivity. He had been doing this twice a day, every day since he first woke up in this room, determined to remain alert, focused. To keep his morale high. He was not a man to give in to despair, no matter how dire the situation. And he was a patient man. The peace negotiations could attest to that—slowly, painstakingly, he had searched, turned every stone, no matter how blood-soaked, no matter how broken, until finally he had found a way to get through to two nations full of fear and hate, and had gotten them to listen.

That was precisely what he was doing now. Searching, slowly and painstakingly. The exercising was a ruse this time. He knew he was being watched every minute, every second of the day. He did not want to let his captors know what he was doing, and these exercises, with the occasional feigned ache, which allowed him to stop and assess, were the perfect way to achieve that.

He was scrutinizing every item in the room and every crevice in every wall. He now knew the door was in fact the only way out. There was no way to loosen a board or widen an opening in the small hours of the night, there were no weaknesses in the walls. The walls were also where the cameras watching him were installed, so disturbing them would alert whoever was behind them anyway.

Then there were the various items in the room, which could, in theory, be used as weapons. But he was in his sixties, and not nearly as fit as he should be. He had never found the time, nor did he have the inclination, to exercise regularly. And he enjoyed food, wine, the company of people in a merry dinner. Dieting was not his choice.

He sighed and sat down on the chair beside the

desk. Then reconsidered and went into the bathroom, washed his face, checked the faucet. No, no good, it could not be taken apart, used as a sharp edge, perhaps. But then, again, he doubted he could overpower his captor, or the bulky young man who had replaced him in his absence. No, the only man he could perhaps overpower was the old man who was caring for him, but what good would that do? Surely it would alert others, and he could not hope to fight them. And in any case, he could not bring himself to harm the old man. He had been silent, kind. Sendor doubted he had any more choice in being there than he himself had.

Still, he must try to escape, there had to be a way. What was the worst that could happen, they would kill him? They would do that anyway, at their convenience, his captor had already admitted that. No, he must find a way to leave. It would, he knew, be best to try to slip out at night, in the dark, but he wasn't sure when that was. He had no idea what time it was, they had taken the vintage pocket watch his wife had given him for his sixtieth birthday. The first meal provided to him after he had woken up in this room had been breakfast, but he doubted he could rely on that to accurately assume it had been morning, although he had elected to treat it that way, creating his own timeline through his meals for his sanity. He could dim the light in the room if he wanted, to sleep at what for him was night, they had allowed him that. But that was it. No, he had no idea about anything, and no obvious way out.

Still, he had to try.

His eyes fell on the pen.

Lara walked to her office, deep in thought. She passed the conference table in the outer office, the screens embedded in its multitouch top still active after her meeting with the extraction overseers and showing the same views as in Mission Command. She didn't even glance at them. Instead, she walked into her inner office and sat on her chair, turned it around and leaned back, her eyes on the window, although she saw nothing of the view outside.

She was already working, already stepping into that place in her mind where she would seek what she came here to find. She had been here before, just outside it, taking the occasional peek in, making initial attempts to find the end of a thread that would lead her where she needed to go. That was all she could do while she was needed elsewhere. This, finding one man who could be anywhere, was different. It required more of her and she needed to be able to focus as much as possible of her attention on it.

By now she had so much in her mind. The events since the ambassador had vanished. The information she had received since from everyone, everywhere. And Donovan's investigation, the details he had given her when he had updated her earlier on Bourne, Yahna, and the extremists. He had spoken to her as Oracle, knowing she would need to know everything if she was called on to act. She liked that, that he updated her as Oracle, yet had turned up in her office later with his eyes on her as his Lara.

She began to shake it off. Him, off. Then realized with a bit of surprise that she didn't need to. These thoughts, with him in them, weren't in her way. They were walking by her side. Reminding her that she wasn't alone, that no matter where she needed to go, he would be there when she returned. Giving her something new, even as Oracle. Something she had yet to define, in this context, but it was adding. That was it, it was adding to her, to what she was.

She let him stay there, in the background. Where she could sense him if she needed, let him, perhaps, guide her back from where she was going, knowing she would have to go in deep this time. Because the fact was that even with everything she had, she still had nothing concrete to go on. Other than the image of George Sendor, whose smiling face she had etched in her mind, she simply had nothing useful to lock on to. He could be anywhere by now, there were a million and one places he could have been whisked to since he was taken. A million and one places where search and rescue teams and under-cover agents and satellites and drones and security cameras and biometric seekers and all the people and technology in the world could not find him.

Worse, time was a factor. Certainly now that the Russians were also looking for him, and for those who had taken him, and who just might know that they were being searched for. And then there were the raids on Pohnpei and on Yahna that had to take place, and that were waiting only for her go.

George Sendor. Had he been killed already? Was she too late to save him? Had they been too late to begin with?

No. He was alive. And where there was life it had to be saved.

I'll need to do this one differently, she thought. This was new. In missions, there was always something around the people she was there to guide that she knew about beforehand and could use to help her lock on to a spatial and temporal point in existence that she could then place herself in, see from, work from. Not this time. This time all she had to lock on to was a man, a life, with no other tangible context.

I'll find you, she thought, already deep in her mind. I promise I will find you.

She gave the command, and the window disappeared, the glass-to-screen technology embedded in it turning it into smooth darkness. She then swiveled in her chair, slowly, thoughtfully, blanking every wall screen, utilizing the design of her office that could be made to imitate that place she went to in her mind, doing so with a pace that matched the strengthening of what she was awakening within her.

Finally, she ordered the door closed and transformed it too and the glass divide it was set in into a seamless dark surface. Around her the room plunged into silent dimness. She settled back in her chair, her eyes open in the dark.

And gave all she had to her search for George Sendor.

Donovan signaled to Scholes that he was leaving and followed Lara. By the time he got to her office, the inner door was shut. He moved toward it but stopped when Aiden approached him.

"Sir, you can't go in," the aide said. "When Ms. Holsworth closes the inner door, no one may disturb her."

Donovan didn't insist, knowing Aiden wouldn't stop him without a reason. He turned to Scholes, who came up beside him, peeked in, and, on seeing the closed office door, nodded.

"Oracle is working," he said.

Donovan didn't get it. He hadn't had many opportunities to see Oracle at work, but when he did, she had worked in Mission Command, using its substantial capabilities to connect her to anyone, anywhere, and let her see any situation worldwide on command.

"Her office has Mission Command capabilities,"

Scholes said, "and it's also designed to allow her to cut herself off from everything and everyone, to work alone. If she's in there, then whatever she is doing is challenging." He turned to leave. "That's that then, let's let her do what she does."

"Just how challenging?" Donovan asked, thinking back to his earlier conversation with the vice admiral.

"I honestly have no idea," Scholes said. "As I said, she's never done anything like this before. Nothing this extreme with so little information, and so little time now that we're moving on the people who took the ambassador. Think about it. How the hell do you find one man who can be anywhere in the world by now, and do so before the person who might have been sent to put a bullet in the back of his head gets to him?"

Donovan frowned. "If he's dead when she finds him..."

"She'll feel it. And take it on herself. That's who she is."

Yes, Donovan knew that. He'd been there with her before and had seen what it did to her. He sent a concerned look at the closed door. "Why can't we be in there with her?" he asked, and realized even as he did that he really had no idea how Oracle's mind worked.

"We would be a distraction that she doesn't need. Oracle takes precedence here. If she hadn't had to be alone, she wouldn't have closed herself in her office." Scholes frowned. "And, you know, I don't think we can go with her where she goes anyway." He waited for Donovan to join him, and the two men returned to Mission Command, each deep in his own thoughts.

"Minister."

Rostovtsev's eyes remained on the map. He had barely moved from it since he had set his plan in motion. This was his destiny, the ultimate achievement that would, he was sure, make him the next president, despite the hitches encountered on the way. The clever takeover of Bosnia and Republika Srpska right from under the hateful United States' and Internationals' noses, the beginning of the end of the alliance, finally checking the Internationals' stubborn progress, and all this with little force. This was the ultimate win.

Gone were the days of forceful invasions, the Internationals had changed all that. They had faced up to Russia's acts of aggression—that was what they had called them—and those of its peers by fearlessly proclaiming that they would not stand by while aggressors took over nations, repressing them, killing and destroying where an attempt was made to resist. Enough death, enough fear, enough wars, they had said. Enough of any form of oppression. People had the right to live in dignity. They had the right to speak without fear, to walk the streets without harm coming to them because of their gender, their race, their beliefs and opinions, their nationality. They had the right to choose.

It had sneered, Russia. Rostovtsev had been a teenage boy then, and he had seen his father laugh at this folly. They speak, his father had said, but they are but a scattered group, short-lived, powerless. The true powers, the countries that had governments and armies and weapons, they would continue to do nothing, just make empty threats and impose useless sanctions in the face of Russia's bold acts. His Russia would be great again, his father had been so certain, together with its old allies and with new ones it had cleverly cultivated in every land where the West, with its empty promises of protecting its allies, had lowered its head instead of defending and had stepped back, leaving those who had believed in it to understand they were alone, to fall, and those who chose to defy peace and conquer, to prosper.

But instead, the boy had grown up to see the Internationals achieve numbers, recognition, respect and widespread support, as governments understood that the newly formed nation was not threatening them nor the structure of the countries they headed, that while there were those who elected to take the international citizenship, chose the new global way of seeing the world as their home, others still needed their national identity, the ways they had always known, and that these two views coexisted well in a reality of patience that taught tolerance.

He had grown up to see not his father's Russia rise but the Internationals' alliance form, as the world learned that the new nation stood adamantly behind its words. The Internationals acted. Not just talked, not just waited for others to do, not set conditions for their help. They had stepped in where needed, at times paying a price and yet never wavering in their resolve. In their actions they had changed the reality of a tired world, and governments and their constituents alike finally understood that they could work alongside this new global phenomenon to do better. Words had meaning once again, and confidence in the prospect of a better future was gained. The world really was changing.

And throughout the years in which the hateful Internationals grew, Russia had stopped. Simply that, it stopped. Its excursion into Eastern and Southeastern Europe to regain hold of the lands it had lost when it had fallen from greatness the century before, initially made easy by the toothless response of the struggling union that had long failed those it had promised to make a part of a strong Europe, could no longer continue as the Internationals' small but smart military positioned itself strategically behind their unrelenting diplomatic force, signaling tenacity and strength. And this made country after country in Europe, and then others across the globe, raise their heads and stand beside the Internationals, who stood strong in the lead. But worse, Russia itself, his father's Russia, which his father and his grandfather had fought for, could no longer control its own people. Those who objected to the ways of its regime would no longer be easily silenced, they could now find refuge among the Internationals in friendly lands on the other side of the crumbling country's borders.

But this, this plan of his, it would bring his father's Russia—now his Russia—back to power. The Internationals would finally be reduced to silence, and without them, without the driving force of their convictions, the alliance would be gone forever.

"Minister," the man at the door said again. The new director of the Foreign Intelligence Service, appointed instead of the one who had been reassigned—at least that was the official word following his disappearance—after failing to find those who were supposed to kill the ambassador.

"What is it?" Rostovtsev grumbled, his eyes still on the forces he was moving. Disturbances were not welcome.

"We are picking up some movement."

Rostovtsev finally turned to him. "Who? IDSD? They were forced to take their people out of Brčko, they are mistrusted by everyone. They cannot do anything."

"No, sir, not the military, just . . . our spies report that the special forces of the alliance were asked to be ready in several locations that we know of. There are indications that the request came from IDSD."

"So?"

"They have put their own special forces on alert, too, they are leading this, Minister."

"So?" Rostovtsev was becoming impatient with this man. He had more important things to do than to think about the Internationals' desperate attempts to—

"Wait," he said, apprehension seeping into his voice before he could hide it. Could they have an idea where the ambassador was?

Could they find him alive?

Chapter Twenty-Three

Where are you?

Her eyes were now closed, and in her mind she was suspended in nothing. She had no idea how long she'd been in here, didn't dwell on it. It was she who had done that, cleared everything away. She needed it to be like this, didn't want anything pulling her in any direction. At least anything that would stand in her way. With nothing to lock on, nothing pertinent that could be useful for what she needed to do, this was the best way to go.

Patience was all she needed, patience and to let it be. It would come to her, what she was seeking, she would never allow herself to think otherwise. And so she waited in the silence, let herself know beyond doubt that it was, it existed, all she had to do was find it, be there with it.

With him.

Where are you, George Sendor? was the question with which she had come here and was now contemplating in the endless depths of her remarkable mind, and she had no intention of leaving without it being answered. Where are you? was the echo an indeterminate distance into the temporal dimension later, even as something finally tugged at her attention and she confidently reached for one end of the thread, followed it, knew.

In the comfortable, dim silence of her office, she opened her eyes again. Her line of thought did not react, was not in the least affected. Darkness and silence had the same peace without as she had within and tended not to disturb her focus.

It was why she had her office designed this way.

She ordered a random wall screen on and accessed IDSD Legal. Not under her visible Missions authorization, that of the formal identity she held, of critical mission expert, but under her confidential, untraceable one. The designated mainframe tagged her entry, revving up, ready to alert, then recognized who she was and stepped back obediently, clearing her way through. She pressed on, searching, until she found what she wanted, then rushed through international records, fast, faster as the pieces fell into place in her mind. Finally zoomed in on Europe, went back a decade, then another year earlier.

Centering on Croatia, on the earthquake that had devastated the island of Cres, taking hundreds of lives and literally breaking it apart, large chunks of it falling into the raging sea.

The island had remained uninhabited, the tragedy that had occurred on it hindering anyone from attempting to start a new life there. The surviving population had been relocated at its request with the help of the Joint Europe Civilian Command and IDSD Diplomacy's peacetime ops force, and Cres, or what used to be Cres, had been redesignated for use as a transitional port and airport for both civilian and military uses. This prompted the idea, quite ambitious at the time, to extend its intact remainder by building on its edge and into the sea a fully usable artificial extension. But although the extension was built, the plan for the island didn't pan out. Everyone was reluctant to use the place, even fishermen didn't go there anymore. Not even youth looking for a place to party or to swim. It was as if nothing that might represent the continuation of life was allowed there, as if forbidding spirits were standing guard, demanding to be remembered.

The place was deserted.

In her office, records were now running on the screen, alongside press releases, internal notices and hearing minutes. The first thing she searched for in these was who had been behind the construction of the artificial platform. That took a deeper look. Most of what she found discussed the disaster itself, the lives lost and the relocation of the too few who had survived. Croatia itself was cited as the final decisionmaker as to the fate of the island itself, and its then prime minister had taken credit for the rebuilding. For all intents and purposes, Croatia had done it all, from start to finish.

But something tugged at Oracle's mind, something that had been there for a while and that had prompted her to add to her mental database all information Missions had about Yahna as soon as she had heard about its extremist faction. Yahna's fall happened at about the same time as the earthquake, in fact when the trials of two of its rogue leaders began the earthquake's consequences were still being dealt with. Shortly after, the two leaders—and Yahna —were let off on the condition that Yahna immediately cease all its activities against the Internationals. And not only them. Other than the trials of those who had caused bodily harm through acts they themselves had committed, all other trials had ended with a warning, not much more than that.

She contemplated this, then ventured further in, toying with a theory. She ran assorted data on four views on the same screen, as if limiting the space they occupied would focus them better in her mind. She wasn't sure what she was searching for, but she followed that sense of uneasiness that was lurking deep in her mind.

She didn't believe in coincidences.

An obscure reference in the ruling in the trial of one of the two Yahna leaders sent her backtracking, then opening a new hidden path and proceeding unseen through IDSD Legal to a junction where she piggybacked on a high internal authorization, one that brought a small smile to her face, then dove into past records of the financial accounts of the Croatian government. She found what she needed in records that were closed to public scrutiny.

The money for the artificial platform, a substantial amount, came in its entirety from Yahna, in a gesture made by it to prove its intention to mend its ways. It would no longer harm and destroy, but build. Its official statement, made in confidence to the then government of Croatia, went so far as to say that the Croatian members of Yahna, who had previously opposed Croatia's intention at the time to join the alliance, wished to show their appreciation for the Internationals' help with the Cres relocation as well as with the severe economic repercussions of the earthquake for the entire region. Apparently the Internationals had, through IDSD Diplomacy, sent search and rescue teams to the devastated island, had paid for the relocation of the evacuees, including doing their best to replicate the homes they had lost, and had provided the survivors, those of Cres and others in the region who had felt the effects of the disaster, with all the help they needed, striving to allow life to return to normal, to the extent possible under the circumstances. Yahna, the statement said, was volunteering to do as the Internationals had, and to find a way to rebuild Cres.

Oracle closed the statement and frowned. Since then, Yahna had remained out of trouble, keeping its head down. Or at least apparently so. As recent events had shown, that wasn't quite what happened. Instead, the extremists within it had used it to maintain a low-key facade, while in actual fact working covertly to create a new, more sophisticated and violent faction. The question was how early on they had begun planning their eventual return, and just how they had been preparing over the years. However, that was something that time would determine, time and the kind of intelligence work and investigation that were not part of what Oracle did, nor what she needed right now.

All she needed was what she now had, the connection that she had found and that was tangible enough for her to focus on. That and her unique capability, which she trusted to lead her down the right path out of infinite possibilities, toward that which she was seeking, which was no longer hidden in the endless fabric of space and time but was now within her reach.

Cres's reconstruction had begun two years after the earthquake. She removed the data from the screen and brought up the construction plans for the artificial platform. Useless. She went further in, searched, and eventually found what she was looking for in the records of the construction company, which in her opinion should have been destroyed long before if what she thought the extremist faction did was in fact what they had done, if they had influenced the construction and had added something that wasn't supposed to be there, something they had meant to keep hidden. But then, people were careless at times, or perhaps wanted information saved for later leverage, and this, fortunately, was one of these two cases. It was simple, really.

The construction company that Yahna had contracted with—and that had been just a little too well paid for the job they had done, a comparison to their other jobs showed her—had kept the blueprints. Archived long ago, and well hidden, granted. But not hidden well enough from her.

She made a copy of all the available information about the reconstruction and backed out all the way out of IDSD Legal, and was still digging into the blueprints when she made the call to Brussels, to IDSD Special Missions Command. Next was Emero, who would be passing on to Southern Territories the go on the raid on Pohnpei and following it in real time. She called using her critical mission expert ID but received no answer. Not surprising, all considering, she thought, and called again using her Oracle code. The call was picked up immediately, the screen before her showing her it was awaiting maximum security mode.

"Emero," was all he said, prompting voice identification that completed the security check.

She gave a quiet command, adding an unanticipatable security layer, and then addressed the agent. "Marcus, there's a structure under the Cres artificial platform, propped on a part of the island that sank and partially integrated with it. Underwater access only. Extremists hot spot."

"You're kidding," he said after a shocked silence. "They were under where they landed the jet the whole time?"

"Look at the blueprints I'm sending you, there's no way you would have found it." And there wasn't. No search could have identified the existence of the hideaway, which was entirely submerged and connected to the underside of the platform and was surrounded by a larger frame that was a legitimate part of the artificial structure. This frame made it invisible unless someone managed to go down a substantial depth and then up again on the inside of the frame, which no one had a reason to do. And the internal structure, the information from the construction company had told her, had been designed to have no footprint that would allow it to be tagged by electronic means.

"Unbelievable." He didn't ask how she found it. He never did.

"Special Missions Command is mobilizing our units at Split, they're the closest. I've already sent them the info."

He nodded. "You'll guide them in?"

"Yes." That, she had no doubt she could do, guide them through any security measures, hostiles included. She had enough context in her mind and by now this type of thing came naturally to her. "But not just yet. They'll stay away from Cres until I give them the go. And Marcus," she added, her eyes locked on his, "you do the same with Pohnpei. Don't move yet." She wasn't finished with her new finding. Whatever it was that was tugging at her mind was still there, still not entirely clear.

Emero confirmed without question and signed off. He knew she would never give such an order without a reason. He trusted her without reservation. He had been at the heart of an investigative operation gone very wrong at one time, and she had saved him. But he hadn't known that until the day he had first been asked to be in charge of her protective detail. She had saved quite a few of his people, his friends, since, and what he had seen her do cemented his trust in her in a way that could not be shaken.

In her office, Oracle was already immersed in thought again. She still hadn't found George Sendor. Except, she thought she knew where he might be.

She called Scholes to briefly update him and the war room outside, and then shut down her communication system. She still had some time before the Special Mission Units arrived near Cres, and she wanted to use it. She didn't want to stop what she was doing, was too far now into that part of who she was that she needed here, too close to be sidetracked.

Her office dark and silent once again, she dove deeper into her mind.

And focused on the life of one man.

Mission Command shifted its focus even as Scholes's phone indicated an incoming call. He took it, and Donovan saw him frown, the frown deepening as he ended the call and issued a series of orders to the mission coordinators before turning to Donovan.

"This"—he indicated the new views on-screen, the step-up in activity—"came from Oracle." He was already walking to the door of Mission Command, Donovan at his side.

The door to Lara's inner office was still closed. This time they stayed there, sitting at the table in her outer office. While they waited, Scholes checked on all the teams standing by to close in on those who were behind the events that were threatening to destroy everything his people had worked for.

With its presumed destination now known, the Air Assault Team of the Special Mission Unit that was moved to the air-sea base at Split in the recent redeployment of IDSD's special forces was ready to be in the air and en route to Cres on command, although it would remain on the tarmac until the order was given. Since Oracle had not yet given a go, the assumption was that its destination could still change if Oracle determined there were no persons of interest currently there. At the same time, the Amphibious Ops Team of the Special Mission Unit permanently stationed at Split was already being deployed to Cres in underwater transports, because of the somewhat longer time needed for their departure from Split and arrival at Cres, but it would also remain a safe distance away until the go or a redirecting order would be given.

In the western Pacific Ocean, the IDSD and US

Combined Special Ops Task Force-Micronesia was in position and ready to move in on Pohnpei, its Electronic Warfare Detachment prepared to disable the island's power grid and all communications through a network of combat stealth drones carrying long-range offensive jammers and flying at a pre-designated perimeter. On command, Pohnpei and its surrounding islands would go dark.

And in the United States, Yahna's members did not realize that the people walking alongside them in corridors, standing with them in elevators, or driving on the same roads as them, were US Global Intelligence agents, who were constantly coordinating with their peers in intelligence agencies worldwide doing the same with Yahna members elsewhere.

Both Donovan and Scholes stood up when the door finally slid open. Oracle came out, her eyes intense, focused. "Cres, they kept him in that zero-comms underwater structure," she said. "He and his abductors were there the entire time, hidden and untraceable." She walked to Mission Command, putting on her headset.

Donovan's concern that she would not, could not accept the possibility that the ambassador was dead, surfaced again. "You need to consider—"

"He's alive," she said without turning back, and the way she said it made both of the men following her know not to argue.

When they entered Mission Command, a mission coordinator informed Scholes that the transports carrying the Air Assault Team that would be serving as the Amphibious Ops Team's backup were in the air. On the screen, two blank views with off-comms signals were added, one for each of the teams. And in Micronesia, the task force was inching closer to Pohnpei, preparing to raid their targets.

"When did you give the order?" Scholes asked, and Donovan was taken aback. He had no idea she had the authority to do that.

She didn't answer. She had done it earlier and had then taken the time to refocus her mind on all active fronts—Bosnia, Srpska, Brčko and Russia, where tensions had reached a peak, Pohnpei, where she would only step in in an emergency, although she had her reasons to expect the raid teams would not encounter significant trouble, and Cres, where the spearhead of her attention was now that she had a lock on the ambassador. It was crucial that nothing would be missed now.

"What are these for?" Donovan indicated the two blank views.

"They have their orders. They will only be in contact with each other and with Oracle until this is over. All eyes are off them," she said quietly, then addressed Scholes. "They won't need additional air or underwater support."

Donovan looked at her and was surprised to see that she wasn't looking at the screen, where IDSD secure satellites were tracking all active fronts, all but Cres. Instead, she stood with her head down, her eyes closed.

"Where are you?" he asked, half expecting her not to hear.

"Sendor," she answered quietly. "I'm with George Sendor."

Donovan turned to look at Scholes, who shook his head. He had no idea what she meant, he had never encountered anything like this before.

Hold on, she said deep in her mind. We're coming for you.

He couldn't hear her, she knew. Didn't know she was there. But she could see him, was with him, would not leave him there alone.

Hold on.

Sendor took the pen apart during his meal, doubting anyone would bother watching him eat. And he had been eating alone since his captor had, apparently, left, which made it easier. He had decided on that specific meal because in his mind, in that timeline he had kept for his sanity, it was in fact supper. And it was now, today, that he intended to finally take action.

He read a little after his meal, in one of the old print books they allowed him to have, as he did on every what he thought was evening. He waited impatiently until the old man came to clear the dishes, and as soon as the man left he dimmed the light as low as he was allowed to and went to bed, feigning tiredness. He waited as long as patience would allow him, hoping whoever might be watching him would get bored and look the other way.

Eventually he got up and dressed quietly in the near dark, staying as far out of view of the cameras as he could. He then inched along the wall to the entry door, holding in his hand the pointed edge of the pen he had taken apart, and reached for the handle. Then he halted, reconsidering, and walked over to the desk. He took the notepad they had given him, tore off the many pages he had written in the duration of his captivity, rolled them up and put them inside his shirt. They were important to him, these words he had written. They recounted everything that had happened to him since he had gotten on the jet and everything that his captor had said to him. They included words for the people he had taken under his wing and had fought to achieve the peace treaty for, told of his dreams for them, the future he so wanted them, their children, to have. There were instructions in them for those he knew would do everything in their power to follow in his way. He wanted them to try to make peace happen, no matter what, no matter how long it would take. And last, but by all means not least, there were words there for his family. For his sons, for the grandchildren he might never see grow up.

He wasn't sure anyone would ever see them, his words. Although he would try to escape, he placed little faith in his ability to do so. He knew enough to understand that he was not being held by amateurs and that it had taken an elaborate plan to abduct and hold him this way, to use him to hurt whole nations so effectively. But he thought that if they killed him and his body would be found, perhaps returned to his family, those he cared about might find what he had written.

With the papers safely tucked in his shirt, he returned to the door. It took him some time, but he managed to unlock it with the pen he had taken apart. Whoever was holding him had apparently not imagined him trying to get out, certainly not after a time in which he had been nothing but obedient. As it was, he did, and this door was not electronically locked. It was an old manual door, the type he had not seen since he was a child.

A child who spent much of his time grounded in his room because of mischievous acts, quite a few of them in fact, and who had soon learned to unlock doors and windows when he was bored.

He opened the door and stepped out.

At the Bosnia, Srpska and Brčko tri-border, the riots were out of control, the people forcing their own militaries back into the Brčko District safe zone in an attempt to get to the besieged Internationals. Where Bosniaks and Serbs happened to chance upon one another, violence broke out, too. The Russian Federation's defense minister hastened its forces' advance into the district, citing no choice lest people of the two nations meet and clash, instigating war, lest the violence seep to his own country, which had the right to protect itself, and lest the remaining peace-keeping force be harmed, which he felt compelled to prevent, of course. At the same time, the forces he had deployed along the Russian Federation's border with Srpska began their determined move forward.

In IDSD Missions' war room and in the IDSD HQ, Joint Europe Commands and White House situation rooms, there really was nothing to say, nothing to do, as the most volatile area in Europe erupted in violence before the eyes of those watching.

In Mission Command, silence reigned alongside tense anticipation as Oracle spoke last words to the teams prepared to move in on Cres, deep in the water and high above in the air.

Chapter Twenty-Four

It's all black, was the first thing Ambassador Sendor thought. And it was. He was surrounded by blackness—black walls, a black ceiling. And there was no one there, even though he had steeled himself to face guards, guns, an onslaught. He took a few hesitant steps forward, not understanding. There was nothing there. He seemed to be in a huge, square room, with nothing but walls and a high ceiling far above him. The only light came from what looked like scattered spots where the ceiling met the walls. Spots aimed at him. Or rather at the wall behind him, the wall of the room he had just left, and the door, now open, in it.

He walked along that wall, perplexed. Reached a corner, turned and continued to walk. Another corner, another wall. Another corner, then another one, and there was the open door just ahead. He walked to it and peeked inside the room, his prison cell, then took several steps back away from it and looked up. At the ceiling. His ceiling, which he was looking at from the outside, the ceiling of the larger, black room looming above it. He had been held in an especially built room within a much larger structure, he realized in surprise. Like a set in a film, he thought. And where was everyone?

He rounded the impromptu room again, heading to where he had seen the entrance to a wide corridor in the wall, the real wall of this huge black room or whatever it was he was in. He stood in place for a long moment, looking at the corridor. It didn't make sense that he was here alone, surely there had to be someone else here.

But no one was coming, he heard no footsteps. He was surrounded by silence. He braced himself and stepped into the corridor, constantly looking over his shoulder to see if anyone was coming after him. Like the room, the corridor was spotted with lights built into the ceiling at regular intervals. Finally reaching its end, he stopped, and his jaw dropped. He was standing on a strip of rough concrete stretching to both his sides, and ending, a short distance ahead, at the edge of dark water. He looked up. The ceiling here was also black, but ahead, on the other side of the water, it met a wall that was not, nor was it neatly smooth like the others in this odd place he was in. It looked natural. Chiseled rock perhaps? He couldn't begin to guess where he was. There seemed to be no way out, but there had to be one, whatever way his captor had used to come and leave, him and the others Sendor had encountered in his captivity.

He took several hesitant steps forward, to the

edge of the concrete strip he stood on. Just under him, beside steps that led down, a miniature submersible bobbed silently in the water.

"Is that what you were looking for?"

Sendor started and whirled around. His captor was leaning on the wall behind him, to his left, an amused smile on his face.

"The way out, isn't that what you want?" his captor asked again. "A one-person submersible will do the trick."

"I don't understand. What is this place? Where is everyone?" Sendor asked, too confused to be afraid.

"There is no one. They are all, let's say, gone," his captor said with a coldness that made Sendor's skin crawl. The captor pushed off the wall and walked along it, never veering off to approach him. Taunting him. "I suppose I should not be surprised that you got out, George. You are, after all, a resourceful man."

"Is this when I die?" Sendor found himself strangely calm.

"Yes." His captor pulled a handgun from inside his jacket, then looked at it with interest. "I don't use these much, you know. That really is not my job, I have people for that. But I know how to use one. Quite well, in fact." He stroked the gun with his other hand. "IDSD-issued. IDSD bullets."

"You are framing IDSD for my death?" Sendor, unaware of the full details of the events that had surrounded his disappearance, tried to put what few pieces he had together.

"That we did days ago. I suppose you could say this is the final touch."

"Why now?"

"Sorry?" His captor turned his eyes back to him, his eyebrows raised.

"Why are you doing this now? I thought I was leverage. You said you intended to keep me alive." Sendor found that he needed to understand, to somehow make sense of his own death, of the pain that would be caused to so many who needed him. To the people he loved. Anger bubbled inside him, anger at the futility of it.

"Yes"—his captor sighed with regret—"I had hoped to keep you here longer. Much, much longer. But things have become too complicated. And I have my orders."

"Orders?" Sendor focused. "I thought you were the one giving the orders."

His captor's eyes turned cold. "It seems I have said too much. No matter, you will, after all, die here."

The captor motioned for Sendor to move to the wall, while he himself walked to the edge of the water, toward his way out, the submersible that awaited him.

"Turn around," he said.

"You want me to stand with my back to you? Why? Are you afraid to see my eyes when you kill me?" Anger mixed with bitterness.

"I couldn't care less. But you need to die like they did."

Sendor took a step forward, horrified, as he realized what his captor meant. "You killed them. You killed everyone on my jet."

"Yes. Well, no, not technically. My people did. I was . . . otherwise engaged, you could say. My job was you." Abruptly, the captor stepped forward, pushed the older man back roughly, turned him around to face the wall, and pointed the gun at the back of his head.

"Say your goodbyes, George. For yourself. For the world, you have been dead for days."

Sendor held his head high and closed his eyes. So be it, he thought. He braced himself.

The shot came.

He heard it on the backdrop of the rustle of water but felt nothing. Next was the sound of the man behind him falling on the hard concrete.

"Go, go, go," he heard the urgent shout, then running footsteps, and someone turned him around forcefully and held him with his back against the wall. He opened his eyes to see guns pointed at him by two men in full combat gear, another held by the man who was holding him against the wall with one hand. On both his sides, more armed figures were coming out of the water, running past him into the corridor.

The nozzle of the gun came down sharply. "It's him, it's him," the man shouted, "got him," and the ambassador heard the words echo all around him.

He looked, dazed, at the men who were now re-positioning themselves to flank him, their backs to him, guns pointed outward, to protect him. More joined them, surrounding him in an impenetrable half-circle.

The man who had spoken was patting him down, "Sir, are you injured? Do you require medical attention?"

"No, no, I'm . . . no." He tried to focus, turned his head at shouts coming from inside this place where he had been held captive as the other men cleared it.

"Who are you?" He pushed at the man, inching back into the wall. He'd had enough of captors.

The man grinned, white teeth a stark contrast to his camouflage-painted face. He reached for his arm and ripped off the cover that hid the Internationals' flag. "Captain Reynolds, IDSD Defense Force-Europe Fourth Special Mission Unit, Amphibious Ops Team, sir. It's all right, we're here to take you home." He motioned to his people, and they began to lead the ambassador toward the edge of the concrete, where two underwater transports had come out of the water.

"No, I have to go, I have to . . . where are we? What is this place?"

"You're on Cres, the Croatian island, or rather under it, in a concealed hideaway built by the people who took you on the rocky foundation created when the island was destroyed." Reynolds waited until he was sure the ambassador understood what he was saying. The elderly man looked disoriented. Not surprising, considering what he'd been through. He spoke soothingly, mistaking the ambassador's rambling for fear, a need to escape his captivity. "First Special Mission Unit's Air Assault Team is topside securing the area. You're safe now, sir. And we'll be leaving soon. Part of my team will stay here to finish clearing this place, but I've got orders to get you to safety and then to Brussels."

Sendor grabbed the captain's arm. "No, please, the treaty. I have to go to them, that man said . . . I can stop it, I can, is there really a war?"

The captain looked at him. "Pretty damn near, sir. They think you're dead, the Russians made it look like we killed you, to create a mess."

So what his captor had said was true. "How long has it been? What day is it? No, it doesn't matter. I can stop it. I have to try. Please."

The captain scrutinized him, then nodded. "Let's see what we can do, then, Ambassador."

In IDSD US's Mission Command, Oracle broke simultaneously from Sendor and the Special Mission Units at Cres and nodded at Emero, now on-screen.

"We have a go," he relayed, and in the Federated States of Micronesia, Pohnpei and its surrounding islands went dark, losing all communications and power, its defense systems rendered useless for a long enough time to allow Combined Special Ops Task Force-Micronesia to launch simultaneous raids on the historical mansion above Kolonia and on the gated community containing the homes of the Yahna extremist faction's members. Minutes later, US Global Intelligence confirmed it was moving on Yahna inside the United States, its counterparts in the additional designated arrest sites worldwide following in cascading order.

In Mission Command, Oracle never took her eyes off all active fronts on the screen.

On the platform that formed the artificial addition to the island of Cres, IDSD Defense Force-Europe First Special Mission Unit's Air Assault Team canvassed the area around them, but there was nothing to find, no danger there, nothing to do but secure the place. In the structure hidden under their feet, their peers found the room the ambassador had been kept in. Behind a concealed entrance in the corridor he had gone through they found well-organized quarters that would allow a large number of people to remain hidden in this underwater hideaway, including well-stocked storage rooms. The only technology found was the closed system that allowed the prisoner in the internal room to be watched, there were no means there of communicating with the outside world. But then, the structure had been built in the first place to have no footprint that would allow it to be detected from the outside. Nor was there any way to physically access it other than by using submersibles such as the one the man they had killed had intended to leave in.

By himself. They found the bodies of three apparent guards and an unarmed old man in the hidden quarters.

No useful intel was found. What little was discovered and taken would be examined at a later time, in more appropriate settings, but would lead to a dead end. The guards and the old man were easily identified but turned out to be obscure individuals, registered as being Croatian citizens with no families and no known affiliations, nor any identifiers in their backgrounds that would have raised red flags. It looked as if they had been carefully chosen for the roles they played in the extremist faction's plans. As for the man Captain Reynolds had shot, and whom Ambassador Sendor had confirmed was his main captor, he could not be immediately identified.

The Pohnpei raids, on the other hand, produced significant results. Not only the arrests, but also information, including elaborate plans, past and future, found in the basement floor of the mansion overlooking Kolonia. The findings were also enough to connect the extremist faction to the ambassador's abduction and to the theft of Sirion, and included the names of at least some of those who had helped replicate the technology, some knowingly and some without knowing what they were helping to build.

The Sirion copy itself was not found.

In Washington, DC, the unmarked cars escorting Richard Bourne from USFID Plaza to the IDSD airfield, from where he would be flown to a secure facility in Brussels, skidded to a halt as a single missile from a UAV camouflaged as a civilian delivery drone hit the SUV he was in, instantly killing him and the USFID agents in the car with him.

In IDSD's Mission Command, Donovan's phone signaled an incoming call. He silenced it. It sounded again immediately, bypassing the lock with an emergency signal. He took the call and ended it after a brief conversation, his face set in a grim frown.

"I have to go," he said, turning to Scholes. He stared at the phone, remembering Bourne's warning. You don't know them, they will find me, he'd said. "Bourne is dead."

"ARPA's Richard Bourne?" Scholes gaped.

Donovan nodded and glanced at Lara, who was facing the screen, speaking to Emero on her headset.

"Go," Scholes said. "She'll be here for a while. And Aiden knows what to do."

Donovan looked at Lara again. Then he turned and left.

The underwater transport that carried Ambassador Sendor and several of his rescuers, Captain Reynolds included, was far too small in his opinion. And despite the heavily armed, dangerous-looking soldiers around him, this did not seem a vessel that could fight an onslaught.

"Are we safe in here?" He looked around him and shifted uncomfortably, still reeling with the realization that he had been held captive underwater all this time.

"We're deep underwater," the captain answered. "No one knows we're here and we're masked." He glanced at a console beside him. "And we're moving faster than you think, sir."

Sendor was more worried about the small transport breaking apart in the water. He wasn't very fond of small spaces. And he couldn't swim. "Where are we going?"

The captain smiled. "Wait for it."

Moments later the transport shifted. Going up now, it seemed, although Sendor wasn't sure. He started with surprise as the upper half of the transport gradually became transparent, and he saw that they were indeed moving up, inside a much larger compartment, a huge one, in fact. Before long they were above water and moored alongside a dock, and the transport opened. He was helped out and stood gawking at the sight around him. Busy sailors moved around the transport he had arrived in and similar ones that hung suspended above water. It looks like a shipyard, he thought curiously.

"This way, sir." Captain Reynolds led him, the rest of his team moving away in a different direction and two naval officers taking their places behind him and the ambassador. They stepped into an elevator that opened again almost immediately to show an austere passageway. The woman awaiting them was imposing in her captain's uniform.

"Welcome to *International Unity*. Good to have you back safe and sound, Ambassador. I'm Captain Gaines."

"*International Unity?*"

"We're an IDSD Defense aircraft carrier. You're now on Internationals territory, Ambassador. You're among friends. I suggest we get you to the infirmary, after which—"

"Please. Thank you, but I have to go back."

"Go back?" Captain Gaines frowned at the distraught man and glanced questioningly at Reynolds.

"The peace treaty. I have to go back. I have to complete it. The treaty must be signed."

"I'm afraid that's a bit complicated," the captain said carefully. She had been briefly updated about the conditions of the ambassador's captivity, the isolation he had been kept in.

"I don't . . . what day is it?" Sendor finally remembered to ask. "How long was I held captive?" He realized Gaines was regarding him with concern. I must sound confused, he thought. He couldn't afford to have them think he was incapacitated, he needed them to listen to him now, before it was too late.

He forced himself to calm down and collected his thoughts. "I was held in isolation, captain, told nothing of what was going on in the outside world," he explained. "I was not even told the day and time. Please, I need to know what is happening."

Gaines nodded slowly and assessed the sober determination in the ambassador's eyes. "All right then," she finally said. "Why don't we all go to my stateroom? I will update you, and we will see."

"I have to go back," Sendor said again once he was told everything. "I can do this. I can save them." The passion in his voice was no longer the result solely of his belief in the treaty. It was, now, also a reflection of his anger and bereavement at the confirmed loss of his loyal assistant, his protective agents and the crew of his jet, who were murdered to prevent him from completing his work. They, and those who had died in the days since his abduction in the renewed hostilities instigated through the destructive actions of those who had taken him in order to instill fear and chaos in the people he had sworn to protect. Enough, was all he could think, now more determined than ever. Enough death.

His words had Council Head Ines Stevenssen, on-screen in the stateroom of IDSD *International Unity's* captain, sigh. "I know you can, my friend." She tried to soothe him. "But we just got you back. Those people meant to kill you, please understand, and we must first make sure that you are protected from them."

"So I am to be protected while the people I promised peace die in war? Ines, please, I gave them my word. I told them I would help them. I was going to accept your offer. To remain with them, to be their ambassador. I owe it to them."

Stevenssen knew he was right. He had always been the key to stopping the escalation in Bosnia and Srpska, and now, finally, he was here to do it. And he could probably succeed, bring peace, even now. If anyone could untangle the situation and get the two nations talking again, it was him. She had known George Sendor for many years. The kind, patient man had a rare way with people, and it could not be argued that he had been the only one able to get the two nations to talk in the first place.

And the reality was that she had no real choice. If the ambassador would show he was alive and would speak out, this alone could make the difference between life and death. After all, it was his disappearance that had sent the two nations reeling, and it could only be his return, and the truth as told by him, in his own words, that would calm them again. And not only the two nations that depended on him would gain from his return. Her people, the Internationals, would be vindicated, as would the United States. The alliance would be saved, and the Russian Federation would be stopped.

This was the only way.

She turned her eyes to Reynolds, who was standing quietly not far from Sendor. He nodded. "I can have the Air Assault Team that assisted us in the ambassador's extraction meet us here, ma'am. We'll get him to our base at Split, he'll be safe there until we can get him to Brčko. I'll arrange it, no one will know we have him until we're there," he said.

"Brčko District is not safe," Stevenssen began, but then paused. "But then, that is the whole point here, isn't it? Very well, Captain Reynolds. Once you get the ambassador safely to Split and he speaks, I suppose our peacekeepers can be returned to Brčko, if that becomes possible. And only then," she addressed Sendor, "we will reassess the situation and see if it is safe for you to return there, George."

"Yes, yes, I would like that, I would like to speak to them, to the people," Sendor said eagerly.

"We will find a way for you to do that, show them and the world you are alive. But George," the council head reiterated sternly, "you will only return to Brčko District if we see that things settle down there. The riots must not endanger you. And," she added, frowning, "neither must the Russian military, they are already too close to our remaining people there."

Reynolds was already making the necessary plans in his head. "In the meantime, sir," he said to Sendor, "you must speak to no one. If you want us to fly you to the region, we cannot run the risk of anyone attempting another attack on you on the way." Reynolds knew from Oracle that the raids on Yahna and its extremists were still ongoing, which potentially left rogue elements still on the loose. Nor was the Sirion copy as yet accounted for, and they could not risk the air transport the ambassador would be in being downed again.

"I will do whatever it takes," Sendor answered.

Chapter Twenty-Five

The carefully worded news was delivered to all media outlets worldwide at the same time. Ambassador George Sendor had been found alive, rescued by the special forces of the Internationals' IDSD following a joint investigation with the United States that had tracked down his abductors, the same people who had downed his jet using life-saving technology stolen and manipulated to suit their goals and had cold-bloodedly killed his personal assistant, his protective detail and the jet's aircrew.

The ambassador himself gave a lengthy statement, in which he confirmed what had happened to him and called for the Bosniaks and the Serbs to rally behind the peace treaty. "I am coming back," he announced. "I am coming back to you, to finish what I started. And I will stay with you for as long as it takes. You know I will," he said, his eyes boring into those of the viewers his statement was meant for with the full strength of his conviction, his caring for them. "I promised you and your children peace. I promised you a new future, a future without war. And I stand by my word. Despite this attempt to stop us, you and me, from achieving our common dream, we will not stop, we must not stop. We *will* do this, *together*."

When the broadcasts were aired, the ambassador was already safe with the abundant defense forces at IDSD-Alliance Jadran Air-Sea Base at Split, Captain Reynolds and the rest of the soldiers of the two Special Mission Unit teams that had rescued him never moving from his side.

The news only hinted at who was responsible for everything that had happened. But within hours of the broadcasts, the media was discreetly leaked information pointing to the Russian Federation—and specifically to its president and its defense minister—and to the anti-Internationals group it had hired, which had used the opportunity to frame the Internationals and the United States in an attempt to destabilize the alliance that had brought nothing but hope to a broken world since its inception. The implication was clear—neither the Russian Federation nor the anti-internationalists had cared that the price could be, and had in fact come so close to being, war.

In Brčko District, the safe zone was still flanked by military forces from Bosnia and Srpska. But the soldiers were no longer careful to keep themselves apart, each from the soldiers of their neighboring nation. If they happened to meet, intermix, in the tri-border area, they did not raise their weapons and were once again civil to one another, even friendly, as they had been before the Internationals' ambassador had been taken.

Behind the borders on both sides, the riots had stopped, the protesters shamed into backing off by their own rash judgments, their own lingering intolerance. The realization of how close they themselves had come to starting a war, of how they themselves had to learn to listen, not be quick to let past hate take over, of how the last days might easily have been different had they themselves rallied, stood together, insisted on peace instead of putting the responsibility for it on others, now made all the difference. They had failed the one person who had fought for them and had suffered for it yet was adamant that he would return to help them, and were eager to make it up to him. The future now had a real chance.

To the east, the Russian forces advancing deeper into Brčko District found themselves facing Bosniaks and Serbs who had gathered to help protect the peacekeeping force and the negotiators, standing side by side as the determined protectors of the flame of hope once again rekindled. Realizing what continuing forward would do, and that the eyes of the world were now expectant on them, the Russian forces retreated. A quiet warning was delivered by the Internationals' High Council, and the forces moved all the way back across the Brčko-Russia border. A combat-ready IDSD defense force then immediately deployed along the Brčko side of the border in an unmistakable message—no more.

On the Russian Federation's border with Srpska, the Russian forces found themselves facing the country's soldiers. These soldiers would not normally be nearly enough to stop them and did not have nearly enough firepower. But between them stood people, tens of thousands of Serbs, among them Bosniaks who were still crossing the border from Bosnia to join them, to help. The live chain of two nations conveyed to the Russian troops a single message— go back. This is our home. Our choice. Our peace.

The Russian forces retreated. Above them, alliance jet fighters hovered in warning. And on Bosnia's and Srpska's western borders with Croatia and on the Montenegrin borders, the alliance forces finally stood down, and leaders across the region gave a sigh of relief.

As the region finally calmed, air transports traveled along the border between Bosnia and Srpska to return to Brčko District the Internationals' peacekeepers evacuated from it. They no longer needed combatant air support and were greeted with cheers upon landing. The peacekeepers, those returning and those who had remained with the negotiators throughout the crisis, found themselves in the midst of hectic preparations as the people of both nations prepared the area for the festivities that would mark their ambassador's return.

Ambassador Sendor asked to travel all the way along the border between his two protégé nations on the ground, instead of arriving at Brčko District by air. Considering the change in sentiments and the reason for the ambassador's request, to put his trust in those he was coming to help even as he was asking them to blindly put their trust in him again, his wish was granted. As his convoy traveled on the joint border, the Special Mission Units escorting him found themselves superfluous. Along the way, the convoy was flanked by welcoming people from both nations, who had had, in just a few days, an unwelcome whiff of what their lives would look like without the ambassador.

The treaty was signed immediately, no one wanting anymore delays, everyone eager to embark on a new path and put the near miss behind them. The Internationals' peacekeepers remained in Brčko and the alliance was still watching the region, but reason seemed to once again prevail. Ironically, now that they had come so close to war again and to losing their independence to a third country, voices were being heard within both nations that called for the two countries to become one again.

And they were not the only ones who would not easily forget how wrong things could have gone. The internationals and the alliance had almost had the work of decades destroyed. Within days of the ambassador's return, the heads of the alliance held a summit to discuss what nearly happened and new ways to protect themselves and the Internationals among them, and, no less important, their efforts to bring peace and unity in the presence of those who benefited from disputes. It would no longer be as easy to put a wedge between the nations of the alliance.

In Russia, a news broadcaster somberly announced a reshuffling of the administration. The defense minister's name was excluded from the new government. The president was replaced, too, a statement delivered in his name citing that he was withdrawing from political life for medical reasons. Behind the scenes, the entire upper echelon of the country's Foreign Intelligence Service was removed. Failure was unacceptable. So were split loyalties. Russia's new president was no fool.

Throughout this time, Emero's agents identified several instances in which men and women turned up in morgues across Europe, people who, thanks to the documents discovered under the mansion overlooking Kolonia in Pohnpei, could now be identified as members of the extremist faction that had originated from Yahna. The information retrieved also indicated that every one of them had been somehow involved in or at least aware of the ambassador's abduction. They had all died in what looked like accidents or botched muggings, and all deaths were timed within the day before Ambassador Sendor's planned killing by the man he had identified as his captor.

One person of interest who remained unaccounted for was the owner of the mansion and the apparent leader of the extremist faction, as the information found and the man's clout in the Federated States of Micronesia attested. He was absent during the raid on Pohnpei and no clues were found as to his whereabouts. Any attempt to find anything about him other than his identity in Micronesia failed. He simply did not exist outside it.

It was only when all information from all parts of the Sendor operation came in and was analyzed that the discovery was made that he was, in fact, the man killed by Captain Reynolds in the hideaway under Cres, Ambassador Sendor's captor.

But that wasn't all that was found. The abduction and the way it was done had been the most important act yet in advancing the extremist faction's agenda, so it was no surprise that one of its prominent members had actively taken part in it. However, there seemed to be someone else behind the faction, someone only obscure references were made to in the information found in Pohnpei and who had been in contact only with its presumed leader, someone whose existence was supported by the ambassador who, when debriefed, indicated that his captor had mentioned having acted under orders.

Someone who was apparently powerful enough to set in motion the chain of events that had almost brought the alliance to its knees and destabilized Europe. And who was still out there, free.

This was not over.

Lara entered her house from the garage and stood at the door, deep in thought. The ambassador was safe, the crisis over. Normally she would feel the past days in her body and mind, but the adrenaline was still there, fueled by the near miss, and ultimate success, of the days' events.

And her worry for Donovan. When she came out of Mission Command, she found Aiden waiting, and not moving from her side. He was always there, but this time he had specifically been asked by Donovan to watch her, make sure the lack of sleep and the exertion of what she was doing didn't harm her. But Donovan himself wasn't there.

At the sound of a car turning into her driveway, she went to the front door. Donovan walked up to her and buried his face in the side of her neck as he returned her embrace. He breathed her in, let the feel of her take the day away.

"I'm sorry about the agents," she said softly.

"Yeah." He walked with her inside and sat on the sofa with a sigh, leaned back, rubbing his face, then turned to her with a furrow in his brow as she sat down beside him. "Wait, how did you find out?" He hadn't had a chance yet to update Scholes on how Bourne died, with the events both at IDSD and at USFID taking precedence.

She shrugged. "We had satellites tasked to us already, so..."

"You put a satellite on location."

"Easy to intercept the USFID chatter, it wasn't hidden."

He shook his head. "Bourne told me they would kill him. I should have listened to him. Damn it, three people. Three good agents. These people simply... a missile. They used a drone to hit a federal agency car with a missile right here in DC."

"And just weeks ago another group destroyed a high security data center here and then tried to—" She didn't finish the sentence. The eyes that turned to her were intense, the memory too strong. He remembered very well what they had done, felt it still. She moved closer and kissed him, wanting to give him what he had been giving her almost from the first day they had met.

He answered her kiss readily, drawing strength from her, and rested his forehead against hers. "They knew. That we arrested him, when and where we'd be handing him over to IDSD, how we'd get there and the route we'd take. Despite all we did to keep it quiet, they knew."

"We're only beginning to understand just how far these groups have infiltrated the alliance," she said quietly. "We'll get them all, eventually. They can't win, we won't allow them to. The price would be unbearable."

He leaned back again and looked at her. "You have a different view of this, don't you?" He'd spent his entire professional life so far striving to identify and deal with threats to his home country. He was finding that with Lara he was learning what it was like to have a view of the threats to the entire world. It was, to say the least, enlightening.

"I'm an International."

"The ultimate International," he said to himself, closing his eyes.

"You're tired," she said softly.

"Look who's talking." He smiled, his eyes still closed.

"It's been a difficult week."

"I can think of some pretty great things that happened in it." He put his arm around her and drew her to him.

In the middle of the night, with darkness mandating silence and gentle rain tapping on the bedroom window, the woman who was Oracle lay awake. Her eyes were open, her thoughts on what the world she had a unique insight into would have looked like if things had turned out differently that day, on what they would look like in the future if those who would try to stand in peace's way would win.

She had been with the ambassador in the moment that nearly led to his death, had felt it all. It had almost been too late. *She* was almost too late. It had taken her too long to find him. Next time it might not be enough. True, in that time she had also dealt with missions, prevented the loss of other lives. But this would not do, she could not, would not allow herself to settle for just enough. Oracle's abilities had grown since she had begun, since she had first discovered what she could do. She could now go deeper, wider than ever in the play of space and time that was her mind's extended reality. But she needed more.

If they were to win this, if those who valued life were to prevail, Oracle would need to be more.

She turned in bed and looked at the man being who she was had brought to her life. He was deeply asleep, his arm draped over her as if he was reluctant to let her go even in exhausted slumber. He, them, what they had, were already doing to her what she had thought impossible, already healing wounds that had kept so much of who she was subdued, already freeing her from the debilitating confines of pain.

Allowing Oracle to grow stronger unhindered.

Chapter Twenty-Six

Donovan didn't like this.

Four days had passed since the events related to Ambassador Sendor's abduction had ended, and the activity level in IDSD Mission's war room was back to normal, although relief was still evident in many of the conversations that dominated the main floor's enclosed workspaces. Donovan was in Vice Admiral Scholes's office, asked here to meet with him and with US Global Intelligence Director Paul Evans. He didn't know what he had expected, but this certainly was not it.

"Because you looked beyond Major Berman's obvious guilt and made the connection to Bourne, and we got what we needed to solve the major's murder and the Sirion theft, and to finally bring Yahna and its extremists down," Evans was saying, "your role in the resolution of this crisis—crises, I should say—was critical."

"The fact that Bourne kept trying to involve himself in the investigation helped," Donovan said, his brow furrowed. Where was this going?

"Why do you think he did that?" Scholes hadn't

been as involved in Donovan's investigation as Evans had and still hadn't had a chance to ask him about it, beyond the connection to Yahna.

"I think he panicked," Donovan said. "To get his part of the extremists' plan done he was required to shoot in the back of the head a man he'd known, the first person he'd ever killed. That was too much. Bourne was a loyalist, but he was a white-collar operative, not a cold-blooded killer. And then he had to stick around, exposed, for the investigation, and because of the eyes on him and on ARPA he couldn't contact his people, maybe get from them the strength he needed. Add to that his vanity—he never thought they could be discovered."

"Good for us, I suppose." Scholes shook his head. "Unbelievable. The damage he caused."

"And then some," Evans concurred.

"How're you going to deal with the fact that your technology's existence is now publicly known?" Donovan asked. "Especially considering how it was used."

"Technology. That's just it," Scholes answered. "Its name was never made known, nor any technical information. Or functional, for that matter. All that was said was that it was used to bring down the ambassador's jet, without specifying how."

"You're going to continue hiding it."

"Yes," Scholes said simply. "If anyone asks, we'll release some of the information about it, say it's a technology that's still in the development stages, designed to communicate with a manned aircraft's flight systems in order to safely land it if it's in trouble. Something like that. Sirion is needed. And with its copy still missing, we need to be able to try to reconstruct how far it was developed and perhaps find a countering technology, without prying eyes."

"What about ARPA? It's taken a serious hit, with the security breach."

"It'll get all the help it needs. Both ARPA and IDSDATR will, and especially the Sirion team," Evans said.

Donovan nodded, then waited, silent, looking at the two men.

"Right. Coming back to the point. Between you and Emero, your roles in this are certainly more than enough." Evans glanced at Scholes, who nodded emphatically.

Donovan frowned. No, he didn't like the feel of this at all. "Enough for what?"

"You found Bourne and through him the group behind Ambassador Sendor's abduction. This led to IDSD Intelligence intercepting communications between the leader of the group and Russia's defense minister and through these Emero was able to decipher the ambassador's whereabouts and ensure his timely rescue." Evans fell silent, waited.

"That's not what happened," Donovan said. "We didn't find him—" he stopped abruptly and turned to Scholes, who nodded, his eyes somber. "You need to hide the fact that Oracle found him. You need to hide Oracle."

"This thing is too high profile, Donovan," Scholes said. "Everyone in half the world, hell, in the entire world, wants to know what happened. The media, politicians trying to ride the wave, everyone."

Donovan didn't like this at all. "So what, Emero and I—"

"Have the gratitude of the Internationals' High Council and the US Administration for all you have done," Scholes said.

Evans nodded. "You're going to be publicly commended for this. And you deserve it."

"No, no way. What we did would have come down to nothing, would not have prevented a war, and Russia never would have pulled back, if Lara hadn't found the ambassador, and on time. And the way she kept an eye on the situation the entire time, the things she seemed to know that she told you about on the way, how many people did she save?" Donovan was angry. This wasn't something he would ever be willing to do, even if the person they were talking about leaving out of the credit here wasn't Lara.

"True." Scholes had expected Donovan's anger. "And yet, this must never be publicly known."

Donovan stood up and turned to leave.

"Donovan." The huge man came to stand in his way. "Those who need to know, do. They always do. Do you think Oracle can be protected the way she is without the support of some very powerful people in very strategic places? You think they don't know her role in this? Who do you think was the first to ask that she step in?" He spread his hands. "She gets the recognition where it really matters. And she'll be commended too, she'll receive the Internationals' highest commendation from Council Head Stevenssen personally, not to mention the ones from Joint Europe and the United States, they've already stated their intention to do so. She'll receive her commendations, just not at the same time as you, and not in the presence of the same people."

Donovan turned to Evans, who nodded, repeating, "The right people, in the right strategic places, and that goes for our administration, too, Donovan. How do you think Oracle works here so easily? How do you think everything Oracle or Lara is accepted in the United States without question? Here she can do everything she needs or wants to, and still remain hidden. Here she is under Internationals *and* US *and* alliance protection."

"And," Scholes added, walking over to his desk, "if you think she cares about recognition or commendations, think again." He punched in a code, and a panel opened in the wall.

Donovan stared.

"These are all hers. There are more, but I ran out of space."

Donovan moved closer, astonished. His Lara had been awarded commendations from more than a few agencies, militaries, diplomatic corps. Countries, all belonging to the alliance. They were all there, the High Council and IDSD, the United States, Joint Europe, he saw the Southern Territories there, the Asian Territories, some others he didn't recognize. She'd never said anything about it. But then, she really wouldn't care. That's not why she was Oracle.

Behind him, Evans spoke. "Donovan, I know you don't care about commendations either. You don't even bother turning up to receive them, do you? But we need you to, this time. You need to be there, along with Emero, to receive these. If they look at you—"

"They don't look at Oracle," Donovan completed the thought. He nodded his consent.

Nothing in the huge hall was understated. Those present enjoyed luxury as much as they enjoyed the unlimited power at their fingertips.

They spoke freely in here. In the entire estate, in fact. There was no danger of their being heard, or seen. Electronic means gave them hermetic protection, and the airspace above them was closed. Not even satellites could penetrate the security measures here. The world was literally blind to the existence of this meeting, to its participants. It would never know the words uttered by them. No money was spared to achieve this. And money was not a problem. They were a combination of the richest and the most powerful people in the world.

One by one they sat down, fell silent. Waited. The man who had called them here looked at them, met their eyes.

"The events of the past days are most unfortunate. I regret that they happened, however we have always had to contend with the existence of rogue groups that have their own agenda for this world, an agenda that conflicts with ours. We should see ourselves fortunate that those responsible have been identified and stopped. This had, as you well know, the potential of causing great damage to our cause, and I assure you that my people are collecting all information relevant to these deplorable events, and we will study them." He paused. "Now, let us proceed with our meeting."

Around the table, the participants of the unique gathering all nodded their agreement. But among them, one thought otherwise. One voice that would not speak up, not betray its true loyalties. One mind that was trying to understand how it could have happened. How it had all fallen apart.

How on earth did they find Ambassador Sendor?

"I can't believe everything that's happened." Lara turned around in Donovan's arms and looked up at him. "Everything's changed." No, not just changed, she thought, everything is so much better.

The glimmer in his eyes and the smile that

played on his lips told her he knew what she wasn't saying. This time she was glad about it. What they had was still too new, it was too soon. For her, the feelings were still difficult to put into words.

"Love does that, apparently." His wonder was no less than hers. He had no idea it could be this way.

This time it was she who put her arms around him, who drew him to her for a kiss. His arms tightened around her. He wanted more, needed more. This, now, was only the beginning.

"And I can't believe we're on a first date." She laughed. "We're already quite a bit past that."

"We're changing the rules. All considering, I think we can make our own." He kissed her. "Come on, let's go."

"Where?"

He smiled, not answering. Their date, on an uncharacteristically warm autumn eve, had begun at one of his favorite places, a restaurant in a marina he frequented. The chef owner was a good friend of his, and their evening had so far consisted of a pampering meal on a terrace above the water, rows of boats below them. Now they were walking along the pier, her hand in his, toward a row of private boathouses up ahead.

"Look at all these boats. Imagine taking one, a sailboat, old school, and just going out to sea. Must be so peaceful." She looked dreamily at the water. She was, finally, relaxed. This was the first day in months she had taken off, the first one in years that she was, unbelievably, happy in.

"You've never been on a boat?" He enjoyed seeing her this way, seeing this side of her he knew he was awakening, just as she had awakened so much in him.

"Not like these, no." Warships didn't count as fun.

"First time for everything." He turned left at the pier connecting the boathouses and approached the farthest one. He stopped, letting the security system identify him, and the door slid open.

"Really?" Lara said, and Donovan laughed and followed her in, the door closing behind them. A short walkway with two storage rooms, one on each side, became a wide dock leading into the water, on which the lights that shone in the high slanted ceiling played. But Lara saw nothing but the two sailboats that bobbed gently in the water.

"A boat. You have a boat. You have two boats."

He laughed again, enjoying how that felt, loving the wonder in her voice.

She came to stand on the dock between the boats and looked to both sides. The left boat was obviously older and was being worked on. The right one looked modern, new. The name on the hull read *Sanctuary*.

She turned to Donovan, who was standing immediately behind her, his arms around her waist. "Is that what it is? Your sanctuary?"

He looked at the sleek boat. "Yes. The only one I thought I needed, thought I would have." His eyes were thoughtful, and when he looked at her again, she felt her heart flutter at what his gaze held. She moved closer to him, her arms tightening around him. Do you know that I love you? She wanted to say, but it didn't come out, not yet, just lay deep within the gaze that held his. She kissed him instead, and it was, for now, enough, he thought, understood that she needed time.

And she was, after all, finally his.

"What's the name of the other one?" She pulled away from him lightly and turned to have a closer look at the faded, hand-lettered name on the older boat. "*Christine*," she read.

"My mother's name," he said, and she turned her eyes to him.

"This was my father's boat." Donovan came closer and touched it, almost gingerly. He put his hands in his pockets. "He loved boats. And he got started on building them when my mother was stationed in Ireland. This one was his favorite. He gave it her name, always said that the two of them, his boat and the woman he loved, gave him peace." He smiled, reminiscing. "Except that my mother didn't care for boats, and she never actually set foot on this one. When she was busy, sometimes for weeks on end, my father would take me out of school, and we would take it out to sea." He was quiet for a long time, and Lara went to him, seeing the memory, the pain. She took his hand in hers. He looked at her, drew comfort.

"When my parents died, I returned here, to the United States, to live with my uncle." It was a bit more complicated than that, but he didn't want to go into it now. He would, with her, but not now. And he knew it was okay, she would understand. "I thought the boat had been sold with everything else. There was no reason to keep it. It hurt me, but I didn't say anything about it. I thought it was too late, and, anyway, I was a kid and had no say in it." He smiled a little. "I'd been in some trouble, and my uncle kept me close to him for a while, straightened me out. That's why he hadn't told me he'd asked my grandparents, my mother's parents, to keep this boat for me. They wanted it gone, it pained them to keep it. But they agreed to do it for me. And when I was sixteen, my uncle took me to the mooring near his house, and there it was." He looked up at the boat. "I've been restoring it. It's an old boat, and I haven't had as much time as I used to."

Lara wanted to know more, to know everything about him. But she remained silent, knowing this wasn't what he needed now. She would wait for him to tell her, as he had waited for her.

He looked at her, coming back to the present, to her, and smiled. "Come on, we haven't finished our first date." He led her up the gangway to *Sanctuary*. "I had this one built a couple of years ago," he said, stepping on the deck, "and I take it out whenever I can."

"So this is where you bring women when you want to impress them?" she teased with a smile.

"This is where I come when I want to be alone, when I want some peace. I've never brought a woman here."

She halted, just as she was about to step on the deck, and looked at him. This was his sanctuary. "I'm a woman."

He turned to look at her, saw her hesitate. He walked back to her, took her hand in his and pulled her that last step onto the deck and into his arms. "You're *the* woman," he murmured and kissed her, lingering, feeling her in his arms, basking in the way her body moved into his, feeling so right.

He loved the way she explored the boat, touching it in wonder. Absently, she let the soft wrap she had on slide down her arms and drop on the deck, let it lie where it fell, walked on.

He couldn't take his eyes off her.

Wondering at himself, at the effect this woman had on him, he went inside. He was busy at the security console when Lara joined him.

"This is absolutely beautiful." She walked in slowly, peeking around her.

"Go ahead, have a look around."

She explored the tasteful saloon, a well-stocked galley, then continued on, looking around, until she reached the master cabin, its cozy colors and design befitting this man she loved, who valued the peace this second home gave him. She returned to the saloon, and Donovan saw her and beckoned. When she approached him, he put an arm around her waist and pulled her to stand before him, and had the system scan her biometrics and program her in.

"There. Now the security system will recognize you. You have full access to the boat," he murmured near her ear, his lips brushing her neck.

She turned in his arms. "Are you sure? Donovan, this is your sanctuary."

"No, you are, my Lara." He touched his lips to hers, and she answered the kiss readily, deepening it. He drew her closer to him, and reached behind her to touch the console and remotely secure the boathouse. He didn't want any disturbances any time soon.

"So, how comfortable is that bed back there?" she mused.

"Good for sleeping, let's see what else it's good for," he said, backing her up toward the cabin.

**Look for the next book in the
Oracle series**

Join our mailing list on www.authorandsister.net
for additional books by A. Claire Everward

9 789659 258420